FOLLOW that CARAVAN

BASED ON
A TRUE STORY

Much has happened since a young couple with three small children sold everything to buy a remote Cornish Valley, there to live in a tiny caravan by a stream without mains water or electric, hoping to create a very special holiday park.

Follow that Caravan is the final book in this true story. How will the sudden touch of wealth affect them as the children grow, seeking their own independence? There is continuing laughter at the strange things caravanners and campers do - and an insight into those peculiar creatures, caravan park wardens and owners! More fun with officialdom too, and a desperate legal battle. But can the park keep abreast of a changing world. Moments of triumph are mixed with occasional sadness, a touch of romance, some strange friends and a love of nature. - Oh yes, and in one small chapter, something unique that might be just the thing for a mother or wife?

Reviews on the previous book.
A Buzzard to Lunch.

A fine companion to the first three books
THE CORNISHMAN

I have much enjoyed the books... now is the time to try
one...   MOTORCARAVAN MOTORHOME MONTHLY

I enjoyed this latest novel
THE WEST BRITON

...pokes a little fun at officialdom
BH & HPA JOURNAL

...a firm favourite with nature lovers
PRACTICAL CARAVAN

... inexplicable embarrassing things that visitors do.
CARAVAN INDUSTRY & PARK OPERATOR.

buy a remote valley... splendid romance... humour... a love
of nature   Series display showing all four covers
MOTORCARAVAN MAGAZINE

Article in LANCASHIRE RAMBLER

...set in idyllic but threatened valley...
THE CARAVAN CLUB

True story of this family's struggle to turn a remote
Cornish valley into a Caravan Park.
THE CARAVAN AND CAMPING CLUB

...wry dig at officialdom... peppered with laughter ...
WHICH MOTORCARAVAN

Series has over 40 reviews including **Daily Telegraph**.

FOLLOW *that* CARAVAN

by

GORDON CHANNER

Valley of Dreams series

CORNISH BOOKS
5 Tregembo Hill
Penzance, Cornwall, TR20 9EP

A WORD OF THANKS.

River Valley was modelled very much on the sites of the
Caravan Club, and of the Camping and Caravanning Club,
my sincere thanks go to them both.

Thanks too, to the County & District Councillors and their
Officers over the years, in spite of some differences.
Much of the detail in this Valley of Dreams series has
come from talking to caravanners and campers and
listening to their expertise in a wide range of subjects.
I hope these books will give everyone a chuckle.

08750224

DEDICATION.

*To Magazines and their Editors, who over the
years have supported and given pleasure to so
many people. Before writing this series I never
realised how difficult their job is!*

Bound and printed in UK
Cornish Books
First Published 2001
Copyright © Gordon Channer 2001
IBSN 0-9537009-4-1

Contents

THE FAMILY

Gordon	Father
Jan	Mother

Children's ages at start of this book.

Chris	Seventeen years five months
Sharon	Fifteen year nine months
Stephen	Twelve years eight months
Jim	Grandfather (Jan's father)
Audrey	Grandmother (Jan's mother)
Frank	Grandfather (Gordon's father)
Ivy	Grandmother (Gordon's mother)
Katie and Jack	Chris and Lesley's children

Bod, Min & Lady Di   The three owls

Period.   Apr 1978 - Apr 2001.

Sketches and notes – see end of book.

CHAPTER 1

As Agreed

For a moment there was silence, disbelief in three young faces changing to excitement.

"I do!" Sharon gasped, eagerness showing; at fifteen she had not yet learned to mask her feelings.

Chris, two years older and more restrained, made as if to speak but changed his mind. A young man in that difficult period, searching for more independence, he looked across to the letter lying on the desk, something obviously on his mind, waiting, turning to his mother for confirmation.

Catching her son's glance, Jan held a hand towards Gordon, asking for the cheque with a snap of the fingers, taking it and inspecting the figure. "Ten thousand pounds," she read aloud, turning with a smile of pleasure to Stephen, her youngest, standing silently on one side. Twelve years old and in the second year at senior school it was typical of his quiet nature that he too, should be suspicious. A small arm rose, a question clear in the gesture. She offered the cheque; he gazed for a moment at the figures, passing it back without comment.

"Let's not get carried away," Gordon warned, alarmed by his own rashness. Surprise on opening the envelope had triggered the offer, 'Anyone fancy a shopping trip?' He regretted that now, worried it had raised the children's expectations too high. "Most of this money is spoken for... don't look so disappointed; we can still afford..." He broke off, looking towards Sharon, "What had you in mind; clothes?"

Sharon nodded, her smile broadening, "How, er, how

1

much can we..." she made a little circular motion of the wrist, not quite able to bring herself to utter that deliciously wicked word - 'Spend!'

"There's a caravan coming," Jan pointed to the track running alongside the little stream. "Your father and I will work out some figures. Chris, Stephen, I guess you both have something in mind? We'll discuss it later."

The family dispersed as a car and caravan drew up, its driver remaining seated with the engine still running. A woman alighting quickly from the far side, hurried to the office door.

"Have you a place we can park on a hill? Trouble starting the car; hope to get it fixed after the weekend."

It was not the first such request. Obviously they wanted to be safely on a pitch before stopping the engine.

Gordon rose from the desk. "Sure, several. The site won't get busy until Spring Bank holiday. Follow me, you can book in afterwards."

As the caravan drew away, three customers walking together approached the little shop attached to the house. Jan opened the communicating door to serve them, it was mid-morning - most visitors would leave for the beach before long, many already on their way. The shop would be quiet then, until the rush back for tea that evening. When the last had been served, Jan moved back to the lounge to find Gordon already returned and standing by one of the windows looking out towards a granite bridge arching across the small river.

Owning and running a caravan park was a great life - if you didn't weaken! Always something different, a little crisis here, a minor triumph there - old faces returning and new ones appearing as visitors came and left; their behaviour sometimes bizarre, even embarrassing. Conditions were ever-changing too; early and late season bringing slack times with a chance to relax, but in the school holidays, busy as hel... really busy! Winter was different again; the valley lonely and deserted, a time for heavier, noisier work.

Now in April, life was easy, the valley splendid, clothed in rich spring greenery, trees and bushes bursting into leaf.

2

Most caravans were out of sight behind the house, only four and a single tent visible from the window, a few dozen ducks resting peacefully on grassy banks beside the stream; mallard, muscovys and large, fat fluffy aylesburys. One in particular Sharon regularly picked up to put on her knee, snuggling a cheek against its white feathers, the duck happily tolerant so long as food was offered.

In the river near the waterwheel a fight was in progress, two shelduck attacking each other. A group of five young ones had been accepted the previous season from Mousehole Bird Hospital. For the first year they caused no problem, indeed a certain elegance endeared them to visitors during that summer, standing tall for their body size on pale legs and walking daintily along the riverbank. Now they were just a pain, chasing the mallard away, not letting them stay on the river near the house, doing the same to newly introduced pairs of carolinas and mandarins, spoiling the valley's happy harmony. Being migratory, their final departure was likely in July, an event anticipated with relief rather than sorrow - an absence that would undoubtedly delight every other duck! A TV wildlife program on shelduck in Australia had shown the male bird defending small freshwater seepages into saltwater lakes, a defence of territory vital to the ducklings' survival, indicating perhaps the source of this belligerent streak.

Quite suddenly the battle stopped as one drake fled, the other following with outstretched neck until its rival left the river and peace returned. The house was quiet too, Stephen and Sharon off in search of friends, and Chris upstairs probably reading.

"This money," Jan moved away from the window looking to where the big cheque still lay on the desk. "We can afford..." she broke off as Chris, now a tall young man, entered the room, making to leave the house by the adjoining office door.

"Chris," she stopped him. "The money; was there anything special you had in mind?"

"Um... a motorbike?" Seeing his mother's shaken head,

Chris shrugged, waited a moment then slipped through the door and left. He was still working locally at the Music Museum but it was Sunday. She watched him go, thinking of his application to join the Police cadets. Would a reply come soon and take him away, three hundred miles up-country to live in London. He would leave anyway before long... her eyes followed the receding figure walking upstream beside the river.

"You were saying we can afford something?" Gordon prompted.

The voice close at hand broke through Jan's thoughts, swinging her back to reply. "Afford to finish the third toilet building? You won't try while we've people staying, will you? How much can we spend on ourselves and the children? Our site fees are up this year - that should help."

The nightly charge had indeed increased, partly from continued high inflation and partly in the hope of remaining unchanged for the next three seasons. Gordon tried to work out in his mind how it might affect the takings, but who could tell?

"The third toilets? No, we need a floorlayer first - too much noise and mess. Let's do it next winter when we close. I can buy the loos and the basins though, plenty of storage room now and prices will only increase. The tarmac must wait 'til winter too."

"What about mains electricity?" Jan glance upward. The house lights worked fine on waterwheel power but people still asked for hairdryers.

"Too expensive for a few years yet, even with that big cheque." He shrugged; who could tell how long it would take? "That Best Site award we always wanted to win; this money could help. Anyway we'd better be careful for a while yet... Ouch!" Jan's pointed finger jabbed at him and he stepped backward, "Okay, spend whatever you want - within reason."

The season had commenced well enough, several old customers reappearing as the days passed - good to see them again after the winter. One visitor however, triggered more dubious emotions - the fire officer, requesting a series of fire points around the site. Perhaps that word might give the wrong impression; a request from the fire officer seldom left one any choice!

A typical design was sketched out. Each fire point must have a long hose, some way of fixing it to a tap and instructions clearly displayed... oh yes, and a warning device, usually a metal triangle and something to bang it with - the kids would have fun with those in the school holidays!

That same afternoon, a hose was bought and a prototype constructed in marine plywood, adequate for any emergency and small enough not to intrude on the landscape. Fire equipment might be important but so was the valley's beauty. A visit to the fire station secured the chief officer's approval - hardly surprising, it was mainly his own design. In a matter of days the fire points were made and fixed, such little diversions not uncommon, life on a park never running entirely as expected.

The morning's post brought a letter addressed to Chris. Returning from work that evening he opened it, scanned the single page, shouted "An interview!" and raced off to show Jim and Audrey, his grandparents in their bungalow at the site entrance.

"It's a good life." Jim, an ex-policeman himself, encouraged Chris to accept the offer and join the force, sitting down to talk over old times "When I started, back in the 1930's things were simple, just catch the criminals! Today that's secondary; the main aim now is paperwork - to line the pockets of the legal profession."

They talked on for a while, Jim finishing with a warning. "You'll see plenty of action, meet all sorts of people - help them where you can but never mind if they're black, white, toff or tramp, if anyone attacks you, clobber him hard and ask questions afterwards. I'll tell you one thing - you're too young to think about it but the pension is index linked; rises every year. I get more money now than I was earning before retirement."

A few days later Chris headed for the train to London

and that crucial interview, a young man full of hope and expectation, shielding his excitement under a mask of coolness as Jan ran him to the station, watching him walk away along the platform, suitcase in hand. Returning home mid-morning, she found the house somehow empty and wished there were more visitors to chat with.

Gordon too had watched Chris leave and wondered about the future, but showing new arrivals to pitches and various other jobs kept him busy. Later he chatted to two motorcaravanners, Penny and Michael from Cheltenham. With River Valley's own unusual source of electricity it was natural that visitors should show an interest, the waterwheel much photographed and admired - a favourite question, 'What does it do?' Chatting about the possibilities, Michael suggested a lathe and thought he knew where to lay his hands on one; an ancient belt driven machine of considerable size.

Learning of this at tea, Jan was doubtful, "Where will it go?" However, seeing enthusiasm in young Stephen's face and hearing the lathe would live in the basement, she relented. "All right, provided it really does go downstairs, not out in the service passage in everyone's way. You say it's belt driven; it won't take all our electric?"

"Will it interfere with the television?" Sharon asked suspiciously. Even with the bigger battery recently purchased, power was still limited, particularly later in the year when more caravanners brought their batteries in to be charged. "Anyway, how much will it cost? What about my new clothes? Does it mean..."

"No," Jan cut in. "It won't interfere with the outfit I promised, because it's cheap." She looked across at Gordon, challenging him to deny it. The children twisting in their seats to follow her gaze.

"How..." Stephen stopped, aware that his parents were not listening, just staring at each other, both with smiles on their faces.

Breaking the contact, Jan turned to her son. "How did I guess? Because I know your father! That little grin he tried to conceal when he asked if we should buy it. Can you see him even considering this lathe if it was expensive? Of course it's cheap! I'll can tell you something else too." She stopped, not immediately offering this piece of information, letting the interest rise around the table, flicking an amused glance towards Gordon, knowing he had probably guessed her intent. Pity Chris was still away in London. Leaning forward as if imparting some secret, she whispered, "Can you guess what will happen if we all say 'No'? I'll tell you. Nothing! He's already made the arrangements - go on, ask him to deny it." She rested back content, sure now from his expression that her suspicions were true. Listening to the children's questions and his evasive answers, she knew too, that he was not about to admit it.

The subject was temporarily forgotten when a ring on the doorbell had Sharon jumping from her seat. "Probably for me."

Stephen left shortly after, pausing outside to speak with Sharon and a group of teenage girls still chatting on the doorstep. They had all disappeared and the quiet of evening approached when a tent arrived, a car with German number-plates. A man in his early twenties emerged from the far side, walking towards the office.

"Two days?" Gordon asked, moving to sit at the desk.

Standing nearby, Jan looked out at the approaching figure. "Three, or perhaps, 'How much is the cost?'"

These suggestions were not entirely over length of stay; by mutual consent the little wager included a guess at what the first words would be. Tourists were to some extent predictable, especially the Germans - nice people but somewhat stiff; economical with words, set in their ideas. Jan slipped into the lounge to an armchair, taking up a magazine as if reading but not actually doing so.

Entering the office this young German halted smartly at the desk, flicked a glance into the adjoining lounge, and back again. For a moment he stood silent, then leaned slowly forward to speak with just the right amount of accent.

"Listen carefully, I shall say this only once!"

The effect was shattering. Gordon and Jan glanced across

7

at each other amazed. That particular expression from anyone else... but Germans didn't make jokes! They looked back to find the man smiling, pleased with the effect - a smile hard to resist, the three soon deep in conversation. Jan was right though, he did book three days and was eventually led off to a pitch, choosing a high terrace on the valley side.

'I shall say this only once,' entered several times in the conversation next day, to be repeated again at tea when Chris returned from his interview. He was in confident mood, expecting his starting date to be notified shortly. Having given every last detail of his trip and heard briefly the latest from home, he sought to find more about the lathe but Jan had no definite information. "Dad's looking at the possibility, trying to arrange it - at least I'm pretty sure he is. It may come to nothing."

A telephone call two days later confirmed a lathe was available for £150 as agreed. Jan, alone in the office, took the call, writing down the details but decided to wait until tea when the children were home to impart the news. Beans on toast, which because it was cheap had been a regular evening meal when they first arrived in the valley, still remained a favourite.

As they ate, she spoke casually. "I had a phone call today." They carried on eating; one thing this family were not short of was phone calls - it rang constantly with bookings. "A man rang about the lathe." She took another mouthful, chewing slowly, cutting another tiny square of toast and adjusting the number of beans, sliding the fork beneath ready to lift again to her mouth.

"Mum!"

"Yes Sharon... Oh, the phone call. You want to know what he said?" Jan waited for the eager nod, lifting another mouthful, taking time to chew and swallow before saying more. "Well, he said the lathe was available... at £150 *as agreed*. Yes, he actually said those very words - *as agreed*! I told you Dad had already arranged it."

"Wonder how big it is?" Gordon quickly addressed the children, distracting their thoughts. "Did he say when?"

"No. You're to ring him, he left a number. Apparently it's the same machine you discussed; rather old but in good condition, with a screw cutting gearbox. He's persuaded the firm to deliver for a nominal fee but doesn't know exactly how much."

Gordon looked at his watch and hurried to the phone, returning shortly to the remaining lukewarm beans with the single comment. "End of the week."

"What day?" Jan asked.

"The man said delivery is cheaper if we leave that open, so I thought..."

"Oh, of course!"

A truck with two men arrived late one afternoon. The driver pulled up, leaned from the window and shouted, "Where is the crane?" On finding there was no such thing, his expression changed.

"Oh dear, how shall we get it off the lorry?" were definitely not his actual words! Hearing the language and not wanting it repeated within ear-shot of any customers, Jan emerged from the house to join them looking at the load, hoping they might be more restrained with a woman present.

Gordon gazed up with a mixture of delight at so much costing so little, and a feeling that the driver had a point! How on earth could it be unloaded? The short answer was that he hadn't a clue but if the lorry was not to disappear again, whisking this new toy away, then someone needed a brain-wave fast.

"Don't worry. Easy enough... I'll manage." Not exactly the truth, as the men clearly knew. They needed distracting. "Hungry are you after the long drive? Jan will cook a meal and make coffee."

As she led them into the house, he managed to whisper, "Don't hurry," before dashing off to find tools. Somehow the weight must be split down, everything removable stripped from the lathe bed. The tailstock was weighty but manageable, working alone Gordon eased it to the ground. The carriage however, proved too heavy. Striding quickly across to the nearest group of caravans, a call of, "Help! Anyone feeling strong!" yielded two volunteers. With this extra muscle the hefty metal carriage was lifted clear. Dismantling continued, various bits of gearing, brackets, guides and guards followed. Finally the headstock came away, the total commitment of three pairs of hands easing it to the ground. A small group of visitors had gathered to watch; wives of the men already helping and three other couples. Only the lathe bed remained - standing there on four cast-iron legs but its weight was immense. Commandeering the three watching husbands gave a slight chance of shifting it; their wives left chattering in a cluster. With three men at each end, they heaved upwards - unsuccessfully!

Reorganising, five men lifted one end while the legs were removed. Treating the other end similarly left this heavy chunk of metal lying flat on the lorry's floor. Dragged across to the edge, it slid with some resistance down stout timbers to lie on the grass below.

Well it was off the lorry! A little cheer rose from the wives; hearing it Jan looked from a window to catch the men congratulating themselves. "As men are inclined to do whenever they manage some little achievement," she thought, turning back to the driver and his mate at the table. "It's unloaded. More coffee?"

Seeing the depth of pleasure this accomplishment had caused, Gordon looked at the debris lying on the lawn. Collecting five good men might not be so easy another time, better to take advantage now - if they would agree! What was needed? Well, the journey across the lawn for a start, then up three steps, across the threshold of the front door and through the hall. The basement stairs would certainly offer a challenge, especially the two right angle turns at the bottom, then along one passageway, round a corner into yet another corridor, arriving finally at the workroom! Perhaps he wouldn't mention all that to start with.

"Do you think we could get it indoors?" They would scarcely say no in front of the women.

Round steel bars rolling across the planks and a six-man propulsion unit, forced it forward. Twelve hands lifting together dragged the front end up the steps, one at a time, then more roller work across the hall to the top of the basement stairs. Now to get it down!

The planks from outside were quickly placed to form a slide, but no one present had the natural insanity required to descend ahead of the lathe-bed and support its weight from below - just as well perhaps! If it got away down the slope this metal billet was quite capable of disappearing through the basement wall. In spite of many ropes and everyone hanging on, the speed could not be entirely controlled - it drew up with a solid clunk against the blockwork below. As men climbed and slid down the plank covered stairway, Jan beckoned the wives inside, gathering at the top of the flight to look down, amused by a surfeit of conflicting instructions from below.

"Push it this way." "No, pull it over here." "I'll go past and work from the other side." "You're too fat, let me try." These and similar niceties rang backwards and forwards as men scrambled round like ants from a disturbed nest. These efforts achieved little; the lathe remained pinned on the winding bottom steps, resisting attempts to force it round.

Still standing in the doorway above, the women watched, seeing it jamb solid in the struggle to turn a corner that so obviously had insufficient clearance. This impasse precipitated a renewed outburst of verbal abuse at the offending object, an occasional unsavoury comment directed towards the laughing wives above.

Lifting one end high in the air, over and down solved the problem, lowering onto a pile of strategically placed newspapers, a safety precaution in case the weight slipped. With the men now out of sight, the women waited, odd remarks still floating up, but after a while they moved off.

Below things were better, the final corridor easy by comparison, just another steel roller job, then on with the legs, fetch and roughly remount the various pieces - the finer details left to be figured out later.

"Thanks." Gordon patted the top of the lathe as the helpers lounged against benches and walls, the scene dimly illuminated by a single small waterwheel light in the ceiling. "I'll show you when it's working - not necessarily this year though. Come on, let's join the ladies." He led the way back along the corridors and up to the kitchen/dining room.

Serving coffee and biscuits, Jan produced a bottle of whisky kept especially for Jim. The ladies had apparently listened with care. Repeating the men's words they held forth at some length on how males make such a fuss over any little job. The merry gathering around the dining room table was stopped when an arriving motorcaravan called attention back to the office.

Enthusiasm is claimed to be no substitute for knowledge, but coupled with perseverance it did yield results in this case! By the following evening the fully assembled lathe was working, all minor bits and pieces now refixed in their proper positions. Working might be an exaggeration; it would be more accurate to say, it could be made to work, for it had no motor - the belt drive must be pulled by hand, a function at which the family was to become involved whenever a machining task demanded power. River Valley could now claim to have the biggest one manpower lathe in the country and probably the oldest, for on the name plate appeared the inscription, Hendry Machine Co., Torrington CT. USA. Patent March 8 1892, a machine reputed to have been supplied on lend-lease during the war.

***

Departure day was fast approaching. Tomorrow Chris would leave home, probably forever. All was packed and ready as the family sat in the lounge, the two younger children not exactly excited but curious, wanting details. Knowing that her own turn to meet the wider world lay not too far ahead, Sharon asked questions to which for the most part Chris could offer no answer. Stephen, still in his second year at senior school, had as yet given little thought to leaving, but envy showed in his face. Discussion turned to earlier times, to their arrival in the valley in the little caravan, to building the house and to the waterwheel - Chris particularly, remembering the events of his younger years as if reluctant to lose them, like an anchor, an escape route if all should go wrong. As the evening progressed, the parents looked at each other often, small things triggering memories, a life left behind, disappearing now, never to be recovered.

"Like I felt that time in the old empty caravan, seeing that phone number written on the wall," Jan thought, "the day we first moved into the house. How many children have built their own house? Will it always be with them or fade in their memories?" She turned back, listening as Chris recalled the day he cycled to Falmouth and back, twenty miles each way, a little more probably. The memory drew a small sigh. Last autumn after shopping in the town she had accidentally left something behind in a shop. Chris, at a loose end with no friends left on site as the season drew to a close, had offered to ride over for it. That was only a few months ago but such times were now past; he would never do so again. Jan turned away, pretending to look at the cover of a magazine.

That feeling of loss returned the following day while sitting waiting in the driving seat as Gordon helped to stack cases in the boot. The last one loaded, she saw father and son stand looking at each other, a brief handshake, a word of good luck - then they were apart, Chris climbing into the passenger seat. Starting the engine, she eased forward and drove off, looking up at the car mirror to see three figures still standing by the house door. Reaching the platform at Penzance station, no words would come and they strode on in silence. Unsure what to say, Chris slowed, setting the cases down and turning. Standing facing each other, a moment of doubt passed between them, an embarrassed pause as they sought to say goodbye in this public place. He was the taller now; she looked up slightly into his eyes then realising the move must come from her, reached forward to hug him. The embrace was brief enough, she would have held him longer, forever perhaps, but knew he would pull away and hated the thought. Then he was walking on along the platform again, setting down one case to wave briefly before entering a carriage. That was it. She waited, standing there as the train became a toy in the distance but no head appeared at the window.

"What are you doing?" Returning from Penzance, Jan rounded the corner of the centre toilet building, drawn by the sound of hammering. A small hole was being knocked in the wall halfway between the Ladies and Gents doors.

"Ouch!" The chisel flew sideways, struck by a glancing blow from the hammer. "Don't creep up on me like that!" Gordon bent to retrieve the tool. "You wanted a place for motorcaravans to empty their waste-water tanks and top up with fresh water. This is a hole for the water pipe, half-inch copper... well it's actually twenty-two millimetres now."

"Bit near the building isn't it? Where will the waste water go?"

"The drain is already in, I laid it across the road before the tarmac came. Just need to uncover it, then add a concrete dish for the splashes. You're right, it is a bit near the building but it's easier here; all the pipework close at hand and a wall to hang the hose on... be all right I think. We'll need a sign."

The arrangement proved successful, nicely timed as Spring Bank holiday brought an increase in visitors.

CHAPTER 2

Alan

June was a fine month, long hours of sunshine spreading good humour through the camp. People were sitting out, lounging around, feeding the ducks, happy in the valley and perhaps reluctant to climb into cars with seat and steering wheels hot to the touch. Many a windscreen was draped in towels, held in place under the wipers and intended, not too successfully, to lower inside temperatures. Visitors were mainly couples, many elderly, the school holidays not yet started and children still scarce. Strawberries and cream and Wimbledon ensured a spell of idleness when the site owners sat back, acknowledging hands that waved in pleasure from various cars as happy visitors passed the office - a little rest and relaxation before the busy period to come. Fortunately grass grew slowly in midsummer, the idleness only relative, confined mostly to the middle of the day for there was still the early morning cleaning, the shop, a few caravans and the odd tent arriving - and now and then a little flash of more energetic activity when a tap went wrong or a drain blocked somewhere, but in general these were golden days.

Billy Jean King was on court when a car drew up in the yard, a man on his own, his dress and demeanour not that of a holidaymaker.

"My turn," Gordon rose, stepping round the chair, taking a few backward steps still watching the screen until a winning lob finished the rally. As half expected, the man on the doorstep was an official. A fire had occurred at one of the coastal parks, sweeping through a whole swathe of tents, so every site was being rechecked for the proper spacing.

"Twenty feet apart; all of them" Gordon insisted. "I pitch each one myself. I go with them and check the spacing is right; help them push their caravans into position too, very often."

"It's six metres now, not twenty feet, we're supposed to be European!" the inspector lectured with a raised finger. "What about people travelling together? We find they prefer to be closer - so nobody sneaks a small tent between them, one couple told me."

"Okay six metres then, and travelling together or not, no one get closer than that - at this time of year it's more like twenty metres. Go look for yourself." Gordon waved a hand across the valley in invitation, hoping to return to the match, Billy Jean his favourite player. The inspector had other ideas.

"Not on this one; we're in a hurry, I can't afford to go round again showing the infringements. Come with me please." About to stride away he remembered something. "Better bring a pad and pencil."

"I won't need one. You'll find everything in order, all the spacing correct."

The sceptical look suggested otherwise. Perhaps it was fair enough - with the weather hot and dry, brush fires were still likely and some camps did tend to let people pitch wherever they felt like, never mind how close. Grabbing a pad, Gordon hurried to catch up as they marched off together, the inspector a pace ahead.

To an extent the man was disappointed, for not one caravan or tent encroached on the six metre spacing but in one place he stopped, pointing to a strip of bushes running behind three widely spaced caravans.

"Gorse is one of the worst fire hazards, think about that."

Probably it was not within his powers to enforce its removal but he did have a point. The first bonfire they had ever burnt in the valley all those years ago, had proved that. A little farther on they stopped again.

"That screen, the windbreak between those two caravans,"

the man pointed to a canvas strip some three or more feet high fixed to a series of posts spanning most of the separation space. "That could transmit fire - we don't want to be unreasonable but tell them to... well, shorten the length or change the angle."

The man left with a few departing words, hurrying off to his next call.

Jan turned as Gordon entered the office. "Billy Jean won the first set and it's going with service in the second. What did he say?"

"Bit stern on the way round, found a couple of things but paid us a nice compliment when he left. We're the best yet on his site visits."

"He probably says that to them all."

"No, he only started this afternoon, we're his first." Gordon dodged the cushion, bending over to pick up and return it, leaning over to kiss her forehead, then sank back into his own chair, content to continue watching until the children returned or the shop bell rang.

Sharon had sat most of her O levels, one remained but she was still at school for a few more weeks with little to do. In her various classes were several boys that with some understatement she described as 'not bad', but who her friends classified as 'dishy'. Several girls in her group were already dating lads but Sharon, while well aware of the boys, was not unduly impressed.

"Some are so big headed, particularly Alan!"

"Teenage boys usually are; some men too..." Jan paused glancing directly at Dad. Sharon's expression signalled agreement and the two girls smiled at each other, well aware that Gordon was watching and had understood.

"These boys at school; big headed in what way?"

"Every way Mum! Sitting there with a group of girls around them, reaching out a hand to touch one, expecting her to swoon with..." Sharon drew the back of a hand across her forehead, closing her eyes in imitation of fainting away. "Holding forth on the best way to do this and that, as if girls were helpless. We were talking about holidays - he tried to tell *me* how to pitch a tent, as if I couldn't possible know such a masculine thing! Wish I could take him down a peg!"

"How much nerve do you have?" Dad asked, "This, what was his name... Alan. What would happen if some anonymous poem appeared on the school notice board, something poking a little fun..."

"Poem?" Sharon looked doubtful. "I'm not very good at... we could try though. Might be fun standing with my friends, pretending not to know - listening to their comments."

The year's serious study was over, a little light relief welcome. The plan that hatched around the table might or might not serve the purpose of denting certain egos, but at least it would add a little mystery in the common room now the exams were mainly finished. To be effective they must exaggerate, that would be part of the fun. Jan was torn, disapproving but not really wanting to spoil the family spirit this little scheme had engendered. She did however insist that Stephen should not be allowed to find out. Sharon approved, fearing that if her younger brother knew, then her own identity might be revealed to the lower school. The plot developed therefore, intermittently and in secret, Sharon and Dad working together when an opportunity arose. It would be cheeky and ego boosting to start, but the final verses should bring him to earth with a bump. Four episodes would be ideal, everything depending on how the first was received. After many trials and alterations, the poem, not perhaps one of great literary merit, read as follows.

My legs go limp when he comes near,
His gentle eyes so blue and clear.
My heart it thunders at his smile,
I yearn for him to stay a while.

Oh let him reach and touch my finger,
What thrill, what pang of joy will linger.
I shall not wash that limb so rare,
My love for him's too strong to bear.

If he should speak this name of mine
A shiver will enshroud my spine.
I am his servant to command,
Now what is it he will demand?

In all my dreams I feel his lips,
As to my arms he quickly slips.
Oh Alan, come to me dear heart,
Hold tight and let us never part.

The finished verses, marred with many crossings out and corrections, were recopied in Sunday best handwriting, the heading ALAN added in big letters designed to draw attention! Sharon looked at the work, a glow of excitement mixed with doubt in her expression, then folding with extreme care, she hid it in her satchel. Next morning while her parents were still cleaning the toilet buildings, she rose, restlessly anxious and unable to settle - taking a slice of bread to feed the ducks from the bridge, tearing off small pieces to throw, then suddenly impatient tossed the rest of the slice on the water and hurried back indoors.

"Sharon, whatever is the matter? Stop fidgeting and eat," Jan shook her head, not connecting her daughter's behaviour with the events of the evening before.

Hurrying up the road later, Stephen found himself first running to catch up, then way ahead as his sister, overtaken by doubts, suddenly slowed to saunter along lost in her own thoughts.

At school the common room was crowded before the first bell; Sharon mingled with friends talking in groups, suddenly aware that someone had asked a question. Swinging round without a clue what had been said, "Yes," she replied automatically nodding agreement, then realised from the expressions it was the wrong answer. "Er... I mean no."

They turned to her, one girl asking, "This boy, who is he? Go on, tell us - don't pretend you were thinking of something else!"

The other girls were waiting, attention sharply keen.

Sharon looked at the faces, wondering for a second if they knew - had somehow seen the folded paper in her bag? She looked down towards it, her colour rising. Nothing could more convince her friends that they had hit the mark, that it was indeed a boy in her thoughts.

Sharon made an excuse that no one believed and wandered off, waiting her chance but someone was always nearby; she could find no way to plant the paper undetected. Only later in the morning did an opportunity come, just before lunch during one of her free periods. Quickly she stepped into the corridor heading for the common room but at the last moment changed her mind and walked on by, stealing a glance through the open door in passing, a glance achieved with eyes swivelled sideways and hardly a movement of the neck. Taking three more paces, her feet stopped; the room had been empty!

In a second she back inside, hands scrabbling for those drawing pins so carefully placed in one corner of the bag, pulling out the paper and holding it to the notice board, glancing nervously over a shoulder, heart beating fast. Hit momentarily by indecision, she hesitated... then with sudden determination pushed the pins quickly home and swung away, racing to the door, controlling her speed with great difficulty and making a somewhat breathless escape. The deed was done!

For a long time Sharon sat alone, pretending to read a book. The lunch bell was due but in spite of a burning desire to know her friends' reaction, she was uncertain; unsure of keeping a straight face, unsure about returning to... to... the scene of the crime? The thought had come suddenly - was it a crime? The headmaster would probably think so. When the bell did sound, the whole building bustled with movement but eating had little appeal. Later three friends rushed excitedly up, '*Come on!*' Despite a pretended reluctance, they dragged her away to the common room. A throng of girls and boys crowded round the notice board; Sharon pulled up sharply at the sight of Alan, standing talking to the others, a smile showing his pleasure, obviously enjoying the burst of attention, the distinction perhaps, that it gave him. Pretending her hesitation had been surprise at the crowd round the board, Sharon managed to gasp, "What has happened?" and pushed forward appearing to study the text with interest.

"Quite good isn't it?"

She turned sharply, dumbstruck to find herself looking up into Alan's eyes; eyes that shone with pride.

Quickly she looked down, worried about discovery but determined. "Damn! He's even more conceited." She had wavered when first seeing the attention this note had drawn, but no doubt remained, the attack must continue.

A week later a second poem was smuggled in and attached to the board. It proved no easier, her heart racing, hand shaking slightly as a new set of pins were pushed in; her breath held as the quick steps of a hurried departure carried her back to anonymity - an elation within defying the danger as she thought of the words and the reaction it might bring!

> My lashes downward turned will be,
> When Alan stands so manfully
> Beside me, and my cheeks will flush,
> First pink then crimson as I blush.
>
> My heart will pound within my chest,
> With bosom heaving 'neath my vest.
> My voice is gone my throat is dry,
> If he leaves now I think I'll die.
>
> Oh Alan dear, please treat me fair,
> For I am yours and do not care
> What ecstasies of joy we reach,
> What ways of love you will me teach.
>
> And when I rest within your arms,
> My body quivering to your charms,
> My lips so hot and moist for you
> To kiss, with burning passion true...

At the page bottom a single line demanded, "Don't miss the next instalment!"

It quickly attracted a huge interest, Alan again grew visibly in stature but had no inkling as to their source. Sharon watched him from a distance, smiling to herself, looking forward to what was to come - not knowing that things were to get more difficult!

The next attempt was almost a disaster. Such intense interest had been created that the notice board was under constant scrutiny. Teachers too, now visited the common room more frequently, striding in suddenly for no apparent reason, to prowl quickly round and smartly disappear. When Sharon entered school one morning with the third edition safely in her satchel, three days had passed since the last such venture but the board was crowded with youngsters. A better way of directing pupils' attention to notices would be hard to find! Mid-morning arrived before she found herself free and entered the now empty room intent on the increasingly risky task. A few seconds was all it required to perch the satchel on a nearby bench, whip out the paper and turn to the board. On the very point of pushing in the first of two drawing pins already held in her hand, she froze... footsteps were approaching from the corridor outside. Snatching away the paper, losing a pin in the process, Sharon stuffed it in her satchel, pulling out a textbook and swinging into a nearby seat. There she sat with head lowered - apparently pouring over the text, sneaking a glance to the left as one of the male teachers stood before the notice board scanning the contents.

At home that night tea was unusually quiet. Having watched, offering a few suggestions the previous evening when Dad and Sharon worked on the new verses, Jan guessed something had happened at school. Whatever it was probably involved the poem but she could ask no questions with Stephen present.

As the meal finished, Gordon left to greet an arriving caravan. Jan wanted to get Sharon alone to ask what had happened but Stephen sat waiting, sensing perhaps a desire that he should leave, such a move typical of his nature.

Unfortunately, no other twelve-year-old lads were on site at the moment who might attract him away.

Jan rose, making for the bathroom, calling back over one shoulder, "Would one of you like to start the washing-up?" On her return, Sharon was at the sink and Stephen had disappeared. The girls grinned at each other.

"Well? How did it go?" Jan asked quietly, reaching for a tea-towel.

The description that followed was graphic, Sharon struggling for the right words to portraying that panic as the footsteps approached, and the lengthy period afterwards when she had sat, wrestling with herself, bolstering courage for another attempt.

"Well, did you succeed."

Instead of replying, Sharon reached for her satchel, opened it and withdrew a creased paper sheet, waving it with a little shrug. "It's more difficult now; everyone is watching, trying to find out who... perhaps I shouldn't..."

The weekend passed, Sharon finding a friend in one of the arriving caravans and the matter was forgotten. Packing her bag on Monday she almost left the folded paper behind but at the last minute tucked it down one side, adding another drawing pin - the dropped one had never been recovered.

At school the common room was crowded; fifteen minutes still to go before the first bell. Sharon lounged against a window with three friends looking idly out when the door flew open, a boy in the corridor shouted "Fight!" then disappeared at a run. Almost the entire population of boys made for the door, breaking off conversations, to dash away - the girls they were talking to looked at each other, not pleased but following anyway as the room rapidly emptied. Sharon too made to leave, stopping to retie a shoelace, signalling her friends on, "Go ahead, I'll catch you!"

Left on her own she reached for the satchel, pulled out the paper, searching urgently in one corner for the pins. A few seconds later it was on the notice board.

But school is not the time or place
To hold me tight in your embrace.
Come fly with me through meadow and field,
And let us to temptation yield.

Soft billowy grasses bow to the breeze,
Bright new foliage gracing the trees,
We step together 'cross springy turf,
And thrill to the sound of distant surf.

Our own little heaven, with birds all around
Still clasping hands we sit on the ground,
No words are required as we hold one another,
'Tis plain in his eyes there is no other.

The wind sighs his name, Alan it breathes low,
As his fingers run through my hair, soft and slow.
I know it is love when my heart beats this way,
I trust him, I need him forever to stay.

At the page bottom appeared the words, "Final episode coming shortly!" No time to take in the effect; anyone might come! She ran headlong for the door, pulling up short as a master appeared directly in her path.

"Why the rush?"

Sharon hesitated, he must see it, almost impossible to miss... "A fight Sir, down below. Someone called from outside. Everyone's gone to watch; my shoelace came undone." She made to leave, the master too heading down the corridor - she hurried to stay with him, wanting to branch off to one side and disappear but fearing that to do so would only cause suspicion. They arrived together to find a mass of students outside but whatever was happening had already stopped. Sharon rejoined her friends, drifting slowly back but left them and went to her classroom to await the bell.

Over lunch talk among the girls was all of the poem, with many a whispered fantasy and outbreaks of laugher, the mystery catching young imaginations. All those returning to the common room before lessons had read it, pleased at the chance to quote, or more often misquote, small snippets to others around the long tables. After eating Sharon hurried off, safe in a crowd of others, but the verses were gone. Who removed them no one knew, but it only served to increase the speculation as to their origin.

The following morning's assembly contained a sermon on time wasting, with a stern lecture about immoral poems and notice boards. Never had the young audience been so attentive; wide eyes anticipating a revelation. Sharon felt certain the headmaster was looking straight at her. That teacher who caught her alone in the common room before dashing off to see the fight - had he said anything? She stood, oblivious of the whispers around, dreading... expecting to be named - but an excitement rising within at the notoriety it would bring!

The lecture droned on but no name was forthcoming. An uncomfortable afternoon followed, waiting for a call to the headmaster's study - but that too never came. Perhaps the staff had discussed it and considered the verses beyond her capability - who knows? It was true enough, she could never have done it without help. Probably the warning was only as a deterrent, the staff apprehensive as to episode four's contents. That final part was already written, Sharon longing to achieve her purpose of 'bringing him down a peg or two', but even for such a desirable cause she was not at the moment prepared to take the increased risk. It lay temporarily hidden in the drawer in her bedroom - she took it out one evening, reading again the words.

> Now Alan laid me gently down,
> On billowy grasses sweet,
> And I prepared with baited breath
> My Waterloo to meet.
>
> You must not think me libertine
> If I resist him not,
> His size twelve feet quite turn my head,
> He's really got the lot.

His eyes are funny muddy blue
They look in both directions,
And roam around without control
I think they've crossed connections.

His teeth do shine like ivory towers
So fine and white they be,
Dazzling perfection in his smile,
He took them out for me.

His dark and wavy hair so thrills
How me it does excite.
This flattering toupee that he wears
Is really quite a sight.

He has a brain above us all,
His marks no hope to catch,
And with that fine colossal head
He has the ears to match.

So now you see why I must let
Him have his way with me.
It's not just love that burns so deep,
It's more like sympathy.

Having built Alan up to quixotic heights, the chance to bring him to earth with a bump was almost irresistible; she had not forgotten his lofty explanation of how to pitch a tent! But Sharon, feeling herself already under suspicion, had noticed several teachers look searchingly round the room as class began, stopping suddenly when their eyes met her own - then seeming satisfied, the lesson commenced. Once when she arrived late, the mistress in charge left the class, hurrying off, to return shortly. Had she been checking on that notice board?

After tea one evening when Stephen had rushed off to

join a newly arrived friend, Gordon enquired as to progress and quietly hinted that Sharon should try again but receiving a cold look from Jan, he desisted, returning to the shop to finish compiling a list of items needed from Cash and Carry. Trade was increasing, time to stock up before the peak season was upon them. More caravan spares were needed too; one woman had asked for a cover for the towing hitch - apparently someone pinched it at the last site, causing the oily ball to stain her dress as she reached into the car boot. They were simple enough things to stock - not expensive, about three pound for a box of twelve and selling at fifty pence each - double the cost! Of course it might be five years before the last one sold so the apparently high profit margin was hardly likely to make anyone rich. It offered however, another little service to the customer - a convenience that should have been thought of before, the need anticipated. What else could be stocked to make people more happy? Canvas repair kits for tents and awnings were added, and little submersible pumps that dropped straight into an outside water carrier and worked from the caravan battery. Those batteries were becoming a problem, so many now brought in for charging that at times the waterwheel had difficulty keeping pace. Increasingly caravan electrics no longer worked directly from the car, but from separate batteries carried in little lockers near the hitch, being charged up automatically as the caravan was towed. Naturally, when stationary on site for many days these batteries ran down. Recently special extension leads had become available giving a connection back to the car battery to overcome this problem. A stock of these leads now rested on the shop shelves.

Something else had been added too. The stream with its crystal clear water attracted not only children; visitors of all ages enjoyed sitting on the bank, some just to watch as it babbled over rocks or ran placidly through deeper stretches, others with a fishing rod in their hands. From time to time someone would walk by, following the footpath to St Erth, and just occasionally among these infrequent ramblers, the River Authority bailiff stalked his prey. Being caught without a local fishing licence was common enough - many folk believing the licence they held in their home county was also valid in the westcountry. Fortunately, Cornwall being an hospitable county, the bailiff merely sent these people off to town, to the nearest fishing tackle shop for a proper licence. However, that was no longer necessary; they were now available in the site shop.

Another line recently introduced was books. Caravans with televisions were still a rarity, so books for evenings or for relaxing in the sunshine should be popular with visitors. A firm called Bookwise had delivered the first consignment, complete with a bookshelf, and would change the stock over at intervals.

Later that evening as Sharon lay reading in her room, her parents talked quietly in the lounge, Jan again referring to the poems.

"Stop encouraging our daughter to misbehave. She should never have started. Can't think where she gets it from; must be you, I was never disobedient at school."

"No? What about that cotton wool? Poor nuns, bet you girls gave them a terrible life."

Remembering, Jan smiled. "Saved them from boredom perhaps - but that's no excuse for Sharon! Anyway you were no angel. Who put linseed oil in the ink so it spread out across the page instead of drying? Dim too - doctored every ink-well in the class except your own, a serious error as your teacher pointed out."

"That's going back a few years! Who told you?"

"Ron, you remember; your old class-mate. We went as a foursome to some celebration, back in our courting days... he came square dancing too, I think?"

Gordon eased deeper into the chair with a smile of surprise, recalling those early days, and another memory came to mind. "Yes, we were at school together. Did I ever tell you about young Ron's stroke of genius in one of our English lessons? The master, a Mr Coles - remember that name, it's important - had the task of improving our writing, an uphill struggle I suspect. Anyway, he contended that no matter how difficult it might seem, an essay could be written on any subject. Just a single word taken at random and a good writer could produce an essay. Did you know someone once wrote six pages on 'Carrots'?

"Anyway, as an example this teacher wrote in chalk on the board, 'Dustbins'. That's a subject I could easily write about now but as young lads it seemed impossible! Picking up his long cane and tapping on the word for emphasis, our Mr Coles turned to the class. *'That's your subject. Now, who can suggest good sentence to start off with?'*"

Gordon eased himself again in the chair, looking up at the little waterwheel lights above, then back across at Jan.

"I remember it so well; the desks, the layout of the class, everything. For a few seconds silence reigned, we pupils looking at each other and shrugging - then Ron sitting next to me, shot his hand in the air, the arm bolt upright, stretching to the limit of reach in his anxiety to be the one chosen, a glow of eagerness on his face. Disregarding the custom of waiting to be asked, he could not contain the urgent plea, *'I've got one Sir!'*

"There was a pause in that classroom, Ron's young face in the bench beside me alight with pent-up impatience. We all looked up at the teacher, waiting; he was an elderly, rather kindly figure. Slowly the cane dipped forwards, pointing, *'Go ahead lad.'*

"At those words, Ron inhaled a long breath of relief, *'Sir. In the dustbin one finds anything, from old rags to old coals!'*

"Of course, orally Coles and coals are identical; the class was in hysterics, even our Mr Coles himself couldn't keep a straight face, pointing again with his cane, *'Very good my lad but be careful.'*"

Gordon stopped, the nostalgic little memory finished, then reached out taking Jan's hand. "I think that bit of fun in the classroom produced a better set of essays than we ever wrote before - all of us trying to better Ron's achievement - a little bit of inspiration you might say. So you see, Sharon's misbehaviour as you put it, may actually give an incentive for her classmates to improve. I bet a good percentage wished they could have written those poems."

Rising early to clean the toilet buildings had, over the years, become the normal way of life; it no longer seemed arduous, just an ordinary start to the morning. Nevertheless when Sharon offered to take over this task for part of each week in exchange for an increased allowance, it seemed a great idea. The funny thing was that having at long last the chance to lay in, neither parent now found they could do so. However, those more leisurely breakfasts were splendid. Jan's father, Jim was still helping too, running the shop for a while later in the morning, cycling along the half-mile of road on his tricycle. He declined afternoons as being too boring, not enough customers to keep him busy. Trade in the shop was not increasing so fast as in previous years, at least not on the food side, partly due to increasing supermarket shopping and partly from caravanners bringing stocks with them; understandable enough but the cost of petrol was rising - would that be an incentive to buy groceries on arrival rather than carry the extra weight? More shelves were now filled with caravan and camping spares; a greater selection of water carriers, pegs for awnings and tents, gas mantles and black buckets for waste water, to name but a few. Ice packs were still frozen down at the bungalow in the village, keeping Audrey busy as visitors came daily to drop in used packs and pick up frozen ones.

Journeys were still being made regularly to Cash and Carry to replenish stocks and Jan was away on such a trip when a car drew up near the office. Out stepped Bernard Leach, the famous Cornish potter, a young Japanese companion with him. Gordon alone in the office welcomed them in, and the three sat talking. Bernard whose eyesight was failing, used his fingers to sense shape, running those sensitive potter's hands over the wooden bird carvings, particularly liking the big buzzard. Before leaving, the Japanese girl produced a small flowery card and pen, and with his hand guided into position Bernard signed it as a memento. After a spell on the riverbank with the ducks gathered close, they departed, the girl showing great devotion to the old master - Japanese respect for age and talent - he had certainly earned it. You never knew who would turn up on a caravan park, a big rumour went round once that Elsie Tanner from Coronation Street, was on site.

As the school holidays approached, numbers were increasing rapidly but so was something else. The wasp population had grown alarmingly, especially on the grassy section in front of the house, an area used mainly by families with children. Wasps are pleasant enough creatures, a little nest that lost its queen was found some years earlier in a topsoil heap, its occupants befriended and taken to live in the house for a while before being released to make the best life they could farther down the valley. Bigger things were now on the horizon. Another nest had come to light - and this was no small community as the last one had been! Right next to a caravan with the nest entrance almost underneath, the inmates flew in and out by the dozen. The caravan's occupants, finding it shortly after arrival, rushed to the office in a panic! Offered another pitch, they made the transfer smartly, smiling happily at this quick relocation but still apprehensive of the nest's proximity, now some eighty feet away.

"It will be dealt with," Jan assured them.

Seeing Gordon return from pitching a caravan farther downstream, she headed back to the office, explaining about the nest and her promise but he sought to avoid the task.

"I don't actually need to destroy it, they're not doing any harm - we'll just not use that pitch. The poor things won't sting anyone."

"Oh yes they will! And it's not only one family, everyone on that area will know by teatime; that nest entrance faces directly at several caravans."

"I can fix that. All it needs is a length of waste pipe and a bend to send them off towards the hedge. Simple." His hands spread in a gesture indicating how easy the solution was.

"You…!" Jan hesitated, shaking her head, "are an idiot! It may surprise you to know that most people hate wasps...

despise them. More children will arrive soon - it has to go!"

She was right, it *did* have to go. Children would play near it, tread on the entrance probably, then they were bound to get stung. No good attempting anything during daylight, half the winged residents were out collecting food for the next generation of wasps and on returning would not take kindly to finding their home destroyed. Better by far to take the necessary action after dark when all but a very few would rest inside. The advantage that darkness would veil their activities from watching eyes had also been considered, for as they say on TV, some of what must follow could be distressing to sensitive folk.

As dusk descended, the necessary tools were gathered: a spade, a gas blowlamp, several boxes of matches, an aerosol tin of wasp killer and a bucket with a lid.

Reluctantly, Jan agreed to help and together they prepared for battle. This was not something one undertook in shorts and a T-shirt! Gordon stuffed trousers inside sock tops, donned a thick jacket zipping it up tightly over a large scarf, then pulled a woolly hat down over his ears. Thick red rubber gloves and large plastic goggles completed the defence. Jan, similarly dressed, wearing a pair of men's socks pulled over the bottom of some old thick slacks, donned her own knitted headwear, becoming almost unrecognisable under the hat's rolled down edges. Defensively dressed in this sinister and inelegant disguise they picked up the equipment, left the office and crept off towards their target with heads lowered, hoping not to be recognised.

Arriving at the nest, tools were quietly and purposefully laid out, all carefully positioned to come quickly to hand - preparations for the dangerous assault ahead. Stealth and silence notwithstanding, the approach of this strangely clad pair had already been noticed. An audience began to gather, curiosity drawing them close. That could be unfortunate! However, whispered comments by the caravanners who briefly occupied that pitch, changed the situation. As news spread of the little expedition's purpose, the circle of spectators magically dispersed!

With roaring blowlamp in one hand and a light spade in the other, Gordon quickly marked and removed a square of turf centrally around the entrance hole. Jan stood at his side shining the torch, a box of matches ready in her other hand, one match clamped firmly in her teeth in case the blowlamp went out. That was the greatest danger! Taking a deep breath and still working with a single hand, he dug the spade in deeply, removing a chunk of soil.

The entrance tunnel might turn in any direction, all that could be done was watch for emerging wasps! Carefully, another shovelful swung clear. There was not long to wait; a slither of soil fell away and little defenders were boiling from the ground. Seeing them scramble free Jan almost dropped the torch and ran. Friendly they might be under normal circumstances but with their home under threat these escaping wasps were angry! Crouching low, Gordon's grip on the blowlamp tightened; quickness of the flame was essential now. If this nest was to be removed as it obviously had to be, then of necessity all the adult wasps must be killed - sad but unavoidable; essential for the safety of everyone, including those half-hidden onlookers who falsely considered themselves beyond danger.

It took time to reach the nest, one or two wasps escaping. With a yell, Jan dropped the matches, snatching up one of the aerosol cans and spraying frantically at some assailant, invisible in the darkness, zooming about her head. The ring of watching eyes stretched farther round caravan corners as she ducked and weaved in a strange moonlight dance.

"The light!" Gordon shouted. The beam had disappeared, cutting intricate patterns in the darkness as Jan gyrated wildly. Hearing the urgency, she steadied the torch and he dug again until one edge of the nest appeared, a creamy brownish colour against the darker soil, its size somewhat less than a football.

The hiss of the gas flame, people peering from behind caravans just visible in the circle of light, and the greater darkness beyond - that, together a total absence of other sounds gave a sinister slant to the scene. Body snatchers in the cemetery at midnight! They worked on, no further word spoken.

As had been expected, extracting the nest in one piece proved impossible. It consisted of an outer paper shell covering layers of honeycomb-like cells filled with eggs or grubs. Most of these layers were recoverable but Jan had no idea of his intention to save any part of it. Reaching into the hole, his free hand probing down among the steaming soil that still crawled with a few surviving wasps, he lifted out each layer separately, slipping them into the bucket and replacing the lid. Stirring the soil, the lamp roared again in an attempt to leave no injured ones alive and suffering, but a few were already in the air - a quick retreat advisable! The debris must be left until daylight.

Jan, standing farther from the nest, came away scot-free. Gordon was less fortunate. One intrepid defender planted a sting right through his sock just below the ankle. "Ouch!"

A bad reaction to stings meant discomfort tomorrow but he said nothing more, unable to resist a feeling of respect for the small wasp's courage; a sense that Justice had been done. He always hated himself a little when circumstances forced such severe remedies as that necessary to remove its home. The sting, the punishment - it was well deserved. Somehow the insect's success pleased him, not only to salve his own conscience but in some strange way he was proud of the valiant spirit that assailed the greater enemy, driving its attack successfully home.

Collecting the equipment, they beat a hasty retreat, still watched by curious faces from afar. The tools would stand in the shed overnight; the bucket could rest there too. Jan failed to notice how carefully it was lowered onto the wooden bench, totally unaware of its coming significance.

In the morning while she visited the hairdresser, the bucket was quickly transferred to the kitchen, its contents lifted onto a small drawing-board, each layer carefully spaced apart, cells downward and covered with a plant propagation dome. This clear plastic bubble was not actually dome-shaped but rectangular, looking very similar to those big sandwich covers seen in take away restaurants. To ensure adequate ventilation, matchsticks were placed under each corner to create an air gap all round the bottom; a gap too small for any wasps to escape. Being intended for propagation, this dome had two ready-made adjustable vents in the top. Opening one vent fully, Gordon placed a large clear plastic tub above - it looked like an oversize upside-down tea-mug. A movement caught his eye; surprised to see one wasp already hatched, he paused, fingers rubbing chin - hatched? Was that the right term?

Several times rings from the shop doorbell interrupted the work; Jan should be back anytime now. Although the arrangements were not yet finished, at least it was fairly safe. The whole creation rested on a small section of worktop in the corner of the kitchen between cooker and sink. She'd be pleased, wouldn't she?

He stood for a moment figuring the next move but a ring on the doorbell cut across these thoughts, drawing him to the office. A woman wanted extra nights; as the lady left, another car arrived. Quickly he reached for the ledger, a pen and a sheet of paper, pretending to concentrate on some figures.

Jan, her arms full of shopping, pushed the door open, stepped inside and slammed it shut with a foot. Looking across to the desk, she received a curt nod as he bent again to concentrate on the books - but something about his expression she couldn't quite place. He made no comment, no offer to help as she struggled on towards the kitchen.

Watching from the corner of one eye, Gordon stopped writing and waited.

A shout rang through the house. "No way!" Her arms still full, she stood looking down at the new guests with a smile on her lips - a smile carefully hidden so no one else should see.

Almost immediately a head appeared round the door, peering in but not entering. "Your hair looks nice."

"Flattery? Forget it! That's not staying there; one's alive." She pointed at a dozy looking wasp crawling slowly around.

"It can't get out... well it could at the moment but it

won't be able to when I've finished."

She moved closer, inspecting more carefully. "That plastic beaker thing on the top; there's a hole in it."

"Of course, that's why it's in the corner near the cooker. Wait a minute." Hurrying to the shop and cutting off a length of plastic that caravanners used for water pipe, he took it to the kitchen, pressing one end into the hole in the beaker. "You're safe. It can't escape now."

"What about the other end... no, don't tell me, I guessed already. That hole in the wall where the gas pipe comes in; this tube goes through there, right?"

"Right. Given a sufficient IQ, they find the open vent, crawl into the upturned tub, along the tube and off to the outside world, bringing back goodies for the next generation of grubs." With a nod and a broad grin, he pulled clear a plug of cotton wool, stuffed in the wall to keep out draughts.

Watching, she hoped the tube would not fit, but was disappointed. The hole had been made long ago and lined with a plastic pipe. In an argument at the time he had insisted, "It will stop our gas pipe chaffing on the blockwork and it needs to be big; we may want more pipes someday."

Remembering, she muttered, "Typical!" and turned away.

By midday several more wasps had appeared. Gordon, delighted at the early success, fed a few on his finger until increasing numbers made it difficult getting them back under cover. Both food and water were placed in small containers inside the dome; none seemed interested in the water.

Discovering a route out through the tube took the little striped guests longer than expected. To help them find the way back, a short piece of copper pipe was cut open, straightened and hammered flat, then bent at right angles to form a tiny shelf. Fixed to the outside wall just under the exit hole, it formed a wasp landing platform. Showing this latest addition to the family that evening, Gordon mentioned casually that he was thinking of marketing it.

"Guaranteed to ensure plenty of space each side of the pitch! I'll call it a Wasp Air Landing & Lift Off Platform, a WALLOP! Everyone will want one."

Rolling her eyes, Jan glanced at Sharon, both turning to Stephen. Heads nodded in agreement and together they turned, walking off. "We don't know him," Sharon whispered.

Inside the dome, building work started right away, the wasps scrapping wood from the board on which their new home stood. Their strong jaws chewed these scrapings to pulp, a soft workable material used for repairing and extending the nest. It became clear then why so often wasps appeared on the shed door on sunny afternoons. Going outside, waiting until one arrived and bringing an ear very near the wasp - moving slowly not to frighten the little creature, it was possible to actually hear wood being scraped off; the sound surprisingly loud.

Returning indoors, four small holes were drilled in the top of the plastic cover and short lengths of string poked in, knotted at one end to prevent them falling right through. Wasp numbers had increased rapidly and they were not listless like the small nest found years before. These were busily repairing the damaged sections, building an outer shell round the nest, fixing it in several places to those hanging pieces of string - like they would fix a normal nest in the ground to the rootlets of a tree. When one wasp died, others appeared to eat it in preference to food made available around the nest. Stephen caught a bluebottle and dropped it in through the adjustable vent. They pounced like a hawk on a mouse, devouring the unfortunate fly in the bat of an eyelid.

Jan watched when she was alone, becoming increasingly intrigued with the industry and continuous movement, some wasps working on the nest, others apparently cleaning up, and yet more feeding the grubs. Other grubs were weaving silken webs across the opening of their cells and young wasps constantly emerged, eating their way out from where white grubs had been only days before. Often she leaned on her worktop, her face close to the nest watching with a faint smile, a pleasure never admitted to or indulged in when anyone else entered the kitchen.

"Those things," as she called them to other members of

the household, were allowed to stay, not from affection but just because she was such a reasonable and tolerant Mum. "But don't push your luck, I could easily change!"

Sharon and Stephen, like young people do, soon accepted the arrangement as a normal feature of the room, sometimes watching or dropping in an item of food but mostly ignoring it. Occasionally Stephen would bring a friend in to view the growing nest but Sharon seldom did. Jan asked her once when they were in the house alone, if she didn't want to bring her latest friend in to see.

"No thank you! Alice thinks we're odd enough already with waterwheel lights - I don't want her knowing just how weird some people can be! We shouldn't tell anyone; visitors talk in the toilet buildings, look at you sideways when you pass by."

After a while, to see how far they ranged, a hole was drilled in the clear plastic tube, a super-thin artist's brush painting a splash of white on each as it passed. These wasps certainly got around; in the dustbin yard, the garden, and it wasn't long before they started flying round the house, entering by the office door. And this was Gordon's big mistake! To guide them home he tempted each wasp onto a finger with jam, and while they ate, took them gently back round the house to their landing platform. They have a sweet tooth, any flavour of jam will do but best of all is syrup from the bottom of a tub of glacé cherries. Wasps learn very fast. Within hours it was like pension day at the Post Office. They were queuing for their syrup! Incoming campers were just not convinced or reassured when told, "Don't worry about them, they're ours, you can tell by the white marks on their backs."

It did however, seem to divert attention from the wasps. Gordon noticed the customers tended to back away smiling with a kind of uneasy nervousness - people can be so strange.

More days passed and numbers continued to grow; worse still, a few flew into nearby caravans, expecting to be fed. Hearing this news while serving, Jan slipped through from the shop. "Your wasps are settling on other people's fingers now. They've got to go, stupid things!"

"They're not stupid. It's just that... well," he hunted for a reason, "I... er, overheard one talking yesterday - she said all humans look alike."

That lame excuse may have held some truth, humans probably did look alike to a wasp, but the school holidays would start tomorrow and it was time to act - or so Jan insisted! As night fell, Gordon sealed the top of the wasps' dome, and early next morning took a spade some distance down the valley, carefully removed a large turf and dug a shallow hole. Returning to the house, the nest on its drawing-board base with the plastic cover still in position, was carefully lifted and carried off along the riverbank. Arriving at the prepared hole, he severed the strings holding the nest to the cover, then using a long sharp knife brought along for the purpose, cut the nest free the drawing-board. So far so good; now for the tricky bit! The wasps had also attached their nest to the sides of the plastic dome and these attachments must now be severed. To do that the dome must be lifted - releasing the residents!

Reaching forward he lifted, and with a long knife broke those attachments. Taking the nest carefully in gloved hands and kneeling, he placed it in the hole, put a short piece of plank across the top for support and protection, then replaced the turf. The air all round hummed, thick with yellow and black striped bodies but not one stung! Wasps are such affectionate insects.

CHAPTER 3

Dillon

Jan rose, moving to push aside the curtain and peer cautiously out. The yard was full, caravans and cars blocking the way. Good! Today, the first Saturday of the school holidays was always busy. Just as well, numbers needed a boost - so far the month had been disappointing, only sixty-six families staying the previous night and seven of those due to leave.

Chris's help would be missed this year; she wondered momentarily when her eldest son would next come home on a visit but another engine outside pushed that thought away as she reached over to shake the sleeping form, then hurried to dress. Right now some of the waiting vehicles must be moved.

Ten minutes later, four caravans had been ushered away onto hardstanding.

"It's only temporary, the office opens at seven. Come and book in then and we'll find you a proper pitch."

Three more caravans and several tents remained in the yard, all asleep in their cars, but a space had been cleared allowing vehicles to pass. That was essential as some visitors left early, those with a long homeward journey or catching the boat to the Scilly Isles or for a variety of other reasons. More would be arriving too, but they must wait - cleaning the facilities and a quick breakfast had priority.

Some forty minutes later when Jan arrived back at the house, Stephen appeared. He had a room to himself now and was growing fast, getting taller, his thirteenth birthday in two months time. No doubt this early rising anticipated a return of old friends from previous years.

"Couldn't sleep?" she looked at him in surprise and not expecting a reply, asked, "Eggs?" At a slight nod she placed another on a tablespoon, slipping it into a boiling saucepan - they were quick and easy. "Dad's still doing the dustbins, will you clean the waterwheel?"

Stephen left, returning almost immediately. "Caravan outside got a puncture, its tyre's flat; one of those in the yard. Shall I tell Dad?"

"No, wait until he's eaten - we won't get chance later. Go to the basement and find that old foot pump. Might be able to get it to a pitch if the puncture's not too fast." As he left Jan added another egg, stepped into Sharon's bedroom and gave her a shake. "Sorry, meant to let you lie in today but we need help. Do the shop for a while after breakfast, will you?"

The morning proved hectic. That punctured caravan tyre was quickly inflated, the old pump lodged on the hitch as it towed away, barely making a pitch in time - not an ideal choice, just the nearest one available. The elderly couple were depressed, a bad start to their holiday, but with a queue waiting there was little Gordon could do. Promising to come back later, he hurried away and arriving at the office without the foot pump, asked Stephen to fetch it.

Mid-morning came before he finally returned to the punctured caravan, but the wheel was missing and the car gone. Recognising the site's own bottle-jack propping up the axle, he guessed what had happened. The couple must be off getting their puncture mended. Making for the office again where another caravan had already drawn up, he saw Stephen with a friend near the bridge and taking a few steps towards them, called, "Did you fix it?"

"Yes, he should be back soon."

"Was he pleased?"

Instead of replying, Stephen held up a fifty pence piece.

By nightfall there were ninety-four caravans and tents; thirty-five had arrived in that single day. As they lay in the bed, pleased but not yet able to unwind enough for asleep, Jan ran a hand lightly over the warm body beside her and resting a head on his shoulder, asked, "Tired? Everyone seems happy, don't you think?"

"Most of them - especially that couple with the puncture. They finally chose a pitch right downstream, a place all on its own. I warned them the third toilets weren't working yet but that's where they wanted to be. Great when everything works out, isn't it. Busy though - what will happen when we get old?"

"Never mind getting old - how do we manage when Sharon leaves?"

It was Sharon who three days later took a phone call from the RSPCA. A swan was in trouble at the Clowance estate at Praze-an-Beeble. It was being attacked by younger swans, which drove it from the lake. "Could you arrange collection and look after it?" the man asked.

"You want my father; hold on," she stepped to the door and called.

Arrangements were quickly agreed; they had taken big birds before and were getting a reputation. Transportation would be difficult; a person could drive one-handed while holding the wings for a short distance but not on public roads. Bad time of year for them both to leave the site; never mind, the bird needed help. Besides, holidaymakers would love another swan, it was years since the last one recovered and flew off. Ringing Jim for help and leaving Sharon temporarily in charge, the two parents hurried off. Jan drove on the return journey, the swan on Gordon's lap not entirely happy, leaving hot little deposits all over his right thigh. Arriving home the big bird, a male, waddled down the front lawn to the river's edge. Having no mate for whom to defend territory, it tolerated and ignored the other ducks, certainly causing less trouble than the five Shelduck that disappeared a week earlier. That departure, expected from their migratory habits, had been a relief to everyone.

When fully recovered, this swan too would probably fly off in search of bigger waters. At the moment however, contentment showed in every movement as it eased into the water, something denied for several weeks, constantly driven away by younger swans. At first it was shy, waiting in the mid-stream for bread to be thrown, but with the site so busy it rapidly became used to people. Climbing the bank to eat from those hands brave enough to offer food directly, it progressed quickly, approaching nearer caravans, tapping a big beak on windows for attention. Most people responded with food, which of course perpetuated the habit.

As another week passed and August arrived, over 120 families were now living in the valley - an ego-boosting rise; a constant stream of juicy cheques giving some members of the household an inflated opinion of their financial position. August brought something else too; a liberal scattering of brand new T registration cars. Sharon came through from the shop to find her mother standing near the office window.

"Look at that," Jan pointed to a shiny Jaguar passing by. "Our visitors are getting very prosperous. The cars shine more this year."

"The tarmac - not so much dust." Sharon prompted, leaning against the desk. "It's not so good farther down-stream; my friend Betty, the one with the black and white collie - she says people down there are grumbling. Dust off the road is bad; their cars don't shine!"

"Dad plans to tarmac that section when the season ends. Pity we don't still have Max, our old excavator. You remember that very dry summer when we loaded the trailer with dustbins full of water, then put a line of empty ones at the back and drilled little holes in a half circle round the bottom. I drove the excavator while your father stood behind in the trailer dipping bucketfuls of water from the other dustbins and tipping it into those bins with the holes, so it sprayed out damping down the road surface."

"I remember how quick it dried. You're not thinking of doing it with the small trailer behind the mower?" Sharon's voice held disapproval. "Waste of time! I could tell my friend she can borrow our watering-can."

"Tell her we'll fix it this winter. I'll ask Dad to mention it when he pitches people in those areas; we don't want them staying away next year. Anyway it's not just the tarmac that makes this season's cars more shiny. Have you noticed all the new numberplates? Ours must be the oldest on site. Perhaps we should..." Jan paused, putting a finger to her lips and nibbling the end thoughtfully.

"No chance!" Sharon shook her head. "He'll say we can't afford it."

"Maybe, but it's not really true any more. With that big cheque in the spring and this season's takings, one new vehicle shouldn't break the bank."

At tea that evening, Jan mentioned casually that rust spots were beginning to show on the car. "They're not too big yet but getting worse all the time. Should have anticipated it I suppose - with the garage converted to a shop it stands out in all weathers. Can't really expect it to last so long?"

"You're not having another new one!" Gordon spoke defensively, already aware of the rust; there had been several faults right from the start, for instance the petrol gauge failed to work when first driven from the showroom. A warning of things to come - the car should have been refused there and then! Nevertheless, knowing the coming winter's work would be expensive, with tarmac and the third toilets to complete, he thought it should last a while longer.

Jan stared back at him for a moment, then catching an '*I told you so*' smile on Sharon's face, swung round with finger raised, but the shop doorbell rang. Sharon jumped up, escaping, hurrying off to serve the customer.

"You don't keep bacon, do you?" a lady asked.

Sharon opened the door of the tall gas fridge. Inside was mainly milk, forty or so bottles packed closely together taking most of the space. On a single narrow shelf stood bacon, cheese and sausages, just a few sealed packets of each. People asked for milk but sausages in particular were often unsold when the date expired, left to be used in the house. Hidden away in the fridge with no way to display them, sales were poor, not many people asking.

Another lady wanted tomatoes; only a few were left. Fresh produce had recently been introduced; tomatoes, potatoes, lettuce, the odd cucumber, mainly salad stuff and fruit - apples, bananas, a few oranges, sometimes plums or cherries, and punnets of strawberries. People enjoyed them but the shop was warm and some soon went off. To combat this, only small quantities could be purchased; new supplies frequently needed.

"I'll get more tomorrow," Jan promised, on hearing stocks were low again.

Fortunately a small wholesaler operated two miles away in Goldsithney. This barn-like warehouse was entered by a long passageway rising steeply from the road and flanked on both sides by stone walls. Jan visited next day for more supplies, reversing up the narrow track, for it was difficult to turn.

"Run out again have you?" A man waved a greeting, then collected the various bags and trays together as they chatted. Heaving a sack of potatoes into the boot, he turned away for the next item. Standing to one side Jan saw the car move, rolling away on the slope, gathering pace even as she sprang forward, swinging the door wide and trying to reach the hand brake. Thump! The passenger side front wing contacted a stone wall, hitting a glancing blow and continuing down the steep incline, the whole left side now scraping along the stony surface. Still unable to grasp the hand brake and with the sound of tearing metal in her ears, a touch of panic caused her to swing the wheel over. Without the ignition key it promptly locked! Thump! Colliding with the opposite wall the right-hand wing crumpled, headlight shattering - the car stopping abruptly. A demolition expert could scarcely have done better at ten miles per hour!

Squeezing in through the door, the engine still worked and with a little help from two men, wings were levered away from tyres, the other goods loaded and the car drove slowly away. Arriving home she parked it, called Gordon outside and pointed to the dent.

"I had a spot of bother."

He looked to check she was unhurt, then at the crumpled metalwork. Really, the lengths to which a woman will go to get her own way. "Expensive potatoes! It needs a new front wing."

"I don't think so."

"Why not?"

"You haven't seen at the other side yet."

They walked round the car. "Hm. Two front wings, one rear wing, two doors and possibly a bonnet. How come you missed the roof?"

"Didn't want to bruise the tomatoes." She lifted the boot lid.

Unloading, he picked up a jacket, jumped in and drove to Falmouth stopping at three garages on the way, finally doing a deal for a new VW Polo. The garage would take the damaged car just as it was, handling the insurance claim themselves, a factor improving the trade-in price considerably. Fortunately he knew Jan would approve of the Polo; it had been test driven at the same garage earlier in the year, not on his part with the intention of making a purchase but just to give the impression he was seriously considering it. Never underestimate a woman!

This was their first foreign vehicle but with the garage converted into a shop and the car standing permanently outside, the paintwork reputation had been an overpowering factor. Believing now that Jan would invariably find a way to secure her new car when she wanted it, he made a mental note to agree more quickly next time.

***

"Mum, what are these sausages?" Sharon stood by the open fridge.

Returning from early morning toilet cleaning, Jan had entered the kitchen to the smell of bacon. "Sausages? Dad must have put them there to use up - out of date I expect. Look on the packet."

"There *is* no packet. They're not wrapped."

"Been removed has it? You know what that means - probably weeks old. Don't use them, he's doing the dustbins, be back in a minute." Jan checked the clock; nearly seven, not bad. Someone had been ill in the Gents; it took extra time to clean up using a short hose specially made to screw temporarily in place of any shower head, giving easy access to hot water as well as cold; that had helped.

He appeared a few minutes later as plates of bacon and fried bread were placed on the table. "Dad, how old are those sausages?" Sharon wrinkled her nose as she glanced towards the fridge.

"Fresh. Only came this week."

"Pull the other one." Jan turned to Stephen, already sitting eating. "Do you believe him? Why would he take the label off otherwise?"

The small head shook solemnly as he continued to chew.

"I'm not eating any. Throw them away," Sharon urged.

Watched by the three faces, Gordon took another mouthful and rose, leaving the room, returning with a wrapper, the name 'Bowyers' in brown and underneath in blue, 'Pork Chipolatas'. Jan took it, examining the sell-by date; still four days to run! Passing it across, she watched as Stephen studied the printing carefully, nodded once and passed it back.

"Unwrapped food is unhygienic, Dad. Why take it off at all?" Sharon lectured.

"Just thought it would save you trouble." Pushing away an empty plate, he scooped up the wrapper as the office bell rang.

A woman stood on the step, a young child grasping her hand. "Someone's engine was running until almost midnight last night. Can we move our pitch?"

Noise on a caravan park often demanded attention, tents and caravans certainly not soundproof. Even with well-spaced pitches friction sometimes arose; a new challenge to be met, a balance to strike. Thankfully, few outside sounds ever penetrated the valley but radio and television could carry a long way, particularly at night. Why is music always so much louder than the spoken word, making it difficult to hear unless the volume is high? Often those listening were not even aware of other visitors being kept awake. Making his last walk round at night, Gordon frequently faced a choice - to act or do nothing? Knocking on someone's caravan door or calling through the canvas of a tent late at night was never a happy task - done only if essential; when to walk on by would inevitably yield a spate of complaints in the morning. The trick in such cases was to get the sound reduced without giving offence. In the early years it had seemed this might be difficult but in practice it seldom was; perhaps visitors were pleased that someone cared enough to come and see them. Occasionally too, the family would tell each other off when their own radio was unintentionally loud - it was easy to do. This present problem was therefore not so surprising, though from an unexpected source.

But the lady on the doorstep was waiting. What to do? It was early for moving pitches. "Certainly you may, can I come and see you in an hour?"

More customers commented later and it turned out to be a portable electricity generator with a small petrol engine. Having apologised for keeping neighbours awake, the motor-caravan concerned left. In spite of having paid in advance for three further days, it failed to reappear that evening. Unlikely now, that they would ever come back; a customer lost? Another source of trouble for the future no doubt? As generators became more popular, conflict between visitors was bound to arise - and guess who must sort it out!

Sharon and Stephen were still off with friends when later that evening the doorbell and phone finally stopped ringing, giving chance to relax; it was already past nine and there might yet be more interruptions. None the less, sinking back into armchairs was great. "Have you noticed how much more comfortable they are after a day like that?" Jan asked.

Gordon nodded, it was easy to agree. He reached down beside the seat, hands reappearing with a small block of wood and a Stanley knife. Shortly a pile of shaving began accumulating on the floor.

She watched, turning to look towards the tree of wooden birds in the office. It was ages since the last one was carved. What was it this time? Unusual shape. Would tomorrow be as busy... her thoughts drifted off, head slowly falling back. Seeing an arm slide forward to hang limply down, he smiled and continued whittling away, another hour yet before his final walk round.

The following day proved equally hectic, it was that time of year. They dropped into bed at night exhausted. Morning, it seemed, came five minutes after their heads touched the pillow, an arm reaching out automatically to stifle the alarm and for a few short delicious minutes while still half awake, they clung warmly to each other.

Remembering something, Gordon rolled from the bed, executed a jump, rotating in the air to land facing back towards the bed, arms outstretched, "It's a great morning. Time for action!"

"Drop dead," with a whispered sigh the still prostrate form drew the bedclothes closer around her.

Five minutes later they were both downstairs. Retrieving a yellow duster from under the kitchen sink, Jan prepared to hurry outside but stopped, pulled up short by the sight of another pack of Bowyers chipolatas on a plate, this time with their wrapper on. The plate lay at her own place at the table, as if someone was offering raw sausage for breakfast. Why weren't they in the fridge? What went on here?

Reaching, she picked them up, surprised at the hardness. Pressing the surface with a finger they were solid, solid but not frozen. "Must be a year old!" Looking more closely in search of an explanation, a voice came from behind.

"It's wooden."

"Wooden?" She turned, "Why? They're the right colour!"

"Painted yesterday, after I finished carving them - for show in the shop so people know what we sell."

As the first week of August passed, Sharon rushed to meet the postman each morning, grabbing the mail to search for exam results. They arrived a few days later. Dumping the rest in a heap on the desk, she dashed to her room, bolting the door - emerging a few minutes later shining and elated. Top marks had never been expected but the grades were okay; pretty good might not be the overstating it - certainly a relief to Sharon and quite sufficient to start A-levels at the girls grammar school. That was all she really wanted.

Chris rang that lunchtime with a brief update on his course. His fellow students had been broken into groups, some acting as an abusive unruly crowd, others trying politely but firmly to contain them - 'Don't lose your temper training,' Chris called it. As the conversation drew to a close he mentioned casually, "I've a motorcycle now, 175cc."

Jan, sitting in the visitors' chair, chatted on briefly, then reached over to put the phone down, starting to repeat Chris's news but was interrupted.

"Dad!" Stephen burst into the office, throwing the door wide. "A motorcaravan just smashed the toilet guttering."

"Damn!" Gordon rose from the desk, moving quickly forward to clear three steps with a leap and raced across the yard, rounding the corner, a smashed section of guttering immediately apparent. Just a few inches clear, a tall motor-caravan rested; one glance at the numberplate confirmed it to be German. Close by a man peered nervously upward, turning with a gesture of apology.

For a while they stood together surveying the damage. The guttering had shattered, cracks extending outwards for some distance, broken pieces lying in the drain below. The fascia boarding to which the guttering was fixed had suffered little damage, just a few scratch marks in the paintwork. Annoying all the same - "Damn Germans trying to blitz Britain again," - the thought had come subconsciously, a safety valve releasing momentary aggravation. Realising how stupid it was, Gordon smiled, wondering whether he dare suggest the idea aloud. Would this man laugh?

"So sorry." The visitor spoke quietly, ill at ease, seeming not to know what to do with his hands.

"Never mind, it's not too bad. I'll fix the gutter; go ahead and fill your water tank. No need to get so close next time, the hose is plenty long enough to reach." Unwinding a few coils he stretched it out demonstrating the length, but the man held up a hand, rotating the wrist back and forth in a 'No' motion.

"Not fresh water. Empty my tank." He knelt beside the caravan, pointing underneath to a big cylinder. Fixed near the bottom was a tap and short length of hose.

"Ah?" It was clear now why he drove the vehicle so close. Glancing up at the clearance above, it would obviously be impossible to reverse within range. "Wait, I'll be back." Hurrying to the service passage that separated Ladies toilets from Gents, Gordon looked around. This corridor, some five feet wide, held an array of pipework passing through the walls on each side to serve the basins and showers. Having the pipes hidden in this way allowed a neater arrangement inside the building, but this passage was also used for storage. A length of light plastic pipe some four-feet long came quickly to hand; searching a box on the bench yielded a right angle bend. Forcing this bend onto the pipe and running back to the waiting man, he knelt again, holding it under the caravan, demonstrating its purpose. While dirty water from the storage tank ran along this pipe to the drain, the driver rose, reaching in a pocket and pulling out a purse. Extracting two ten-pound notes, he held them out.

"I pay for the damage... it is enough?"

Gordon took the money, looking at it; twenty pounds - tempting! He glanced again at the guttering above.

Seeing the direction of this gaze and taking it as doubt, the caravanner reached again into his purse.

"No, it's plenty..." Gordon hesitated, wondering if he was being foolish, but shook his head, his hand signalling the extra money away. It was fair enough to accept proper payment but something else to take unfair advantage, particularly of someone not familiar with local money or costs. For a moment longer he stood undecided, looking up at the roof edge, fighting an instinct to... what was the word... make a quick buck. The repair would never cost twenty pounds. Peeling off one of the notes he passed it back. "Look, we'll pay half each - partly my fault for not thinking of that pipe before. I'll clip it to the wall for everyone to use."

Back at the office, finding Stephen and Jan waiting, he waved the ten pound note, putting it in the till. "Our motor-caravan man paid for the damage."

By the time they sat down to tea, a length of guttering had been cut from a bundle of spares in the toilet building loft and the damaged section replaced. Discussing the little incident as they ate, Gordon made no mention of that returned ten pounds - they might think he was going soft.

The valley as usual, was full of birds; they seemed to increase each summer, tempted no doubt by knowledgeable holidaymakers leaving favourite foods nearby, enticing various species closer to their caravans and tents. Even those not interested in human offerings, the martins, swallows and swifts for instance, swooped along the valley, with warblers, buntings, the woodpeckers, wagtails, various raptors, herons and even an occasional kingfisher. All came and went at intervals, darting, hovering, gliding, all forms of flight - and one who arrived on wheels!

A small car drew up opposite the office; a couple probably approaching retirement age climbed out, the man carrying a duck. They moved across the yard and for a while stood near the bridge watching muscovys and mallard on the river.

"Mum," Sharon standing by the window, called quietly across to the office desk. "That duck; he isn't really holding it - it's standing on his arm. They're coming over."

The couple walked towards the office. Jan rose to meet them but seeing Gordon appear round the toilet building and stride forwards, she stopped, beginning to turn away, back to the desk again then changed her mind, intrigued by the new arrival. "Come on Sharon, let's join them."

"His name is Dillon," the man announced as they met, holding out his arm to display the bird and stroking a hand over sleek feathers.

As to breed, Dillon could scarcely be called rare - smart standard colouring, green head, white circular neck stripe, brown chest with a hint of a reddish tinge and a generally greyish underbody. Anyone could tell at a glance he was a mallard drake; anyone that is, except Dillon himself.

"He thinks he's a person!" the woman whispered as if not

wanting the duck to hear. "We've reared him from a chick; our little house in Falmouth doesn't have much garden."

They had decided Dillon would be happier on a river with other ducks rather than dodging cats that occasionally visited their home. This new recruit had one outstanding trait; he wanted to be picked up, a thing most ducks cordially detest. To gain a normal duck's confidence don't chase after it, let it come to you, which it will, given patience and a supply of food, though the process can take weeks. When it eventually takes bread from your hand, don't pick it up - a duck likes to be free. After a long association when sufficient trust has developed, it might not mind, but touched too soon it may never come back.

Dillon however, was no normal duck! He actually wanted to be held. By way of demonstration his owner put him on the ground then strode off. Dillon ran to catch up. The man turned right, then left, then ran back to where the waiting group stood, all of which movements the duck mirrored faithfully. Having finally caught up, a series of little two footed jumps the like of which the family had never seen, showed its eagerness to be lifted.

One thing *really* not required was another drake. However, it did need a home. "You'll have to hold him until we drive off; he'll follow us otherwise," the lady took the duck, passing it over. As the car disappeared along the road, Sharon descended the sloping bank, lowering Dillon carefully into the water. Quickly it climbed back on the bank and stood waiting to be picked up. Several younger children with bread in their hands were feeding other ducks. Seeing this strange behaviour they moved forwards, intrigued. Watching from a window, Jan was not in the least surprised to see Sharon organising the youngsters to look after Dillon, before heading back to the office.

Being so tame, there seemed some danger that the other ducks might bully him? Not a bit of it. Dillon was dominant, immediately becoming undisputed 'top duck'. He was used to having his own way and had no intention of changing! In spite of thinking himself a person, with an obvious preference for human company, he found no difficulty in understanding which of his own kind were females and what they were for; becoming a touch promiscuous as top drakes are inclined to be, his efforts at first clumsy and comical to watch.

The ducks received these advances with varying degrees of enthusiasm or reluctance, being as with females everywhere, fairly unreliable. Often they appear to appreciate the attentions of only one mate with whom they pair, and make up to him with neck stretching movements; at other times they seem happy to accept more than one drake, often in quick succession. Even when a duck makes every effort at evasion, she is sometimes unsuccessful and forced to submit to apparently unwanted attentions. Often the offending male is simultaneously mating while fighting off an attack by the duck's steady partner but they still seem to succeed; natures way possibly, to ensure fertile eggs?

Visitors loved the ducks and this season, just as with all previous years, they were fascinated by one thing in particular - the way a drake after successfully mating would swim round the duck in a big circle, neck outstretched and exuding an aura of triumph! Ignoring this performance, the female's head dipped beneath the surface to throw water over her back and outstretched wings. Standing with a group of campers on the bridge, Jan and Gordon were surprised by the laughter it caused; they had become so used to the ritual it was hardly noticed any more until someone else drew attention and asked for an explanation. That night when retiring, Gordon tried the same drake movement round the bed. Jan caught on immediately and threw the clock at him - which fortunately he caught.

"Beast!" she grinned broadly.

He did another circuit back to his own side of the bed. Two slippers followed in quick succession. These were great days, exhausting but happy. It was already well past eleven and they must rise before six as usual. Catching the second slipper he jumped into bed and five minutes later both were asleep.

A little after midnight, the doorbell sounded! How many

times it had rung Jan had no idea; coming groggily awake she stepped gingerly from the bed, not switching on the light, three steps taking her to the window. Fumbling with the handle, she eased it open, looking down in the darkness at a dim figure holding a gas bottle. The bell rang again.

"Hey," Jan's shout was hardly more than a whisper. The person below, it might have been a man, took a backward step looking around then upward.

"Can I change a gas bottle?" The voice was definitely male.

"Not a this time of night!" The muted refusal made up in scorn what it lacked in volume, not wanting to wake other visitors.

"But couldn't..."

"No! You don't clean toilets at six every morning. Go away!" Closing the window, she heard a noise across the landing and hurried to the door. "Stephen? Go back to bed... only some stupid man wanting a gas bottle."

Wearily she crawled into her own bed, reaching to touch the nearby shoulder - Gordon was still fast asleep.

At breakfast the following morning, Sharon too asked about the bell in the night but was not overly concerned; there were more important things at this time of year, her attention turning to friends and how much longer they were staying. No one was sure, too many comings and goings to remember the dates for any particular caravan. Excusing herself Sharon made for the office, sat at the desk and reached for the Daybook. Looking up three girls, she found one due off tomorrow, the others not until next week. Good. Flicking a glance over one shoulder, her finger ran down the column again, finding two other names, not girls this time. Turning three pages both names still appeared, three more days at least then. She was turning the fourth when a noise behind caused her to close the book sharply and push it aside.

Coming into the room, Jan caught the movement and evasive expression as Sharon looked away. Dropping into the visitors' seat across the desk, she smiled at her daughter.

"A boy?"

Sharon glanced round, checking the corridor that led towards the kitchen. Although the toilets had already been cleaned and breakfast eaten, it was early, just after seven; Dad and Stephen must still be in the dining room. She looked back at her mother, doubtful but not quite able to keep her thoughts secret.

"No, Mum. Not *a boy*, two boys!" It was spoken quietly, leaning forward across the table.

About to ask more, Jan saw movement in the corridor and said urgently, "Pass me the booking forms."

As the male half of the family left by the office door, going to check the dustbins no doubt for they wore rubber gloves, the two girls were apparently studying what caravans would arrive that day.

"Well," Jan asked as the door closed. "Two?"

"Just... er, friends." Sharon spread her fingers in a gesture, but the little smile that lingered on her lips said otherwise.

"You prefer one," Jan paused, remembering her own adolescence, "or feel safer with two?"

"No... well, perhaps. One is very keen but somehow I prefer..." Sharon stopped; she felt close to her mother but this conversation was turning more personal than expected - more revealing than she felt comfortable with. "Didn't you ever have...?"

Jan smiled, "Have two, you mean? Yes, I suppose so."

"What made you choose Dad?"

"I didn't always want too; he was, how shall I say... unpredictable. At college we were supposed to wear subdued clothing, something suitable for an office. He turned up once in a bright tartan shirt, the top part in creamy white with white tassels hanging all round, bouncing about as he walked - got called to the office and told not to wear it again."

"Did you ever try to... make him jealous?"

"Is that what you're doing with these two boys?" Seeing Sharon turn away, Jan guessed it was true. One of the pleasures of being a young girl, getting fellows to fight over you - well not fight exactly but it did seem to increase their desire. She ought to disapprove but... "I did try once. Your father and I had been going steady for some time - not serious you understand, that was all of four years before we eventually got married, but nothing seemed to be happening. This other chap was interested in me too, and he had a motorcycle! Well I let on that he was taking me on his pillion for a weekend in the country. What do you think your father did?"

"Forbade you to go?" Sharon had turned back now, face alight with interest.

"I know boys can be fools, but not that stupid! No, before the weekend came, a parcel arrived. You'll never guess what was inside."

Sharon shook her head, waiting, having no clue what the contents might be.

"The address was in your father's writing, I recognised that straight away and whisked it off to my room to unpack, so Jim and Audrey wouldn't see. Inside was a pair of trousers, slacks... the brightest red you ever saw! I tried them on, they looked great!"

"Did you go on the motorbike?"

"Of course. I had to then, a sort of a dare - and I wore the red slacks too, but I wasn't really thinking about the chap I was with."

**

Weeks were passing, August well on its way. The Council's 'spy in the sky' had flown over taking photographs, a man had come to service the shop scales, adverts were already booked with the Club and other magazines for next year and more toilet rolls arrived. All was going well, except perhaps for dustbins - something needed to be done, but what? Gordon looked at them again, stopping to pick up some rubbish on his evening patrol. This last walk round to check for anything that might spoil visitors' enjoyment, was getting earlier each night. It was easier too, darkness terminating the children's outside games at a more reasonable time when no one cared too much about loud noises and the occasional shouting voice. A gas mantle in the Gents side of the first toilet building had disintegrated, or maybe someone had given it a poke; whatever the cause it had thrown the building into darkness, the gas still burning harmlessly with a small blue flame. This lamp, not visible from the office, had been fine when lit over an hour ago. Entering, he turned the valve, allowing it to cool, hurrying back to the shop for a mantle. Only a dozen or so remained in the box - it should be enough. All the stock was being run down now; they had learned their lesson the previous year, eating leftover tins and packets for half the winter.

With these shortening days came a little peace in the evenings, and perhaps more important, a touch of extra energy! There had been no time earlier in the season to make much use of the lathe. It still rested in the basement, hardly surprising - six men had struggled to place it there; goodness knows how many would be needed if it ever came to be hoisted out! The mode of operation was still only one-child-power, maybe a tenth of a horse-power, one of the children pulling hand over hand on the belt - but with the latest technical refinement, they pulled more effectively. Previously the belt had hung loose; the person providing the power must stretch it out horizontally, pulling while simultaneously keeping it taut. After Chris left, Stephen had done most of the pulling, Sharon finding it difficult to master the knack - or that could have been just a clever pretence. Now a set of pulleys hung from the concrete ceiling above, the belt from the lathe passing over them and keeping itself tight. With this arrangement, even Sharon could provide the necessary power while her father cut a screw thread or turned some metal bar down to size. Fine, but continuously pulling the belt tended to raise blisters on the hands and with the family growing up, this system had little future!

"Something should be done about our lathe," Gordon suggested as the family sat at tea one evening. "I know the children love pulling the belt but..." He stopped in pretended surprise at groans of protest round the table.

"You needn't think I'm helping!" Jan warned, spreading bramble jelly on another slice of bread. "I always said it was a stupid idea. They'll all be working in a few years - what will you do then?" She cut the bread cornerways, lifting it to take a bite.

"I er... thought we might breed some more?"

Jan looked up, mouth open, bread falling upside-down on the cloth. Sharon turned sharply to her mother in surprise. "Mum, you're not..."

"No! I'm not!" She turned to Gordon. "You can put that idea right out of your mind if you don't want to wake up one morning slightly handicapped."

"Okay! I'll think of something else."

CHAPTER 4

In Uniform

Sharon opened the door and hesitated, looking back round the room checking nothing had been forgotten, then down at her skirt, fingers tentatively brushing away some speck or crease. "'Bye Mum." She stepped through the doorway walking towards the bridge, a slightly self-conscious young lady in neat, almost elegant new clothes; an outfit purchased soon after that big cheque arrived earlier in the year but saved for this special occasion. More surprising, Stephen who left a few seconds later, dashing to catch up, also looked smart. The return to studies had arrived; Sharon now sixteen and starting A-levels was nervous, unsure what to expect on her first day at the Girls Grammar school. Stephen, three years younger, had no such worries. He knew well enough what lay in store, returning for his third year at the same school - his seniority increased.

"And then there were two!" Jan murmured, watching from the window as they walked away, remembering again when Chris had been with them. Turning away, her eye fell on long lengths of steel recently dragged out from behind the house. The windmill dismantled more than a year before still lay in pieces, but galvanising had been arranged - at Charlestown forty miles away. This treatment works contained a large vat of acid for cleaning the steel, and a long heated trough of molten zinc into which the lengths were dipped. She had been shown round when taking smaller items for treatment on a previous occasion - they had a large waterwheel there too, the lower section hidden below ground in some sort of channel.

"We use it during electricity cuts," a man claimed, but it was not running at that time. Galvanising was a great work saver, all the site's steel manhole covers and most other steel sections and supports had been dipped; expensive in the short term but a boon as time passed, saving hours of repainting. A lorry would collect the windmill pieces - they were far too long for the car; the same lorry would bring them back too, but only when it had other deliveries in the area - take about a month, the man suggested.

Jan explained to the children at tea. "When he heard it would cost extra to have the pieces returned more quickly, guess what your father said?" She paused but gave no time to speculate, "He said, *'No hurry, we'll wait for the free delivery!'* Well what did you expect - that he'd pay to get them here straight away? You'll be lucky to see them by Christmas."

The delay was of little consequence with a few caravans still on the site, mostly on hardstandings chosen now from preference, perhaps having found soft ground elsewhere on their travels. Those few needing grass because of awnings had been encouraged to choose a spot with a hardstanding conveniently near to park their cars on. Jan handled the incoming visitors now; the shop, the phone calls and the midday toilet cleaning too. It was easy, only the centre toilet building remained open and that hardly used enough to get dirty.

Gordon worked way downstream on his own; the yearly trimming. Banks were strimmed, hedges cut, trees kept in check; a severe pruning, no trouble spared - none would be cut again until next winter except maybe the odd bramble. For two people running a big park it offered a sensible division of time; tend the bushes in winter, tend the customers in summer. Under this regime the wild flowers flourished. Here and there in remote corners, clumps of nettle were left to host next year's black peacock caterpillars - pleasant enough work but lonely, good to get back to the house now and then.

"Had a tent in this morning," Jan waved a hand towards Area 2. "How much longer before we're safe?"

They had just eaten lunch and wandered through to sit in the lounge. Gordon rose, stepping to the window, glancing at a smallish tent pitched on the back field, its car parked on the curved track. The original planning permission had not included tents, a fact no one realised at the time. "Let's see, last autumn we joined to the sewer, that means one more year until it's safe. We've established a right then; after that if the Council find out, there's nothing they can do - unlawful but immune, that was the wording, wasn't it? I see you made them park on the road."

"The woman thought it a good idea. It's not dusty now, not like in summer."

"The final tarmac is due in November; I've a bit more work on the levels and drainage..." seeing a lorry come into view some distance along the entrance road, he rose, heading for the office door. "That'll be sand for the third toilets; I'll show the driver where to tip."

This extra toilet building was badly needed for increasing peak-season trade and to stop complaints of walking too far. Three loads of topsoil were also on order, the first they had actually paid for. That big cheque received earlier in the year meant visitors would see a difference next spring!

By midday just a week later, the new building's internal walls were finished with a smooth cement render but not yet dried out enough to start decoration. A roomful of bright new toilet pans and wash basins were ready for fitting but the floors must come first; a specialist job. Charles, who laid the previous floors, would be available in a few weeks. Lunch break over, Gordon collected his tools and moved on; many hedges and banks still to be trimmed - there would be little time later in the winter.

***

"Here they come!" Stephen's voice brought Sharon bounding off the bed where she lay reading.

A small red car approached along the road, crossed the bridge and swung round to park beside the shop. As it pulled to a halt, a uniformed figure swung from the passenger seat to stand tall, the sun glinting off polished buttons and cap badge, light blue epaulettes denoting him a police cadet. Chris had arrived home. The younger two rushed forward, drawing up a pace short of their brother, suddenly unsure. He was not the same; the uniform made him... pushing the fleeting impression aside, Sharon took his hand with a welcoming squeeze. Prompted by the action, Stephen reached forward to finger one of the buttons.

Leaning against the car with the door still open, Jan stood watching the little reunion across the roof; she noticed the hesitation. Did police uniforms have that effect on everyone? She had felt the difference herself when first meeting him at Penzance station.

"Don't you think your brother deserves a coffee after his long journey?" Jan addressed the question to Sharon, breaking the still uncertain reserve between her children. "You get it ready, Chris and I will walk down for Dad."

Later the camera came out for photos by the river, Stephen borrowing Chris's cap, then Mum dressing up in both cap and tunic - she looked like a traffic warden, the tunic's length, well below her hips, emphasising how much taller her son had grown. Another shot showed Chris in full uniform standing beside the car, leaning forward as if giving directions to some passing motorist.

A few brief days and Chris was off again. Arriving back after running him to the station, Jan parked the car and walked towards the house, shopping in one hand, a rolled up magazine in the other. An elbow on the bell-push fetched Gordon from where he worked in the adjoining shop. Modifications were being made to hang smaller items of camping equipment from the ceiling, saving shelf space. Putting down a screwdriver he hurried to open the door.

Placing her shopping basket deliberately on the covered billiard table, Jan took a step forward and with a fierce expression, lifted the rolled up magazine to hit him hard, a heavy blow directly on the head.

"I've read it! Yes, you may well back away," the magazine swung threateningly again but with no real intention of making contact. "Hm," with a little snort, she unrolled it, straightening the cover. The title read, *Caravan Monthly, Dec 78.*

The article had been secretly written and posted, and had unwisely included a passage of which Jan might well disapprove. Remembering this, he moved carefully to one side as she opened a page with the bold headline 'I am a Site operator'. Four pictures of River Valley lined one side of the second page but it was not these that had caught her attention. Pointing to a paragraph part way through the article, she read aloud.

"Running a site is not difficult if you make the right preparations. I have a special gadget for cleaning toilet blocks at six o'clock each morning. It's called a wife - no site operator should be without one - they are almost a necessity in our occupation. Try to find a reliable model that's not too expensive to run. I got mine for seven shillings and six pence (borrowed from her father) 20 years ago, and have been well satisfied ever since."

The magazine closed with a bang and she swung away marching off to the kitchen in apparent anger. In truth, the sudden departure concealed a smile that she had no intention of letting him see - at least not yet!

This little dispute came at a bad time. With Chris's departure it had been planned to start painting together inside the third toilet building. Working alone next morning gave him time to reflect, any regrets compensated for by memories of her stamping off - he never suspected the real reason for those sparkling eyes was amusement not anger. Warming as the memory might be, he had no wish to continue painting alone! How to sweeten her? A trip into town on the pretext of buying more paint provided the answer.

The colour television was in no way an inducement. Pure coincidence explained its sudden appearance, or so Gordon insisted - but the effect was to instantaneously restore his popularity. This purchase had actually been under discussion ever since the big cheque arrived that spring, the family pressing for action but Dad holding back. A month ago Jan and Sharon had looked at sets, choosing a Ferguson Moviestar as the one to buy, and combined forces trying to persuade him.

"We'll see in the January sales," had been his non-committal response.

The TV's arrival then, at this particular time, might certainly be viewed with suspicion; only one day having passed since the magazine article's discovery. Actually, quite a lot of fun had been created, the matter not so serious; his professed sorrow obviously not felt - her pretended offence slipping often in little half-hidden smiles of joy. She was already seeking some excuse to pardon him even before the TV appeared.

"An early Christmas present because you're so irresistible I can't wait," he had said, arriving back from town with the set. Equipped with a 12-volt adapter, it consumed only 85 watts of waterwheel current.

Next morning they rose, ate a quick breakfast and hurried outside to collect the equipment. Painting seemed somehow so much better - that little disruption of the previous day emphasising the pleasure of working together again. At one point their hands reached out and touched, a spontaneous moment before turning back, one slapping more paint on a wall, the other stepping up to reach the ceiling. Romance is where you find it. Returning for coffee earlier than normal, Jan immediately moved to turn on the set - time for ten minutes viewing.

"You can watch but it's not really for you," Gordon felt on safe ground now.

"What do you mean it's not for me? Didn't I start painting those toilets with you this very morning?"

"Yes... but that's woman's work anyway."

"I'll show you one woman who..." she stopped, aware he was smiling. "Well? Go on then, who *is* it for?"

"The customers, for demonstration purposes. Those who grumble about reception - how else could we prove the signal here in the valley is good?"

"Well... yes, they do complain at times; but some have those stupid little loops on top of the set. How will it help them?"

He smiled broadly. "Yesterday I ordered a dozen proper

aerials for the shop next season!"

"To be sold at a good profit no doubt. You devil, you let me think that set was just because you loved me... and I fell for it! Anyway, those aerials will never cover all the cost, so it was partly for me - go on, admit it."

"Of course, though there is another little matter."

"Oh? What?"

"It's now a necessary part of the business. Therefore..." he waited, seeing understanding dawn.

She pointed an accusing finger, "You're claiming it's Tax deductible - my present!"

He nodded. "Well, partly anyway. I'll try 25%; write it in the ledger in big letters, then if the inspector disagrees he can say so."

***

"Look, it's the only way. We're spending a fortune on tarmac and new toilets, we can't let the dustbins spoil it. There's foxes, crows, the occasional squirrel; everything will keep attacking them whatever we do. We need one central place surrounded by walls."

The waste problem had been worsening for years - growing in volume with more people, and increasing as manufacturers used extra layers of wrapping, selling the packets rather than the goods inside. Animals and birds in the valley were getting far too clever, learning where to find this easy food supply.

Experiments had been made placing groups of bins farther downstream but the rubbish spread far and wide. Worse, at mid-season they filled up quickly, demanding attention many times a day, something that proved impossible with only two people running the site, even with help from the children. A fence round each set of bins might contain some of the rubbish but not solve the problem of continual emptying. It had to be one central spot, somewhere within calling distance of the house. The place chosen was convenient; every visitor passed nearby on their way in and out. Nicer too, to store rubbish well away from the pitches - less flies and wasps, and less chance of rats. Even so, Jan baulked at the solution.

"Isn't there enough to do this winter without concreting a base for a hundred dustbins?"

Those bins were already washed and packed away in the basement - a late autumn ritual guarding against the vague possibility of frost. Some had survived eight years already; given care they would last as long again.

Work commenced, mixing the lazy man's way; maximum concrete from minimum energy. Make a pile of shingle and sand, split a bag of cement over the top then turn the whole pile over with a shovel. Turning once more while Jan sprinkled with a hosepipe, saw the mixture well on its way. Not too much effort so far. Finally, dragging the long steel point of a pickaxe in two directions through the resulting pile and adding a dash of water when necessary, almost finished the job. By the time it was shovelled into the barrow, wheeled off, tipped and levelled at the other end, the texture was as good as any mixer could make; a fine drop of stuff!

By late afternoon as muscles tired it didn't seem so quite so easy, but the children arrived home and evenings were drawing in, darkness preventing a resumption after the meal - fortunately perhaps. One disadvantage of being your own boss was a tendency to work harder than you ever would for someone else! Not many days passed before the base and surrounding walls were complete.

"We can relax now?" Jan suggested as they stood looking at the finished enclosure, but she spoke too soon. A lorry arrived with the windmill parts all galvanised and ready. As it unloaded and drew away, the tower's concrete base seemed to beckon for attention. Jobs were ticking off but so were the weeks; not long now until Christmas.

"I'll be home late tonight," Sharon spoke quietly. That was not so unusual; evening visits with classmates before coming home were common enough, but something in her manner as she turned away apparently to move a cup on the worktop, was evasive - coy perhaps?

Standing by the cooker preparing breakfast, Jan wondered

what had caused the whisper. "Why so secretive? Who is it this time."

"Oh, just a friend." Sharon turned away, fumbling with her satchel, a touch of colour in her cheeks. "Will Dad, um..."

"Will he mind, you mean? Doesn't usually, does he."

"This is our disco again. When I asked him last week, told him I was going with all the girls - he disapproved."

"Probably thought you'd want picking up around midnight. Do you?"

"No. Already got a lift. His parents..." Sharon paused again, a nervous smile concealed as she looked away. "Er, somebody is picking me up."

"*His* parents? A boy?" Jan waited as her daughter slowly turned, both smiling openly now. "That should make Dad sit up and take notice."

"I'm going anyway; whatever he says!" Sharon punched a hand downwards, emphasising her determination, then looked less sure. "Mum, could you, er, just mention it casually, during the day?"

"Why me?"

"You could persuade... I mean, well, you always get your own way."

"Nearly always. I thought you didn't care what he said?"

"I don't! But John may want to come in."

"John? Supposing I don't approve?" Jan raised an eyebrow and as they laughed together, neither heard the approaching footsteps, softened as they were by the hall carpet. Suddenly Gordon appeared in the doorway, looking in surprise at wife and daughter. "What's so funny?" Even as he spoke, he moved to open a drawer, took out a fresh pair of rubber gloves and made to leave again.

"I'll be out late tonight Dad, at that disco. I'm going with a boy!" Having forced the words out, Sharon glared at her father, waiting for an argument.

"Good. Much better arrangement. Tell me about it later." And he was gone, hurrying off as if those few words had delayed some vital job.

Sharon, unable to gather her thoughts, lifted one hand in

a gesture that asked, "Fathers, who can understand them?"

"Perhaps he's trying to get rid of you?" Jan suggested as they laughed together again.

The tarmac had been delayed, promised now for early January, but Charles arrived on time, starting immediately on the third toilet building floors. Following the success of his earlier work he handled this job with equal skill. It takes an expert to lay a floor so well that the slopes are too small for most people to notice and yet every drop of spilled water runs quickly away. Two days later it was finished but not yet hardened enough to walk on.

In spite of the various jobs in progress, the children were now seldom asked to help. Sharon had her own problems. Busily coping with more homework and the naturally higher standards of Grammar school and A-levels, she tried frantically to accumulate good marks and stay in the top group in her class. The absence of boys she claimed had raised levels of achievement, making it harder to keep up.

Noticing this new dedication, Jan watched one evening as her daughter worked longer and more intensively at her books, and wished enthusiasm were catching. It was dark outside but Stephen, going through an idle spell with more excuses than willow seeds in May, had slipped off somewhere shortly after arriving home. He did his homework after a fashion since both parents insisted, but with little real effort except in Technical Drawing, a favourite subject that caught his interest, his exploded views of machines quite excellent. He had acquired too, a skill with freehand drawings of futuristic themes, fantasy figures, dragons and space fiction characters.

Within a week, floors in the third toilets had hardened and Gordon left the still unfinished trimming to install basins and loos while Jan repainted walls inside the first two buildings where she could still run for the phone if it rang. Apart from the children in the evenings and a couple of quick trips to her parents' bungalow, she had seen no other person for three days. Dipping a big brush in the paint again, she straightened, reached to make the next stroke but stopped - her fingers squeezing on the handle. All afternoon the feeling, the isolation, had grown. Clenching hands even tighter she turned lifting an arm... fighting the impulse. Suddenly with a downward swing that carried every ounce of her strength, she hurled the brush at the opposite wall. Splosh!

Ah, that felt so good! She watched a shower of white droplets spray out as the brush fell, and wished it had been Gordon not the wall!

There would be no more painting today. Five minutes later the spots had been washed away and a white blob where the brush fell cleaned off the floor. Carrying the tin to the service passage and dropping the brush in a bucket of water, she leant back, wondering, seeking some human contact. A trip in the car? Pretend to have run out of something perhaps? Yes!

Entering the house for the car keys, she looked at the phone and swore softy. Right! Grabbing paper and pen she wrote, '*Run out of milk. Make yourself a black coffee. Stay in the office in case the phone rings.*' That would fix him!

Locking the door, she skipped lightly down steps to the tarmac yard, happy now, her spirit lifted at the chance to get away... wait! Quickly retracing her route, she unlocked the door, ran through to the kitchen and opened the fridge. There stood two bottles of milk, one half empty. Without a second thought both were tipped down the sink, the bottles washed and put away. The feeling of deception was delicious! Smiling, she ran again through the house, intent on escape, driving up the road, looking the other way when passing her parents bungalow, somehow feeling they might disapprove.

In town a still rebellious mood forced aside the normal need to hurry back; looking in windows and browsing through shops pleasant enough - making a few purchases, a low-cut blouse far too thin for winter might be effective in another way; she would wear it one evening to see if... a girl at the counter interrupted the thought. Jan paid and took the parcel; it would slip under the driving seat to be smuggled indoors later. Heading back to the car, another shop window caught her eye. "No girl should have to buy her own flowers," the resentful thought flashed to mind - a recklessness that had grown in those lonely hours of painting, pushed her inside. Choosing expensively she felt even better, an attractive mixed bunch with roses. That would teach him! Carrying them back to the car, the milk was almost forgotten.

Arriving home, the office looked deserted. He had gone back to work despite the phone. Typical! Yet she was supposed to stay listening for it. Grabbing the milk and flowers, pleased now to have bought them, she entered the office.

"Buying spree?"

Jan swung round. He was sitting in an armchair, hidden in the corner of the lounge. Tilting the flowers away, she sought an answer. "No... er, just luck. I was their five-thousandth customer."

***

Mid-January had arrived; opening day six weeks ahead but things were coming together. The new toilets were almost finished, the windmill base concreted, dwarf walls about a metre high surrounded the dustbin yard - progress on all fronts! Living in the valley was still great despite the hard work; lonely sometimes but good when they worked together - that new blouse quite a success; life had lost none of its passion. Shorter days left long evenings to relax, to visit Jim and Audrey or chat with the children on schoolwork and on progress at home. Sharon particularly liked the larger showers in the new toilets and looked forward to a trial run. Hearing the tarmac was due tomorrow, Stephen asked quickly, "Can I stay and watch?"

'Easier than studying,' Jan thought, and was about to refuse but a small nod of the head across the table made her reconsider. Stephen had shown an interest in building work. Might it benefit his future career?

"Dad thinks you should." She saw a smile spread on the young lad's face as it turned for confirmation.

"You might as well. This final section is your last chance to see a quality, machine laid road." Gordon turned, "You don't want to watch too?"

Sharon's eyes opened wide, "Huh!" Her expression said he must be mad to ask.

Breakfast was long over when the machine arrived shortly after 8.30. Stephen raced on ahead, expecting work to commence where the previous tarmac finished but the machine drove past, one of the men pointing onward. It stopping eventually near the site's downstream end where the stone road faded out, Stephen in hot pursuit.

"If we started where you were waiting," the man called, "then the next lorry would run over the hot tarmac already laid, and mark it."

While talking, the men lit burners to pre-heat the apparatus, odours of diesel oil and hot tar hanging in the air. A loaded lorry appeared and laying commenced; this first coat in a coarser stone size leaving a rough, rather knobbly texture. A workman on the machine's rear platform pressed a metal probe into the hot surface, winding the control gear up and down to adjust the depth. Gordon pointed him out to Stephen.

"That's the man to watch. He controls the thickness. It's difficult to check later."

More lorries arrived, the machine returning to the road end, starting again spreading a second layer of finer material to leave a smoother surface, a big roller giving the final polish. Other sections of road were also completed before men and equipment departed.

Back at the house for coffee, Jan asked, "Would you know how many lorry loads to order?"

Stephen shrugged, stretching his arms out in a 'Search me' motion, listening as his father explained the method of calculation, using the length and width of road, and depth of tarmac. The lad learned a great deal that morning, both the practical side and the planning. Perhaps he would concentrate more on mathematics having seen it had real uses.

The following day he returned to school with a note explaining his absence. Jan could have written that he was ill but gave the true reason - why shouldn't she? Three days later a letter arrived threatening prosecution for keeping him from school.

"Pompous Idiots!" The words came out with feeling as Jan read. Being told by other people what was best for the family did not go down well! Things other children had said made her aware of the school's truancy problems but this seemed totally ridiculous.

"Pompous Twits!" she repeated between gritted teeth, laying the letter aside.

Sitting drumming unconsciously on the desk top, her temper rising, the remarks when she did speak were scathing. Probably referees who missed a vital foul have been called worse but not by much! She cast doubt on their intelligence, their ability to read, their truthfulness and their common sense. She was so angry that had it not been for a natural distaste of bad language, the little tirade might well have included more unladylike words.

The reply to the education authority was polite but only with some effort. Didn't the master concerned ever look at attendance records before writing stupid letters! Could she keep her son off school for three weeks holiday but not for one day to learn something that might help his future career? Jan slipped the letter in an envelope, stuck on the stamp with a thump of the fist and stomped off up the road to the post box!

Nothing ever came of the matter, a few off-the-record words by a friendly teacher revealing Stephen's attendance to be excellent. She couldn't check but felt sure it was true, and the anger had gone - quite a good school really.

The third toilet building was finished; almost identical with the earlier ones but with seven instead of six loos in the Ladies, and two considerably larger shower compartments. An expensive stainless steel urinal had been purchased for the Gents. Since it would never need repainting, Jan approved but could not resist asking, "What about that porcelain urinal trough still stored in the basement? How come you left it standing there doing nothing rather than use it and save money?"

"Well, er... I thought perhaps..." He stopped with a gesture, "we might need a spare?"

They stood for a moment, grinning at each other before Jan spoke. "Don't you think I'd guessed that? Never mind, the painting's done, the water all turned on and we're open. Where are the customers?"

True enough, not one caravan or tent had appeared. In early March, that was scarcely surprising, but after lonely winter months some company would have been welcome. This lack of visitors came up again at tea.

"They would only be old people anyway," Stephen brushed the matter aside, not expecting any of his own age group to arrive.

"Old like us, you mean?" Jan looked across at Dad, then back to her son, waiting.

A grin spread as the young face looked down. A reply was hardly expected but shortly the head rose again, "What about the windmill then?"

Stephen's question had been asked before and with good reason - the foundation was finished, four short lengths of steel already sticking up from the concrete. Alongside lay several dozen recently galvanised sections, which once assembled would project the tower skyward - far higher than any building in the valley.

"You prefer it to homework?" Jan's comment brought another grin to the young face but no reply; it hardly needed one. She turned to Dad, "I'm not helping; you realise that!"

Instead it was Stephen who gave a hand next morning, taking advantage of the weekend to slip in the bolts while his father held the first tall leg sections upright, waving in the breeze. Eight horizontal braces went in without difficulty but the diagonal tie rods proved unusable, the threaded ends eaten away by rust. Work was temporarily abandoned.

In due course, new rods made by the blacksmith arrived but needed galvanising. At six o'clock one morning Gordon and Jan set off, Jim and Audrey minding the empty site. The Torpoint galvanising works, smaller than Charlestown and eighty rather than forty miles away, had agreed to dip the steel that day, saving a double journey, and more importantly, saving days of waiting. A box of nuts and bolts was also taken.

"Could you find something to do until after lunch?" the foreman asked. "Come back at two o'clock, it should be ready by then."

Crossing the ferry from Torpoint to Plymouth instead of the Tamar bridge, was pleasant, a chance to wander round the shops, then lunch at a big department store. The invitation to waste time was novel, a feeling somehow carefree and relaxed; chance to make a few purchases including some gold material to re-cover a chair, before heading back. The time estimate however, proved over optimistic for at two o'clock those long rods were still being treated. Asked about the nuts and bolts, the foreman shook his head.

"They need fixing on wires, about a dozen on each so we can dip them - haven't had time. I don't think..."

"Can I wire them up?" Gordon stepped in quickly. Coming back tomorrow was not an option with eighty miles to travel. A nod of agreement and a rapid demonstration were interrupted as an overalled figure working nearby, lowered what he thought was a solid bar into the zinc bath. It floated to the surface.

"Hollow pipe!"

As this sudden yell echoed round the enclosure, a hand clamped on Gordon's sleeve dragging him clear, men rushing headlong from the shed. Reaching a safe distance, they turned, waiting. Nothing happened. One man went back, pulling the tube clear with a long pair of tongs.

"Hollow tubes tend to explode," the foreman explained. "Air inside them expands, or tries to. Depends how strong the tube is. Last week one threw out a hundredweight of molten zinc, showering it across the floor."

A little later while watching the bolts being dipped, a concrete building block used as a support, fell into the trough and floated away across the surface. All finished at last, the lot weighed, the bill paid - and they were off, beating the rush hour, their strange extended load sticking out fore and aft below the car bumpers.

Reaching home, the valley remained empty, no early caravans appearing - disappointing but only to be expected. The following morning found more pressing demands. Four lorry loads of topsoil unexpectedly arrived and jobs changed, hurrying to catch the spring growth. Earlier in the winter when other soil was spread, a strange companion had become ever more bold, a large cock pheasant, beautifully coloured and with a proud strutting step. Now it appeared again.

Standing in the kitchen telling Jan about the bird, Gordon mentioned the way it walked. "All men should have a strut like that." Seeing a raised eyebrow, he explained what should have been obvious, "To show our superiority of course." By way of demonstration he strutted across the room, shoulders back, chin up, stopping as their bodies met and looking down at her, a touch of arrogance in the stance - as if expecting eyelids to flutter and have her fall into his arms. Instead she smiled and punched him straight in the midriff, not hard but it caught his breath.

Doubling over in a mock display of injury, he looked up a moment later to find a tea-towel tossed over her shoulder, cloak fashion, head thrown back, one hand on a hip, doing her own toreador impression, a little smirk on those lips as she met his gaze. Not at all what he intended!

This new pheasant companion had a special mannerism, a series of quick steps then one leg reaching out, long talons scraping the surface, beak bending to peck up any food exposed. A few more brisk steps saw the whole procedure repeated. When spreading topsoil and setting seed a spring rake was used, the sort that drags moss from lawns. Would this action look perfectly normal to a pheasant? Is that why it became so tame?

The work took several days, then with no more soil available and no customers yet arrived, it was back to the windmill tower which soon reached half height, the new diagonal rods vastly improving stability. Even so, standing some twenty-five feet in the air, balancing on slender horizontal steel angles with nothing to hold on to, was daunting, the shake in the knees not entirely due to movement of the tower. However, by late afternoon the top sections of all four legs were in position.

"Right. The rest should be easy," Gordon claimed at tea, "Provided you don't mind clambering about on thin steelwork only two-inches wide."

"Five centimetres," Stephen corrected. "In metalwork we use metric."

"Okay, but this windmill was made in... I'd guess before 1910, over fifty years before you were borne. Everything was inches then - in this country at least."

Jan, who had listened without interrupting, frowned. "You're sure it's safe?" Seeing Stephen nod, she turned to Gordon. "Will you both be wearing a rope?"

"Stephen will but not me. I'm safer than he is."

"Why?"

"Afraid of heights. My hands will cling on so hard, the steelwork may bend! Anyway there's very little to do. We're only finishing the tower and the high platform, not mounting the actual blades that turn in the wind."

This task quickly finished, the windmill stood untouched as more weeks passed, other jobs taking precedence. For instance, scattered round the park were many standpipes - the taps from which caravanners and campers drew their water. Attached to each tap was a short length of hose perhaps six to eight inches long. These allowed water to be aimed better, filling water carriers with less running to waste down the drain. Some had become sticky and as a result, all were changed for lengths cut from a brand new hose - only the best for River Valley customers. With this, some window cleaning and a dozen other small things, the windmill was forgotten; it was safe enough now - could be happily left until autumn.

CHAPTER 5

On High

"Hello, which side can I walk?" A solitary female rambler striding down the valley stopped to watch ducks being fed from the bridge.

"In front of the house," Jan pointed and they fell naturally into conversation, leaning over to look at the clear water and the ducks below. A muscovy approached, waddling up from behind, beak reaching to pull the hem of the woman's dress and they bent together, stroking the feathers while offering the last few crumbs.

Standing again the woman asked, "Was this a military prison once?"

"No. Whatever made you think that?"

"The tower..." she looked up across the house roof, "Oh. You can't see it properly from here. Walking along the road I noticed that little platform at the top..." she stepped back a dozen paces to the far side of the bridge and pointed. "Yes, there. I thought perhaps a soldier with a gun stood on guard."

Jan moved to the woman's side, following her outstretched finger; it did look a bit like that. Now the idea had been planted, she wondered how many other people would see it in a similar way. Explaining that when finished it would pump water, like the old wind pumps on many rural farms, she saw the woman's expression change; no longer instinctive disapproval but something much more benign. One could easily imagine her thoughts switching from a place of retribution to a pastoral scene, a farmyard perhaps with a Jersey cow, a milking stool and hens contentedly scratching the ground. Once the fan, the circle of little blades that caught the wind, was in position, people would instinctively associate it with bygone days, the rural scene, the nicer things of life. In that moment, watching a soft smile spread across the woman's face, Jan resolved to find some way to get the tower finished.

At tea, having repeating the conversation with the passing lady, she turned to the children for support. "I think Dad should leave the other jobs and give this priority."

"He should do it tomorrow." Sharon looked towards her father. "The other parts have lain beside the house so long that some ducks sleep on them in the daytime."

"I could help in the evenings," Stephen offered.

Gordon looked at the three faces, knowing he should have done the job some time ago, wondering why he had avoided it... the height perhaps? "Yes, tomorrow. But only if it doesn't rain overnight - too dangerous otherwise."

"Why should it be dangerous?"

The parents looked at each other, smiling quietly. Jan turned to Sharon, "Rain can make the steel slippery. We'll wait for a dry day." Seeing her daughter's disapproval, she elaborated. "Don't want your father slipping off and breaking a leg, he's useless enough already."

Sharon's frown disappeared, the jest bringing grins to the children's faces. Watching these changing expressions, Gordon warned, "You can joke but it's serious. Didn't I tell you once about that multi-storey car park at Southwark Bridge in London when I was a young engineer?"

Heads around the table shook.

"Well, we were building in steelwork, no floors or walls, just steel girders in every direction, and quite high... I forget how many storeys but the cars were taken up in lifts, then rolled along conveyor belts and into a parking space, or at least they would be when the job was finished. Everything was to be automatic.

This happened many years ago; I was young, hadn't left college very long, still not much experience. When we started, the building grew quickly, just big steel joists that bolted together. The erection team were on bonus - that means earning extra money if they fixed the steelwork quicker. This was a real tough gang, columns and beams went up so fast you'd hardly believe it. Each beam was fastened to the columns with six bolts - sometimes it was more, eight or ten, the holes already there, made at the steelworks. Anyway, these men didn't put all the bolts in; they could get more beams up that way and earn more money - but it wasn't safe, dozens of empty holes where bolts should have been. That was my job." Gordon sat back, reaching for his coffee but it was still too hot.

"Well, I was never keen on heights but you couldn't let a gang of men like that see you were afraid. I had to climb up the ladders and step straight out onto those beams - they were much stronger and more solid than our windmill but longer too, and nothing to hold on to. Everyone just walked across from one end to the other, maybe twenty feet, balancing on a piece of steel six inches wide. When I started making them go back to put in the missing bolts, it slowed the work down. They tried to intimidate me then, to make me afraid. Nuts or heavy bolts would suddenly fall from high overhead and thud down just missing me as I started to climb a ladder. No one ever did find out who threw them. I'd look up and find several faces watching from above, waiting to see if I'd turn round and go back to the office. That's what I wanted to do but I couldn't - they'd have the upper hand then. Instead I climbed up with my pen and little pad.

After a while as the building grew, we were many storeys off the ground with nothing but more steelwork underneath - and way below the hard concrete base. They used to watch and wait for me then. As I balanced across the beams their biggest man would start from the other end, so we crossed in the middle. One push would have killed me - there was nothing to hold on to. '*You mind you don't fall,*' a man coming from the other end of the beam called. I wanted to go backwards but he would easily have caught me, and if I did back away, then they had me. I'd be useless after that.

"*We might both go together,* I made the suggestion to

him sound a good deal more casual than I felt. I still didn't like heights but this was no time to admit it! We crossed over very carefully; one of my hands gripped his overalls as we passed, the fingers wrapped tightly - he looked down at the clenched knuckles and then our eyes met. I was only a lad really, about the age Chris is now. How we continued to balance, looking straight at each other, I'll never know but suddenly he stepped aside - we passed and parted. I made a point of staying longer and hunting harder, finding extra empty holes, asking for the torque spanner and checking some of the existing ones, even a whole row that had been checked before.

"Their foreman complained; wanted me replaced. My boss, the man in charge, turned to me. '*Does every hole have a bolt in it?*'

I said, '*No,*' and was about to explain but he cut me off with a gesture of the hand and swung round angrily to the steelwork foreman. '*Right. All erection work is suspended until every bolt is in place!*'

"He spoke to me afterwards, told me how important those bolts were; if anything moved when the lifts were installed, the whole system would be useless. Things went better after that, they stopped trying to threaten me. I suggested that if one of their men came with me carrying a bag of bolts, I could show him straight away which ones were missing; it was easy enough, I had them all listed in my notebook. They were a tough crowd but when they found it saved time, I became one of them, they looked after me, covered for me if I missed anything."

Gordon paused, waiting for comments and picking up his coffee, it was cool enough now. Stephen asked if anyone did ever fall; Sharon wanted to know if all building workers were like that because some on a building in Penzance made wolf whistles and passed remarks when she walked by with a group of sixth form girls from school.

"Men in the building trade tend to do that. Did you disapprove?" Dad asked.

"Well..." Sharon hesitated, "No, not really. My friend

wears a short skirt; she pulls it a bit higher every time we walk past that building site now."

Jan sat back waiting, and in a lull said quietly, "You know what I think?"

Eyes turned in her direction. She looked at Dad. Guessing her intent, he grinned; she smiled back. "I think that tale made you all forget what we were talking about - why he won't finish the windmill if it rains overnight."

"Guessed you'd remember. Funny you should ask; I was just coming to that. This tough gang I spoke about - even though it affected their money, they never worked when the steel was wet; it voided their insurance. If they went up in the rain they weren't covered against accidents."

Sensing the story was over, Sharon carried cups to the draining board, Stephen quickly slipping away. Fortunately no rain did fall overnight, the next day dawning clear and dry. Nevertheless, a heavy dew made the steelwork slippery, postponing early work. A trip to Cash and Carry ready for Easter and some small preparation jobs in the shop delayed a start until mid-afternoon.

"What will be first?" Jan asked as they stood looking up at the tower from some distance away in the yard.

"That gearbox," Gordon pointed to a big iron casting on the ground. "Will you give a hand; it's too heavy for me alone. This is when I miss not having Chris around... no, I didn't mean it to sound like that. I miss him for more than the work he could do; particularly at teatime when Sharon and Stephen are here - it never seems quite the same around the table. Was it my fault?"

"Probably." Jan sat for a while, looking out the window. "Why do husbands and sons both want their own way? You might have prevented it; then again you might not. Young men like to feel their feet, make their own decisions... without transport he found it difficult here, away from everyone, his friends, things going on in the area - particularly weekends when we were both busy."

"Might be good for him, do you think... the police I mean? He never wanted to work here."

"He might, if you let him have his way... but I doubt it could ever succeed. If he brought home a crowd of rough looking mates in mid-season, you'd throw a fit - want them properly dressed or hidden so the caravanners didn't see. It may all be for the best but when you're working and I'm here alone..." Jan stopped, no explanation needed.

Gordon laid a hand on her arm. "Sorry. I..." he hesitated as she reached out, a finger touching his lips, telling him to say no more.

"Don't tell me you'd do it differently if it happened again. You've put too much into this valley, trying to make it perfect. No way could you change. Forget it, things will come right in the end - maybe! What about this gearbox?" She looked upward. "I'm not climbing that tower!"

"You don't have to. It weighs about a hundredweight, at least that's what we guessed when dismantling it, and the shape is awkward with that long tube sticking from the end, but we'll manage. Come on, I'll show you."

The casting already had a rope firmly attached; Jan followed with her eye where it rose to the very top of the tower and over a steel member, then fell again to the ground. Understanding, she reached for the loose end that hung down, pulling it tight and taking some of the load as he lifted. Even so the gearbox proved no easier to raise than it had once been to lower. Friction on the rope where it passed over the steel beam high above prevented her lifting much of the weight but conversely, helped to prevent it falling.

Holding the casting, Gordon heaved up the ladder one rung at a time, resting it against his chest between lifts. Even with help from the rope it proved impossible to raise with a single hand. Standing on one leg, gripping the side of the narrow metal ladder behind the other knee to stop himself falling, he forced the gearbox up another nine inches with both hands. Wedging it hard against the steelwork and relying on Jan to hold most of the weight, he moved up another rung - at least this time there was no damaged finger! How long it took before the gearbox lay on that high wooden platform, neither could say - but the relief when it rested safely down was immense.

Undoing the rope and tying it temporarily to a handrail he leaned over the side to shout, "Put the kettle on, call me when it's ready!" Now, with both feet on a solid surface, it should be fine. The platform floor had been rebuilt using new timber, treated with preservative of course. It gave confidence. He squatted down, took a good grip and lifted with a straight back, letting his thigh muscles do the work. The casting rose to chest height, but it was already clear that he could never reach from the platform and needed to step upwards onto the short cross member some twelve inches higher - even then a prodigious lift would be needed. Quickly, an unpalatable fact became obvious; he was neither sufficiently tall nor strong enough. Strain as he might, it was beyond him.

A call wafted up from below. Coffee break was later in the afternoon than usual. Lowering the weight back onto the boarding, he descended the ladder. This could be tricky.

As they sat drinking, he asked casually, "How do you feel about climbing to the top and helping me hoist that last piece into position?"

"Reluctant!"

"Can't lift it on my own, I've tried. I'll keep a rope on you all the way up."

"I said I wouldn't do it."

"Okay, perhaps Stephen..."

With a sigh, Jan shrugged her shoulders, "Blackmail? Come on."

Draining the cups they headed outside. Raising her arms she let him tie the rope securely round her waist then watched as he raced upwards, surprised how much taller it suddenly seemed. Never before had she climbed the tower, not so much as placed one foot on a single rung, never wanted to. Her eyes swung to the ladder close by, a hand moving out to touch - never wanted to was right! She didn't want to now. A movement at her waist broke the thoughts; she looked up again. He had untied the rope from the platform handrail above and passed it round the main mast. "Okay!" the call floated down. Unwillingly she placed a foot on the first rung.

With each step up the ladder the rope moved, the slack taken out, a comforting safety net but not tight, not pulling at her waist. Some twenty feet in the air, she paused, taking a quick look at the ground below, body clinging tightly to the steelwork. Only halfway but already higher than the toilet building roof! Sliding a hand carefully upwards, fingers tightening, her body hugged the metal ladder as one foot lifted, gingerly feeling for the next rung. Heaving up and reaching out again, a small flexing of the metalwork cause a moment of total panic, a gasp as she clung there, muscles frozen. Seconds ticked away before the tightly closed eyes opened; no tug urged her on - a glance to his face above revealed concern, not impatience. Steadying herself a foot moved cautiously towards the next rung. After an age that might only had been a few minutes, she reached the little hole forming an entrance to the high platform, sliding through to stand slowly upright, both hands grasping the short length of tower above.

"There." She felt pleased, glancing down through the opening at the concrete base nearly forty feet below, her heart still beating fast. "Now what?"

"Now you climb up above the platform, and stand on that little ledge. Hold on very tight."

"No need to tell me! I may never be able to let go!" Easing her way to the far side of the central column, she reached up, moving one hand at a time and placing a foot with care. Two other hands touched from behind, helping as she pulled herself up to the high perch.

"Comfortable?"

"Oh sure!" She looked down again, following the line of the entrance road towards the village, then turned slowly round as far as her neck would allow. The site looked different from here, smaller somehow, and yet everything fitted, areas joined just where they should. "Naturally," she told herself, turning gingerly back. "How am I going to help; my hands are not free?"

"They will be, when I tie you on."

The tower was narrow here, coming to a point, she gripped tighter as it moved in a gust, feeling him lean against her as he passed the rope round and back behind her waist, then round again several more times. The contact was good; just for a fleeting moment she wondered if it would be possible up here, exposed and in the wind? A stronger gust pushed the pleasurable thought aside.

"Now let go with your hands... you can't fall."

"Gee, thanks."

Stepping down, Gordon stooped for the heavy cast-iron gearbox, heaving it up, lifting high. "Pull it tight against the steelwork." He climbed onto the ledge with a struggle, forcing himself upward, using his chest to steady its weight against the tower. They were less than a foot apart, facing each other. "Heave!" Together they lifted, hurrying now - it had to be quickly done, before muscles tired.

The gearbox rose, forced upwards until that long metal pipe sticking down like a tail, slid at last into a hole in the tower's topmost piece. As it lowered with a thump, they smiled in relief - but too soon.

"I... er, hardly like to mention this," he murmured sheepishly, "but we've forgotten the bearing washer."

"*We've* forgotten? Don't include me, you're the one who... Hey! This doesn't mean..." seeing his nod of confirmation, Jan glanced around hunting for a missile but nothing was loose up here! For a moment they stared at each other, grins slowly spreading, a feeling detached from reality, close to lunacy perhaps engulfing them both.

Peals of mad abandoned laughter rang across the valley, the man and the woman high in the air leaning back, letting their combined emotions, frustration, fear, a touch of insane delight, drift away on the stiffening breeze. After a few well chosen words concerning husbands in general and this one in particular, Jan helped again to lift the gearbox clear, balancing it precariously across the tower while the washer was slid on - then lift and lower again to its final resting place.

As they relaxed, cramped arms recovering, he whispered, "You do remember I promised never to let you get bored. It takes a good husband to think of exciting things like this for a wife to do."

"Oh, of course. I love being tied to the top of windmills! It's a wonder you didn't have me hanging from a helicopter."

"You know, it never occurred to me. If you don't like the tower here and want it moved, perhaps we could..."

"I like it here!" She made to untie the rope round her waist but the knot was on the far side - within reach since the tower here was narrow, but awkward to undo.

"Hey!"

At the distant call, she stopped struggling with the knot, looking outwards to see two small figures part way along the entrance road. Sharon's arm was pointing towards the tower, and then they were running, both racing forward until they stood out of breath in the yard.

"Are you coming down?" Sharon's words held a certain awe as she gazed at her mother high above.

"Can't. Dad tied me the tower!" Jan pointed to the rope then leaning backwards, threw both hands in the air. "Help!"

Stephen dashed towards the ladder but his mother's voice came again from above. "No, I'm fine. We'll be down in a minute. Go and get tea ready."

As the younger family members made for the house, talking together and glancing back over their shoulders, Gordon moved to untie the rope, helping Jan descend onto the high platform and leading her to the corner.

For some time they stayed, arm round waist and head on shoulder, looking across at the river at young spring grass and trees beginning to leaf. The Elderberry was already fully out, pussy willow showing early spots of colour that would later become a mass of yellow, and among the hedgerows in bigger or smaller patches, the dark green of gorse. Fields of neighbouring farms were visible from up here, and along the valley, south-eastwards, Godolphin and Tregonning hills some five and six hundred feet above respectively and four or five miles distant. In a northerly direction, an extra hundred feet or so of height might reveal the sea in St.Ives Bay across the top of Tremelling Wood. Reluctantly Jan climbed through the small hole and down the ladder, the rope round her waist still held from above.

Over the next few days the cogs, fan, vane, brake, and all the rest of the gear were assembled. The main rod too was hung down and connected to the pump, its suction pipe placed temporarily in a five gallon drum filled with water. That final day was absolutely still, it always is if you want wind - part of the natural cussedness of life, but towards evening in only a slight breeze the fan began turning. Gradually at first, the central wooden rod rose and fell, speed increasing until it pumped merrily away, water splashing out from the open pipe to run across the yard and away. As they watched, some mallard waddled over to dabble in a tiny pool formed by a depression in the tarmac. Marvellous! With a whole river to swim in, they preferred this muddy puddle.

Standing now, hand in hand, looking at the ducks then upward to where the blades spun leisurely round, it was clear their neighbour had been right; they did need a windmill! Sadly he had become ill and died soon after it was first dismantled.

"Pity Melville can't see it," Jan said quietly.

"He would have liked it; would have liked the ducks too." Gordon nodded at four more muscovys waddling over to drink at the small puddle, then looked up again as a puff of white cloud sailed across behind the tower. "Perhaps it stands as a salute to his memory, looking over the fields he once planted. I know we sent a wreath but I regret now not going to the funeral. As children we were taught to stay away, not intrude on a family's private grief. I'm no longer sure that's right; perhaps attendance is more support than intrusion?"

Over the following months it was strange that people commented more on the windmill than about the newly opened toilet building. One visitor asked to take his camera to the top but was refused. "Our insurance company doesn't allow it. Tell me what you want and I'll take them for you." Gordon offered. No one really knew if the insurance would disapprove, for they had not been informed yet - a matter quickly put right.

Other things were noticed too. A couple who had stayed in previous seasons pitched their tent as usual on Area 2 not far from the house, but came back to the office later enthusing on the new roads and requesting a pitch at the site's downstream extremity.

"Sure, but there's no one else down there - mind that old badger doesn't nibble your toes at night!"

Far from putting them off, the couple nodded with pleasure, hurrying away to re-pack their tent.

***

"Good morning Dr Johnson." Jan opened the office door wondering if one of the campers was ill.

"Hello. Public Health visit I'm afraid. Not a complaint, just a normal site inspection. Come with me if you've time?"

"Gordon will." She pointed to a figure approaching with a broom. At this time of year the strongly growing grass stuck to mower wheels, coming off when crossing the tarmac roads, being swept away later with a stiff brush. Explanations of the visit quickly made, the men walked off together, entering the nearest toilets to find nobody inside; not surprising at mid-morning in April.

"My first visit." The doctor glanced round, looking in various cubicles. "I'd heard they were good. Push taps?" he placed an elbow on one, feeling the water temperature with his other hand. "Hygienic. Not many pipes showing either."

"A service passage between Ladies and Gents takes most of the pipework."

"Am I imagining it or does the floor slope?"

"Towards that drain point under the sinks. Tip water anywhere you like and it runs away."

The doctor nodded approval, not asking for a demonstration and pushed open a shower door. "You might like to think about those shower mats; they can spread verrucas - some authorities prefer bare floors. I usually say, if you want mats fine but don't choose ones with a deep pattern that holds pockets of water; not smooth either of course in case people slip, just a slight pimple effect and disinfect them regularly."

"We do, twice a day but I see what you mean about holding water. I'll get new ones," Gordon promised. "Some people turn them over."

"Shower slippers are best but not many use them - what about that cobweb?" He pointed to the black cistern above the urinal.

"I clear them once a week - we've a list of things for each day. Webs are a Wednesday job but without disturbing the spiders. See that square hole where the chain lever enters the cistern; that's where they live."

"It's okay; don't move them on my account. Nobody catches infections from a spider - not in this country anyway."

They moved on, heading downstream to the new toilets but apart from the shower mats, no further suggestions arose. Walking back with the trees in bright spring green all around and small birds hunting among the branches, the doctor spoke again. "Several of my friends are into wild life; I've found a way to keep up without too much effort. I study harvestmen, the spider-looking things with long legs and little round bodies. There are only five varieties in Britain - you can be an expert with no real effort."

New shower mats took longer to locate than expected. The previous set came from a car accessories shop, the mats that go under drivers' feet; similar shops were visited in search of replacements. Although plenty were available, all had a system of box-shaped markings that would obviously trap water. After several days searching, some were located in Truro. Arriving home, Jan parked beside the shop, taking one mat from a pile on the passenger seat. Entering the office she tossed it on the billiard table, its mahogany covers already partly obscured by various pamphlets for the visitors.

"There! That's what you want isn't it? The rest are in the car."

Gordon rose from the desk, picking it up and inspecting critically. Satisfied he made for the door. "I'll take them round now."

"Don't I get any thanks?"

He stopped, turning back to see her standing, a cheek held slightly to one side. Quickly scanning the yard to check no one was near, he stepped towards her, planted a small kiss then hurried again to the door.

"I may swoon," she muttered quietly but he had gone, opening the boot and grabbing the other mats. "Ten minutes," she thought looking at the clock, then corrected herself, "Unless there's anyone in the Ladies; then he'll probably come back for me."

It seemed unlikely; early May was quiet, down to six units tonight, their owners off somewhere - sightseeing no doubt, it was cloudy today, hardly beach weather. Shortly Gordon reappeared carrying the old rubber mats, water still dripping from the ends. Mounting the steps but unable to open the door, he leant a shoulder on the bell-push.

"Put them in a dustbin!" the call came from inside.

Shaking his head and signalling again for the door to open, he waited, then carried them through, laying the lot in the empty bath.

"I thought you said this type were no good any more." Jan stood in the bathroom doorway watching.

"Well, not for the showers perhaps but there must be some other use."

"Dump them!" she urged, then changing tack, "Wasn't I clever to find the smoother type?"

"Not very. There's only twelve."

"We've only got twelve showe... Ah, the spares, yes?"

"Yes. Still, you're moderately clever - for a woman." Seeing Jan's smile he stepped forward, taking her wrist and reaching to plant another small kiss, using the movement to slip by and through the door, calling back, "At least you will be when all those are washed and put in the basement."

An arriving motorcaravan saved his bacon as she caught him in the office. This somewhat disreputable vehicle was difficult to refuse with the valley so empty; no way to say they were full. Only the driver came to the office, a roughly spoken man, baulking at the price but he paid and was shown to a pitch.

The couple left just before noon the following day and cleaning the toilets a little later, one of the new shower mats was missing!

By June the site grew moderately busy but easy enough to run, the visitors predominantly retired couples. That last walk round was just before darkness now; even so the light evenings tended to cause later bedtimes. On one such night shortly after darkness fell, a strange pick-up truck shunting about then parking in the yard, had Gordon hurriedly dressing and dashing downstairs. Some sites in the area were rumoured to have lost caravans; stolen, towed away by some thieving villain - it wasn't going to happen here! As he left the office door, the vehicle's engine sprang back to life and it made off hurriedly up the road, a group of people talking by the bridge jumping smartly to one side.

Crossing to apologise in the darkness, he found the two couples more interested in something else.

"We came to see the ducks," a woman pointed at several just visible on the water, some apparently asleep, "but on the way from our caravan we actually found a glow-worm! Come and see."

Glow-worms had always been part-legend to some caravanners; like everyone else these people had heard of them, but until now had never seen one, half believing it to be an old wives tale.

"Do you get many?" a man asked as the group headed back into the site.

"A few, if it's already dark when I do my last walk round." Gordon looked up to see Jan, wrapped in a gown, standing anxiously in the office doorway, and gave a wave to show everything was well, the motion indicating she should go back to bed.

Not turning at the toilet building but walking straight ahead towards Area 11, the five people entered a section of road with a tall hedges on one side, and there, a few paces along, a greenish-white spot glowed in the verge. As they stood together looking down, the shorter lady whispered, "Listen."

It was already past eleven but even so the quietness was amazing - all the little lights in caravan windows and the tents lit from within, like being in toy town or some Disney set - another world, a place at peace. The four visitors gazed around, listening? No sounds, nothing. They glanced at each other in the dim light, "You're lucky," someone murmured in a hushed voice, as if not wanting to breach the silence - the valley's peacefulness on that warm still night, affecting everyone.

"Thanks," Gordon's reply was no more than a whisper on the air as he sank down on one knee. The verges generally were uncut, full of campion and other wild flowers but just here the soil was poorer, shorter grass, the texture more open and sparse. Reaching for a stone no bigger than a fingertip, he laid it gently by the road edge, marking the spot, then plucked a young sycamore leaf and gently eased the glow-worm onto a protruding lobe.

The light did not go out immediately; another couple walking in the darkness strolled quietly up, watching as the glow faded before the man produced a torch. Under its beam the little creature resembled an armoured caterpillar, dark brown bordering on black, a series of little flat platelets covering the curving back - the shape explaining perhaps the 'worm' part of the name. Rather ugly now, without the glow.

"That's the female," the man with the torch spoke, his voice low but distinct, one could almost say polished. "She uses a substance called luciferin which glows in the presence of oxygen. Little tubes in her body walls let oxygen flow in and she can close them, stopping the flow and turning the light off - like just now. It's to attract a male."

Gordon bent down, using the marker stone to place the insect back exactly where it had been found. Good camouflage; it could hardly be seen against the soil. Rising he saw Jan standing in the background and wondered how long she had been there. Saying soft good-nights to the visitors, they walk arm in arm to the house.

Undressing for the second time that evening, Jan paused, looking across the bed. "This stuff, luci... whatever it was; I could use some - might attract a *real* man."

The challenge could hardly be ignored. Tossing the trousers aside he looked her up and down, taking in the part naked figure, "It might work but don't you think that female glow-worm was much prettier?"

Casting the final garment aside, she slid into bed. Days might be long but there was little pressure in June, still leaving enough energy to enjoy a small argument together - and its consequences.

Another family milestone arrived that week. News came that Chris was now a police constable undergoing training at Hendon before posting to his first station, and in celebration he had a bigger motorcycle, a 250cc. Stephen, nearly fourteen was envious, wishing for both the independence and the transportation. His father's suggestion that more study might pave the way to such things, met with little enthusiasm. The promise of more money for helping on site in the school holidays however, was better received.

In spite of continuing encouragement at home, Stephen's interest in school failed to improve. On Friday night his satchel was thrown in a corner, not to be touched until the following Monday, his time spent away at the beach or out with a friend. One weekend, roaming local woods somewhere upstream, the two lads came across a lake and an old boat. Struggling, they dragged the small craft overland to the river, crouching out of breath at the water's edge, keeping low to scan the ground behind for any sign of pursuit. Nothing moved, this part of the stream and surrounding land, wild and neglected. At a nod Stephen clambered aboard, reaching back to grasp handfuls of vegetation on the bank and steady the boat while his friend climbed in - and they were off, going with the current, dipping in the paddles to cruise the boat forward, leisurely unhurried strokes, pulse rates dropping as the banks slipped by. Floating along in silence, the sound of a heavy engine ahead had them back-paddling, finding the bank and hanging on. Through the trees ahead a large bus moved slowly along a rough track, rolling from side to side on the uneven ground; they watched it swing left, the engine note changing as it drove off at speed. That must be the main road; they were approaching Relubbus bridge. Slowly they eased forward, letting the current do the work - this was one of the danger points where they might be seen! A dark rectangular opening where the water rushed through lay dead ahead and simultaneously voices were heard. Someone was near! Stopping the boat in that small gloomy space where the river ran directly beneath the main road as difficult, the current more concentrated here - and there was no way to tell if the coast was clear. Easing into water that reached his knees, Stephen peered cautiously out on the downstream side, climbing the vertical bank to check briefly along the road in both directions. Returning quickly to the boat, they shot off paddling frantically, brushing the shallow bottom once on a pebbly ridge, keeping heads low past Jim and Audrey's bungalow and within fifty metres were hidden again from the road by overhanging branches. Sailing on they relaxed, laughing, enjoying the risks, knowing what they were doing was wrong - and revelling in it!

Next hurdle, the site - and that was coming up fast, round the very next corner.

"What happens if your Mum or Dad spot us?" Stephen's friend called urgently.

"They mustn't! I'll get extra work for the next six weeks. If any visitors wave, just wave back and keep going."

The arch of the bridge lay ahead now, ducks scattering as they sped quickly beneath, charging on towards the weir. Paddling both on one side, turned the boat bringing it to the bank. That was right in front of the house windows, but there was no option - shooting the weir could puncture the bottom and they had no intention of causing damage. Half scrambling, half rolling onto the bank, their dinghy was dragged clear, carried at a run twenty metres downstream and slid back in with a splash. Wet to the waist they were under-way again, jumping aboard and speeding off, paddling like crazy, thrusting through the water still within sight of those house windows, easing off only when a bend masked the view, then drifting on, crouching and hiding their heads when people passed along the footpath. Floating at this leisurely pace carried them northwest, nearly three miles downstream to St Erth, the boat safely moored and abandoned, none the worse for its little adventure but inconvenient nevertheless, for the person who must find and recover it. This little misdemeanour did not go undetected! The two boys found themselves cleaning out stables each weekend for a month - a most suitable penalty.

Towards the end of July, other lads and lasses of Stephen's age were arriving; these new friends and the work he did for extra pocket-money would hopefully avoid further mischief? As usual in the school holidays, life changed gear; no time for anything but looking after customers and taking their money - almost entirely in the form of cheques. Financially things began to look acceptable, even rosy by the family's standards. Having no immediate neighbours to keep up with, spending requirements were not extravagant, no one wanting swanky furniture or antiques, although as Gordon told Jan, "I do like some old things."

Making a sudden move as if to lash out and laughing when he flinched, she looked straight at him. "Yes, they're not bad when you get used to them."

These little verbal duels relieved the tension, but even as they spoke a man was walking towards the office door with a toilet roll in his hand.

"It's your problem," Jan swung away, "I must go, there's a lady heading for the shop."

The man strode in, moving to the desk and reaching over to put the roll firmly down. "Tear a piece off that."

Gordon glanced at it, puzzled then back at the man. They had gone upmarket, a new batch of rolls, a really soft twin ply.

"Go on, tear a piece off!" The visitor lifted the roll again, holding it so the ragged end dangled. Gordon grasped it, pulling a square free. Instead of breaking evenly it frayed apart, leaving another rough edge, the two layers of ply breaking in different places, the piece unusable. He was trying again when Sharon entered the office, took a step and stopped, glancing back at three other girls standing by the doorway, all turning to stare at the men with the toilet roll. Quickly backtracking, Sharon rejoined her friends and hurried off, giggles of laughter floating back to the office.

"Ah," The man, his eyes following the girls, put the roll down. Not quite sure what to do with his hands, he half gestured, moved them towards a pocket, changed his mind and said, "They're all like that; every cubicle."

Inspecting the uneven ends again, Gordon rose. "Must be a bad batch." Leaving the office, he made for the service passage, beckoning the man in and breaking open the plastic wrapper of a new case.

"Try these." He passed one over, taking another himself, both men easing the first sheets away where they were stuck, then tearing off an experimental square. Perfect. A new roll quickly filled the empty holder in the Gents, those in the three other cubicles also having to be replaced, but not the spares stored behind the cistern flush pipes. That was not so strange, the spares were topped up regularly, they could well have been from a different batch. Another caravan rolling into the yard had Gordon hurrying back, the three bad rolls, still in his hand. He dumped them temporarily on the office billiard table.

"Throw them away," Jan urged as the shop bell rang, calling her again.

He nodded, but three people from the caravan came in and after it was shown to a pitch, things suddenly started to happen. A strange car was roaming around the site, at least its registration number was not one of those listed in the book - perhaps it had been entered wrongly but someone must check. It turned out to be three people having a picnic under some trees near the downstream boundary. Gordon charged them a pound each, making a great show of writing down the registration number. After all, the car did have a hitch;

they could be just casing the joint with the intention of towing away someone's caravan. They wouldn't do that now, knowing their number had been recorded. Jogging back towards the office, a red tag showing outside the third toilets, indicated an empty gas cylinder. That did not immediately affect the hot water since the gas valve switched automatically to a second cylinder but the empty one must be changed and the spanner was back in the office! The possibility of feeding each toilet building direct from an enormous central gas tank had been considered. It would avoid the need to change these smaller cylinders but any fault could put all three toilets out of action together - not worth the risk. He hurried on to collect the spanner and in passing the telephone kiosk saw fragments of glass on the path. Opening the door, more lay inside; someone had dropped a bottle.

By early evening of a somewhat frantic day, those four faulty toilet rolls still lay together on the billiard table. The office had been busy, crowded at times but no visitors had seemed to notice or passed any remark. Certainly the family had little time to think about it, only now finding chance to draw breath - but a scream from outside drew them quickly to the office door, then rushing towards the river as a lady climbed the bank with a very wet child. Her son had obviously fallen in the stream but it was only a few inches deep at this point; no danger.

"Shouldn't have rivers on a camping park!" The words came tightly as the woman strode by without pause or hesitation, no break in her angry step, her own clothes now well and truly wet.

Gordon and Jan looked at each other. This lady chose River Valley and now grumbled because it had a stream? What a day! But another couple were waiting by the office, standing at door watching the little drama, an explanation unavoidable. The conversation that developed was somehow relaxing - the couple sympathetic, laughing at the day's events. Their names were Alec and Anne. Somehow the toilet roll episode came up, Alec reaching across, lifting one.

"May I?"

"Sure. Go ahead."

"Twin ply I think." Alec fiddled with the frayed end, separating the two layers of tissue, then peeled back the outer one, unwinding a single turn and pulling. The paper broke off cleanly. "Try now."

Gordon took the roll, pulling another piece. It came away easily, nice square end, no fraying.

"With the two plys out of step, the perforations don't line up." Alec reached for another, unwinding the single top ply and tearing it off to bring the sheets back level; holding up the end to demonstrate.

Jan reached across for a roll, unwound the outer layer herself and pulled it clear, looking gratefully at Alec.

"He's not so clever," Anne smiled back. "He works in paper - toilet rolls, cardboard, paper bags, you know... did these four suddenly happen all at once?" She pointed to the rolls and receiving a nod of confirmation, added a warning. "Sabotage. Someone else knows the trick; a child probably."

Not until late August was there time to draw breath or give a thought to the winter ahead. Sharon was already preparing to return to school, her second year at the Girls Grammar, others probably doing the same for families with children began disappearing, a normal and expected autumn decline - but could anything be done to boost numbers? A few people during the season had asked for electric but the cost was outrageous. Attention turned to more reasonable ideas, special postcards for one.

Earlier in the year in June, a painting of the site was commissioned by Barbara Wills, a well known artist living in the parish. No instructions were given as to what views should be included; she was the artist after all. Not much point in employing someone with flair then trying to dictate how it should be done! The picture that developed was a composite, several features of the valley shown together in a way impossible to do with a camera - an overall impression but with such detail - a variety of small birds, flowers, a dragonfly, a red admiral, several ducks and a heron, all cleverly hidden in a scene with the waterwheel, windmill and a general view of the valley.

The original now hung in the lounge where visitors to the office could see it through a large opening that joined the rooms. A photo of this painting, another of the ducks and several more shots of different site views had been sent to Dowrick Design, a printer of postcards. If all went well the shop would sell them next season.

Still seeking ways to boost the autumn trade, another use for the painting came to mind. Many caravanners displayed triangular pennants of places they had visited - a chance for more publicity. Drawings were made but the painting proved unsuitable, too much detail.

"If sold to caravanners and hung in their windows," Gordon argued, "our pennants will appear all over the place, so we need something simple and easy to read from a distance - something eye-catching."

A duck motif sketched out as a trial, seemed suitable.

"Looks great don't you think?" Jan stood admiring it.

"Sure, besides there's a good mark-up on pennants. I already made enquiries in the trade; they should sell for perhaps a pound."

"How much will they cost us?"

"Depends as I say, on the design. Ones like this, about fifty pence."

"You mean, sell pennants in the shop at one hundred percent profit, so visitors can ride around the country carrying our advert? Make a second profit when other people see them and come to River Valley? Not very ethical?"

"Well... Ah... It's not the money..."

"Really? We'll be giving them away free then and..."

"No!" Gordon cut in sharply, the look of alarm on his face suggesting any such thing might be sacrilege. "We could..." He hesitated, then forced the words out, "reduce them to ninety-five pence?"

"Golly gosh! You be careful." She stepped back, mouth open in mock alarm, then shook her head, sighing, "And this is the man who claims women are devious."

The mallard duck design was agreed and drawings made by a good local designer. A phone call later that week settled a price, promising the flags for two months time.

Hearing about it at tea, Sharon sounded a warning. "One of ours at Guides got wet and the ink ran. When they get here, hang a sample on the windmill, right at the top - to test its weather resistance. Someone is bound to ask."

"I can do it," Stephen was standing by the window looking at a picture that arrived in the morning post; Chris's passing out photo - rows of uniformed young men about to be released on the streets. "When will he be home?"

"Tomorrow the letter says; before he starts duty as a proper policeman."

Stephen would have preferred an arrival by motorcycle but as usual Mum picked Chris up from the train. He had travelled in ordinary clothes, carrying the police gear in a suitcase and changing into them soon after arrival. The new uniform, particularly the helmet, was impressive, or it may just have been his sudden maturity. Whatever the cause none of the remaining caravanners recognised him. Meals round the big table however, recaptured a touch of the old life. As they talked Jan felt good, glancing often at her big son, wishing for a moment it was possible to go back ten years or just that he lived nearer, but she was happy enough - he had done well. This visit would last only a few days, some of it spent visiting old friends, but the family felt whole again. Sharon challenged him once about studying and ambition but Chris professed no desire for promotion to a desk job. Gordon asked about the basic training, wondering how it compared to his own squarebashing days, listening with interest to the details, the tests of initiative and stamina.

"What about your first posting?" Jan wanted to know.

"Notting Hill. People say it's a rough district - we'll be walking about in pairs." There might have been a touch of apprehension to Chris's grin but he was bigger now, not just in height - the past months had built more muscle and a self-assurance not seen before. Stephen certainly noticed; his own yearning for independence increasing. Jim and Audrey too, were delighted when Chris arrived at the bungalow in full uniform. Those few short days were pleasant, father and son finding common ground and getting along well. Jan drove Chris back to the station, sorry to see him go but watching the departing figure with a feeling of pride.

Back at the site, falling visitor numbers gave chance to try something more with the dustbins. The new single enclosure was a complete success as far as visitors were concerned, no complaints of rubbish around the caravans during the whole season. People seemed to prefer one central point well away from their pitch, more than one person commenting that it lessened the number of wasps. However, although not being spread around, the dustbins still came under attack, many knocked over and the contents spilled. True, this was now contained by low walls, but someone still had to pick it up in the morning and make the storage area look neat.

Foxes had mostly been responsible, reported several times as racing off into the night - badgers too may well have played a part but had the good sense not to be seen. Even during the day the bins were not safe; from eleven o'clock to almost teatime the site lay largely deserted, with people out at the beach, the ideal time for mowing and any other noisy jobs, but it left the dustbins vulnerable. One old crow had developed a technique of grabbing the lightweight plastic lids and by beating its wings could find enough lift to tilt a cover clear, drop it and perch on the rim. Picking at the contents, it dropped various bits to the floor before flying off with some choicer morsel. Though no longer so important now fallen rubbish did not reach the caravan or tent areas, some action to deter the raiders seemed desirable. As a first attempt to catch the fox, a cage was purchased from a mail-order catalogue. This cage had a special mechanism. When an animal walked in, the door would spring closed behind it. Fine - if you get the right animal! The only creature caught so far was the neighbour's farm dog, a good-natured creature who promptly curled up and went to sleep - it was released next morning, made a fuss of, then sent on its way with a wagging tail.

CHAPTER 6

The Bus

"It's going!" Stephen pointed at the screen. A black margin was forming around the edges.

Sharon glanced up at the little overhead bulbs; she had thought earlier that they were dim but pushed the idea aside, her attention on the television drama. There had not been a winter electricity shortage for over a year, not since purchasing the bigger battery. No other house lights were on - standard practice ensured the switching off of everything not in use. Rising, she pulled a cord dangling from the ceiling and the room darkened, the black border round the screen diminishing. Ten minutes later the dark edge had grown again and shortly after, the picture failed.

"Fetch a candle, Stephen. They're still in the usual drawer, the matches with them." Jan spoke in the darkness, turning to Gordon. "What happened?"

"Something floated down and stuck in the waterwheel perhaps - I'll look." He rose, feeling a way through and leaving by the office door. Outside there was moonlight enough to see but it was hardly necessary - the wheel's characteristic splash telling immediately that it still turned. Entering the house again, a candle's warmer light now flickered in the lounge. "The wheel is okay, must be the alternator brushes, I'll fit the spare. Where's the torch?"

Ten minutes later the house batteries were charging again, running on a spare alternator; the faulty one left in the basement for servicing tomorrow when the lights recovered.

"I thought you said the big battery would give no trouble?" Sharon asked, resuming her seat in the candlelight.

"Not the battery's fault; probably not been charging properly for days but no one noticed - pity it doesn't recover more quickly."

Idle chatter speculating about the film's possible end, about the season and friends who had visited, passed away the time, rather like those first days in the house before the wheel existed. Sharon spoke about a girl of her own age, staying with her parents in a tent. "Something was eating the groundsheet, little holes appearing but they couldn't find out what. Each time the family went out another hole would appear; they showed me; a funny crinkly type of groundsheet, thin and brittle but something was definitely eating it, a mouse probably. Anyway she heard a faint gnawing sound one night and threw a slipper, but her father had heard too and was crouching nearby - the slipper hit him instead. Wish it had been me!" Sharon grinned.

"I bet you do," Dad glanced towards the candle, seeing smiling faces around the room in its soft light, everyone lying back, somehow cosy and contented in the armchairs, obviously expecting him to say more. Nodding, he glanced upwards to the little lights no longer working in the ceiling above. "I threw something myself once, not exactly a slipper but the light was dim there too - years ago in the forces. It was late, nearly midnight, our group had been on exercise. Some other lads in the billet were playing cards, just two lights still on, high up near the sloping ceiling a good ten-feet above; one directly over my bunk. Someone called *'Put those damn lights out, we want some sleep!'*

"The lads around the table carried on playing; *'Get lost,'* one called. Other voices round the room joined in, words sailing back and forth, things beginning to look ugly. I reached for a boot, black and highly polished, and threw it with force at the light. It hit the shade, they were like chinaman's hats - the bulb fell, landing on my bed, not even breaking - the odds must have been a thousand to one against. A little cheer went up, the whole atmosphere in that room changing. There, that was my little moment of fame, so what happened to your slipper throwing friend?"

"Her Dad was annoyed, grumpy; you know, like Dads are," Sharon grinned again, "but her mother woke up, said she should have thrown it harder, knocked him out and got some peace in the tent!"

Jan asked casually, "By the way, are we safe for tents now that..."

"What about tents?" Sharon's attention sharpened, aware her mother had suddenly broken off, not finishing what she intended to say.

"Mum means will we have enough camping pitches next season." Dad cut in quickly, then changed the subject. "These lights, I thought I'd try to improve them before visitors start arriving."

"How?" Doubt sounded clearly in Stephen's one word question.

"In two ways. Take these," Gordon pointed to a cluster of three small 12-watt bulbs high up in the corner. "We can stick mirrors to the wall. That's almost like doubling the number of bulbs, and I can paint the top of the bookcase white..." seeing Sharon's expression change, he turned towards her, "No need to look like that; it's too tall for anyone to see on top."

"And the other way?" Jan asked critically.

"We should replace the waterwheel's wooden breastwork with a concrete one, closer fitting and smooth - make more use of the water's weight to give extra power. Replacing those cheap bearings in the gearing would help too - use better quality roller bearings instead. We'll need more power next summer for all the batteries caravanners now bring in to be charged."

Later, when the children lit more candles and retired to bed, probably to read, Jan stretched out to kick his foot.

"What was all that rot about having enough pitches? You know what I was asking. We are safe for tents now aren't we? The time must have passed when the Council could stop us. It has hasn't it?"

"Yes. About three months ago... at least, I think so."

"So the children can be told?"

"No. Tell no one! Don't even discuss it when you think we're alone because..."

"Someone might overhear? Don't be ridiculous! We're miles from anywhere, inside our own house; who the hel... who could possibly hear?" Seeing him about to protest, Jan shook her head, "One of last year's customers might have bugged the place, yes?"

"Well it's possi..." he cut off sharply as she hissed a very rude word.

"Let them listen to that! All this talk about the wheel - will it really increase the current or was that just a diversion too; something to take their minds off tents?"

"How could you think that?" A small smile on Gordon's face admitted she had hit the mark; he hurried on. "Yes, it should improve the power, possibly quite a bit. Anyway, those cheap bearings are beginning to wear. Did you realise our wheel does more than seven million revolutions a year? I was calculating it while trimming the hedges last week."

January was windy, the whole country swept by severe storms, warnings of possible structural damage broadcast for the coming night. Being in a valley always cut the force, only the more violent winds felt to any extent. The family saw no reason to be worried despite the dire forecasts, and spent the day indoors cleaning and repainting the shop for the coming season. The postcards had arrived and needed a display stand, the scales were repositioned and various other adjustments made.

During the afternoon, the wind rose, gusting so that even inside the house the intermittent noise whistling past windows drew the eye to events outside; leafless trees swaying wildly as if bent by some hidden power made it obvious a more than normal storm was building. During the night the force increased further, rattling tiles on the roof. Jan and Gordon on the house's windward side, lay close together listening, talking occasionally in low tones, concerned about damage and unable to relax until in the small hours exhaustion took over, both drifting into uneasy sleep.

They rose the following morning to find the wind dropped but drew back the curtains with some apprehension. Leaving Sharon to start breakfast and Stephen still getting dressed, the two parents hurried off to check outside. Every tile on the house remained in place, not one missing. Great; a sigh of relief expressed their feelings. The toilet buildings too looked in good shape but just round the corner a different picture lurked.

After converting the garage to a shop, an increasing number of tools and other bits and pieces had either been squeezed with the mower in the blockwork shed beside the Ladies toilets or pushed into the service passage. Their presence in either place had been a nuisance, but leaving tools outside exposed to the winter weather was not an option. Nor could they be left out during summer; a hundred little hands would investigate with uncertain consequences. As an alternative, a cheap wooden shed had been purchased from a mail order firm, arriving after dark one evening, delivered flat, ready to be assembled. Erection and treating with preservative had taken most of the following day - nine feet long, six feet wide with double doors, and all for £79; hardly surprising the timbers were flimsy and flexible. Never mind, for many months now it had served its purpose. In practice, storage had been swapped around so the mower alone lived in this new shed. It stood not far from the toilet building, or at least it had stood there the night before. At this moment it lay some distance away in a crumpled heap, the mower still standing untouched where the shed had once been. Taking in the scene Jan's expression changed, calling out, arm raising to point in alarm, and they ran forwards together.

"Ooh! I didn't do it - honest." She put a finger to her mouth, looking up under lowered eyelashes, her amusement justified. Although the damage looked terrible, the whole thing had been cheap enough not to matter - comic rather than serious.

Calling Sharon and Stephen, the family approached with care, walking around it on tiptoe, as if not to wake some sleeping Grisly, afraid a sudden movement might precipitate the final collapse. Forty minutes later with Stephen's help, those tangled sections were separated and neatly stacked. The shed was never re-erected, but advertised cheap as, "In need of slight attention, has tendency to fly."

***

The dining room table lay covered in books and paper. At one end, Sharon scanned a textbook, scribbled some notes then studied the textbook again. Beside her, Stephen struggled with his maths homework, while Dad wrote continuously on several foolscap sheets.

As the kettle boiled, Jan put her book aside, rose from her chair and made for the stove, pouring boiling water onto cups already laid out for coffee and bringing them back to the table - a signal for everyone to unwind. Turning to Stephen she asked, "Working hard tonight, aren't you?"

"Maths. Double homework for misbehaving."

"What did you do?"

"Not just me, the whole class, talking and shouting - someone used their ruler to flick an ink pellet; it hit the wall just missing the teacher, made him jump - he can't keep order anyway."

"He should give you all the cane."

"They're not allowed to Mum," Sharon lectured. "Can't keep them in at night either; they have to catch the bus. Good teachers make the lessons interesting, control their class like that."

"There are other ways." Gordon leaned back in his chair. "Be sinister, intimidating. We had one that walked up to your desk, clench his fist as if about to hit you, appeared to restrain himself with difficulty, then walked back to the front of the class - it felt like you'd had a narrow escape."

"That was in your day Dad." Stephen spoke as if of another century. "Everyone knows they can't hit you now."

"Pity, some could do with it. Anyway, there are other ways to be sinister. Listen, at one time a fingerprint craze hit our school; everyone was dipping fingers in an ink pad and pressing them onto paper, something to do with a detective series on the radio. A few teachers joined in - for a laugh I suppose, but this particular one refused. We were all a bit frightened of him anyway, but had gathered by his desk just before the lesson. '*No,*' he shook his head, then looked carefully round, kind of furtive like, and leaned forward to whisper. '*A fortune teller reading my palm once told me that at sometime in the future I would commit a murder! So I'm not letting anybody take my fingerprints.*' He looked round again, staring at each of us with wild looking eyes, slowly raising a hand, then in a sudden movement brought it crashing down on the desk, shouting '*Back to your places!*' We shot off like the devil was after us and never said a single word the whole lesson." Gordon held out a hand as if asking their opinion.

Stephen's eyes glowed with interest, but Jan disapproved.

"I don't believe a word of it! Stop leading the children astray. Anyway, what are *you* doing?" She pointed at the sheets of paper spread before him.

"Preparing another magazine article, or trying to. Actually I've just written a good bit, things the children once said, things that showed their intelligence; my own too of course..."

"Oh sure! What about mine?" Her eyebrows rose, waiting for an answer.

"Yours? Well to some extent, but I didn't want to get too out of character."

He had not escaped that little episode unscathed, the family supporting Mum but all in fun, life easier now. In spite of the departing shed, this winter's work program was light, with no tarmac and no more building to worry about. A few extra standpipes for campers farther downstream were already erected. Naturally the water pipes to feed these new taps had been laid inside larger stronger pipes for protection and easy replacement. The rear tent field, Area 2, had also received attention. Lifting the turf on a sloping section, then levelling the ground and replacing the turf again was still under way but with no urgency; a job to be done at will. Civilised living at last; time for hobbies, time to be idle, time to experiment with the lathe. This machine, though proving versatile, still needed someone to pull the belt. Now that Sharon's A level course demanded more time, this task usually fell to Stephen but the power he could generate was limited, the help not always willingly given.

There must be a better way! Provision of alternative power had proved difficult. Attempts to work it from the windmill, using a long steel tube passing through holes in the basement wall, drew ridicule from the female half of the family when it failed to work. Waterwheel power would be better - but how?

Quite by chance, early in March while talking to a caravanner, a solution presented itself. Apparently, dynamos from old cars could be run as motors. Normally a car engine turns the dynamo and produces electricity. However, if current from a battery if fed to the dynamo instead, it will run as a motor - and should therefore turn the lathe?

With a little improvisation, such an arrangement was constructed. The family stood watching as the first test was made - Mum and Sharon looking for another chance to laugh; Stephen hoping fervently that it would work and consign belt pulling to history! In the dim light of that basement room, a blue flash crackled as the wires touched. Slowly the lathe began to turn! For a moment no one breathed, all willing it go, and as the speed increased a cheer rang out.

Over time, as visitors started to appear, the efficiency improved; one advantage of running a caravan park was a vast font of knowledge regularly passing through.

"Offsetting the dynamo brushes about 10 degrees will make a big difference," one camper offered, "give you more useful power for the same battery current."

Another visitor who had worked for a transport firm advised, "Some dynamos are better than others, don't think they're all the same. Use the C42 models from old Rover cars; small Bedford lorries had them too, they handle 360-watts without overheating."

Two such dynamos mounted together gave 720 watts, about a horsepower. From the biggest manually powered lathe,

River Valley had improved to the biggest battery operated version, one could even say the biggest water-powered lathe since the batteries were charged by a waterwheel.

Stephen particularly liked this move in self-sufficiency, enabling school metalwork to be done at home, giving him a special advantage. Very few of his classmates had a lathe, certainly none had one of such prodigious size and driven by a natural source of power. In this subject and the allied technical drawing, he moved ahead, enjoying his leading position in the class. No member of the family was really expert at machining, but here again specialist advice proved readily available from visitors, who even provided odd bits of equipment, a dividing head and various small tools. A long fly-cutter arrangement that fixed to the face plate, also made milling possible.

Everyone had originally believed work on the lathe would be limited to short periods to avoid running down the batteries, and in summer with the river level lower and so many caravanners batteries to be charged, that was certainly true. It didn't matter, for nobody had time to use it in summer anyway? Dad was bound to be busy and Stephen would acquire a host of new friends. At the moment however, in the quiet of early spring, the lathe would quite happily run for an hour. In practice, setting up the work usually took more time than actual machining, so the system was quite satisfactory. Its main limitation was speed; with the power available, high speed working was impossible - one just had to be patient. Never mind, in Cornwall life itself moved at a slower pace.

The basement workroom had accumulated so many small tools that finding any particular one tended to be difficult. The solution - more shelves and suitably sized tool bins bent to shape from aluminium sheet purchased cheaply at a local scrap yard - part of the sides of a wrecked Western National bus. A few further bins were still needed and discussing it at tea one evening, Jan suggested, "Those buses with the top deck cut away, the ones that run along the coast for viewing the scenery; do you think the company would notice if one more were to appear?"

"I think they just might?" Gordon smiled, and seeing approval on Stephen's face, turned to offer, "Let's visit the scrapyard again, but in the autumn; we're getting too busy now."

However, the opportunity was to arise sooner than expected. A caravan arrived one morning driven by a lady. Coming slowly over the bridge, its occupants obviously looking at the river, the car rolled across the yard to stop on the far side, the lady stepping out and making for the office.

"Do you have a pitch very close to the toilets?" She spoke from the doorway, not entering the office but waiting, giving the impression that if the reply was negative, she would leave again.

"Sure. Right alongside if you want. Come in," Gordon motioned towards a chair, then on a thought, asked, "Your husband...?"

"Hip replacement. That's why he stayed in the car."

"Our toilets have steps; we did think about ramps but people can slip on them."

"He's not in a wheelchair. Just can't walk too far yet. Can I book one day to see how we go?"

The caravan was soon pitched close to the third toilet building, Gordon staying as always to help push, his offer to adjust the steadies declined but appreciated. Towards midday the same car stopped at the office on the way out, the lady entering, waiting her turn until a couple asking about beaches, left.

"The showers are fine. Only one thing my husband finds difficult - putting his trousers on. Can't balance, falls against the wall because there's nothing to hold on to. He'll get the hang of it. Can I have five extra nights?"

Recounting the story at lunchtime, Jan asked, "Can we fix a hand rail?"

"Probably. Need to find something suitable; I'll pop out after we've eaten."

The afternoon was moderately busy. Jan took one caravan round, led it to a pitch, saw it manoeuvre into position and having answered various questions, set off back to the office. When the man opened his caravan, picking up a wrench to wind down the legs, a dog jumped from the door and raced across the grass. Catching the movement from one eye, Jan swung round in dismay.

"Damn!" Turning quickly, she headed back to the caravan. "I'm sorry, you didn't say you had a dog." As the man looked up sharply, she hurried on. "The dog section is farther down, near the riverbank footpath. Makes a nice exercise walk - and dogs must be on a lead." Seeing the couple glance at each other, she guessed there would be trouble, and steeled herself to be firm. This was the part she hated.

"Okay, sorry about that." The man reached to wind up the caravan leg again, the lady kneeling down, a move which had the dog racing towards her. Five minutes later they were on another pitch, pleased with the new position and the nearby walk along the riverbank. Relieved, Jan hurried back to the office wishing she had made a call earlier to ask her father's help - it hardly seemed worthwhile now.

When their own car returned shortly after, she hurried out to meet it, gazing through a window to find the back seats folded down, the rear loaded with various junk including a bundle of shiny bars. Turning off the engine and hurrying to lift the boot lid, Gordon reached inside, pushed some smallish aluminium sheets under one arm, grasped an oily looking dynamo in each hand and made for the office, calling back, "Bring the bars!"

She caught up in the basement, "What is this lot? The metal sheets are for tool bins, I know that, but why those filthy dynamos?"

"They're spares - the lathe wouldn't work properly if one of the existing pair breaks down. Cost very little so I got a couple... well you never know!" He spoke the last word defensively, seeing her smile spread and head shaking.

"And *these*? Handrails? I expected something small and neat; people won't want anything this big! They were cheap too I suppose?" Jan held one up, obviously stainless steel, over two feet long, both ends curved round and flattened with four holes for fixing.

"I disagree. Fixed vertically they'll be the ideal height for everyone, little children right up to the tallest adult. For a start I'll fix just one in those bigger showers in new toilet building."

"In the Ladies all on your own? Brave? You didn't say where they came from."

"An old bus; these are the grab rails from the seats - and yes, I *will* do the Ladies, provided there's nobody inside, otherwise it can wait, because..." He stopped, a gesture of the hand saying 'you know.'

Jan did know - he didn't consider it safe! Turning away with a smile in the dim basement light, she headed along the corridor, up the stairs and finding no one waiting returned to the kitchen to a cake, a special sponge in the shape of a waterwheel being prepared for the St Hilary Country Fair on Whit Monday. The wheel itself was a circular Victoria sponge, hollowed out to show each paddle separately then covered in chocolate icing to resemble wood. Below this a series of thin rectangular sponges joined together and iced in blue formed the river, contrasting with cream coloured supports marked out to look like stone blocks. That left only the final touches - flecks of white to give realism to water gushing from the downstream side. Every part was edible but how would it fare in the decorated cake competition?

June was hot and with little rain but this dryness no longer caused a problem. The final road surfaces, including the stretch leading steeply up to the top terrace had been tarmaced eighteen months ago; no more dusty roads. Better than that, there had been time and traffic enough since then for the first blackness to wear off, recently laid sections mellowing, blending better with that of earlier years. The site was looking good! Those grab rails in the showers had been well received, particularly by the chap with the replacement hip - that one had been installed the same day, before he arrived back for tea. Trees planted along the terrace edges had flourished this year too; in fact the whole valley looked great!

On 12th June 1980 a letter arrived from the Council inviting participation in the first ever competition to find the western tip of Cornwall's premier caravan park - a chance at last to win that *'Best Site in the Southwest'* award so often talked about. At tea that evening, the children were interested, pleased even - but without the excitement they would once have displayed. Five years ago it might have been different but priorities were changing - concerns for the future lying in different directions. "Sad," Jan thought as interest in the competition quickly changed to talk of a new friend Sharon had met, and a motorcycle just bought by one of the older boys at Stephen's school.

The competition entry form was prepared and sent off, three site postcards attached, one showing the ducks. A few weeks later a group of Councillors and Officials gathered at the house, asking to be accompanied on their inspection - standard practice apparently, so each site owner could answer judges' questions. That was sensible. On the tour of inspection they seemed impressed, one looking at the grass and saying to his colleagues, "It's more like a golf course than a caravan park."

No indication was given of course, how well River Valley compared with other parks, and within the hour they were off.

Towards evening the phone rang. Sitting in the lounge alone reading one of her study books, Sharon put it aside, crossed into the office and lifted the receiver. A well-spoken foreign accent asked, "You have room for a motorcaravan this evening?"

Sharon glanced automatically at the area across the yard, though that was not where a motorcaravan would go. The site was busy but nowhere near full, there should be no problem providing a pitch but this vehicle might be 300 miles away and arrive in the night, waking other customers. She answered carefully.

"I think so. What time did you intend to arrive?"

"We park at Hayle, finishing our meal. Half an hour... it is okay?"

"Yes. We'll be expecting you."

Ten minutes later when her parents returned from their evening walk, Sharon explained the call and the expected arrival, then collected her books, carried them to her bedroom and closed the door. Stephen returned briefly, leaving a young friend on the doorstep, hurried down to the basement, reappearing quickly with something in his pocket and the two raced off round the toilet building.

The next big vehicle to appear was not in fact a motor-caravan but a very long garishly painted bus, the engine noise telegraphing its approach.

"If this is the one, you won't like it. What does our licence say?" Jan rose to stand watching at the window.

Joining her, Gordon tried to remember. "The actual words... let's see, 'excluding any railway carriage, tramcar, or omnibus body... er, with or without wheels and howsoever adapted.' You see, to be a caravan it needn't have wheels but it can't be a bus! That certainly excludes this one! About as long as the house would you say? I'd better go - could get stuck on the bridge."

Two cars were already following and if this vehicle had to reverse back to the village, real problems looked likely. Moving to the extreme right and brushing the bushes on final approach, the driver inched forward. Judging by faces peering through the windows, it contained at least a dozen teenagers. When the vehicle stopped in front of the office, only the driver and three others emerged.

"I'm sorry, we don't have a place for you." Gordon felt ill at ease.

"We telephoned..."

The explanation about permissions and licences did not go down well. Apparently the group had already been refused at a number of places in the area and were tired. That was not too surprising - parties of young people, particularly teenage lads, could be a problem on sites, especially ones with no entertainments. They got restless, tried to liven things up - not helpful to older folk or to young families. The advice to try a coastal site met with ugly looks but the moment

116

passed.

Climbing back in, the driver executed a series of turns in the yard, then rolled again towards the bridge. Quite a few visitors from the nearer caravans had now gathered in the yard, a quick scan of their faces showing approval that this bus had been sent on its way. Feeling relieved but sorry not to be able to help the young people, Gordon ran ahead to signal clearances to the driver, an unnecessary gesture intended to end with a wave of good luck to the occupants, but the engine note suddenly rose, the bus surging directly towards him. A wild leap backwards into willow and gorse that edged the road only just avoided contact, the vehicle's side scraping against the branches as it gathered more speed along the road. Angry young men with murderous intent or just having a laugh? Back in the office he was still not sure, and not entirely happy with his own conduct.

"Should I have taken a risk, let it stay?"

"There's a few people around who would love to photograph it here; a chance to prove we've violated our licence. Not worth the risk; they wouldn't have been happy on a site with no activities. Anyway, it's not your fault; he could easily have said on the phone what type of vehicle he was driving and how many lads inside. He wasn't being open or honest, so why blame yourself? Not many people here would have liked to see them stay."

**

"We're having boys!"

"Yes Sharon, you told us before - anyway, what's so special about boys?" Jan winked at Stephen.

"Nothing! They'll be a nuisance, slow the class down." Sharon spoke with certainty, sneaking a glance towards her father.

Gordon looked up, inquiring of nobody in particular, "How many hours has she spent today getting ready, pressing clothes, washing her hair... was that lip-stick I saw on the dressing table? It's girls that slow a school down, throwing themselves at us chaps!"

Seeing Sharon about to explode, Jan stepped in quickly,

suppressing a smile. "Ah, but these particular chaps as you call them, are good-looking and young, not like some around here, eh Sharon?"

Good humour preserved, discussions turned to A levels, then to Stephen's coming school year. The following morning Sharon did look smart as she walked up the road for that first day at the re-named 6th Form College, no longer the Girls Grammar school.

In mid-afternoon a week later, tidings of the Best Site competition came by phone. Jan took the call while sitting at the desk talking to a lady customer, and even with another person present, could hardly disguise her delight. "We did? Really? A letter this week you say?"

The visitor was obviously curious but replacing the receiver Jan merely said, "Bit of good news. You were asking about ironing facilities. Not here, I'm afraid; we have no electric... they work off the waterwheel."

The woman had glanced up at the lights. Hearing the explanation she nodded, "Someone told me but well, everyone has electric; I didn't really believe... they said something about irons that go on the gas?"

"In the shop. You go round, I'll meet you there."

Back in the kitchen a little later, Jan worked with a smile, laying out the best tablecloth and preparing a special tea, but when Sharon and Stephen arrived home she gave nothing away. "Go and tell your father tea is ready."

"Mum! What... " Sharon wanted an explanation but seeing Stephen make for the door to fetch Dad, she broke off abruptly, charging after him.

Gordon saw them approach at a run, and listened to quick excited words that something was going on, they didn't know what - Mum wouldn't explain. Then the pair were off again, racing to be first back, leaving him to follow behind. Entering the house, he peered round the dining room door to look questioningly at table. Seeing a shrug from Stephen but getting no other answer, he turned to the bathroom.

When all were seated, Jan joined them, picking up a slice of bread as if nothing out of the ordinary was happening.

Everyone waited; the two parents looked at each other, both trying to keep straight faces - had they been alone the little game might have lasted some time but Sharon's pent-up impatience was about to burst.

"Well?" Gordon asked.

"Well what?"

"Why all the finery?"

"Only fitting for our station in life." Jan made a fine gesture, a little flourish of the wrist with one outstretched hand.

"Mum!" Sharon thumped the table unconsciously with a tightly clenched fist.

"Did we get a place?" Dad asked, suddenly guessing the cause.

"A place? No... we won!"

"Won? What outright?"

"Yes." Jan turned to her son and daughter, "We are now officially the best caravan park in the southwest!"

"What must the others be like?" Stephen mumbled doubtfully, a small grin spreading as the family turned on him.

The promised letter arrived on 17th September. Opening it, Gordon read the brief text, drew a magnifying glass from the drawer and examined the heading minutely, then waved it towards Jan. "So we really did win!"

"Did you doubt it?"

"Thought someone might be pulling our leg."

"So that's why you wouldn't tell the customers."

Almost a month passed before the presentation Ceremony. That was held at the Council offices on Friday 10th October at 3 o'clock. Apart from Chris, the whole family was present and the local press, a picture of the group appearing in the Cornishman with Herbert Lutey the Council chairman presenting the winning plaque.

Gradually the season drew to a close, with no grand schemes for the coming winter. Sharon at least was now working hard, battling with a mountain of homework in her final year. Stephen too had made progress, though he lacked any real determination except in those subjects that appealed to him. His parents could scarcely complain; they were themselves taking life more easily. A whole winter lay ahead with little to do but trim back the ever-growing foliage and perhaps a little painting. The facilities were now complete - at least *they* considered it so, and having won the best site award, were perhaps just a little complacent. However, they did start attending a first aid course to help visitors in the event of accidents. Money was no longer tight and earlier in the year in an uncharacteristic urge to spend, Gordon had bought new clothes for the children and some skirts for Jan, but when she raised again the subject of mains electricity, he shook his head.

"I did enquire again. I know a few people ask and money is easier this year but we still don't have enough. In any case, we could never cover the running cost. The Electricity Board have a minimum usage clause; they charge for quite a chunk of current, whether it's used or not."

CHAPTER 7

Three Owls.

"One could get to like idleness?" Jan looked out across the field. This winter had certainly been easier, no great strides made but a little work here and there passed the days usefully. March arrived, time to get grass seed in the ground - more energetic than some of the winter's activities, but short-lived. Only one load of topsoil had arrived, a lorry looking for a place to tip; it was quickly spread and the seed set. Free loads were rare but no matter, not many areas needed grassing now, and in any case, another job beckoned. A small well must be dug so the windmill could pump water properly.

"Behind the house out of sight!" she insisted, sceptical of the project.

"I thought in the front, near those Camellia bushes in the Cornish wall?"

"Okay... if you must; but make it look good for the customers, a wishing-well with a thatched roof and a winding handle for raising buckets of water, like the wells of olden days."

Half an hour later walking casually outside carrying some bread as if to feed the ducks, Jan saw him levelling a patch of ground behind the house and smiled to herself. Good, that was where it should be! She had guessed when suggesting the wishing-well that with people beginning to arrive, he would go for the simpler option.

Gordon looked up as she passed, caught the little smile and understood; pausing with a grin of his own to follow her movements as she crossed to a gaggle of ducks, letting them take bread from her hand. Clever and pretty. He turned back to the task in hand. She was right, starting behind the house *was* better, the woody dell already several feet below general ground level. With the water table not too far down, a hole less than ten feet deep should be sufficient; some heavy sleepers dumped by the sewage men would cover the opening safely. It should be quicker, less than half the work of the alternative. Besides, built where he had originally intended, the wishing well and its little thatched roof would be in the way if they ever wanted a warden's van next to the house; extra help might be essential one day if the site became very busy. Yes, Jan had been right, and that little grin as she passed showed that she knew it! Never mind, if it had made her happy he would keep quiet; content enough to let her win.

Right! To work! Anyone can dig a well... if they can stop the sides falling in! On this loose ground it could be dodgy digging down to water level then crouching inside, building up blockwork to form a lining. Never mind, he had an idea - build the sides first and dig the hole afterwards. Marking a square on the ground and removing a few inches of soil, provided a level surface on which to start. Four layers of blocks were quickly built with a strong cement mix then left to harden.

Jan looked at it. "Wells are supposed to go down, not up!"

"Ah. But I'm doing a special well; it's for sloping water."

She recognised the old family joke, memories from a time long past. When first married, way back in that secure but slightly boring suburban existence, they were contemplating building a swimming pool. Standing on the patio of their bungalow looking at the upward sloping garden, she had said, "Build the pool with the back higher than the front, then I can see the water from the lounge."

Remembering that previous lecture about sloping water, she gave a dirty look, strode away and sent Sharon and Stephen out to inspect the new well.

"You'll never get any water in it," Sharon said positively.

"'Corse he won't," Stephen agreed.

"Yes I will, all it needs is a lot more courses on the top. It's not finished yet. Wants to be bigger."

Stephen made a screwing sign with a finger against his head, a motion first learned from his sister years before. Sharon just sighed and rolled her eyes upwards in a 'Heaven preserve us' expression - something copied long ago from her mother. Gestures do tend to pass down through a family.

A week later with the blockwork properly hardened, the children out and Jan off shopping in Penzance, Gordon climbed inside the well and started digging. The ground, a mixture of clay with lenses of sand and gravel, proved easy enough. When the depth reached eighteen inches, he started prising out soil under the blockwork, letting it slide downward. Digging evenly all round proved impossible, the stack tilted, but working preferentially under the high side soon adjusted it back to level. Proceeding in this way, digging centre then edges, the lining sunk little by little until only a couple of inches remained above ground. He was mixing mortar for the next three layers when Jan came back with the shopping. She went over to the well, looked down, then turned to find him watching her, a smug expression on his face.

"Clever Clogs!" Nose in the air, she sniffed loudly and marched off indoors.

The next three courses of blocks only needed to set for four days before they too were lowered into the ground; another three courses followed, each set deepening the well by just over two feet. Having seen the method, Stephen became interested and gave a hand, though only one person at a time could dig. At one stage, friction against the surrounding earth stopped the lining settling even though nothing supported the bottom blocks. Water from a hose trickling gently down outside the blockwork soon induced a slide but made the bottom sticky, a matter of little importance for in another six inches, water level was reached.

Two foot below water was as deep as could comfortably be worked; a dryish spell made it unlikely levels would fall much farther. If they ever did... time enough to worry when it actually happened! With the work now complete, the pump was connected. An old bucket sunk in the bottom should stop the suction hose clogging up. High above, the fan blades were stationary, turned out of wind by a rope system at the bottom of the tower.

"Okay, are you ready?"

Jan called back that she was; a caravanning couple had joined her.

"Right!" Gordon gave a jerk, releasing the rope to swing the blades back into wind. Slowly the fan started turning, the main rod rising and falling, its speed gradually increasing - up and down rather like a large bicycle pump. At first the water was muddy with silt and fine material disturbed during digging - why is it that ducks, with a sparkling river nearby, prefer to drink from a shallow puddle, behaving as if the output of that pump trickled across the yard solely for their benefit? Checking again later the silt had gone, the miniature stream flowing crystal clear.

Among a handful of bookings in the morning post, one envelope contained a £500 cheque. Its arrival stemmed from the previous autumn when the stainless steel urinal in the third toilet building received an end of season clean with a proprietary brand of detergent; a product that succeeded in discolouring the metal. A company rep sent to inspect the damage took notes and photographs, and this cheque was compensation.

Very good! However, the arrival of Easter coincided with another surprise, one with less chance of a favourable outcome! Rubbish collection was to change; bad news - this service no longer free.

"Free! It was never any such thing. What do they think we pay rates for?" a voice on the phone demanded; another site owner canvassing opposition to the change, but as usual the Council had its way. Henceforth special plastic bags must be purchased, the price to include collection. Anything not in such a bag could not go on the dust-cart. Special holders were available at extra cost but as a concession, parks could use the bags as liners for their existing dustbins. Ah well, be thankful for small favours, at least the site's 100 bins would not be entirely obsolete. Anyway, the cost could now be afforded, the finances in good shape considering it was Spring, usually a low point in the family's resources. Jan took advantage, increasing her wages by £5 to £45 a week, claiming to be worth every penny as she helped carry a consignment of something over 500 toilet rolls down into the basement.

Those rolls were unlikely to last long; as the season developed they disappeared with increasing speed. Each set of toilets had its own waste bin, a place for old razor blades, empty toothpaste containers, discarded ends of soap and most of all, the cardboard tubes from used toilet rolls. Counting these tubes revealed the rolls were not being stolen - well, the odd one might have been but in general the number of tubes tended to match the rolls used since the previous day. More rolls were on order, usage increasing markedly as the school holidays approached. Thoughts of returning to cheaper scratchy types of paper were rejected, keeping customers happy was more important. In general they succeeded but on occasion the strain would tell! One morning there had scarcely been time for breakfast when an urgent call came to look at duck feathers on the riverbank. A brief inspection confirmed that one must have been killed, the body taken off, probably by a fox. Depressing. At about this time too, the urinal in the centre toilet building became blocked and apparently people continued to use it. By the time someone at last had sense enough to mention it in the office, the trough was full! Hurrying out to stand looking down at the smelly liquid, Gordon was vaguely aware of the outer door opening.

"You know how to clear it?"

He turned at the voice to see Norman, an old customer, standing at his shoulder. "Hello. Not really; it's never blocked before. Where's the alsatian?"

"Back at the caravan with Iris. You've a hand drill?" Seeing a nod, Norman continued. "Get one of those old curtain wires, the coiled up type you hang nets on. Cut off about three feet, open the end slightly, put it in the drill then keep turning the handle and feed it down the drain."

It sounded simple enough - attractive compared to the

alternative of groping about in rubber gloves.

Back in the shop Sharon was in trouble over newspapers. Someone's favourite had sold out and he was not pleased. Knowing Jan was in the house, she called through. "Mum, speak to a gentleman about papers."

As Gordon reached the house door, a three way argument was underway in the shop and simultaneously the phone rang - and there was still that blocked drain. Tension! This was the month for it.

"I'm sorry but you should get up earlier!" Reason having failed, Jan was losing her temper - she had been trying to prepare a mid-morning snack to make up for a skimped breakfast. Repenting the outburst, she offered, "I'll increase the order for tomorrow. Call at the shop in Goldsithney, they may still have one left."

Heading back for the kitchen as the man departed, she was stopped by a command from the office, "Find me some curtain wire, will you."

"Find it yourself!" She clenched a fist and stalked off.

A trip down to Audrey and Jim's bungalow finally located a length, but even there some people collecting ice packs caused a delay and a caravan rolled by heading for the site. Driving back down the road and telling himself off for going too fast, Gordon swung round the caravan now parked in front of the office. It proved to be an American - usually easy going people, and not too difficult to please. Anxious to see all of the country, they general stayed only a day or so, making the pitch less important. This one however had other ideas and after being shown a dozen places, finally chose one far downstream in an awkward corner. Conversation was brief and a touch unfriendly; this chap either one of the strong silent type or the journey down from Plymouth had left him tired and frustrated. Deciding that his awning should face out into the open, he declined any advice, growling "I do know how to back a trailer, mister!" and with that jumped in, running a bit too fast onto the grass, correcting clumsily and bringing the caravan tight but reasonable well against the hedge. The only trouble - this was an English caravan. The door, not on the side he was used to, was now totally blocked. After more manoeuvres to adjust the position, the American climbed down, grumbling about stupid pitches.

Gordon, anxious to get back to that blocked drain and guessing other caravans would already be waiting, was himself feeling anything but friendly. "If you hadn't been so damned impatient for independence we'd have taught you which side of the road to drive on!"

For a moment the two men stood watching each other, expressions hard with anger, then a smile slowly spread across the American's face. "That's something I can tell the folks back home, anyway!"

"We're short of basins." Sharon waved a letter from the morning post as her mother came through from the shop and dropped into an armchair.

"Phew, the queue is finally gone. What did you say about basins?"

"We need more. Dad tossed me this as he went off with that last caravan. Said to work it out." Sharon rose, carrying the letter across and passing it to her mother. "It says the third toilet building increases our licence by sixty, based on two WCs and two wash basins per thirty pitches. That's just for the ladies. We've only twelve ladies basins, so that makes 180 caravans we can have - more if you count the three deep sinks."

It seemed unlikely that this figure would ever be reached, although permission did exist for 250. There were already more than enough toilets; a few extra basins could easily be arranged if ever the need arose, but a piece of information of more immediate importance arrived that morning.

News of the owls first came from Bertie King, an authority on birds of prey; an old friend who visited the valley from time to time. With the season reaching its peak and the site busy; mid-afternoon when visitors were out at the beach would be the time to collect them. These were tawny owls, recently arrived at Mousehole Bird Hospital, a worthy organisation supported by voluntary contributions. It had operated over many years to the benefit of all types of bird; injured ducks from this source had several times finished their recovery in the Valley, the river providing an excellent habitat.

On this occasion, three owls needed training for release; two of them celebrities in their own right, having been the subjects of a naming competition on TV - the eventually choice of 'Bod' and 'Min' followed naturally, the abandoned fledglings having been found on Bodmin moor. The third owl, unnamed, was very gentle. As she arrived in the month of the royal wedding, Jan christened her 'Lady Di'. Although Di was smaller than Bod or Min, she was actually older, this fact obvious from the feather development. A blow on the head while young had left her with a damaged left eye, the iris slightly displaced. Whether sight in the affected side would ever fully return had been assessed as doubtful but with luck, time would see some improvement.

By arrangement, the owls were collected from Mousehole on Wednesday afternoon after their last TV appearance. At the hospital, three comfortably sized transport boxes lay open on the bench. Olga, the assistant who cared for them, wisely used rubber gloves to lift the first one. Taking it from her, Gordon was quickly reminded how much sharper were young owl's claws than those of the buzzards previously looked after and successfully released. There was no malice in the punctures, just fright, nervous tension, like humans cling to the arms of a dentist chair.

All three were soothed into boxes, loaded in the car and driven gingerly back to Relubbus, trying not to catch them off balance on the corners. As owls habitually perch on trees in a gale with no trouble, this concern was probably ill founded.

At home arrangements had already been made; they must live in the bathroom with its easy-to-clean floor. A stout hook screwed in the ceiling provided a hanging point for a perch, a free swinging trapeze suspended over the bath where droppings would do least harm. Removing a few loose objects and sliding the linen cupboard doors closed completed preparations. These precautions however, underestimated an owl's curiosity; first the bath mat, then a small mirror came under attack and were rescued and hidden away. Toothbrushes in a little chromium rack, the towels, various bits and pieces of cosmetics and combs, quickly followed.

Later the curtains had to go; owls are efficient at shredding anything from newspaper to dishcloths. A loose bar of soap thought to be owl proof, proved not to be so - leaving only the soap on the magnetic holder which they had not yet found. Oh, and the toilet roll was safe - so far! The bathroom contained the only toilet in the house (it had seemed superfluous to provide another with thirty more loos not far away). At first the loo seat cover was left down, fearing one would fall in, but being smooth, they tended to slip off when landing, their claws scratching the surface. When both cover and seat were raised, the vitrified rim quickly became a favourite perch. They liked the tiled windowsill too, and the solid top of the low level cistern, and would sit in either place while anyone used the toilet, eventually becoming bolder and settling on a shoulder to nibble gently at an ear, their heads turning to follow any movement. An unusual sensation, tearing off sheets of tissue and... well you know... watched closely by three pairs of eyes!

Certain precautions were taken right at the start. Fleas, flat flies and similar creepy crawlies had, on that first day, made anyone seeking to cuddle these delightful young tawny owls, step back and touch only at arms length. It was to be expected; most animals in the wild have parasites. A hedgehog in the torch beam one night was absolutely crawling with fleas, glistening brown in the light - perhaps it's difficult for a hedgehog to scratch; certainly a wonderfully defensive position for the flea. The owls were put in an open topped box for half an hour with a Vapona stick - it worked well, flat flies and other vermin dropping out. For a bird in good condition, such pests should be negligible; some authorities have even expressed the belief that a few may serve a useful purpose in keeping the bird's skin and feathers in peak condition by devouring moulds - who knows?

As always with birds of prey, the talons were lowered into a dish of dilute Dettol water, counteracting infections naturally present on the nest floor. With this peril removed, dripping a little blood, though avoided where possible, was hardly noticed in the excitement of handling and helping such beautiful birds and the prospect of seeing them fly back into the proper environment, healthy and strong enough to survive.

At first it was prudent to use thick gloves, for they were still nervous and their talons sharp. As days wore on however, gloves were dispensed with, the birds easily handled with bare hands, a slight upward pressure against the feathered chest inducing them to step aboard. Lady Di still needed hand feeding, tucking bits of rabbit into her beak and not forgetting to include some fur, essential for natural digestion - to be regurgitated later as pellets. Bod and Min however, could already tear up for themselves provided the rabbit was opened, which it always was since Jan insisted it be gutted first - they would probably have eaten part of the innards too, but the smell might be difficult to live with. She later found to her surprise, some regurgitated whole pieces of bone which the stomach acids had cleaned, smooth as a beach pebble, the bone itself partly dissolved away.

"Where have they gone!" A call rang out but nobody heard, all busy with customers. Stephen had entered the bathroom to find it empty. Nowhere a single owl in sight, not so much as a feather. The fanlight and double glazing were both open a crack, but surely not enough for an owl to escape. He looked carefully round and seeing the linen cupboard door not quite shut, moved to push it closed but instead, slid the door back to look inside. There they were, comfortable sitting on a pile of towels, not in the least worried - a fine imitation of a hollow tree. Reaching forward to the nearest owl, he rubbed the chest feathers - the bird raised a wing as if in invitation and he scratched the underside gently then lifted it to his shoulder before stroking and petting the next. With one on each shoulder and one on an arm, he slid the door closed, stepping to the bath, spending more time transferring each to the swinging perch, staying for a while, not talking as other members of the family might have done but his fingers continuing to rub and fondle a chest, then a wing, then the back of a feathered head.

With continuing pressure from a site full of holiday-makers, that linen cupboard door was left open again on odd occasions. Whenever the trio managed to sneak in and hide, they looked so comfortable on top of a pile of towels or shirts and so very resentful when taken out, clicking their beaks repeatedly in disapproval. No mess was ever stained the clothes, something to do with not making droppings on your own doorstep perhaps - few birds will soil their own nest. In a short time the owls lost all fear of the family, continuing to preen, or to tear up and eat when anyone was presence.

"Look!" Sharon urged as she carried 'Bod' into the office, one arm held out horizontally in front. The bird was perched in what might be described as a dust-bath stance, crouching on her bare forearm, the full length from chest to tail in contact with the skin, wings lowered crescent fashion dropping loosely below. Fluffing up feathers he shuffled his body about, reminiscent of a hen in dry soil. Finding a comfortable position and ignoring a group of customers near the desk, Bod settled, his posture now similar to a cat lying in wait for prey with its chin close to ground.

Such antics were a thrill; the bird's faith and confidence reward enough for those hours of patience it took to earn that trust - the feel of the beak as it nuzzled a finger, the gentleness of a creature that in nature is anything but gentle! Fascinating; a sensation hard to describe. Several of the watching visitors wanted to reach out and touch, and were allowed, one at a time to stroke the mottled feathers.

The family suspected that taking a bath with three owls looking on might be difficult; in the event it was relatively easy. Being birds of prey, much of their lives would be given to waiting, sitting silently watching for an opportunity, and so it proved in this case. They seldom bothered to fly to the bath rim or onto Jan's head as the last buzzard did - much to her a relief. Three at a time would inevitably have meant two landing on her bare shoulders! However, leaving a trio of owls perched directly overhead at bath times had its own hazards - they were moved one at a time onto the 'loo' seat, covered with a thick cloth for the purpose. There, they sat in a cluster, six great round eyes watched unblinking across the room - the absence of any white round a tawny owls eyes making them seem even bigger.

Matters were different with their own bath. Since the food supply was mainly rabbits, many having been deep frozen and therefore fairly drained of blood, it had seemed prudent to provide another source of liquid - a wide metal roasting dish about three inches deep, half full with water. In a very short time that water was everywhere! Each owl in turn crouched in the bowl, fluffed up like an overgrown winter sparrow; shaking tummies, trying to duck heads and generally becoming as wet as any owl had a right to be - at least Bod, who was first to discover it did! Not too much water remained for the others but it didn't stop them trying. They came out, feathers spiked and bedraggled, looking most forlorn; what little water remained was cloudy, so they must have achieved their purpose - a substitute for the lack of indoor rainfall perhaps?

***

Looking out over the site; it was busy - so it should be in early August. Not many more would come now, late afternoon a time for the shop rather than for new arrivals, except perhaps the odd motorcaravan, still most welcome. Today was special, Gordon and Jan's Silver Wedding Anniversary; the billiard table's mahogany covers spread with pies, tarts, cakes - a whole host of tempting, calorie-drenched morsels. One hand absently stroking the owl on his arm, he turned towards her, sitting at the desk with an owl on each shoulder. She didn't look twenty-five years older. Life was great; not only were they still attracted to each other, but good friends too. There was nobody whose company he preferred. That was just as well, for although the valley teemed with life now, long winter months and splendid isolation must inevitably follow.

Sensing his gaze she looked up and smiled, one hand still playing with soft feathers, the owl obviously enjoying this attention.

Stepping across, he swung the visitor's chair round one-handed and sat astride it, facing her over the desk. For a while they watched as the three owls' heads turned in unison to follow a bird flying by outside, a rook probably... and then it was gone.

"Well, do you still love me?" Asking was unnecessary; she was sure he did but wanted, on this special day, to hear the words. As she expected, before speaking he turned to check no one had approached - the action made her smile.

Sensing immediately what had drawn that smile, Gordon stopped momentarily... then they were grinning at each other, both aware. He leaned forward, "I wouldn't change you for all the young actresses in Hollywood... well, not for more than a night."

But she knew, as he knew, that neither would be unfaithful, although both hinted occasionally at the possibility. They laughed a lot too, perhaps the secret of a good marriage. The turning point had been way back in those early years when they stopped finding reasons to disagree. It was instinct now to approve. Arguments were rare but this was the month for them - the busy season with its constant pressure - not that either would have missed it for the world.

"The chance would be a fine thing." Jan raised her eyebrows. "Think they'll chase you screaming through the valley?"

Almost the exact response he expected. It had happened before, as if they were telepathic sometimes.

"What would be a fine thing?" Sharon entered from the kitchen carrying more food, and seeing her parents smile at each other, asked again, "Well?"

"Your father thought he might go off for the night with some young actress."

"Huh! Who'd have him?" Sharon put the plate down, easing others outward to make space. She had done most of the cooking.

"Cheek. That's an insult to your mother. Let's tell all the visitors when they come, that our daughter might be nineteen now but she not very bright."

"I wouldn't if I were you Dad, not on your twenty-fifth anniversary. I might let something slip."

"What?"

"That I'm twenty-six?" Sharon left with a broad grin.

As the afternoon passed, visitors began to call - a notice in the toilet buildings inviting everyone for coffee, the note explaining their anniversary. As the cake was cut to cheers from those visitors who happened to be in the office at that time, Gordon looked at his wife with a feeling of pride. Given a hundred lives, never again would he find such a partner.

Later that week on another fine evening, a man came for gas. The shop was open until seven during peak season. Jan took the bottle, exchanging it for one standing in the corner; it was the last, only a few kept in the shop because of storage regulations. Laying down a five pound note, he asked, "What's all the music?"

"Music?" She pushed the note into a box under the counter, rummaging among an untidy pile of coins to find the right change.

"Yes. Floating across the site. Quite good if it doesn't go on too long." The man took his change, the shop bell ringing twice as he opened the door and closed it again on leaving.

He was the last. Locking up and swinging the 'Open' sign over to read 'Closed', she returned to the lounge asking, "Know anything about this music?" A blank look prompted her on. "Man in the shop said it's coming from somewhere, drifting over the valley - from the farm perhaps?"

"Did he seem upset?" Seeing a shaken head Gordon rose, heading for the door. "I'll look anyway. Could be just a caravan with a loud wireless."

Jan moved to the kitchen for some bread, stopping to

look in on the owls, stroking and talking to them briefly before walking out to feed the ducks. Squatting just outside the office absent-mindedly popping bread into eager beaks she listened to the music; the man was right, it sounded rather good - for a while at any rate. Seeing Gordon stride back towards her, she called, "Did you find it?"

"No. Not coming from the site - maybe the farm as you say."

An hour later an elderly couple knocked at the office door, not complaining exactly, but not so tolerant as the man in the shop had been. They came to the valley for its quietness and although the music was pleasant enough, they preferred the natural sounds, evening birdsong, the crickets, a soft breeze sighing through nearby trees - things they couldn't get at home in the city.

Even now in the school holidays, a good percentage of visitors were retired people, sitting outside their caravans on a pleasant evening. Those many families with children had also chosen the site for a reason - and that would not be perpetual music, however sweet!

Gordon rose again, hurrying off. The sound was elusive, difficult to place. Wandering around, his footsteps moved this way and that, hunting - drawn inexorably upwards, to the terraces and on into the unused, largely unexplored wooded area beyond. The sounds were growing louder but not harsh; they had clarity, a pleasant roundness of tone not usually associated with radios. Stepping quietly now, he slid past a tall tree and edged round a mass of gorse - freezing in mid-stride.

There on the ground with his back against a trunk sat a man, his eyes closed, fingers caressing the strings of a guitar. Gordon eased the foot down to stand spellbound; the beauty of the playing, the pureness of sound at this close range... captivating. He recognised the player, a big man arriving earlier that day, a man from Holland - someone he had thought of as a shipbuilder or perhaps a rugby player; never suspecting those large hands held such finesse. Suddenly the music stopped, the head turning towards him.

"Cut off in mid... mid what? Mid-flow, mid-melody? What did you call a musical interruption?" the idea flashed to mind as Gordon stood, knowing what was needed but unsure how to... Lamely he said, "Hello."

Insisting the music was great but had to stop, was not easy. Explaining why it must stop promised to be even more difficult! Fortunately, as with most Dutchmen, the player spoke good English, and this one was more sensitive, more understanding than he looked.

With food, love and attention the young owls' condition had improved - training for release could start. Getting birds of prey back to the wild was more than just letting them go. The family followed a system taught them by that famous naturalist from Devon, Dr. Hurrell. They had sought his advice many years before in connection with a Buzzard. The method referred to as 'hacking back,' was based on several essentials. A bird should be in peak condition before release, not too young, and will fare better if familiar with the surrounding landscape and the creatures encountered there. Above all, it must know where food is to be found, then if as is quite likely the first hunting sessions are only partly successful, the bird need not lose condition and die. A special feeding table, chest height with a flat square top, now stood in a quiet corner near a group of tall trees.

Walking the owls outside was stage one; an introduction to the wider world. Sitting on an arm they were carried round the valley, beside the stream, along the hedgerows, into the various clusters of trees, flinching at first at any strange noise, crouching close and taking comfort from the well known body on which they perched.

On one such walk it was not the owls that were startled. A tourist hurrying in the opposite direction, came upon the trio and their guardians suddenly where bushes grew close to the road edge on a corner. Some people are nervous of big birds. Coming instantly to a halt and taking a backward step, he held up a defensive hand, "Ok, so I stayed an extra night - I'll pay." Actually, the man owed nothing and was booked for several days yet, the quip a defensive reaction covering momentary fear and loss of face.

A thin leather lead attached to each bird during these walks prevented premature escape, allowing time to assimilate country noises and find their bearings on the territory. The feeding table was regularly visited, the bathroom food supply simultaneously reducing - a simple procedure but the owls proved resistant to hunger. During the first week only a few mouthfuls were taken in the open air; too many eye catching things distracting their attention. The habit of rotating the head to follow another bird's flight was curious; the neck could turn so far! When watching some distant movement they were hard to distract, a hand passed backwards and forwards in front of those big eyes having not the slightest effect, the bird's concentration still on the object that might represent either danger or food - ignoring the familiar hand close by. They did not swivel the eyes to follow movement; the entire head turned, giving a trance-like impression.

Contrasting their behaviour with the buzzards previously reared, the owls seemed able to rotate the neck much farther but stability of the head was less. The buzzard had an uncanny ability to keep its head in the same place. An arm with a buzzard on can be raised and lowered a couple of inches, or moved sideways and back by that amount without any motion of the bird's head. The body moves and the neck stretches and contracts but the head stays quite still; it can also blink one eye at a time - both features developed no doubt, to keep their prey in sight! These owls while similar, were just that bit different.

Although designed for night use, their daytime vision was good, all three turning again at another small distant movement. A new sound drew their attention immediately but familiar noises were often ignored. Lady Di's bad eye had improved, she was bigger now, growing faster. Because business was busy, it became standard practice for either Gordon or Jan to stay in the office while the other took all three owls. For the same reason, walks were usually in the middle part of the day or towards evening when campers' demands were less. Often enough Sharon or Stephen would take a single owl, showing it to the other children, allowing them to gently touch, even letting it perch for a while on another young arm. It may have stimulated many a youngster to care for wild things - that was very much in accord with River Valley's purpose.

In the course of the evening walks many caravan and camping guests used a great deal of film, but whistling or finger clicking seldom induced Bod or Min or Lady Di, to look at the cameras. Their feathered heads often swung at the sound of a shutter, only to swing back almost immediately as if to say, "Oh, those funny humans again; we're safe enough on that side."

There were no shortcuts to the training; patience needed but no one wanted to hurry. The owls could stay forever if they liked but that would be unfair - they needed the freedom they were created for. Still resisting eating at the feeding table, a good meal at intervals in their bathroom sustained them. They certainly regarded that room as their own, good-naturedly tolerating occasional intrusions. The extra nourishment ensured against any decline in strength. On such occasions three separate portions were given but nevertheless two often disputed the right to a particular piece, squabbling and warning each other in an entirely different voice to their normal tone. On one such occasion Gordon tried to cut a slice off the largest piece to give a fairer share, and as Bod would not let go, he used the knife with great care not to damage those talons firmly gripping the meat. The owl made no effort to prevent this taking part of its feast, seeming quite prepared to share with a person but not with the other owls.

"Strange. Have I taken the place of a parent bird?"

Chapter 8

Blood

Mid-August was busy, the shop running out of several items, but numbers should start falling soon. Slower selling lines would be discontinued now, though some stocks must still be replaced to keep visitors happy. Once the morning rush had abated, Gordon nipped off to Cash and Carry. A quick phone call to Jim in his bungalow at the site entrance, brought a promise of help, he would come right away. With his bad leg, 'right away' was a relative term. How busy would the next ten minutes be. As if in answer to that thought, the office door opened and a woman entered, greatly concerned over a big moth crawling across the floor of the Ladies toilets. She feared it might get trodden on, but had not felt able to pick the creature up.

"I'll come." Jan grabbed a key, locking the door as they left, but saw an elderly couple walking towards the shop, new faces not regular visitors. A quick glance found the entrance road empty, Jim not yet in sight. With only the waterwheel to provide electric, the shop had no proper till, an open wooden box under the counter held all the cash, coins and notes together - totally unprotected. Many of those notes were not even in the box, but lay alongside, spilled over on the shelf and somehow forgotten on this busy morning. She hesitated, torn between the two tasks, stopping to ask, "Did you want the shop?"

"Yes please, just to look round. It's our first day."

On the point of going with them and asking the moth woman to wait, Jan saw another group appear, also heading for the shop, and changed her mind - there was safety in numbers. "You go ahead, I'm just off to do a little rescue; be back in a minute."

In fact, it took rather more than a minute, the moth had disappeared, crawled away, found eventually behind a cubical door. Bending, Jan eased it onto a finger, hurrying back to show the waiting customers, then popped outside to find a hiding place on an ivy covered tree trunk. Five minutes later the shop was empty again and Jim arrived from his bungalow, hobbling in to stand behind the counter.

Sitting now in the office answering phone calls and taking money as visitors booked extra days, Jan dashed off occasionally to pitch an arriving caravan or tent. After one brisk session when a temporary lull allowed time to quietly catch up on some bookwork, voices drifting through from the shop caught her attention. Rising from the desk and taking a few steps to peer through the slightly open communicating door, a regular caravanning couple, Audrey and Charles from Ilkley, another ex-policeman, were chatting over old times. About to turn away she heard the name Ruskin Park - a place from the past where she fed ducks as a young girl. Jim was speaking of someone who snatched women's handbags and how he cornered this young thug in a tool shed.

"Cocky he was, standing there, tools hanging from the walls all round. No chance of getting away, I had him cornered but he knew I couldn't hit him; even in those days it wasn't allowed. He sneered at me and said..." Jim paused, deciding not to repeat the actual words with a lady present, "er, said something offensive. I jumped forward, swinging a fist as if to flatten him. That changed the look on his face. Not so brave then! He leapt back like a frightened rabbit, hit the wall a great clout, something above broke and a whole shelf of tools smashed down on him - made a hell of a mess. Serves him right, nasty little pervert!"

Another caravan drawing up called Jan away and after pitching it, she spent a few minutes with the three owls, stroking their feathers and making a fuss of them. Over the past weeks their training had shown good progress, all three eating regularly at the feeding table. Lady Di, originally the slowest starter, was now the most forward - so much so that she had somehow loosened the attachment for her lead. Fixing these had been a problem in itself! A lead was essential, not just something to please the family and protect more timid caravanners but for the birds' own well-being. Premature escape would probably mean death. The first requirement therefore, of any attachment was strength and reliability. It must be comfortable too, allowing the birds freedom to feel their wings, not injuring them when they tried short flights. There was also the matter of release when they returned to the bathroom. As with the buzzard some years earlier, slender leather dog leads proved best, these clipped to a 'collar' on the bird's leg; this collar made of soft strong leather sewn close to one leg, forming a figure eight shape. You should try sewing a leather ring round an owl's leg - it might be called a memorable task. After Jan finally succeeded on the first occasion in fixing these leg collars, the birds had torn at the newly attached leather with their beaks for a while, then accept it completely. Now the task was simpler, Lady Di tolerating the procedure with scarcely a quibble. For final release it would only be necessary to snip the stitching.

The family now found their charges becoming more active, particularly towards evening, a good sign. 'Min' had taken to making practice pounces on an arm, the stance delightful, the bird rearing up to the fullest extent of its height, head waving from side to side, eyes turned down, to suddenly pounce and grip the flesh but seeming to know it must not actually break the surface. Working its way along the arm in this fashion, the owl showed no such inhibitions when reaching the rolled up shirt sleeve, striking at the material then pulling with its beak. A bird of prey 'strikes' with its talons, its killing weapons. The foot shoots out, contracting on contact, driving claws deep into the prey; the hooked beak merely for pulling off bits of flesh afterwards. Sometimes an owl would follow an outstretched arm to the shoulder, then become gentle again as it sat upright to pull at strands of hair.

"Why do they like to do that?" Jan asked as Bod and Min sat one on each shoulder, running their beaks through her curls.

"Not sure but I do have a theory," Gordon offered. "I think they're looking for fleas or other vermin - they often do it with each other."

"I hope they'll be disappointed." But she made no attempt to stop them. The way they sat close to her face, continuing to nuzzling beaks through her hair, or nibbling so gently at an ear... a delight that must be experienced to be fully understood. The final release was approaching - a prospect both joyful and sad; fortunately that decision need not be faced just yet.

"Women can be so unreasonable," Gordon protested one morning. He carried a live mouse, caught with the intention of releasing it in the bathroom, but had hesitated on the threshold, torn between concern for the mouse and a need to let the owls practice their first kill. The smart money would be on the mouse, to escape down one of the holes that carried various water pipes into the basement. That little moment of indecision on the doorstep however, had been his undoing. Jan spotted the mouse and was adamant.

"Get that *thing* out of here immediately!"

In the interest of marital harmony and perhaps with some relief, he let it go in the bushes behind the house.

River Valley's flock of ducks now included mallard, muscovys, aylesburys, campbells and a few silky bantams, one with chicks. All became used to owls passing by on an arm, and ignored what ducks in other places might normally consider a danger. One evening however, just after leaving the house, 'Min' took it into her head to fly. This was not unusual, all the owls tested their wings at various times - it was standard procedure to run in the direction of flight, bringing the bird gently to ground with no sudden jerk of the lead. On this occasion, Min landed near a silky bantam chick, whereupon the mother silky immediately attacked with such ferocity that the owl fell backwards in surprise, causing the bantam to over run her target, swerving round to charge in again. This flurry of activity put all the ducks to flight, a host of wings flapping in panic, bantams squawking, running in all directions, feathers flying everywhere - as good a simulation of chaos as any film director could ever have wished.

Gordon bent on reflex, stopping the mother bantam's second charge and in the same movement scooped up the owl. Min looked bewildered, gazing round from her safe perch with big eyes and a 'Did I do all that?' expression.

More days passed, Lady Di doing well and in keeping with her greater age was now way ahead of the others; the time for her release at hand. Westward TV wanted to film - a quick phone call to Mr Eastwood the TV cameraman and the release would be next evening, subject to good weather - Jan insisted Di should not spend her first night alone in the wet. After some filming in the bathroom, the leads were put on and Jan, Stephen and Dad took one owl each round to the feeding table where three pieces of rabbit had already been placed. Tommy, a neighbour from Gurlyn farm next door had supplied this rabbit - and many others too, in a battle to prevent them munching his crops.

Film of the owls eating while still on their leads was followed by Lady Di on her own, then a shot of the soft leather ring to which the lead attached. The camera watched as it was cut gently away leaving her completely free but still feeding happily on the table. Time passed, the camera waiting, but she refused to fly. Bod and Min had been taken away on the basis that perhaps once they were gone, Di too would leave? No such thing - she was equally happy with people. Everyone withdrew to stand watching from a distance, the cameraman adjusting his lens for fading light. It would be dark soon... and still they waited. Finally Di was taken on a wrist and moved up and down, gently encouraging her to take flight. She remained totally unruffled, wings opening slightly for balance. Suddenly they opened fully and Di was off, swooping in a big arc almost to the ground before soaring upwards, disappearing between the trees into the wood, there to settle perched high on a branch. Over the next days Di was sighted several times. Meat placed on the table each night after dark was gone in the morning. Later in the week this food stopped being taken but Di was seen twice more, obviously well fed and happy - a very successful outcome.

The loss of Lady Di and the realisation that both Bod and Min must go soon, triggered an expensive move that had been talked over for some months; a new camera, a Nicon FE was acquired complete with tripod. The wish for better quality photos had been discussed several times recently, something to record the valley's wild life for visitors to see and for all those personal things the family would one day look back on. The owls' imminent release had finally decided this issue, clinching the purchase.

Chris's arrival home for a few days gave another incentive. Photographed in his summer uniform, white shirt with dark epaulettes and no tunic, he held an owl on each arm. In the following few days Bod and Min 'sat' for many pictures, campers and caravanners being warned not to take flash photos; no one knew how it might affected those large night eyes. Approaching close enough to fill the frame was no problem with these owls, but for other birds a telephoto lens would be nice. "Could I buy Jan one for Christmas?" Gordon wondered.

That evening the family of five sat again in the lounge, chatting together, the owls with them, 'Bod' on Sharon's shoulder as she recounted her last term at school and hopes about university. Stephen, with 'Min' on his arm, spoke of friends and of fishing. Darkness had fallen outside and overhead the little waterwheel bulbs spread their light across the room.

Suddenly, one of the bulbs flashed with a loud pop and the light dimmed.

"Ouch!" Sharon flinched, immediately reaching up to comfort the bird on her shoulder, "Did it frighten you?" She pushed a wrist up under Bod's chest, causing him to step on, then transferred the bird to the other side. Pulling back her blouse revealed a spot of red where a talon had punctured the skin; she smiled, turning to display it. "Look, blood!"

"Well done, Bod." Dad winked across at Mum, the two

boys nodding agreement, Sharon trying to look fierce but laughing with them, reaching a hand up to stoke the owl gently.

"You know what is important about blood?" Chris asked.

No one volunteered an answer, just as nobody suggested the bulb be replaced. In the dim light of that single remaining bulb, Chris leaned back in his chair and started to speak.

"I was on duty with another policeman in a part of our beat that wasn't always safe. We were watchful, walking with care. It was dark, the street ahead full of empty doorways and passages, a district where it paid to be prepared. Approaching a junction, our feet trod softly - you never knew what might lie round a corner. We were keyed up, ready I thought for anything, but as it turned out that wasn't true. Into the silence, a woman screamed! - a sudden, full hearted, shrill goose-pimpling scream on the night air! It stopped us in our tracks - then we were racing forward as a dark figure broke from cover to flee down the street. My companion stopped to check on the victim; I ran on giving chase. Whatever he'd done this man was fast but gradually I was closing, catching him. I shot a quick glance over one shoulder - the other constable no longer with me. The man in front veered left, heading for the park. I raced on with grass underfoot and after a while, back onto pavement again. He must have heard my steps closing then for he turned suddenly, drawing a knife! But I was too close, no chance of stopping! I was on him already, committed in that final lunge, no way to avoid the contact. His arm rose the blade glinting in a distant street light - about as bright as our lights here. I grabbed desperately at his wrist, striving for a grip as we went down struggling.

"When the other constable rushed up a few minutes later, I already had him under control, wrestling him to his feet, kicking the knife clear. I was worried; we were both covered in blood but in the end it didn't matter... it wasn't mine! Trying to stab me, he'd cut himself."

Chris paused, looking round the faces, continuing in a more relaxed voice. "That's what is important about blood -

whose it is!"

The family enjoyed those few days together with the owls before Chris departed again. Absorbed in his career as a London police constable he came home at intervals, sometimes accompanied by colleagues, looking bigger and more muscular at each visit, but he seldom stayed long.

Sharon too, was restless. In spite of the novelty of boys arriving at the school, she had used her time well at Sixth Form College, working hard to obtain good 'A-level' passes in Physics, Maths and Chemistry. She was still on holiday now but must leave in a few weeks for her first term at Exeter University, a new somewhat uncertain future. What would the rooms be like, and the other students - would she understand, keep up? The prospects left her... not exactly nervous but apprehensive, thinking back often to the comfortably familiar surroundings of the previous year. Sitting in the lounge one evening still thinking about the old school, she recalled an incident from those final weeks when the exams were already over. The other sixth form girls had been reduced to tears of laughter by Sharon's articulation of the word 'grotesque' while reading aloud an extract from some magazine. Her rendition, three separate syllables, grot-es-que, exactly as written, became a word regularly used in the group, and always with that same pronunciation.

Listening, Jan felt her daughter's bubbly excitement, the need to talk, to say something; saw her jump up as she finished the tale, striding off to her bedroom, only to return empty handed a minute later. Quietly watching, Jan knew the cause. Sharon would be gone soon - how quiet the house would be then! She would certainly enjoy the new life with plenty of study and evening activities, and without doubt would settle in well at Exeter; no one made friends faster, they accumulated wherever she went. Jan wanted to reach out a reassuring hand, but with Stephen and Dad present, this was not the time.

She turned towards her youngest; Stephen was studying for 'O' levels, having come top of his class last year in

Geography, Chemistry and Technical Drawing, quite an achievement at last, but soon he too would leave. Jan mentioned the thought next day while washing up after a meal.

"We could start again... have another three?" Gordon ran a finger down her back.

She didn't reply directly but looked down at the carving knife in her hand and stroked the blade with a thumb to test for sharpness; a long, thoughtful look offering the most positive '*No*,' altogether beyond discussion!

***

Sharon put the needle aside, looking at the finished work but she was restless, dismissing it with a nod, her mind elsewhere. Hurrying back to her room to check cases and boxes she looked once more through drawers and wardrobe, a nervous excitement in fingers that touched, drew away then touched again items of clothing to be left behind. Her first day at University approached; tomorrow! Throughout the day she flitted, sitting, standing again, hurrying off on a sudden panic that something had been forgotten, stopping halfway to gaze through a window at the river. Dad was out, gone to Cornwall Farmers for duck food, mother and daughter talking or working together in the kitchen. Several times during the afternoon Jan spoke without hearing a reply, and turning, found her daughter sitting, eyes blankly staring.

When another question met with silence, Jan shook her head, knowing the cause but asking, "Who is this boy that sends you off in a dream?"

Sharon looked up sharply, startled, and seeing her mother smile, she grinned back. "I don't get sentimental over males - not like some people!"

"Some people?"

"Yes Mum." Sharon's hand rested loosely on the table, a finger rising to point, "Why do you keep that single red silk rose by your bed?"

"Oh..." Jan's eyebrows rose. "When did you... it's just something Dad once came home with."

"Are you blushing?" Sharon leaned forward, elbows

moving onto the table to form a support, chin resting on cupped hands - all attention now, the impending departure briefly forgotten. "About time he did something romantic. Probably wanted his own way over some new scheme."

Jan waved an arm, unsure how to reply. "A man can get away with such things; make a grand gesture and that's it for a while. A woman on the other hand, is constantly thinking of her man - little things, doing them for him day in and day out. Both are important in a good marriage, it's what makes ours work."

"Little things?"

"Yes, the meals, things he likes to eat, keeping the house clean but doing it so he doesn't even notice. If he likes a particular cup for his coffee, I see he gets it," Jan paused, thinking.

"Fetch his slippers?" Sharon asked.

"No, never. Anything but that."

"Why not?"

"Standing joke between us - he likes to grumble about fetching his own, pretending I don't look after him, tells his mother I don't sometimes."

"Cheek!"

"Don't worry, she knows. She says 'Oh, it's a hard life that woman leads you' meaning me; but the tone, the manner in which it's said, tells the story. His Mum knows what goes on. Only time he ever picks up a tea towel is when Ivy visits. It's fun, we understand each other... and it's usually me that gets my own way, not just by being devious - your father knows and lets me... well, most of the time."

The two girls smiled at each other, content, talk swinging back to university again, what the rooms would be like, the lectures, the evenings?

The household was still asleep when Sharon rose next morning, bathed, dressed and lifted the office curtain to look out. A dark sky overhead lightened towards the east; sunrise not far away. Gas lamps in the centre toilet building glowed dimly through the glass but no single light shone from the handful of caravans on the front field. She wished her parents would rise, it was already after six, only a few minutes past but they should be up by now. Impatiently she strode to the kitchen, then returned on impulse to the bathroom, stroking and fondling the owls, knowing their release date to be due and regretting she would not be here to watch.

An hour later the toilets had been cleaned and the car stood ready, laden with boxes and suitcases. It faced the wrong direction but Gordon refused to start the engine so early. Caravanners were still asleep; after the meal would be soon enough. Breakfast was eaten with an undercurrent of expectation, Stephen and both parents caught in Sharon's air of suppressed excitement. She rose for the third time, only to sit again in frustration as the others continued eating.

"Finish your meal; food at Exeter may be less appetising," Jan advised quietly.

"You might as well, we're not starting yet," Dad warned. "No good arriving too early. Don't be so impatient - young girls should learn some restraint."

"I'm not a girl! I'm nineteen... a woman." What started as a challenge, faltered, indignation falling away, the last word softer, hesitant, almost a question, eyes looking down at the table.

Departure by mid-morning was plenty soon enough but waiting that long would be cruel. Within half an hour the car was on its way, Jim and Stephen left in charge. Now in September they could manage easily, the site no longer busy. Chatting as the car hummed smoothly along, Jan turned often to Sharon in the back seat, realising that for her, this must be a journey almost as significant as that first arrival in the valley more than ten years ago. Then at least, there had still been parents and brothers for reassurance. Now for the first time she must live in a new place, surround by strangers.

Arriving at the University, a young lady, a second year student, guided Sharon to her lodgings, the cases carried to a small but comfortable room with bed, desk, and best of all a radiator. The campus resembled a disturbed anthill, people coming and going, scampering in every direction, cases dangling from each hand; boxes, tennis rackets, suits tucked under arms - even a motorised trunk-trolley full of cases trundling by.

Sharon was nervous, bubbly, excited - and more than normally talkative. With everything carried in and piled temporarily on the floor, she waited impatiently for her parents' departure, anxious to start finding new friends. However, as they turned to go she detained them on some pretext, then regretting it, chivvied them again to the door and stood waving as they descend the first of many flights of stairs.

"She'll be all right," Jan murmured, reaching to take Gordon's hand. No one had suggested otherwise. He looked down at her and smiled. Losing a daughter, an only daughter, was important to fathers as well but the women had been much closer, cooking together, quietly discussing female things. The house would seem empty, especially now Stephen was out with friends most evenings. Crossing to the car they looked up, scanning the tall building; a small face at a window high above looked down, a hand waved and disappeared.

The journey home was quiet, those few words spoken had a touch of nostalgia; talk of the children as they once were, when Chris was still in his second school year and Stephen only three.

"Did they have a good start in life?" Jan wondered aloud. "I think so, but could we have done better?" she paused again before answering herself, "Yes, of course. Who couldn't, with hindsight."

Gordon nodded, flicking a glance at her then back to the road ahead. "I certainly should have been more under-standing, not come back to the caravan and house so tired in the evenings; taken them more places, not given out so many jobs - but work meant survival then. I'd change that part if I could, but it's too late now for regrets! Did you ever think they would grow so quickly?"

"Never! It's still hard to believe." With a shrug of the shoulders she sighed and for a while silence reigned, the car speeding on past banks and trees with glimpses of a wider landscape, the miles slipping by. Passing a small parking space just off the road, a young family were standing, stretching their legs no doubt as children need to do. Briefly she glanced towards Gordon then turned quickly away.

In that snatched moment before concentrating again on the road ahead, he had seen the brightness in her eyes and knew this was no time to speak.

Five miles passed before Jan had herself fully under control, her words coming with apparent ease.

"We can't have done too badly. Chris has a job with real promotion prospects; he's good with people, helping on site did that, dealing with visitors even back in his junior school days. That would never have happened if you stayed in an ordinary job."

"I suppose, but you were brave too - to give up the house and live in that tiny caravan. Don't pretend it's all my doing. Mind you, I may have given him one advantage."

"Oh yes?" She could hear the laughter in his voice.

"After working at home for me, he may find other bosses a piece of cake!"

Jan smacked his knee, not hard, not wanting to distract his concentration. "Don't joke. There may be some truth in it! They should have had more free time - still you may be right. Sharon knows how to work too, she'll get a good degree." Another silence followed as they drove on.

Crossing the Tamar, Gordon said quietly, "Cornwall."

There was no reply and he said no more. Time passed, the miles eaten up but something was missing. They passed under a railway bridge and down a long incline, slowing as the road narrowed and traffic increased.

Passing through Fraddom, Jan pointed. "There, by that wall. That's where Sharon was sick on the first journey down; she was seven then. Stephen will be gone too, before long; he'll want his own place once he's working. He'll..." Suddenly she broke off, turning again to the window. Gordon slowed, looking for a place to pull over but she urged, "Don't stop." A handkerchief appeared and she blew her nose noisily.

It was true. In a year or so he'd be gone - just the two of them left. The house would be quiet then, the valley more isolated in winter than all those years ago in the little caravan.

Arriving home, the place already felt different, the owls happily providing an outlet on which to lavish affection. Always tended and well cared for, they seemed to sense the need as sad fingers caressed their feathers. But that too, was to stop. Arrangements had been made for Bod and Min's departure; it had been planned that these two, being the same age and presumable companions since birth, would be released together. Once free they would soon separate, but might offer each other company for those first few days in the strange wild world.

The TV cameras came earlier this time, ensuring plenty of daylight. Jan and Gordon stood together in the bathroom, clipping on the leads for the last time, ruffling feathers gently, Bod nibbling Jan's ear. The walk to the feeding table was slow; but for the cameraman's presence it might have taken... who knows how much longer - an hour, a day, another week?

Carefully the stitches were snipped, soft leather circles eased from the legs, feathers ruffled and stroked again in a reluctance to let go - then with determination, they stepped back. The wait this time was not so long, wings opening, seeming to know, feeling the breeze; an experimental flap, a crouch and a small leap and away - one leading the other following, settling as Di had done, in the wood.

The family saw themselves on television on Friday, surprised that from the miles of film taken only a fraction was shown, less than five minutes, ending with a particularly good shot of first one owl then the other flying off to be lost in the trees; hero departing into sunset in true western fashion.

Sharon's absence was indeed felt as winter approached; it would be good to see her back for Christmas. Being the only young person now at home, Stephen too usually left after tea, cycling off to find friends. For the parents, days were busy with pruning and trimming, but longer lonelier evenings demanded new indoor hobbies, preferable of a not too physical nature. Jan elected for dressmaking and embroidery. An adjustable dressmaker's model and material were purchased, and some dressing table runners with various coloured silks. In the event, after making several skirts and a dress, she found working with silks more interesting and started an enormous tablecloth, likely to last for months.

Still seeking ways to improve the business, Gordon purchased a Spectrum computer and printer, hoping to write a program that would calculate each customer's bill and print a neat receipt showing exactly what had been charged for. Perhaps the program could also count how many visitors booked in each day and add up the takings? Normally, people expect computers to run from mains electric, not from waterwheels! However, an improvised device converted home made current to the voltage required. So far so good but what about learning computer languages? Difficult perhaps, but just the thing for long winter evenings.

***

Several months passed; outside it was cold, not freezing but a nip in the evening air. Sharon sat at the desk, she was home again but must leave for university in two days now that Christmas was over. The phone rang; with the new year under way calls were increasing - she reached across lifting the receiver. A masculine voice enquired after vacancies in August, and receiving confirmation started giving his address, breaking off to say, "You do have hook-ups?" It was hardly a question, the tone assuming it must be so.

"Hook-ups?"

"For electric." The voice was impatient now, as if only an idiot would need to be told.

"No," Sharon drew in a breath, controlling what she would like to have said. "No mains electric; we use a water-wheel to..." She stopped, the phone had gone dead.

Her parents were working outside. During the first season on site with no sewer yet in the valley, smells had wafted down from ventilation pipes sticking through the toilet building roof. Extending the pipes high in the air had dispersed the smell. Once the sewer came, smells were no longer such a problem but those tall pipes had never been taken away. Sharon moved to the window, watching her father walk along the ridge of the roof balancing a long pipe, then walk down the sloping tiles and pass it to her mother, waiting below. Another pipe already lay on the ground, each building had only two - he would come down now with the light beginning to fail. Stephen was running across the bridge, just arrived home, school restarting earlier than university. She opened the door, walking across to give the news.

As the family sat down to a late tea, Stephen spoke of his day at school and particularly of his favourite subject, technical drawing, addressing a question to his sister. "You know how to draw a hexagon?" Either Sharon didn't know, or could find no easy explanation.

Seeing the shrug, Stephen reached across for paper and a pair of compasses, making a quick circle. "Draw the circle you want the hexagon to fit inside, then without changing the compass setting, mark off six radiuses round the perimeter - like this."

"Radii," Sharon corrected, "that's the plural."

Sensing an argument brewing, Dad asked, "Do you know why... why your hexagon works out that way? Those marks you've made round the circumference; join two of them to the centre and what do you have?" Watching the lines being drawn but seeing no sign of understanding, he tried again. "What length is each side?"

"Ah!" Automatically Stephen made to raise a hand, withdrawing it quickly "All radiuses... er, radii - they're all the same length, an isosele... no, an equilateral triangle, sixty degrees..." he paused, finger raised obviously calculating, "Yes, 360 degrees in a circle so six will fit - six equal sides - a hexagon."

"Some of my friends still want hair-dryers." Not keen on being outdone by her younger brother, Sharon changed the subject. "What will you do about electric?"

Gordon looked vacantly out through window, a frown lining his face.

"Nothing," Jan gave the answer, "not this year anyway."

The following day Sharon set about packing. She had over the Christmas period been to several parties with old friends, one of them in fancy dress. A costume had come through the post, an intricate Indian costume supplied by Ivy, Gordon's Mum. Photos had been taken when she first tried it on; now it was packed away with care. Placing final items in a case, Sharon rose, collecting bread from the kitchen and going outside. She was restless, torn between home and the new life. A duck sitting by the river caught her attention.

"Stumpy!" She called, walking towards a mallard drake that stood shakily, taking a few forward hops. It had no right leg - cut off in some unknown way at the knee. The wound had healed before it arrived, floating down the river to join the other ducks. There seemed no point it taking it inside - no chance to make the leg better - the best vet in the world could scarcely fit a replacement limb. Stumpy managed tolerable well and seemed happy enough, but assuming the bird less capable of finding food, everyone gave him extra attention. The bread soon disappeared - other ducks that had gathered round, wandering off again. Sharon rose, sauntering back to the house. The following morning she departed, keenly alive and looking forward to the coming term as Jan ran her to the station.

Bookings were coming faster, a handful each day. Late one afternoon just before tea, Stephen took the phone calls while his parents removed those tall pipes from the other toilet building roof. Working together it would take only fifteen or so minutes in the gathering dusk. By chance one of those who rang during these few minutes, again asked for electric. Stephen, tired perhaps of sitting at the desk, went outside, jumping a small hedge and calling the loss up to his father. It was only one out of some twenty bookings that had come in the last few days, but depressing all the same. Shortly after tea, Stephen cycled off to find friends, leaving his parents alone again.

That night as they lay side by side, sleep would not

come; there had been such nights before, some without reason, others from the elements, heavy rain or the wind, but most often over worries for the future. That night was a good example as Gordon lay thinking about the missed booking - it was not the first this year, there had been the call Sharon took, and another a week before. Aware he could not sleep, Jan too lay awake; she guessed the cause, had seen his face change on hearing the news. One moment he was smiling climbing from the roof, pleased with the better appearance that removing the pipes had made, then as Stephen spoke of the phone call, that smile had gone, replaced by a thoughtful frown. He had been subdued all evening but she passed no comment, nor did she now, but lay close giving what comfort such contact could bring.

Many things had happened over the years that left them restless at night - they had discussed it long ago, agreeing just to lie back, relax and make the best of it, avoiding sleeping pills and hoping events would never turn so serious as to make them essential. If the body got tired enough then sleep must eventually come they had reasoned, though it was not always that easy. Often if something exciting or important was due the next day and a good night's sleep considered vital, that would be the very time they lay awake. The cussedness of nature again! Another thing occasionally causing sleeplessness was waking at some unexpected noise.

Against the wall under the bedroom window rested an old settee that converted to an extra double bed. Once used in the lounge it had been constantly in the way and was moved upstairs for want of a better place to put it. In the closed season no vehicles were expected, so if an engine sounded late at night Gordon would crawl from bed, walk sleepily over to the window, kneel on the settee and peep between the curtains. Very convenient, but for some time Jan had wanted the old settee sold.

"It's five years since anyone slept on it - why should you want to keep it?"

"We might need an extra bed sometime, or extra seats. It could be useful."

"When? If we're desperate there's that spare mattress in the toilet building loft - something else you won't throw away. No one will ever use this! Who has a settee in a bedroom anyway? It looks poor... makes the room smaller. No one could ever sleep on it up here, so why..." seeing him about to protest she broke off, pointing a finger, "Go on then - Who?"

"I might want a French maid."

Eventually, of course, the settee was sold, almost given away but time had passed, Jan working quietly for many weeks to achieved her aim. It did make the bedroom bigger. Unfortunately shortly after they retired, a strange car chose that night of all the nights to turn round in front of the house. No doubt it had lost its way, but either from suspicion or curiosity Gordon swung out of bed, feeling his way in the darkness over to the window, knelt on the settee which was no longer there - and crashed heavily to the floor. Thump!

Roused by the reverberating sound, Jan pulled the light switch, jumping from the bed and rushing over. "Are you all right?"

"Oh it's nothing." He flexed a knee, adopting his best martyred expression.

She realised then that all was well; he liked to suffer in silence - provided everyone knew what he was doing! She knelt beside him anyway. Neither wore bottoms with their pyjamas and as she crouched near he put an arm around her waist, sliding it under the soft material; just for support, of course.

Putting a hand down to the injured knee, Jan massaged gently, whispering, "Come back to bed and I'll rub it better for you."

Married life can be very satisfactory. Lying contentedly in the bed later, it seemed even less important that neither could sleep. After a while Gordon rose and dressed.

As he moved to leave the bedroom, a soft voice called, "Where are you going?"

"Out for a walk."

"At one o'clock in the morning!"

"Yes. Why not?"

"It's cold out there - not even February until next week."

"Won't be long." Leaving the house he climbed a path up the valley side and on into a wood above the waste heaps, moving quietly, the torch in one hand not yet switched on. Although more gloomy under the trees it was still possible to see, leafless branches overhead showing darker against the night sky. Locating one large trunk he cupped a hand round the torch, secretive, as if to avoid detection.

It took a moment or two, the concealed beam searching where roots from the trunk bottom spread outwards across the ground. There had been some here last year... Ah, the light fell on a group of early snowdrops; flicking the torch right and left showed more nearby. Careful to take only a few from each clump, perhaps a dozen in all, he hurried back; Jan was right it was cold, either that or they were getting spoiled by the warmer West Cornwall climate. Entering the house again, he slipped a thin elastic band not too tightly round the stems and found a small glass, adding some water but not putting the flowers in, holding them separately and creeping upstairs. Spying carefully round the doorframe, their eyes met - she lay on one side watching and waiting - hearing or sensing the approach. With both hands behind his back, he walked over to the bedside table, placed the glass just out of sight, then sat on the edge of the bed.

Jan, hair tousled on the pillow around her, lay waiting; looking up unsure what to expect but aware something was being concealed. For a moment longer they gazed at each other, then a hidden hand moved forward into view, offering the snowdrop posy.

For a while she looked at it, reaching out to touch his fingers, then rising on one elbow, kissed him gently. "Not many men would be crazy enough to bring their wives flowers at this time of night... and certainly not afterwards."

Chapter 9

Frank

By opening day, everything was in good order, the water already turned on, all services tested and the shower temperatures adjusted as they invariably needed to be after lying unused over winter. The River authority had finished their annual clearing of the stream, Keith, Danny and the rest of the boys making a great job. Everything was ready; the valley however lay deserted, with no great influx expected for much of the month. It was quiet with only Stephen living at home; mostly he came back late, knowing the prospects for finding friends on site varied between unlikely to impossible in early spring. There would be a need of those recently developed evening indoor hobbies for a while yet. Outside work could still be found, always something to improve - a few turfs to lift, level the ground beneath and put back again, but nothing pressing; life so much more relaxed than in earlier years. One thing Jan did want, was a change to the front of the house.

"There's plenty of time now - think of something. You've said often enough how brilliant men are, so go ahead, prove it!"

This was not the first time the unattractively square appearance of the house front had come up. There seemed no way other than some system of planting and maybe a patio - low stone walls perhaps, curved to combat that present squareness. Gordon sighed, "Okay, I'd better do some sketches."

The drawing-board, dredged from a pile of unused articles stacked in the basement, was erected in a corner of the sitting room. The first attempt showed a semi-circle of Cornish wall stretching the full width of the house, with an off-centre gap for a cascade of steps leading to the office door. Sticking too far out into the yard, it failed to impress and was discarded. Not only that but the thickness necessary for double stone walls with sufficient soil between for planting gave a heavy, rather clumsy effect. An hour spent outside experimenting with paving slabs produced a miniaturised version - more in proportion, the slabs cut into narrow strips about the width of a hand. This was only a test piece - more would be needed, lots more; two different colours might be good. Okay, but the line was still not right, the plain semi-circle sticking out like some usherette's ice cream tray. Ah well, back to the drawing-board.

Jan watched as the large paper sheet was unclipped, expecting it to be cast aside and a new length cut from the nearby roll. Instead he merely turned it over, slipping the clips back on.

She grinned to herself, "Silly of me to think he would waste the back." The first attempt had not been totally to her liking but she said nothing, finding reasons to pass close by as the design grew. Two separate semi-circles were now drawn; the larger outside the lounge windows, a small one by the office door. They overlapped, the arcs crossing - how would he join them? The angle at that joint looked clumsy but she knew it wasn't finished yet. A reverse arc solved the problem, forming a transition curve at both ends to give a smoothly changing line, swinging inward, then outward, then inward again. He called her over.

"There'll be conifers along the top, like the other walls. What do you think?"

They stood together, his arm reaching to rest easily round her waist. She leaned against him, gazing at the drawing, turning to the big window and trying to imagine how it would look outside. His voice cut across her thoughts.

"I've still the steps to do - something broad and inviting; make it look as if we want visitors coming to the door. That's why I preferred the walls slimmer, not like a fortress. Let's choose really dwarf conifers... decorative but not forbidding, not a barrier to hide behind - more an encouragement, like the light that shines through our orange curtains at night, right?"

"Right." She squeezed his hand, offering up her lips. He started as if to kiss them but hesitated, looking guardedly round in case anybody was watching, then satisfied, bent towards her. Annoyed by the reservation, she dodged quickly back, evading him and heading for the door.

"Come on, show me exactly."

Outside the distances were paced out, the line of the arc roughly scratched on the ground. It seemed about right. So much for the outer walls, what about the steps themselves? The existing square ones looked really poor, not only those for the office and shop but also at the front door. The shop required only one step; he drew part of a broad circle. Good! The office needed more, four at least; another experimental circle was quickly followed by three more... Hm? Tilting the drawing-board, he stepped back... Fine! It looked okay. The flight of circular steps led both to the office door and down to a circular patio. There remained the steps and a path to the front door but now the choice was restricted; to blend in they too must be circular.

Just before tea, Gordon called, "Okay, it's all finished. What d'you think?"

Stephen, already home, stepped casually over to look at the drawing. "S'alright."

With that enthusiastic welcome, how could it fail?

Following on behind, Jan smiled. "I like it anyway. Go ahead, our visitors will approve when it's finished."

Materials were ordered and small concrete foundations quickly laid - so far so good, but the slabs arrived with a thin layer of cardboard stuck like glue to one side - designed no doubt to stop wet concrete sticking to the mould when they were made. Building a wall on cardboard is definitely to be avoided - the cement would never stick! Wire brushes, a hosepipe and many a tiresome hour followed!

Stephen, raked in to help on some evenings, declared

the wall a stupid idea, and why wasn't it started when Sharon and Chris were still at home? Finding a dozen excuses, he cleverly did very little towards the project.

Once clean, each paving slab was cut with a hammer and wide bladed masonry chisel into twenty-four small pieces. One word described this task to perfection - tedious! Moreover, this was not something to be done at leisure; half-finished walls and untidy piles of paving slabs spoiled the entrance. Gradually the shapes emerged; walls curving every which way and all done with the little grey and yellow home-made blocks. Tapered steps and the patio followed; each step cut to fit the circular shape.

Stephen looked at progress each evening, commenting on how little had been done, then ate his meal and smartly disappeared to seek friends elsewhere. Five days saw the task complete. A day later conifers and heathers sprouted from the top, the effect beating expectations. That evening, just because a few trees had been planted, Stephen was more impressed.

"Shame about the marks," Jan pointed to patches where a brief spell of unexpected rain had washed unset cement down the face.

That problem too was solved - somewhat dangerously perhaps, using hydrochloric acid applied wearing rubber gloves and goggles. Strong stuff! After the first sniff one soon learned not to stand downwind when applying it. The effect was startling. Washed off with a hose, it not only removed cement but left the surface bright, little granules of quartz sparkling in the sun - hopefully a great first impression for arriving visitors.

Later in the week a medium sized, somewhat travel stained motorcaravan rolled down the track, coming to a halt near the house, the man speaking with a southern hemisphere accent. That was no surprise; such long distance travellers unusually stayed in Britain for several months and having studied the climate, naturally chose Cornwall for early spring. In spite of having had a New Zealand friend at university and meeting many Australians since, mistakes about the accent were still occasional made.

"What part of Australia are you from?"

The husband looked up sharply. "Don't be insulting! We're from New Zealand."

Not sure if he was joking, Gordon apologised, promising more care in future.

With every appearance of real offence, the man suggested, "It's safer to assume all people from our part of the world are New Zealanders, then you won't offend anyone. Australians are bound to be flattered!"

"Really?" Gordon murmured, head nodding in apparent agreement, making a mental note to try it out on the next Australian - should do wonders for international relations. An opportunity arose later that same week. It proved quite effective!

When told the full story, the Aussie laughed. "Our offshore islanders can get a bit cheeky sometimes, sport. Pity we missed him. I could have offered some tips on how to play rugby!"

Early May saw the arrival of a new ride-on mower, a tool taking heavy wear mowing perhaps twelve acres of grass - the purchase long overdue. More ducklings were hatching too. Borrowing three from one mother duck, Gordon took them to the village to show Jim and Audrey, stopping on the way back to visit Mini, the old lady at the ancient miners cottage halfway along the entrance road. As they chatted, he asked about children from the site playing in the recreation field next door. "Don't cause you any problem, do they."

"No. I like to hear their voices, it's company. We used to have someone living there years ago, a young couple, they lived in a bus." Min moved her hand to stroke a duckling that pecked at her finger.

"In a bus?"

"Yes, a double-decker! Kept chickens, hundreds of them, sold the eggs to cafes and hotels - the Barretts, Tony and Joan. You know how tall my roof is; Joan climbed up once to fix some slates that blew off in a gale - put a cement wash over it too, sliding the ladders about and laughing out loud. My sister Emma, rest her soul, was sure she'd fall off. Joan helped me collect holly at Christmas time too; I made a little money sending it to market; things were tight in those days. Nice couple, I miss them. They moved to the village eventually, then off to New Zealand."

Hearing this, Gordon mentioned the recent New Zealand visitor then taking his departure, hurried home to restore the three ducklings, watching as mother duck fussed over them.

As the month passed, visitor numbers were increasing but the site remained quiet. That was what most customers wanted, quietness and country things - the valley offered both. A pair of Mergansers appeared about mid-morning; maybe they floated down on the current or just flew in, landing on the water, for no one saw them arrive, only the other ducks' behaviour betraying their presence. Both muscovys and mallard followed these strange arrivals warily at a distance as the stupid creatures tended to do with anything suspicious, including foxes; sometimes even following dogs along the bank. Several caravanners stood on the bridge to watch, one with a camera, others throwing bread but the big birds paid no attention. After a while they flew over the weir landing in the water downstream, letting the flow carrying them off.

That same evening the two site owners strolled along the river, not with any real purpose, just for the pleasure of it but with half an eye cocked for the mergansers. Growing on the bank were a series of willow trees put in some years ago to lessen damage caused by the sewer, each young tree supported by a bare pine post. Something on one post caught the attention; a knot in the wood perhaps, but of unusual shape. Investigation revealed a large moth, its fore wings covering delicate pink shades that partially circled the body, its weight heavy for an insect. Being a night flier, lifting it onto the hand occasioned no difficulty, then showing it to visitors and particularly the few children now on site before fading light triggered the creature to action. Starting with a slight shiver of vibration, it 'warmed up its engines' in the way big moths do, before flying off to be lost in the trees. Consulting South's *Moths of the British Isles*, it certainly appeared to be the very rare Convolvulus Hawk rather than the similar but more common Privet Hawk. Pity there had been no chance of official authentication, but the caravanners were pleased.

Something else fascinated visitors this year, the new computer bills, primitive enough printed on plain paper without a proper heading, but few had seen them before. The dates and cost displayed were accepted without question; coming from a computer it must be right! The shop was different, no such confidence - items added by hand on small slips of paper were invariably checked through by customers. Only machines it seems, were to be trusted!

As visitor numbers continued to rise, children's bicycle problems increased. With all roads now smoothly tarmaced, some youngsters reached dangerous speeds. At one time most complaints came from balls hitting caravans or tents, but that had been solved by directing rougher games to the recreation field along the entrance road. The same could not easily be done for bicycles; mothers with babies and toddlers were grumbling about safety and it was not clear exactly what to do. Those lads challenged generally claimed to be going to the toilet buildings. Girls were somewhat less of a problem, tending to ride slower and more safely.

Apart from this however, people were happy, fresh faces arriving and old friends returning, many with favourite places, like Olwen and Arnold on Area 12, the second terrace. People liked the roads, the quietness of the valley, the ducks, the ample sized pitches - even the ice pack system still run by Audrey and Jim from the bungalow in the village met with approval, a chance to stop and natter. Things were going well. One couple, the man also named Gordon and his wife Marjorie, had returned again as in many seasons before. This year they had their daughter June and her husband staying, and two grandchildren, Ben nearly three, and Sam only five weeks old. Was that the youngest ever customer? Someone almost gave birth in the valley once but was whisked away in the nick of time.

By July the tempo of life had picked up. The University year over, Sharon headed home again to work part time on site. Collected from the station, driven back to Relubbus and along beside the river towards the house, she pointed ahead.

"I like the patio and those circular steps."

The meal that Jan prepared was interrupted more than once by rings on the doorbell, but these demands lessened as the evening rolled on.

"Fancy a game of battleships?" Gordon asked.

"Battleships?" Sharon looked up, then towards Mum.

"He's been playing with the Spectrum again, writing a games program. It's a nuisance, you have to empty the machine first, and load it back again before anyone else can book-in. Should be all right this time of day though.

Sharon walked across to the desk. On the TV screen used with the small computer, were two grids of small squares, numbered 1 to 18 down the side, and A to P across the top.

"I've entered our names. Draw up a chair, then type in a letter and a number to target the square you want." Gordon moved his own chair to one side so both could reach.

Sharon pressed the keys and a square changed colour but no sound came - a miss. As the game proceeded, many squares, changed to light blue, a few changing to yellow with a beep, indicating a hit. Other sounds occurred unexpectedly at intervals, first a long rising sound when a whole row of squares changed colour; that was a torpedo run. A falling sound on the other hand, coloured a group of nine closely packed squares; a depth charge. Three sharp tones indicated a sonar plot, exposing any targets in its path. In the end Dad lost, and across the screen flashed the words, "Sharon is the greatest!!!" The computer sounded a fanfare that ran on for thirty seconds. For the rest of the evening she was insufferable, or so Dad claimed.

The following day, Sharon went off to meet friends and no more games were played but whenever the chance arose, Gordon worked on the program. Jan asked once what he was doing but received a dismissive reply, "Just making a few improvements."

On Tuesday, usually the slackest day, they played again and Sharon lost... and lost... and lost. Each time when the fanfare played, she stamped off.

"I'll get you next time!"

She played Stephen too, and each won several times, but playing Dad, she lost again. It was Wednesday evening, when losing another game, she stayed in her chair with a "Huh!" as the fanfare played, and this is when she saw it.

"Hey!" The screamed word had Mum and Stephen on their toes and dashing to the office to find Sharon pointing, but before they could see, the message had disappeared.

"What was it?" Jan asked.

Sharon, her arm still extended to point, was fuming. "A message came up on the screen, right at the bottom! It said *Gordon is cheating!* I bet he's done that all the while."

An exclamation was asked for - demanded with threats.

"No I didn't know where the ships were, honest - I just made a new sequence the night Sharon was out. Whatever I enter, the computer ignores it - just hunts around for a ship and sinks it for me. I made that little sign about cheating too, it's been there for at least the last twelve games but Sharon never spotted it before. Simple! I couldn't really lose. How about coffee?"

"Make your own!"

Stephen, still at school for two more weeks, also intended giving a hand this year - that would certainly be helpful, reason enough to increase his allowance. In the event, that help was to be needed sooner than expected.

On Friday morning, Friday the 13th July, just eight days before the busiest Saturday of the year, the phone rang.

"Gordon, what's the matter?" Jan saw him put the receiver slowly down.

"It's Frank, my Dad... I never even knew he was ill... he's dead."

"Dead?"

"Heart attack. Died in hospital. They'll let us know when

the funeral is."

Jan flicked a glance out at the front field, now almost full with caravans, then turned towards the corridor. "I'll make us a coffee, we'll drink it in the kitchen. Sharon can manage in the shop for a while, she'll shout if it gets busy."

Coffee never materialised. Three caravans following each other down the road, wanted to be together in a quiet corner because one had a parrot.

"Do you mind not being near the toilets?"

No, they didn't mind at all - would actually prefer it. The more remote the better, away from nosy strangers because the bird was apt to bite probing fingers.

"Right then, I've the ideal pitch. Next week it might have been difficult; you arrived just right. How many nights?"

"We haven't decided that yet. One night to see what it's... to get our bearings - would that be okay?"

The three were booked in and led away. Nice enough chaps if a shade suspicious - their wives had stayed in the cars. Arriving at the pitch, Area 24, a small grassy patch taking only three caravans, they were pleased, the wives too approving. As they parked, the bird appeared in a big cage - no wonder they were concerned; the beak on it could take off a wrist, let alone a finger. Some parrot! Questions were asked, the river walk, beaches, eating places - pleasant enough chat, taking the mind off those funeral arrangements.

Back at the office more customers waited. As they paid and went off to their cars, ready to be led to a pitch, Jan laid a restraining hand on Gordon's arm, preventing him following, looking at him pensively.

"There are plans to make. Should we tell them to wait?"

"Frank would disapprove. He'd say, *'Serve the customers first'*. He would, honest - if he's looking down now, that's exactly what he'll be thinking. I'll go and get them settled."

An hour before lunch more coffee was made, Sharon joining them, the shop now quiet.

"We can't both go, and yet we ought to." Jan shrugged.

"I'll go on my own, after all he is... was, my father - you get Stephen and Jim to help here. Ivy will understand, they've been in business. Frank would agree; Saturday was his busy day too, driving from dawn to dusk, the van loaded with meat to serve his customers. He'd have carried on if the world caught fire."

And so it was done, Jan and Stephen staying to run the site, Gordon and Sharon making the journey, Chris meeting them at Ivy's house. When the hour came, a huge black saloon with multiple rear seats transported the family, following the hearse as it slowed in respect when passing the local post office where Frank had once lived and worked; a sad moment in a sombre day.

Later, people were sprinkled around in little groups with all the flowers laid out nearby. Chris stood with Kenny, another relation, having their photo taken. Sharon looked in surprise at the number and variety of wreaths. Not realising her grandfather had so many friends, she leaned closer to whisper, "Were did they all come from?"

Gordon thought for a moment before whispering a reply. Though no one else was near enough to overhear, the hushed voices seemed appropriate. "Frank was always kind of serious, never laughed very much, at least not at home. He was more jovial with the customers - business I suppose, but he seemed to enjoy a joke well enough with them. Anyway, he helped a lot of people one way and another throughout his life."

"Everyone looks so sad."

"Hm. This is your first funeral, I haven't been to many either. Some people believe in having a wake, lots of drink to send the person off more cheerfully. When I eventually go I want to look down and see you all happy, so find some way to bring a laugh to your mother's face okay."

Sharon looked up doubtfully. Seeing a small smile, she nodded without managing to smile back, changing the subject instead. "I wonder how busy Mum and Stephen are?"

By evening, having returned to the house with Ivy and spent many hours talking, it was time to go. Gordon and Sharon headed west again, towards home, chatting together and remembering things Frank had done, like the horse and cart that bolted with all the meat aboard way back in the war in petrol rationing days. Sharon's memories of her grand-father were more recent, she spoke of them as the car cruised on.

Passing through the outskirts of Slough, Gordon slowed, coasting into a small roadside parking bay and drawing up near a flower seller's barrow. Turning, he murmured uncomfortably, "Better take something back for Mum, hadn't we?"

Seeing the nod he stepped out quickly, hurrying to approach the man, "Some er, red roses?" Buying flowers was not his thing at all. He noticed Sharon approaching and wished she'd stayed in the car.

"Sold out," the man moved to one side, reaching to lift a small bunch of pinkish buds, his attention turning to Sharon, regarding her with a slight leer, holding out the flowers for her inspection.

Gordon cast an eye over one shoulder, hoping no one would approach, his unease measured by the fact that he forgot to ask 'how much' before turning to Sharon, "Will they be all right?"

The flower seller's leer broadened.

"Yes." Sharon spoke through her teeth, pivoting on one heel and marching back to the car.

Relieved to have a second opinion, he pulled out a pound note, wondering how much change would be given.

"Three." The flower man's grin was still there, sure of his ground, drawing the little posy back a few inches.

"Three?" Gordon stopped, caught in the act of passing the note. Three was ridiculous, but he had no wish to go through all this again; didn't want to stop at another stall. A natural caution with money pushed this embarrassment aside - he shook his head, peeling off another note. "Two is top whack. Take it or leave it."

The grin subsided. Mr Flower Seller, seeing his chance of a good profit disappearing, reached to whip the offered notes before they disappeared, passing the roses forward, winking and leering again towards the car.

The meaning of this behaviour dawning at last, Gordon

took the bunch, sweeping the man with a stern warning look. Turning to stride away he heard the flower seller's laughing words, "Ooh, you can be so masterful ducky."

Jumping quickly into the car, the wheels spun and it sped away like the devil was following. Driving as if at Le Mans, shaving corners at some stupid speed, gradually those tensions faded, the car slowing to a normal pace. Sharon was sitting, hands clasped tightly together, staring directly ahead. He glanced towards her. "Expensive, but we got them."

"Huh!" she looked away, then unable to contain her anger, turned back. "You could just see what he was thinking!"

"Eh? Oh yes, you noticed too? Flattering I suppose if..."

"Flattering!" Sharon's savage exclamation exploded in the confined space. "He thought I was letting you..." lost for words, she clenched her hands more tightly, "Beastly little twit!"

"Thought I was pulling a dolly-bird did he? I'm rather proud..." Seeing his daughter's expression, Gordon stopped, then hurriedly changed the subject. "We won't be home 'til the small hours; I'd better buy you a meal later - er, well a snack - if anywhere is still open."

The unexpected offer brought a ghost of a smile to Sharon's lips. She knew he had spoken in haste; the rash offer, the modification, the attempted retraction. Happier now, she chided gently, "You shouldn't joke after a funeral."

"Frank would be pleased - maybe he wouldn't exactly laugh but he'd grin a little, and something else too. That flower chap asked *three pounds* for these." Gordon reached to touch the roses. "I only paid two pounds, Frank would have approved - well, half approved; he'd probably have got them cheaper."

The car droned on largely in silence. What do a father and teenage daughter talk about on a long journey; most topics already well covered on the trip up. Mother and daughter would have found more in common. The past had already been chatted over but fresh little memories broke the silence at intervals. About eleven, they turned into a wayside restaurant, unpretentious enough in appearance but on opening the door, fully laid tables with cloths, glasses and smartly dressed waiters, gave a different impression. Gordon pulled up short, grasping for Sharon's arm to pull her back but she evaded him, moving quickly forward to sit at one of the central tables, knowing her father could hardly back out now without making a scene.

Sitting down, he looked across the immaculate array of cutlery to see amusement in those eyes, amusement and a certain elegance - Sharon, head erect, shoulders back, trying to look as if such dining was a regular habit. Placing an elbow delicately on the table, she leaned forward, chin resting on the upturned hand, spreading the fingers free, fanning them out as models are apt to do, whispering cheekily, "Dad, do try to remember it's the outermost fork first." The pose was quickly abandoned as a waiter approached, white towel draped over one arm. Opening two large menus with a flourish, the man set one before each, stepped back a pace, executed a slight bow and strode off.

Choices were made and a glance towards the waiter drew him smartly back.

"Sir?" The notebook was poised.

"I'll just, er, have an omelette - not very hungry," Gordon having seen the prices, excused himself before hurrying on, "and for Miss... Miss...?" leaning forward he whispered loudly, "What *is* your name?"

"*Sharon*," the word hissed back.

"Ah," He turned again to the waiter, "Yes, the plaice for Miss Sharon."

The man smiled politely, no flicker on the deadpan features betraying any sign of disapproval. Perhaps Sugar Daddies gave bigger tips - an alarming thought, silently corrected. "No chance!"

Seeing the waiter walk away Sharon turned, raising a warning finger, a few choice phrases on the tip of her tongue but the intended words never came, the finger withdrawn, rising to rub a cheek as if that had always been the intention. A woman at the nearby table was staring across, obviously listening. Frustrated in her intention she looked towards the ceiling, annoyed at the shadowy smile on her father's face.

The fish was good, she enjoyed it but wished for some way to... to... she felt at a disadvantage? Those thoughts still churned inside as the plates were cleared, and in ordering dessert she chose the most expensive item and saw her father flinch. Good! She felt better already.

Sitting after the meal, things didn't seem so bad. As the waiter approach she held out a hand for the bill, looked at the total and smiled, passing it back with satisfaction. "My father will pay."

Reaching home an hour after midnight, Sharon rang the bell and waited. Jan unbolted the door in a dressing gown, asked a few brief questions, said the day had been hectic, then still half asleep disappeared back to bed. Those few items taken in the car could be unloaded tomorrow, only the roses rescued, put in water and left as a morning surprise.

Sharon slept-in the following day, rising late and preparing her own breakfast, her parents already busy with the office and shop. Having eaten, she wandered through into the lounge to find the roses in a cut-glass vase on a chest in the front window where passing caravanners could see them. It was mid-morning however before Jan came through from the shop.

"Showing them off," Sharon pointed at the display.

"Why not? I like people to know my husband buys me flowers; don't get the chance very often."

As they sat talking Sharon recounted their journey, the flowers on Frank's grave and all the sad faces of people attending. Speaking of the trip home and the roadside flower seller, her tone changed, still angry, but they laughed together about the restaurant incident.

"Serves him right!" Jan banged a fist on the arm of her chair when Sharon told of her expensive sweet and the final bill Dad had to pay.

A ring on the doorbell interrupted the chat, a woman and her husband wanted to book more days. Jan hoped the roses would be noticed but these visitors were full of their new caravan, anxious to tell of its luxuries and what a difference having a gas fridge made. After a while, seeing another caravan draw up, the couple moved to leave, still talking as they went - the man leading, the lady stopping on the doorstep, signalling towards the newly arrived caravan. "Not as good as ours." Pleased with herself she raised a hand in farewell then pitched suddenly to one side, stumbling on the top step and staggering forwards, fortunately to be caught by her husband.

Jan rushed to the door, "Are you all right?"

Brushing some imaginary speck of dust from a lapel, the woman drew herself up, "Certainly. And I've not been drinking. It's those steps, they're all the same colour, you can't see where one ends and the other starts." The couple waved again and departed smiling.

Speaking to Gordon after he sited the caravan, Jan explained the mishap. "The steps are clear enough if you pay attention, but she could have fallen."

An hour later, a curving line of white, an inch or so wide, coated the outer edge of each circular step, a 'Wet Paint' sign temporarily diverting people to the shop.

At mid-afternoon Sharon opened the office door, bent to feel the paint, and finding it dry strode back through the office meaning to ask if the notice could now be removed. What she saw when poking her head into the shop however, stopped her and she hurried to the kitchen

"Mum, what's Dad doing?"

"Making a list for cash and carry I think."

"No he's not. That hundredweight sack of poultry-corn from the basement... it's in the shop now. He's weighing it out into small plastic bags."

A minute later they were back in the shop doorway. Gordon looked up, smiled at them and turned, filling another bag, dropping it on the scales and reaching in to remove a handful, letting a little trickle back in to get the exact weight before tossing the surplus away in the main sack.

"What's all this in aid of?" Jan pointed to the stack of plastic bags on a shelf by the counter.

"For feeding the ducks. Visitors like to. Excuse me." He

reached out an arm, nudging Sharon to one side and selected a 10p ticket from a plastic holder fixed to the door, then clipped it to the shelf.

"You're charging them ten pence to feed *our* ducks? How much in each bag?"

"Eight ounces. Reasonable price don't you think. We pay nearly four pound for the hundredweight. I've finished now, I'm off to cash and carry for..."

"Dad!" Sharon broke in, the word coming forcefully. "That makes over 200 bags - at 10p each it's more than twenty pounds!"

"Is it really? Well I must be off; watch the shop, will you?" The bell rang twice as he opened the door and slipped through.

Looking at the packets, Sharon reached for a pen and slip of paper from a nearby shelf; a little stock of such slips rested there for adding up customers bills - having no electric meant all adding was done by hand. Jotting down some figures, Sharon turned to her mother.

"He'll make twenty-two pounds and forty pence, that's over eighteen pounds profit on something costing less than four pounds. Do I get a bonus?"

"If any really young children come in, I'll give them one free."

"Better not let Dad catch you!" They grinned at each other.

"You think I might get told off - just let him try! Anyway, he'd probably approve."

"Oh yes?" Sharon's eyes opened wide. "Probably pretend this five-hundred percent profit is just to stop the ducks being overfed."

"Say it's for the children's benefit more likely; stop them spending money on sweets and getting bad teeth."

The two were still laughing when a teenage boy arrived, looking a little uncertain in the doorway, then stepping inside carrying three ice packs.

"Can I get these frozen?"

"Not here. Take them..." Jan's explanation was cut short.

"I'll do it Mum. I promised to call on Jim and Audrey." Sharon turned to the young man. "Come with me, I'll show you."

Jan watched as they left, seeing them stop on the bridge, then stroll off along the track talking together, and wondered, "Could I still pick up a boy with such ease."

As the school holidays drew towards a close, the figures revealed a better year so far, one with few problems and as usual a good proportion of retired couples. That was hardly surprising; they were never likely to draw a mass of children like sites on the beach. Analysing the peak period it was nevertheless pleasing to see the number of young families who enjoyed River Valley's quieter appeal, many finding more fun in the ducks and the open countryside than in spending time at arcades and games rooms.

With the coming of Stephen's seventeenth birthday in September, he mentioned casually at tea that all his friends called him Steve. He made no demand that the family do so but from that day on it became standard practice, both Dad and Mum quickly correcting themselves on the odd occasion when they forgot. As weeks passed, his time at the 6th Form College 'A level' courses, was characterised by a marked lack of enthusiasm. Several of his friends had already given up study and now held jobs - not necessarily ones with great prospects but at seventeen, young men tend to live more for the moment - talk and encouragement about the future by their parents causing only resentment and rebellion. Money was the big attraction - working friends appearing to splash out on things not affordable by those still intent on study. Partly to counterbalance this, Steve began to work part time at home; it gave a small measure of spare cash, a raise in standing with his mates. With the site's improving finances, it would have been possible to increase his weekly allowance without the need to work, but that might encourage too casual a regard for money - or perhaps it was just not in his father's nature. Whatever the reason, things were drifting along, the future uncertain. Watching, Jan sensed her youngest was much more interested in mechanics and would never complete his 'A levels'. Already taking driving lessons, as Autumn progressed he put in more working hours, saving the extra money towards buying an old car.

The Council's 'Best Caravan Park' competition had not been held again, leaving River Valley as holders of the title - this fact clearly displayed on the signs at the site entrance. Seeking perhaps to justify the claim, new gas heaters were installed in the toilet buildings, heaters with a modulating flame to give even better temperature stability in the showers. This being mechanical in nature, Steve enjoyed it far better than cutting up more paving slabs to extend the patio wall and make circular steps at the front of the house - steps to improve the appearance rather than for actual use, the front door hardly ever being opened. With very few caravans left, and all visitors out during the day, the time of year for such jobs had arrived. Later, father and son worked together on a fence beside the river. Dogs running free as their owners walked along the riverbank had caused problems over the years. Many caravans near the river had dogs of their own but kept them on a lead. Sometimes these dogs were bitches, and were in heat. Under those conditions any passing male dog if it be not under control, could rush into someone's awning intent on satisfying its natural instincts. This had proved annoying to caravanners and embarrassing to whoever owned the roaming dog; hard words occasionally passing. The offending animal however, invariably left with a satisfied smile.

Another problem intermittently arose. After being pitched in the proper position, both caravans and tents were, on occasion, moved by their owners nearer to the river for a better view, thereby restricting or blocking the footpath. A fence had seemed the sensible answer setting everyone at ease, but in erecting it the family had no inkling of the trouble that would eventually follow.

***

"I don't care how expensive it is; we can afford it!" Jan pointed to the floor. "Look - over there by the door, the place where everyone walks in; it's disgusting. We need a new carpet, one all the same colour right through the office and lounge."

Gordon frowned. The two rooms joined by a large opening had carpets of different colours, pieces carried from the old house more than ten years ago, but only one part was worn, just a patch by the door. Did customers really notice carpets? "They'll last another year, won't they?"

"Oh sure, and when someone trips over and sues you; what then?" Jan reached out, giving a little shove of frustration, forcing him backward and for a moment they stood facing each other before she turned, stalking off to the kitchen. There were still a few caravans around, the October weather mild; half-term at the end of the month would see more arrive.

"Inflation is high again; I heard it on the radio," Jan mentioned quietly later in the day. "I suppose that means carpets will be dearer next year?"

Gordon picked up the coffee with an almost straight face, hiding a smile and pretending not to hear. What she had said was true of course, and visitors' first impressions were important. A carpet must be bought, that much was now clear but he would show reluctance a little longer before letting her win.

And so it was that leaving Jim in charge, the couple sneaked off for a day's shopping. Not just any shopping, a major spree! With no big projects due this winter to absorb cash, the season's trade had been rewarding, certainly enough to justify a few of life's good things, luxuries forgone over the past years. Even so, this planned spending had the business and customers very much in mind. Jan wanted not only a carpet but to refurbish the office and adjoining lounge; new chairs all round and hinted again that the billiard table should go. Probably what was needed could be located in Penzance or at any rate in Truro, but an urge to get away drove them farther. First stop then, Exeter. A leisurely search through furnishing stores offered carpets galore, Waring and Gillow sporting a particularly fine display, including a heavily patterned Axminster from Belgium.

"How," they asked the assistant, "can you get a Belgium Axminster?"

The story of a genuine Axminster loom exported to the continent sounded very fishy but the colour and design were perfect. Passing on quickly from this explanation of origin, the salesman pointed to a price ticket. "It's fairly expensive but exceptional value for such quality. Last for years."

"Price is not really a consideration now," Jan waved a hand, turning for confirmation.

"I... well, within reason that is." Gordon looked at the pattern again, stretching out a hand to feel the pile and shake his head doubtfully, turning back, "Discount for cash?"

The salesman hesitated, his lips forming to say the word "Five."

"Ten percent?" Gordon asked, before he could speak. The season had been good but expenses had risen too. They might never be rich; no need to throw it away.

The bargain struck included fitting and delivery, to arrive on Friday. The same store had rather nice Ercol chairs, they gave a cottage effect, lots of wood and not too much material. Seeing his hesitation Jan urged, "That makes them cheaper to re-cover."

Gordon looked at the chairs; they *were* rather nice and he knew she wanted them. Turning to the salesman he raised a hand rubbing thumb against finger in that age old gesture, "Your delivery vehicle bringing the carpet, it could carry the chairs too - save you diesel to Penzance and back. Must be worth quite a bit?"

Another discount and the deal was done. By the weekend, those few caravanners still arriving entered a plushier office, the difference in their reactions noticeable. Later that week it became apparent that not only people appreciated the new carpet. Sometime between 7 and 9pm each evening, a large spider marched from one side of the room, right across the centre and under the sideboard. They watched together the first night but never saw it go back. That return journey must have been made however, because the following day the spider, or one exactly like it, could again be seen making the evening trek. It happened several times, not every night but quite frequently. They could hardly believe a tribe of such specimens were making this pilgrimage - had to be the same one. It became the custom to say "Good Evening Fred," when these crossings occurred.

"Why Fred, why not Fredricka?" Jan wanted to know, "how can you tell?"

"As far as I know, you can't," Gordon shrugged, "unless you see both at once."

"Oh, and how can you tell when they're together?"

"Easy. Frederika is the big one!"

Jan, who had been unwise enough to mention the gain of a couple of pounds with the easier pace of life over recent months, drew back her fist and punched him. "Don't be rude!"

"No, it's true. Female spiders are bigger than the male. If he's not quick after mating, she eats him. Honest."

"Spiders are more sensible than I thought!"

As the house had a very dry atmosphere, a small biscuit tin lid filled with water was placed under the sideboard in case Fred got thirsty. After a couple of weeks he disappeared. They never found what happened. Sad really, perhaps a Frederika got him after all?

A month later when the billiard table was at last sold and with the new chairs rearranged, the office did look more spacious and special.

"I'll feel comfortable now about receiving people." Jan executed a little pirouette of delight after moving the last chair into its new position.

With shorter days, hobbies developed over previous winters came into there own again. Working on a cross stitch pattern of flowers and leaves, Jan paused to glance across the room. Seeing Gordon concentrating on a book, she asked, "No more work on the computer program?"

"No more room, the machine's storage space is all used up. I already pretend some figures are letters; that saves space.

Anyway, you grumble if I change things around."

"Naturally! I get used to pressing one set of keys and suddenly, the sequence alters. What are you reading?"

"Flies." He held out the book, *Flies of the British Isles by Colyer & Hammond.* "What do you know about blue bottles? Tell me the difference between a vomitoria and an erythrocephala?"

Seeing the little smirk on his face and aware he was about to impart some gem of wisdom that nobody in their right mind would ever want to know, she sought a way to stop him. "They're nasty annoying little pests - like husbands?"

"One has red hairs on black jowls, and the other has black hair on red jowls."

She didn't ask which was which.

In mid-January with his driving test due and confident of passing, Steve scoured the Cornishman and the West Briton for a second-hand car. Finding an exceptionally cheap mini-van, he asked if someone would run him to see it. Watching husband and son drive off together in the Polo, Jan wondered if Gordon's quick acceptance of the request had been a keenness to help or just concern over what type of vehicle might stand beside the house in the coming season, and what impression it would make on incoming customers. Caravanners tended to be suspicious on their first visit - easily put off by anything out of place, particularly those staying at other sites who came looking round in their cars. That was why so much attention was paid to the road, and the appearance from the bridge.

An hour later, the Polo returned followed by a mini-van of considerable age, the grey colour obviously hand painted, probably to hide rust, its engine sounding moderately awful. As it drew to a halt, a stranger jumped from the driving seat to be picked up by another car following behind. Walking across the yard Steve entered the house with a broad smile on his face, saying nothing and disappearing immediately down the basement stairs, no doubt to collect tools.

Jan looked at Gordon, her eyes opening as if to say,

"Well?"

Sensing the question, he shrugged. "What could I say? It's pretty horrible but we started our life down here with exactly the same model. Anyway he may not pass - we can hide it somewhere away from the entrance then."

Steve did pass; did it at the first attempt - but in spite of his love of mechanics the old car's engine still proved unreliable. Gordon was talking with his mother on the phone one day when the matter cropped up in discussion. Ivy offered a solution.

"Frank's car, the Maxi - it's still standing in the garden. I thought I might drive it after a little practice but Bill took me out the other day and when we came to a roundabout and traffic, I knew I never could. Stephen can have it if you like - he'd need to collect it."

Steve, still working part time on the site, was beginning intermittently to miss school on the pretext that he had no lectures that day, an ominous sign. Taking more time off, he went by train to Buckinghamshire. A day later he was back, the Maxi now standing beside the house - the mini-van remained but plans were in hand for its sale or disposal - probably to some breaker's yard.

CHAPTER 10

Dropping in

"Why not buy ourselves a caravan, a tourer?" Jan threw a handful of broken bread on the river, watching the ducks race for it as she reached for Gordon's hand, hoping he would agree.

"So we can visit Sharon at weekends and stay nearby?" A grimace showed his disapproval - money that need not be spent. "We could visit by car; come back the same day."

"Yes, but it's not just that." Sensing he was waiting for an explanation, she turned away, ostensibly to cast more bread on the water, targeting the ducks individually, trying to fool the drakes that being bigger, tended to hog the food. Why should males always get the best? They were standing on the bridge, facing towards the house and had been admiring the additional shrubs added that morning, new dwarf walls now extending from the patio, right round the garden, separating it from the footpath beside the river. That was really the last of the winter work; trees and hedges that grew forward every year had already been cut back. This trimming was done not with neat precision like a household garden but deliberately intermittent and irregular, a more wild and natural appearance. The riverbank too had been repaired where rising winter water levels had scoured the soil away; grass for resurfacing found by cutting back turf that grew rampantly forward over tarmac roads edges. Like early Spring of the previous year, no further essential jobs needed attention, leaving time for each other's company. She was pleased about that, it took the edge off the children's absence, though Steve was still at home - sometimes. Since inheriting Frank's car, he used the house more as a hotel, coming back to eat hungrily then disappearing again until late evening. Casting the last piece of bread, Jan turned back, feigning surprise at finding Gordon still watching her. He was waiting, that much was obvious, sceptical of this other supposed advantage, whatever it might be - not at all anxious to spend money on a caravan.

She smiled as they stood facing each other; her remark, *'Yes, but it's not just that,'* had been less casual than it seemed; much thought and preparation going into choosing the right moment, picking a reason difficult to resist, difficult for him that is - at any rate she hoped so.

"Taking the caravan to somewhere near the University and having Sharon join us for a meal would be really nice. I've found a site only a few miles from Exeter..." Jan hesitated, still seeing resistance in his face. She had guessed persuading him would be difficult. "We've nothing essential this spring, there's hardly any visitors about, Jim could manage here and Steve is home at night - we could go on a little holiday ourselves..." she saw his head begin to shake. He never wanted to leave the valley; even visits to the family in Buckinghamshire were short and infrequent. Seeing him about to speak, she hurried on.

"How long is it since we visited other sites - how do you know we have what caravanners really want? Isn't it time we saw what others are offering?" Signs of doubt showed in his face as she rushed on again. "When people leave they often ask where to stop to break their homeward trip; we don't really know - shouldn't we find out?"

Seeing his head nod slightly and sensing success, another idea flashed in her mind. "If we find suitable sites on the main routes and recommend them to caravans going home, shouldn't they recommend us to those coming down!" A surge of elation passed through her as she watched his face; they would have the caravan! Sharon would eat with them some weekends, Steve might even come too.

For a minute they stood unsure, then were together - hugging, kissing; right there in the middle of the bridge. On

184

an impulse they leaned apart at the waist, turning to scan in opposite directions then back to each other with an abandoned laugh. The valley was deserted.

"I don't think the ducks will object; they know it's spring, the proper time for courting," he kissed her again. "You're clever. Don't think I don't know when I've been manipulated, but you missed one thing - could have been the clincher if you hadn't already won."

"What?" She was smiling now, knowing the battle was over.

"Can't you guess? Why are we buying this caravan?"

"To visit Sha... No, to make arrangements with other caravan parks! To benefit the business! Yes?" Seeing him nod encouragingly, she continued. "That makes it..." a lifted finger orchestrated the final words, the hand dropping as they spoke in unison, "...tax deductible!"

"Yes, well partly. I'll put a note in the ledger, ask for 50% do you think?"

A van careering down the road brought the conversation to an end. It pulled sharply to a halt before the office, another consignment of toilet rolls hustled to the basement before thoughts returned to the caravan. Like any sensible couple contemplating such a purchase, a visit to Penzance secured every caravan and motorcaravan magazine currently on sale. Where else would you find such a wealth of data to study in the comfort of your own home, comparing one against the other, finding good points and bad; the essentials and those touches of unnecessary luxury in which to indulge? It was not conclusive, only a starting point, but considering the amount involved those magazines probably saved their cost a hundred times. A towing hitch must be fitted to the car but that could wait, it would only take a day and whoever sold the caravan would want time to clear the cheque before seeing it towed away. A few phone calls located the short-listed models, the prices noted and compared, a destination chosen - and off they went. A firm at Ashburton stocked three of these preferred models, a salesman showed them round and seeing their indecision, left them with a wave.

"I'll be in the office, wander wherever you like, sit inside and try them out, fetch me if you have any questions."

Left on their own, Gordon took two strides towards the second-hand section, but was pulled back. With a shrug he moved to a small modestly appointed model, the price tag £3800. "This one is reasonable, we'll just be taking the occasional trip. It's the only one our Polo could pull."

The logic seemed inescapable but Jan demurred; partly from a woman's love of window shopping and partly from an idea forming in her mind.

"Look at this," She stepped towards a bigger model with the name 'Daystar' on a poster in one window, below which in large black print appeared, 'Only £5000'.

"Only!" Gordon's finger pointed at the offending figure. "We couldn't pull it anyway - well we could, just about but not safely and not legally."

"There's no charge for looking." She disappeared through the doorway, leaving him no option but to follow or wait outside.

Climbing the step to find her sitting back in a big bench seat, he looked around; unquestionably more comfortable and luxurious and it wasn't *that* much more expensive - not if you said it quickly.

Jan ran a hand invitingly over the upholstery beside her. "Good isn't it. Something you wouldn't be ashamed of, standing on the site all season. You did promise to change the car this year anyway."

He nodded slowly, there was something in what she said. Caravanners were... not exactly snobby, but very conscious of status; the small one might be a mistake. Something else was worrying too; he decided not to mention it yet, but needed to check.

"Let's look at all the others first." The tour of inspection took in everything on display, ending up back at the Daystar.

"Have to use Steve's Maxi for towing until August. If we're to buy a new car let's have the latest numberplate too. You go inside and sit comfortably while I do a little deal."

Back at the office, Gordon chatted to the salesman again,

emphasising how they were in the trade and this caravan would stand near reception on a site which held the title '*Best Park in Southwest Cornwall*'. More than that, everyone would know it was the owner's own caravan, and from the little plaque that most sales firms attach, the visitors could all see where it was bought! After a while, coming back to where Jan was still looking round the chosen model, he smiled happily, whispering, "Fifteen percent discount, that's about £750 off! It's only a few hundred dearer than the smaller model. They say collect it next week; it still needs an initial service and polish."

"Next week? I was hoping we'd meet Sharon this coming weekend. Couldn't you...?"

"Not really, not after what I squeezed on the discount... here, he's coming, try to look pleased."

"Pleased? You usually say to look disappointed."

"This one is different - he could still change his mind. I've promised we'll be recommending it, so he needs to know you approve."

The journey home should have been good but for one disturbing factor. The chosen caravan had lights that ran on twelve-volt electric! All the current models on show had this system too, only the older second-hand ones on sale were equipped with gas lamps. The salesman had thrown in free a table lamp that worked directly from a smaller gas cylinder, but he said, "You should never need it. This caravan has a big battery of its own that charges up as you drive along."

That was fine. Going to Exeter and staying near the university for two days the battery would surely not run out... but what of other people? What about visitors that came to Cornwall for two or even three weeks without moving? This new breed of caravans was disturbing. River Valley had no mains electric. For more than a decade the waterwheel had provided all the power, but it could never cope with this unexpected demand - regularly charging every-one's battery! In any case a good percentage of customers were retired people, not likely to be keen on lugging heavy batteries about! They would want it recharged automatically from an electric hook-up on their pitch. How quickly would other caravanners find themselves without gas lights. The position was serious!

A restless week passed; worries about electricity causing arguments at home. Dad asked to borrow Steve's car to collect the caravan and make a quick trip farther up country, checking how other sites were preparing for these new all-electric models. Actually he had not so much asked, as insisted.

"Of course I won't damage it, and no, you can't have the keys to the Polo; our insurance excludes anyone under twenty-one. Get your push-bike out, we'll only be gone a few days. And don't go giving wild parties while we're away. Jim will be here in the daytime but it's down to you in the evenings. Time you earned your keep, Okay?"

It wasn't really okay, a resentful Steve left behind when the journey started. The caravan had been collected, towed home and stocked with all the necessities. Now it drew slowly across the bridge and away up the track, off on a trip to investigate other sites.

As cities go, Exeter was on the small side, and in that context small was beautiful - locating a site for the caravan then finding the university, no problem. Parking, they climbed the stairs and knocked on Sharon's door for an excited reunion. That first stroll around the campus revealed a super setting; like every really civilised place it was graced by mallard ducks. The two girls eventually prized Gordon away, grabbing an arm each and dragging him off. Back at the caravan the three ate, Sharon asking briefly about home, dismissing it quickly to talk of friends, university life, the work, the companionship; obviously wrapped up in her new existence and enjoying it - a happy meal! Later with Sharon full of restless energy, unable to sit and relax, they ambled around the caravan park comparing it with their own; the showers, the flowers and shrubs, commenting on the absence of ducks. Sauntering along looking at this and that, more electric points appeared along one side. Their own caravan was already plugged to a similar hook-up - an experiment rather than any worry over batteries running down.

Spending the afternoon in the city centre, they returned later, Sharon staying for the evening, chatting while Jan cooked another meal; far easier now than in the little tourer all those years ago, for this caravan had an oven and a fridge, both working on Calor gas. The television had been brought along too; most people would be surprised that it used 240-volt current in the caravan and 12-volt at home, exactly the opposite of what would normally be expected.

Journeying on towards Buckinghamshire, three nights were spent on three separate sites, none as picturesque as River Valley but all with at least a few electric hook-ups. The visit to Ivy, Gordon's mother was pleasant as always, a chance to talk again of Frank's funeral and his life, to catch up on local gossip, to chat with her great friend and neighbour Mary and walk in long remembered places. But there was something else too. It was not possible to turn on a light, to open the fridge, to boil a kettle, without thinking of electricity. Much as they enjoyed the short stay, a restlessness lurked, a need to return and face this problem now awaiting them.

It was natural that they stop again at Exeter to visit Sharon on the way home, and logic dictated a different location be chosen, to allow inspection of another set of facilities. Pure chance took them to Kennford International with its polished pine toilets and yet more electric hook-ups. They ran Sharon back late in the evening, returning quietly to the caravan so as not to wake anyone, but not themselves feeling sleepy, sitting for a while reading pamphlets that Paul, the site owner had given them on arrival. Paul wife's name was also Jan - so he must be a good chap!

Among the pamphlets one boasted that Kennford was a Best of British site, apparently a series of high quality parks that had banded together to offer better standards to visitors. A list of members from all over the country showed none near the western tip of Cornwall. Preliminary ideas of joining were quashed and the pamphlet cast aside in disappointment when further reading revealed only parks with electric hook-ups were admitted.

The journey home was difficult - not in a physical sense but uneasy in the mind over what had been seen. Before buying the new caravan they were happy with the quality of their site, convinced few in the country were better. Now that was clearly untrue! Looked at any way they might, it boiled down to one thing - find a proper electric supply or the park would be history; left behind by the march of progress.

"Never mind how much it costs," Jan urged, "we've got to have it. If we don't, in a few years we'll be second class. Even our regulars will stop coming when they change their caravan!"

Darkness was falling as they reached Relubbus, a few lights the only evidence of life in the handful of houses that made up the village. Turning to follow the river, a badger caught in the headlights made off down the site's entrance road at a slow trot, rump rolling from side to side in a wobbling gait. Not panicked by the vehicle's presence the badger, still highlighted in the beam, hurried along keeping to the tarmac as if not prepared to tread on the rougher verges. Slowly the car followed, not close enough to frighten but within easy watching distance, expecting at any moment to see it turn off. The badger wobbled on, continuing for some quarter-mile, half the distance to the bridge before veering away to disappear in some bushes.

Emerging from the house, Steve watched the caravan being uncoupled, said briefly "Hope you left it full," and not waiting for a reply opened the car door, turned the key and stared at the fuel gauge. With a few words explaining the week's happenings, he climbed in and drove off, promising to be late back. That was obvious, it was nearly ten already.

The late evening snack was quiet. Virtually everything possible, everything with even the slightest relevance to the problem in hand had been discussed on that long journey home, really nothing left to say. They touched a lot that evening; a hand reaching out, a wistful hug when passing close, taking strength from each other.

Years before they had risked everything for an ideal, taken a chance, worked at times to the point of exhaustion.

Luck had been kind, but it was not luck alone that brought success and turned a dream to reality. In many ways the life they had made was ideal - independent, happy, free.

"No, not exactly free," Jan thought. "There's that phone someone must answer, and the rush and pressure when mid-season comes, but that's enjoyable too...well it is with most people. It's enjoyable when you make them happy - but will that still be possible now?"

Why should having electric be so important? Quality, that was the difference. With new caravans ruled out, the site would see diminishing numbers of older units. Of course there would still be the tents - thank goodness for tents! Thank goodness the period in which the Council could challenge their right to tents was over... wasn't it? Doubts were pushed quickly aside. Certainly it was - long ago! But people in tents often change to a caravan as they get older and better off. Would the present camping customers also eventually be lost? Down that road lay dilapidation, decreasing quality and a rougher cheaper type of trade. They had both believed in their hearts that River Valley was the best site anywhere; but now... now it looked like crumbling about them.

The local Electricity Board were phoned five minutes after opening next morning. "Yes, a surveyor will visit you," a young female voice confirmed.

So far worries had been solely over cost, but a few days later when the surveyor appeared, matters were not so simple.

"For so many caravans, you need an 11,000-volt supply to prevent voltage drop. Where will this power come from? That's something we have to decide then a study must be made to assess the effect on our lines and equipment." A gesture of the man's hand suggested this should all be obvious. Head shaking he continued, "Routes must first be surveyed, then wayleaves for the wires to cross adjoining land; we need the landowners agreement. All this will take time!"

"Yes but how long... and how much will it cost?"

"I can't say, not the time or the cost - not until the route's fixed and these other matters resolved, and even then our

Board's work-schedule is set months in advance. You'll still have to wait your turn." Seeing the solemn faces this warning caused, the surveyor made to leave, hesitating on the doorstep and turning back.

"You do realise of course, that our wires need planning permission."

"Damn!" Gordon murmured under his breath as the man strode off. The bottom line was this; even if the price proved affordable, no one would see a hook-up this year! Never mind, digging trenches in the season was out of the question anyway, but would a start in the coming winter be possible, say in six months time? Past experience of planning procedures gave reason for doubt!

Steve came home from college one afternoon in a mood that was quiet even for him. Throughout tea he spoke little answering questions with evasive one word answers, finishing quickly, to rise and leave the room. Jan made no comment, she didn't think Gordon had even noticed. Clearing the table and finding herself now alone in the kitchen, she wondered again about her son's behaviour. Whatever it was he might tell her eventually - but she wasn't sure she really wanted to know. School had not been going well but...

A head poked round the door, breaking her thoughts.

"I've got a job." That was it, the bare statement - no preliminaries, no warning.

Jan stopped in mid-action looking at her son, taller now than her own height, standing waiting, offering no explanation. Putting the plate down, she moved across and reached for a chair, signalling him to another.

"Where? And doing what?"

"Leedstown way." Steve paused, glancing towards the window with a small smile. "I'm an animal welfare and food procurement technician." Seeing his mother's eyes open wide in astonishment, the grin broadened. "I muck out chickens and collect the eggs. It's only temporary, 'til I find something with engines."

She smiled back, surprised but pleased at the unexpected

explanation; well aware of his desire to work at mechanics. Obviously there would be no more college; not the happiest of arrangements but he would continue working part time at home, and with the season getting busy that help could certainly be used. A ring on the office doorbell stopped further discussion, someone waiting outside, a caravan standing in the yard.

Opening the door, Jan listened then apologised. "No, I'm sorry, we might have some next year."

The man standing on the step turned, walking away. Reaching his car he opened the door, not entering but leaning with one arm against the roof and talking to a woman inside. When the curly head shook, the man nodded, climbed in and drove away. This, the first Saturday in June, had been disappointing, not that it was ever really busy at this time of year but that was the second caravan lost in as many hours, and both for want of an electric hook-up.

"I think we're not only losing them this year but for future seasons as well," Jan suggested, explaining the loss when Gordon arrived back at the office. "We should be more positive, say hook-ups will definitely be available next year - that they're being installed over the winter. That *is* what we expect, isn't it?"

"Expect, yes. Hope for anyway. Surely the Council can't refuse us electric - not in this day and age?"

Scruples cast aside, the line was agreed, customers would be promised hook-ups for the following year. On any reasonable basis it ought to be possible.

***

"Ice packs are still slow, not too many visitors yet, have you?" Audrey had come up from the bungalow ostensibly to discuss the service offered to customers from the two deep freeze chests in her garage. "Some don't get collected; we've fourteen old ones now. People go home and forget, or leave too early in the morning. We just keep them in a cardboard box on Jim's workbench."

"I'll collect them if they're in the way," Jan offered.

"No, he doesn't use the bench now; finds standing too

193

difficult. He's overweight, can't get the exercise, needs something to use his arms on. Could Gordon fix..." Audrey paused, not really knowing what was needed, and shortly after, took her leave.

"I guessed she wanted something," Jan watched her mother walk off up the road, still tall and straight, age not altering her stature.

Over the following week, Jim's bungalow saw changes. Ropes dangling by a favourite chair passed up over pulleys on the ceiling and back down to one gallon plastic containers filled with water. Pulling these ropes gave the necessary arm exercise without moving those painful legs. Passing the rope round more pulleys on the wall behind the chair allowed the movement to be outwards rather than down, a change of exercise - the weight of water easy to adjust when required. Getting up from a chair was difficult too, and here mahogany extension pieces, the top ends carved to fit a hand, gave a hold at a suitable height to thrust the body upwards. In the bedroom, a multiple pulley and rope system, with a broad leather belt, gave a means of hauling himself up if he should fall. Another rope hung over the bath. None of these could be called essential but Jim liked them for that little extra touch of independence.

***

"We bought a car today, the one Dad promised last year," Jan spoke as they sat eating tea, and seeing Steve look up sharply, she warned, "It can't be collected for five weeks. We want the 'A' registration in August, then there's towing gear to fix. Don't worry, we won't be borrowing your car - too many visitors to get away again; that's why we ordered the new one now, before it really gets busy."

"What model?" Steve asked, turning to Dad.

"A Ford Sierra - that caravan dealer over at Scorrier will fit the hitch, he owes us a favour with all the customers we've sent him over the years - especially tents in bad weather."

"Sort of a light creamy yellow," Jan added and seeing no reaction, knew she might as well have saved her breath. Men were seldom interested in colour. Never mind, Sharon would be home soon, helping again during the school holidays.

More weeks passed, continuing good weather helping to increase trade when early one evening with the shop still full of customers, the phone rang yet again. "Can you take it?" Jan's voice called through.

Gordon, standing at the office door giving directions to a customer, called "Yes," then excused himself, took three paces to the desk and lifted the receiver. "River Vall..."

"Dad?" a voice broke in.

"Sharon? Where are you ringing from?"

"Redruth station. I'm stranded, everyone else from the train has left and I'm alone here. Can you pick me up."

"Sure. Be right there."

The man at the door had gone, their conversation already finish. Slipping the catch he hurriedly poked a head in the shop door. "Got to collect Sharon from Redruth - I've locked the office."

Fifteen minutes later after an indecently fast journey, the car drew to a halt where Sharon waited. A quick hug, the cases loaded and they were off, the ride home more leisurely, catching up with the news. Talking about the university's facilities, Sharon suddenly broke off. "And don't send me any more letters like that Dad! I collected it from our reception desk and rushed off to class. Sitting there with all my friends waiting for the lecturer to arrive, I opened it."

"What's wrong with that? Don't your friends get letters from their parents?"

"Not ones written on toilet paper they don't!"

"Ah. I found a few of those old hard sulphite rolls in the basement. Must have been there years. I was just trying to use them up, hope it didn't embarrass you?"

"Fibber!" Sharon tried to look fierce but was grinning; she planned to work at home for a month - extra money for the following term, her help most welcome with the school holidays due to start.

On Saturday morning just before six, a car horn blasted outside. Gordon, on the point of rising anyway, swung quickly from bed and hurried to the window. Below the yard was full of waiting caravans, three cars with small trailers behind and one large motorcaravan; the back windows of two other cars obscured by folds of material, undoubtedly tents and bedding. The bridge was blocked, two more caravans waiting to cross. A car pointing in the other direction and obviously wanting to leave, had squeezed halfway across the yard but could go no farther - probably the one with the horn!

This particular Saturday, the first of the school holidays was invariably hectic, but not usually to this extent and so early. Letting the curtain fall he turned back to dress as Jan called sleepily "What is it?"

"Too many caravans waiting. It's blocked solid. I'll shift some, they can book in later - will you see to the office... Sharon can handle the cleaning can't she? Never mind breakfast this morning." He left without shaving.

Most vehicles showed signs of life, no one likely to remain asleep after that car horn sounded - including visitors on adjoining areas! Signalling the big motorcaravan to follow, he led it quickly to a nearby hardstanding.

"This is temporary, to clear the yard. Book in at the office when you're ready, I'll show you to your proper pitch then." With a smile and a wave of the hand he was off, not waiting for a protest forming on the driver's face. Back near the office, two caravans had rolled forward, filling the vacant space. These must be the next to move, taking both together would be quickest - an idea occurred raising a smile, something from an old back and white gangster film they had laughed at with Sharon the night before. Going to the second driver and tapping on the window, Gordon pointed to the one in front, "Follow that caravan."

Hurrying forward he signalled to the first driver, leading them off to a grassy area farther on and giving the same message about booking in.

Forty-five minutes later the yard was empty, not that it would stay that way for long on this particular morning! A queue had formed at the shop but Sharon was coping. The day continued busy with little time to eat, energy sustained perhaps by the happy flow of money, mostly cheques. About midday a brief clean of the toilets was somehow managed, working round people still using the facilities. Skipping one toilet cubical that was in use, Gordon silently resolved to nip back later, a promise that might well never be kept! About three o'clock he did pop back, finding the cubicle again in use and wondered how long the occupier would be. The sound of another vehicle arriving drew him away.

Just before tea he entered again to find the building empty apart from that one compartment. Strange. He listened... no sound. A gentle tap raised no response. "Anyone in there?" Still no reply. About to bend down and check, he hesitated... gossip would go round the site like a forest fire if someone caught him looking under toilet doors! Guiltily he stepped to the outer door, pulled it opened and scanned the area outside. Plenty of people but none very near. Quickly he moved back, letting go the handle and as the automatic closer swung it shut, knelt to look into the locked cubicle... no feet! Standing on the loo in an adjoining compartment and stretching upward, it was possible to see over; the place was empty. Damn! Some clever lad had bolted the door and climbed out over the top; dirty boot marks on one wall showed where. Still balanced on the loo and making a note to wipe the seat with a cloth later, he turned to stand squarely between the two walls, reaching hands upwards one each side. With a great heave, the body swung up and sideways, legs clearing the blockwork partition to land standing in the closed cubicle. A light pull on the small inside bolt allowed the door to open.

In the office after cleaning the marks off both wall and seat, he warned Jan to be on the lookout. "Don't tell anyone! If some mother mentions it to her children we'll have everyone doing it. Just notice if any are closed and see if you can hear any sound inside."

"Oh yes. And what should I do? Press an ear against the door, tell anyone who enters suddenly that I'm listening for woodworm? I'll watch, you do the listening!"

The chances to keep watch, let alone listen, were limited

with so much else requiring attention, but several times Gordon walked quietly to the outer door, pushing it open to look at the row of toilets. On one occasion, a caravan coming slowly along the road towards the bridge allowed just enough time to re-check the offending cubicle. Hurrying to the door he burst in with such vigour that two men washing at the basins turned to regard him with surprise. "I, er... just checking the waste bin." He crossed over lifting the lid, "Be all right 'til tomorrow," and quickly walked out again.

Towards evening when customer's demands lessened, Jan asked, "Well? Aren't you going to check again?"

"I... no I don't think so. A little later perhaps."

When he did go out, the same door was closed but several people were in the building. Not letting them guess the purpose of this visit, was important. Gossip could spread in no time. Moving to a basin he reached out to push down a tap letting water run warm onto the other hand and asking, "Is the temperature okay?"

One man said "Fine," the other murmuring "Could be hotter."

The ideal answer, Gordon gave a nod, "I'll increase it just a touch." It offered an excuse to come back shortly without it looking odd if they were still there.

Ten minutes later he returned; the building was empty, the offending door still closed. As expected, knocking lightly and calling produced no answer. Entering the next compartment, he stood on the loo, reaching up to the top of the walls on each side. Heaving as a gymnast on parallel bars, feet and body swung upward and sideways over the dividing partition, like an athletic side-dismount. Dropping into the empty compartment he unbolted the door and made for the house, toying with the idea of painting the tops of the walls with acid or lining them with broken glass set in cement.

Back indoors, Jan laughed at his annoyance. "Why not use those big curved bars with sharpened ends like at zoos to keep the animals in?"

"Hm. All right... so I'm over-reacting. Never mind, at least it's not destructive - sort of thing Steve would have

198

done five years ago."

It was not until early afternoon the following day that the door was again closed; Sunday was less busy with arrivals, and with splendid weather most people were out at the beach or sightseeing. Gordon listened at the door, not expecting to hear anything. This was getting monotonous. Ah well, the little perisher couldn't stay forever - some teenager no doubt. Entering an adjoining cubicle, stepping onto the loo and taking a deep breath, he heaved himself up, swinging across... No!! The word almost came out aloud as his pulse leapt, muscles tightening, trying desperately to stop the inevitable. A glimpse had been enough, a lowered head... and then as momentum carried him on, the whole figure of a man seated on the loo below, straining, concentrating on his task, oblivious of the catastrophe about to happen. Gordon had reached the point of no return, fingers grasping to retain a hold and pull himself back, a prayer on his lips "Please don't let him have a weak heart!" The movement would have done credit to an Olympic gymnast; his weight swinging back, dropping out of sight! Wow! For that split second, landing on the man's lap seemed completely unavoidable.

Some years earlier Jan, when she went to clean the toilet buildings, had walked in on a man standing naked outside the showers with his back to her. She escaped without his noticing but had lapsed into little spells of laughter for some time after the event. It was easy now, to understand how she felt. The relief! He leaned against the partition breathing hard. How surprised the chap would have been... how fortunate he never realised what almost happened! And what could one say? 'Sorry to drop in on you like this,' or 'Don't get up, I'm only passing through.'

Hearing the sound of tearing paper, Gordon pulled himself together and hurried away, never having felt quite so guilty leaving his own toilet building. Sidling into the office and relieved to find no customers, he tried to hold down a grin that refused to be suppressed, finally giving way and having difficulty explaining what had caused the amusement. They never did find out who the man was.

CHAPTER 11

Carlos

"Ooh! How the idle rich live!" A woman stood in the shop doorway, pointing towards the brand new car, highly polished and shining, parked close by.

"Idle? At this time of year?" Jan moved out from behind the shop counter, walking to the door, smiling with pride as they looked together at the vehicle. "We started cleaning toilets at five-thirty this morning, three hours ago, just to have that standing here on the first day of the new number-plate! Had to make a special arrangement with the garage to collect it so early; the only chance we'll have today. Good job you holidaymakers don't know how to get up in the morning."

"Cheek, I'm always early; have to be or you run out of my favourite paper."

Jan served the newspaper and milk, watching the lady walk away, then strolled to the door, looking out across the waking site, glancing back at the car and smiling again. Persuading Gordon to stick to his promise and buy it had been difficult; at least that had gone right but still no news on the electric supply front. Seeing three people approaching, she returned to the counter, casting a glance at the postcard stand. Another batch showing a different site view arrived recently; customers liked them and fifty percent of the postcard price was profit!

As caravans started to arrive, the day gathered pace, Sharon taking over in the shop and Steve fixing the dustbins. Later, when the visitors were mostly out, he started cutting the grass.

"Dad," Slowing the mower as he drove past, Steve shouted above the engine. "The last tent that left... I've just mowed the pitch; there's three patches of burnt turf."

"Those damn disposable barbecues again! I put a notice on the board asking people not to - the man who invented them should be tied on a spit over half-a-dozen and roasted like our grass."

But Steve was already moving off, turning his head away so the grin didn't show, happy to have achieved his aim. That grin did not entirely escape notice. Gordon had seen it and guessed the reason - his own fault and well deserved. The previous day on returning to the office, he had sat at the desk to check how much longer someone was staying on a particular pitch, only to find the computer not working and all the information lost. It would be difficult now to find out how long each caravan had booked or when they were due to pay again! A brief search for the cause showed the house battery condition so low it hardly made the desk lamp glow. Dashing to the window, the waterwheel turned at the correct speed so that was okay. Hunting further, the culprit was found - Steve in the basement with a young friend running the lathe. That could be fatal at this time of year with so many caravanners' batteries being charged. Seeing red, Gordon had ranted on a bit, sending the two lads away. Setting to work at the long job of recovering missing records, he regretted the loss of temper, knowing he had been unreasonable, but there was no way to call it back. Those ancient words came to mind, 'The moving finger writes...'. "Why? Why am I more tolerant with customers than with the family?" He looked up, eyes following young Steve on the mower, remembering that concealed grin and thinking, "He was actually pleased to bring the news, would probably like to have burnt those patches himself. Well it just serves me right."

Sharon had returned to university, September a more peaceful relaxing time of year; at least it should have been. However, a lack of discernible progress on the electric front spoiled any such peace of mind, phone calls meeting with evasive answers, an application apparently not yet put to the District Council in acceptable form.

Preliminary enquires from electrical equipment suppliers indicated cable, switchgear and boxes might cost something approaching £2000. To have the system installed, trenches dug and all the gear wired up by the same firm would triple this price. Looking at the figures, Gordon drew a recent statement from the drawer and pointed to the bank balance.

"With what the Electricity Board will charge, there's unlikely to be enough. Pity we bought the caravan... still, without it we'd never have realised how quickly things are changing."

Worry as they might, the matter was beyond their control. Only when the planning authority gave permission for those incoming wires would they know the cost - always supposing it was not turned down.

"Can a Council refuse anyone electricity?" Jan asked.

No one knew the answer; perhaps they could? Keeping busy seemed the best remedy. New signs were needed at the entrance, passing years and hot sun taking a toll on the existing ones. The boards were ready; cut to shape, sandpapered and painted with the proper number of coats; only the lettering still required. Lugging one up from the basement, Gordon laid it on a blanket on the kitchen table; having watched the signwriter work on previous signs, the job seemed not too difficult.

Watching these preparations and realising his intention, Jan was dubious. A little argument developing, the words becoming more heated.

"We want the professional look!"

"And mine won't be I suppose? Well I'm doing it so you might a well give up."

"You..." She pointed a warning finger but aware now of his determination, decided better of it and changed tack, her voice softening, seeking to retire with at least a partial success. "I know you're quite good with your hands at some things but..." she paused, a mischievous glint in her eyes, watching his expression change, then continuing, "I was thinking of that last signwriter, the one with all the muscles and that deep tan - now I won't see him again and he was *so* nice to me!"

Honour satisfied and harmony restored, a squeeze of the hand, and work started. On the white background, letters were carefully constructed in soft pencil, each outline filled with solid black paint to boldly display the park name. Around this central feature other information appeared, mainly in black but with yellow, red, blue and green in places. A line of print along the bottom edge proclaimed, "Winner - best site in the Southwest!"

***

"Look at this! Cheek!" Jan waved a magazine.

Emerging from the basement, Gordon wondered what was so important and followed her finger to a small advert headed River Valley Caravan Park. Not one of their own adverts, another Cornish address but much farther northeast than Relubbus.

He looked up. "Another River Valley in the county? Our reputation must be spreading; someone trying to poach?"

"Perhaps they didn't know?" She glanced at the large plastic jug of corn in his hand, "We should give more, hardly anyone is feeding them now."

He nodded, walking to the outer door, but as soon as it opened the ducks' heads came up, making him hurry across the yard; an attempt to stop them gathering on the office steps as often happened, for they understood well enough where the food came from. Reaching the normal feeding place, muscovys, mallard and aylesburys were running and flying after him. Most had no inhibitions about human contact, a few recent arrivals hung back, still wary; a thrown handful to kept them happy but most were crowding close, jostling each other, several pinned tightly to his legs by the weight of other ducks pressing forward. They seemed not to mind, some reaching in to gobble a beakful directly from the plastic jug but most preferring to nuzzle around in the outstretched hands.

Watching from the office door, Jan wondered if those beaks found it easier or perhaps just more pleasant to eat off skin; calling the idea across, her head shook as a cry floated back, "Personal magnetism!" She was right about needing extra, the jug was empty already - more eaten as winter drew near. Never mind, they were worth it; the flock would diminish by spring anyway, one or two invariably lost by then. For the most part no one knew their fate, certainly not hard weather, the southwest normally mild; a hungry fox probably the culprit, especially as autumn mellowed and young rabbits matured - older, wiser rabbits making less easy prey.

Often a duck would get lame, their clumsy landings conducive to such strains. On water the touchdown was graceful enough but on land they tended to misjudge, hitting heavily, often falling with the impact, some rolling head over heels. With hollow bones as all birds have, this was risky; most did no damage, others recovering after a few days, the odd unlucky duck limping for a week or more. This morning, one Mallard drake dragging a leg badly, struggled but failed to reach the normal feeding place. Gordon filled another jug with corn and leaving it to distract the main flock, wandered over with a handful, offering some to the injured drake, reaching out the other hand to steady its unbalanced body. The searching beak found every grain, obviously hungry; he picked it up and felt the leg. Broken certainly, the bottom part hanging freely, a clean fracture line easily felt beneath the skin.

Back indoors, Jan took the drake, holding it carefully while a large cardboard box was found, corn and a dish of water added, and the bird lowered gingerly in - a temporary touch of comfort while preparations were made. Placing lint and a roll of plaster ready on the dining room table, Gordon descended to the workroom, cutting a small rectangle from an aluminium sheet, a piece perhaps an inch wide and twice as long. Using the shaft of a screwdriver as a mould, he bent a U-shaped trough a little larger than the drake's leg, smoothing ends and edges to ensure no sharpness punctured the skin.

The break was mid-height on the main visible leg bone, a very fortunate position well clear of any joint. Lifting gently, Jan held the drake while the splint was offered up. It slid into place, loose as intended. Lining with a double layer of lint made a tight fit and would stop the leg chaffing. Carefully with pieces of sticking plaster, the splint ends were secured; gentle upward pressure ensuring proper contact of upper and lower sections, leaving no gap that might prevent the bone knitting. Winding on more plaster from a roll, starting at the very bottom and ending up just above the top, fixed the splint firmly in position, the leg now secure and exactly in line - but would stay that way only if the plaster remained dry. During the whole procedure, the drake made no struggle or attempt to escape, content in those soft hands and with the voices that spoke continuously to him.

"We'll call him Carlos," Jan lowered the patient into his box. For two days he rested sleepy, apparently contented and moving little - only to be expected; most animals have a way of lying quietly when injured, waiting for recovery. On the third day Carlos stood stretching his neck to look over the box sides, standing mainly on one leg, touching the other occasionally to the floor just long enough to balance. Towards evening he obviously wanted to come out. Closing the kitchen door and lifting him onto the floor, allowed more freedom of movement. For a while Carlos continued to stand, looking round, bending to scratch some itchy feather with his beak before gradually limping forward to the end of the kitchen where Jan was cooking. He had no fear, having constantly been hand fed. Those three days living in close contact had been sufficient to remove any residual worry he might have about people, or more particularly, these two people - three really, though Steve was at home so little he was almost a stranger.

Over the next week Carlos became progressively more active, moving towards Jan, not liking to be left on his own, shadowing her from one side of the kitchen to the other and back again, making it difficult sometimes not to step on him. Luckily she never did, for his progress was easy to follow, the splinted leg's sound contrasting with a soft 'pat' of the unbroken one. When Gordon stood in the kitchen on his own, which was seldom, the drake showed less inclination to follow, but as soon as Jan appeared he headed straight for her. Once when a small dispute arose, she turned, threatening, "I'll set my duck on you!"

The drake, as if in reaction to the sharp tone, looked up quickly, simultaneously depositing another little dropping on the floor.

"There. I told you this would keep happening," She reached to the bench, then bent to wipe it up. Tissues were clogging the waste bin; not handkerchief tissues, they disappeared too quickly, the lesson had been learned long ago with a baby moorhen - soft toilet rolls were a cheaper, more plentiful substitute, several hundred still stored in the basement and unlikely to be used so near the season's end.

"Not your fault is it Carlos? Same with any bird - instant digestion. When you fly, you can't afford unnecessary weight." Jan reached out a hand, the drake came to it and she stroked the feathers.

"A good wife would house train it?"

"Some chance!" She shook her head. Patience and kindness could work wonders with animals but one thing seemed totally impossible; house training a duck!

"Some ducks can be. Remember in the breeding season how they dash away, holding it inside themselves until well clear of the nest - then whoosh?"

"This one doesn't sit on a nest. Drakes have other duties - you've probably forgotten?" Still stoking the feathers, she smiled up, pleased to have thrown the challenge back.

On one occasion as she bent down letting the broad beak nuzzle around her hand, the office doorbell rang. Hurrying away she pulled the door closed to stop the drake following, but failed to find that final touch of force necessary to click the latch. A couple were waiting on the office step, caravanners of course, all the tents long gone. Not many visitors were left now, the site must close in two weeks time at the end of

October. Opening the door wide she invited them in.

"It's so pleasant here. Could we have three more..." the lady stopped her mouth open, attention now directed somewhere low down on the floor behind.

Jan swung round, knowing what to expect. "Carlos! Go back to the kitchen."

Carlos paid no attention, taking a few quick steps to stand with one wing against her ankle. She stooped, scooping the bird up, making the introductions and then stood talking as it went to sleep, snuggled between supporting forearm and waist.

More weeks passed and Carlos seemed fine. The trouble was, they had no exact idea of the time this heeling needed. They knew how long it should take, but was that okay for this particular duck's bones to mend? Another few days perhaps? Time passed but they hesitated, action put off - and put off again. Finally Gordon knelt one morning looking critically at the now dirty dressing, asking the drake if its leg was really better? Looking up to see Jan watching him, he hurried off to fill the bath, returning for Carlos and lowering him into the water to soften the plaster. The first swim for many weeks, he loved it; splashing wings, fluffing up feathers, ducking and frothing the surface, spreading droplets liberally around, saturating both floor and bathmat. Duck feathers are so resistant to water, such efforts probably necessary to force penetration right down to the skin. After a while, bits of dressing were eased off, little by little, snipped here and there with small pointed scissors, more swimming and water play allowed between. Eventually the little splint came away and was carefully stored - just in case! Neither dare test the leg for strength but the drake seemed fine; after padding for an hour round the kitchen, he was taken outside and mixed immediately with the other drakes, not even favouring the previously broken leg - a most gratifying outcome. Pity other things were not going so well! October drew to a close with still no news of the electric.

The morning post brought a letter, an unexpected diversion taking their minds off the matter. During the year, Gordon had continued to study flies, using odd moments to find new species in sunny hedgerows, drawing the occasional strange look from campers as he crept stealthily among the leaves. Now in late autumn less flies were seen but one had appeared on the lounge window and not immediately recognising the type, he had taken a closer look. It proved fairly typical of many found in houses but something even smaller drew attention; a swelling on one tiny leg. A magnifying glass revealed some minute parasite clinging to the fly - something scarcely bigger than a speck of dust. That had been a week ago. The letter arriving that morning confirmed it to be a Pseudoscorpion, Lamprochernes nodusus, a first sighting for Cornwall confirmed by Stella Turk who recorded such finds for the county.

A little flurry of activity, four extra caravans, marked half-term; a satisfying end to the month - encouragement too for the coming winter. Along with these welcome arrivals came a car with a single occupant.

"Funny time of year for a rep." Gordon watched from the shop doorway. He was standing assessing what perishables they would have to eat over the winter. This man however, was not selling anything, he brought news from the electricity board. Apparently the neighbouring farmer's approval had been obtained for a different route.

"It *is* slightly longer, and therefore more expensive," the man warned, "but it doesn't pass in front of his windows as the original line would. He didn't like that."

"I don't blame him." Gordon looked surprised. "I never realised that it did."

"I think he's pleased now."

A map of the line was produced and discussed. To achieve a less visible route across the site, one that avoided passing directly over too many caravans, the transformer pole was relocated to a less central position. "We'll send in a new application to the District Council," the man confirmed.

"Any idea when we might be able to start."

"No, I'm afraid not. The Parish Council originally wanted it underground."

"What, out here in the country? Why? Who can see it anyway - and what will that mean in terms of cost?"

"Twice, perhaps three times..." The electricity man made a gesture with his hands that said, 'Who knows?'

There was nothing to do but carry on working. A trip to Exeter with the caravan tested out the new car's towing ability for the first time; meeting with Sharon again cheered the atmosphere but on returning home more weeks ticking uselessly away - weeks in which trenches could have been dug and cables laid.

Seeking work outside the house as more days passed, Jan had been tending the grass, noticing the moss would need attention next spring. Commenting on this at coffee, she asked, "It's not growing so fast now. I've mowed most areas, why can't I do the riverbank?"

"Not safe."

"Afraid I'll damage the mower? When you mow it, you don't get near enough the edge. That sloping bit in front of the house, the bit you do with the strimmer - that would look better mown."

"Trying to get rid of me? What happens if the machine tilts and falls in the river while I'm sitting on it?"

"Don't be ridiculous." She turned, striding off to the kitchen.

Five minutes later, a voice shouted through. "Come and give me a hand."

Hurrying through to the office she found the door open, Gordon sitting outside on the mower, a length of hosepipe in his hand - about six feet long as near as she could guess. A finger beckoned her closer.

"Here, take this." He passed the hose over, reaching to grasp her elbow as she turned to leave. "Don't go away. Look, hold the end in one hand and put a thumb over the opening, then stand near the bank while I mow close to the river."

"Why?"

"If the bank gives way, I'll probably end in the water, mower and all - if it lands on top and pins me to the bottom, you jump in and stick that end of the hose in my mouth."

"You've got to be kidding!" There was ridicule in Jan's voice.

"No I'm not. Be sure you keep that thumb tight over the end so I don't inhale water."

"You're mad! Anyway, you'd be breathing the same air over and over again."

"I've thought of that. Breathe in through the hose and out through the nose, it's simple."

"So is someone else!"

November saw a change pending in the household; a change Jan viewed with mixed feelings - Steve had applied to join the army, the Royal Engineers where he would work with engines. He left at six o'clock one morning, catching a train at Penzance and heading off towards Birmingham, to Sutton Coldfield for an interview, not sure if he would return the same day or whether overnight accommodation was provided.

The phone rang shortly before ten o'clock that evening. Steve was stranded in Plymouth. They had booked him a through ticket on a train with no forward connections. He must find an alternative way home or sleep rough on the station. Gordon took the call, promising to come immediately. Jan, reaching for a coat, cursed softly as a six-foot length of hose now kept on the coat rack in the hall, fell to the floor. Pulling on the coat, she hurried to catch up and climb into the car. Plymouth was 80 miles away, darkness already fallen. The tourist season having passed, light traffic left the road conveniently clear. Probably for this reason not one single garage along the route was open. With the fuel gauge registering zero, they reached Plymouth and were fortunate enough to see a stationary police car. Following the directions for less than a mile, yielded the blazing lights of an all night garage.

Drawing up a little later at the railway station, a dark figure emerged, hurrying towards the car. Opening the door, Steve stepped in, sunk into the rear seat and in answer to the question "How did it go?", merely murmured, "Alright," then after a while, "Warmer in here," but said no more.

Jan, anxious but still not sure what she wanted to hear, remained silent too.

Crossing the Tamar bridge, Steve spoke again. "I passed. They'll send for me. Don't know when yet, next spring they think."

The voice sounded normal enough, unconcerned, as if it didn't matter. Jan fancied she heard a keenness, a touch of pride in the apparently nonchalant words, but with no further explanation offered, she couldn't be sure.

More weeks passed, fruitless frustrating weeks waiting for word of the power supply - weeks that should have been filled with useful work.

Putting the phone down, Gordon turned. "Nothing! Everyone passes the buck!" Earlier he had rushed to meet the postman, hoping against hope that a letter would arrive. Now he rose, pacing across the room. "Look, I'm going to start. We've taken chances before; surely the Council must grant permission sometime? At least we know the wayleaves are done and our neighbour no longer objects. Nor does any member of the public, or so we're told."

"If the Parish Council still want an underground cable, could we afford it?"

"No, I wouldn't think so; have to save up for several more years first. Still, if I build the meter house now, the cost won't be wasted. We have to get electric soon - provided the delay doesn't lose us trade so fast that we never can afford it."

There the argument rested. This little electric room involved no great cost, some five foot square with a single door and no windows, its neat pitched roof matching the other buildings. The main control box with all its complex switch gear would hang from one wall, with cables leading off in various directions. The Electricity Board meter too, would be inside - the transformer mounted on a pole nearby - at least it would be if planning permission was ever given!

The work was quickly finished but December had almost

arrived - three months only until the site opened again - and what about those promises? How many times in the summer had they reassured visitors, "Yes, the hook-ups will ready next season; we'll be working on them all winter."

Something must be done! Taking a folded plan from the desk drawer, Gordon looked at the layout of underground cables for the first 54 electric points. So much trench to be dug! In the soft conditions of winter, an excavator would cut up the surrounding ground. That must be avoided! The work would be by hand, but how quickly could he dig? Money shortage precluded hiring in help, at least it probably did - still not knowing the cost of bringing the power in was a nuisance. Looking at the long list of equipment required, he lifted the phone, contacted suppliers and placed the full order, finishing with the armoured cable.

"The cable is urgent!" A few more words were exchanged before he rung off.

"Taking a risk?" Jan, listening as the order was placed, had pushed some papers back from the edge of the desk and half-sat, half-stood looking down at him.

"In for a penny..." a gesture of his open palm said who cares - but both knew that was untrue; they did care. This was important.

"How long?"

"They'll order today. Comes direct, delivered by the manufacturers. Depends when they have a lorry in the area. It's all armoured cable, over a thousand pounds worth but that's a small drop for them."

"Will you start on the trenches."

"Can't really. The material dug out must go back within a week or the grass where it stands will spoil."

"Hand work is slow, will there be time? What about you, can you... how long are these trenches, added all together?"

"Nearly half a mile."

"By yourself? Suppose they refuse our supply, all that money and work wasted?"

"I'd have to do it eventually, might as well be now. At least the boxes will be visible; visitors will know we've kept our part of the promise. If we wait we'll still need to spend the cash next year."

That was true and the gear would probably get dearer - everything tended to. As days passed, the delay proved hard to come to terms with. The first long line of trench was already marked out, the turf carefully lifted then laid back in the same place; a move to save time later, but little else could be done until the cable arrived. Jan watched as he emerged from the basement with a pair of branch loppers and strode off. Shortly after, she watched again as the loppers were replaced and he disappeared with a broom. That was one thing they never did in the valley - sweep leaves away. On grass areas the mower pulverised them and elsewhere they blew away in winter storms. He came back shortly after, throwing the broom against the wall and entering the office.

Seeing the frustration, she spoke quietly. "Why not sit and relax; read a book? There'll be enough hard work later, have a rest while you can." It was good advice but she doubted he would take it. Leaving him standing by the bookcase, she went back to the kitchen, returning later to find him sitting at the desk, a large sheet of paper and sundry drawing equipment spread across the surface.

"What are you drawing?"

"A laundrette. No chance of affording the materials this year, but let's get the planning permission - avoid another delay next winter. Look," he slid the drawing sideways, "We can build over the old septic tank; it's not used any more. The foundations are strong, take anything; save work too, and expense."

"What about size?"

"That's the only drawback; no flexibility. Whatever we want inside just has to be tailored to fit - no way to change the dimensions."

Later that day with the aid of yellow pages, a local laundry equipment supplier was located, rough sizes for various machines obtained. More fiddling with sketches confirmed that the size would be adequate. Three washing machines were shown; two should be enough but better plan for expansion later! Adding two large tumble dryers left masses of unused space. More drawings of wooden partitions showed a separate room with stools, mirrors and little benches set out as a do-it-yourself hair drying salon; space too, for a row of sinks to hand-wash clothes, and an ironing station. A spin dryer might be added later.

"Why is the roof lopsided?" Jan peered again at the drawing.

"Remember when we visited other sites? One had rows of washing up sinks fixed to an outside wall, people using them, chatting together as they did the crockery. I think visitors liked that, somewhere to talk, men and women together; some probably used those sinks rather than their own caravan just to meet people. They like to be in the open air too - not enclosed. Well, we'll go one better... outside sinks and space all round, but with a roof over in case of rain.

The job now was to draw proper plans and fill in all the forms, inevitably in triplicate, the application finally submitted on 7th December, a day before the cable arrived. For the 54 hook-ups there were five main cables; sinking these in the ground would take some energy! It was tempting to reconsider and hire a digger but with the season approaching, grass was a major consideration. The first trench was started, digging five inches wide, just room to stand one leg in front of the other. To change the leading leg and relieve tired muscles, one must step out, stepping back with the other leg in front.

"Out here or indoors?" Jan, holding a flask and two mugs stood looking down at the long length of trench.

Gordon, standing awkwardly with one hand resting on the pick handle, climbed out, walking over to rest against a nearby tree trunk as they sipped the coffee together. There was still a long way to go, and this was only the first cable. After a while he drained the cup, passing it over and walking back to step again into the trench.

"You," she said watching him, "are narrow minded!"

"Never! Haven't you heard that small is beautiful."

"Just be careful that by tonight your voice isn't an octave higher." She walked away, a smile on her lips at having had the last word.

Trenches that will not show afterwards are an art. Placing turf on one side and soil on the other, digging continued. Cables were laid and covered with sand, the replaced soil stamped down in layers, and the turf relaid. A stiff broom removed remaining soil particles, the first rain doing the rest. The idea that a man with a shovel is just a labourer and has no skill, is rubbish.

Darkness fell early now in December and perhaps that was just as well, the effort poured into those trenches hard to sustain! Evenings however, found more work; special posts must be made to carry the electric hook-up boxes. Two-hundred feet of steel angle lay waiting on the basement bench to be cut and drilled. The separate parts needed fixing together too. Fine, Steve had a new job, one involving welding. Life was not looking so bad, the heavy physical work to some extent diverting the mind from that long awaited planning permission.

A few days later however, the outlook bleakened. A sympathetic but anonymous voice on the phone bought news of a recent Council meeting!

"The officer's recommendation was 'No Objections', but when it came before the Development Services Committee on the 12th, they threw it out, asking that the line be put underground."

"That's ridiculous. I don't think there's a single house that can see it. Just take a look at Relubbus; cables everywhere and no one says a word. We can't afford it!"

"This is not final; only what the committee recommends. It goes next to the full Council for a final decision. They might not agree, especially if you get some support. Councillors are reasonable people, speak to a few - put your side of the case. They could still pass the application or at least refer it back to Development Services for reconsideration."

Thanking the caller, Gordon put the phone down, relaying the conversation to Jan. They were alone, Steve away at work and not another soul in the valley. Outside, a half-finished length of trench beckoned but more important things were now afoot. Draining the last of the coffee, he reached again for the phone.

Laying a hand on his arm, she asked, "Who are you ringing?"

"Our own organisation, the park owners association. They know who to approach, where to get support. Improving standards is what they exist for - to make British sites better."

"Will our Council listen to them?" Jan looked doubtful.

"Probably. Most Councils do - tourism is an important source of local income. They can write saying how essential electricity is becoming to caravans, and tell us who else to contact." He lifted the phone.

By evening, help had been sought from COSIRA, the small business organisation and from the Country Landowners Association. Was it enough? Work on the trenches continued but would those cables ever be used?

***

Chris would not be home for the holiday, single chaps usually took the Christmas police duties, but Sharon arrived with several days to spare. Dad was still digging, making good progress, leaving the two girls alone in the house.

"Mum, where's the jug, I'll feed the ducks."

"Down the basement in the corn sack. They've been fed already but another jugful won't hurt."

Opening the basement door, Sharon pressed the switch; a light came on below and she descended, turning the corner, passing a dark opening on her right and wondering why these underground rooms still felt so creepy. Just ahead two corn sacks leant against the wall, the first already open. Taking the jug, and about to fill it with grain, a faint sound made her pause, staring along the other corridor towards more dark rooms faintly visible at the end. Standing rigidly still and listening intently, the sound was nearer at hand, a faint... how could one describe it - almost a grinding sound, close but lower? Sinking silently onto one knee the noise was clearer, she leaned to the side, hand touching the unopened bag of corn sack. There! An ear against the paper confirmed it, a distinct crunching sound - the sack was alive?

Moving back to the first sack, the one already open, an ear rested again against the side - no sound this time. Quickly she filled the jug and hurried towards the stairway, relieved to reach the bottom step with daylight showing above.

Hearing her daughters footsteps, Jan wondered what had taken so long, and looked up to see an eager face appear. Certainly something had happened.

"Did you..." Sharon stopped, expression changing. "Er, did you want to feed them too?"

Jan was taken aback, still sure something was afoot, but with no idea what. "Yes, I'll come." They walked together out into the yard and onto the riverbank, crouching down as the ducks gathered round, Sharon reaching to pick up a big white aylesbury, balancing it on one knee and watching it gobble corn from her hand. "When will Dad be back for coffee?" she put the duck down.

"Any time in the next fifteen minutes. Why?"

"Oh no reason." Sharon turned away, smothering a smile.

"Hadn't you better tell me what's going on?"

"Going on?" Sharon fought to hold a straight face but under her mother's gaze the smile slowly surfaced, changing to a grin. "Come on then," she rose tipping the last remaining corn from the jug and heading back to the house. Leading down the stairs and onward, Sharon stopped near the corn, putting an ear to the unopened sack then rising to step away and point, "Listen!"

Jan knelt, listened and drew back? "Something alive?" Reaching for the thread that held the top closed, a hand touched her arm.

"Mum, er... Dad carried it down here, shouldn't he...?"

"Good idea. Come on, he'll he back soon. Here, pull this half-full sack into the boiler room, and bring back one of those empty ones."

"Why?" Sharon grasped the sack, waiting.

"So I can say we've run out of duck food and need another one opened. Don't they teach you anything at that university?"

Grinning together in the dim light, Sharon grasped more

firmly and pulled the sack away.

When Gordon strode into the office it was later than intended, but he was pleased with himself; the turf on another length of trench replaced and looking good. Announcing this as he walked in the door and half expected some ribbing that the job had taken too long, it was pleasantly surprising to find the two women so attentive, all congratulations and concern. Was he exhausted?

"Well, just a bit - hard work you know." He stooped over slightly with a little sigh and a shake of the head, wiping a hand across his brow.

Jan placed a cup near the armchair, "You sit down, have a rest, make yourself comfortable, let me know if the coffee is okay."

Smothering a grin Sharon dropped into another chair, Jan moving to sit in her own. As more questions flowed about the work, Gordon lay back, enjoying the recognition of his prowess, being careful to sound strained but bearing up as a chap does of course - yes, yes, it was hard, but men were made for that sort of thing!

As heads continued to nod in understanding and agreement, and little smiles passed between mother and daughter, he began eventually to feel apprehensive, a touch uneasy. Little pictures flashed through his mind of them buying Paris gowns, or staying at some health spa with expensive therapy and beauty treatments; he could even imagine a female hand writing out the cheque, noughts flowing across the page!

"All right, what do you want?" He sat suddenly upright, all signs of fatigue disappearing.

"Want?" Jan looked up innocently. "Nothing... oh, you could open a bag of corn, so Sharon can feed the ducks."

Rising with relief, no longer feeling his hair might turn grey, he made for the basement stair, surprised to see the women following. Ah, they were coming to collect corn of course. A thread hanging from one corner would undo the sack; reaching forward he wondered why Sharon didn't pull it herself, and glanced round to ask but she had not followed after all. Some distance away two faces poked cautiously round the corner at the bottom of the stairs as if ready for flight. Catching sight of them made him wary.

Struck by a sudden wariness, he glanced upward at the concrete ceiling close overhead. No place to hide a bucket of water that might tip - even with the dim waterwheel light such a thing could not be concealed. What else? He looked carefully to each side of the sack, expecting some trap but seeing nothing, shrugged and pulled the string.

Peering round the corner, Sharon and Jan watched the top come clear as the sack opened. When nothing jumped out, they approached gingerly as Dad stood waiting, mystified by this unexplained behaviour.

"What about the noise?" Sharon leaned forward looking closely, but the angle of the light obscured the actual corn. "Wait!" Racing off, she returned shortly with a torch, shining it down into the sack.

"Agh," The light wavered, Sharon stepping sharply back.

"Get them out of here!" Jan urged as all three stared at the black flecked corn, covered in hundred upon hundred of tiny grain weevils, their munching jaws generating the sound.

For a moment no one moved, then Gordon stepped forward, lifting the hundredweight sack, keeping it upright and hurrying up the stairs, Sharon racing ahead to open the office door. Trying to get rid of some by issuing extra rations was only partly successful, the ducks not too keen - the taste of weevil dropping perhaps, but it stayed outside in a plastic dustbin well away from any building. Examination afterwards found the basement wall still covered in weevils; most were sprayed with flykiller, but some had obviously escaped.

About to return to trench digging, Dad stopped in the doorway. "Do me a favour next coffee break... don't be nice to me."

CHAPTER 12

Too Big

"Bring them in the office," Jan stood beside a lorry, looking up at the man above, watching him move several large cardboard cartons nearer the edge. When he jumped down, reaching to lift the nearest box, she led the way across the yard. The electrical equipment had arrived; all it needed now was the supporting stakes to drive in the ground, but those were still at Steve's new place of work, waiting to be welded.

Having signed the ticket, she tried to keep the driver talking, a nice young fellow but like all delivery men, in a hurry. As he drove off along the track, her eyes watched the disappearing lorry, then scanned the nearer valley sides following them off way into the distance. Nothing. Just bare leafless trees, their branches not even swaying. Steve was at work and Sharon back at university, the valley lay deserted, not another soul in any direction. A movement caught her eye; the ducks. Fetching some bread she went outside, stooping as they crowded round nuzzling her hand, the slice disappearing into ever hungry beaks.

Gordon was away too, at the Council offices hoping to ferret out the latest information, see if anything further could be done. A recent chat with the Electricity Board had raised the stakes - an underground supply they suggested, might cost £15000, massively greater than the scheme applied for, and totally out of reach!

One bright spot had arisen; the Board agreed to leave space in their work schedule so if permission for an overhead line *was* given, it could be erected with less than the usual delay - a compensation perhaps for so much having gone wrong. More than seven months ago the Board had indicated this application to be a simple procedure, almost a formality. Some chance! Everything depended on the Council's decision, and that was weeks away, due the first day of February; an evening sitting as such meetings usually were - a long time to wait!

A duck pulling at her skirt caught Jan's attention; reaching out a hand she stroked its feathers but the bread was all gone. Returning to the big cardboard cartons, the binding on one was loose. Inside lay white plastic boxes, each with a number stuck to the lid. There were two types, the larger size about like a cornflakes packet. Lifting some out onto the desk she found a bunch of keys and unlocked one. A tangle of wires and switches filled the upper area, several holes in the bottom were obviously where cables would enter.

"Good, make a change from trenching," she murmured, smiling at having spoken aloud - even with a megaphone nobody could possibly hear. She had been helping with those trenches recently, not with the actual digging but fetching sand in a small trailer towed behind the mower, covering the cable then shovelling the earth back in.

Another week spun by. Things were happening! Cables reached the first two toilet buildings; fuse boxes were connected up and a single long strip light fixed mid-ceiling in both Ladies and Gents. They looked well enough but none worked yet; nor would they unless the Council repented!

A cable reached the house too, passing in through one basement wall and out through another, running on to feed more caravan hook-ups along the riverbank. Great, but no hook-up points could be fixed yet; the metal stakes still not arrived! Not Steve's fault; the place where he worked now claimed to be too busy. A phone call threatening to cancel the order did bring some result - a promise they would be ready next Thursday.

"Sounds like a pair of shoes that never gets mended," Jan banged a fist on the desk in annoyance, looking hard at Gordon, "Do you really believe that?"

"I said I'd be over to collect them before lunch that day, done or not. I will too, even if it does cost more elsewhere."

The final trenches were still to be dug and a few more connections made, but the house had been totally neglected. Having survived with 12-volt waterwheel current for the past ten years, it hardly seemed important. However, since all other inside jobs were finished and darkness still fell early, the house wiring was started.

"What will happen if you accidentally connect the mains into our 12-volt lights?" Steve asked one evening, watching his father threading wires up through a duct in one corner of Sharon's bedroom.

"Blow up like a grenade I should think. *If* we ever get connected, you can be the one who goes round pulling all the light switches. Okay?"

Steve shook his head.

Jan, standing in the doorway asked, "Pull switches? Aren't we having proper ones like a normal house?"

"No." Gordon reached over, putting a finger on the wall by the door. "This is where such a switch would be - so how do I get a wire to it? We'll have ceiling switches, just like the waterwheel lights."

Out of the blue, a letter arrived. Taking a handful of mail from the postman, Jan set about sorting through it. The local postmark on a brown envelope caught her eye, the typewritten address suggesting it was not a booking. She slit it open, withdrawing the letter, stopping suddenly as the Council's headed paper came into view. For a moment she sat, wondering what to do; unsure whether to push it back and forget... A quick movement of the hand pulled it clear, opening and spreading the paper, scanning anxiously across the page - had they refused? Why? The meeting was not due for a fortnight... what did it say?

Her eyes rose to the top again and there below the heading were the words she could hardly believe: 'Notice of Conditional Permission for Development.'

"What! We've got it?" A finger ran down the print,

following each line, 'HEREBY GRANT permission.' It must be right, the words were in capitals. The finger moved on to stop abruptly on the fourth line; 'construction of a laundrette.'

"The laundrette!" She shook her head, not knowing whether to cry or laugh. How long had they waited for electric? More than seven months since approaching the board - the laundrette had been applied for less than five weeks ago and it wasn't even wanted this year! That had just been to save time next winter.

Later when Gordon returned, she tossed the letter to him, passing her own comment, "It's Crazy. You won't start this winter, will you?"

He scanned through, "I'd like to, but no... we don't have the money."

That evening Steve came home with a happy grin. "I've started welding your posts but they won't be ready by Thursday."

Surprise, surprise - but he was now working on them most of the time.

"I've done six, but each one is faster. I could go quicker but you said make them really strong. If they leave me alone, I'll finish next week."

Under the circumstances it seemed unfair to take the work elsewhere.

"I've been thinking..." Gordon started.

"You be careful," Jan's warning brought a smile to the three faces.

"...thinking I'll dig a trench to the terraces. I intended connecting up the other hook-ups first, in case time gets short, but with the posts not finished, I might as well dig it now."

"What about the Council meeting?" Jan asked.

"It's due next week. I contacted quite a few councillors; most seemed sympathetic, surprised we only have the water-wheel and no mains electric. We might get that decision overturned, but well, if not..." he never finished; there was really no answer. Days passed slowly until the meeting.

***

A number was called, a few words floated on the air

and a circle of hands rose. Looking down from the public gallery at the Councillors seated below on a ring of chairs at temporary tables, it hardly seemed possible - someone's dreams realised or perhaps shattered with such speed. There was scarcely time to find the item, read the small print and see what had been passed of refused. Another number rang out, papers were rustled... more hands were raised; another decision taken.

The Councillors of course, knew exactly what they were doing; had read the details beforehand and made notes on anything they disapproved of. After all, their own committees had made these recommendations - this meeting largely a rubber stamp operation giving the whole Council's approval, spreading the responsibility perhaps, but allowing any members to object, as was their right.

Jan and Gordon sat close together looking down at the scene below. Around them in the gallery were other members of the public, each no doubt with their own worries, affected to a greater or lesser extent by the proceedings below.

On a raised platform at the far end of the hall several figures sat behind and around an elongated desk on a raised platform, the middle one, the chairman Councillor Daniel, contributing a word from time to time; various officers taking notes or passing relevant papers.

Another number was called and passed without a word of debate.

"Next page," Gordon whispered and felt a hand squeeze tightly. Would their own future be passed over with the same speed and apparent indifference.

Minutes passed, papers rustled.

"Number C55, item B," a voice called.

This was it! Lights in the toilets, hand dryers, perhaps a washing machine for the visitors, TV that could be watched for any length of time even in summer, and most important of all, those electric hook-ups to keep the caravans coming - all depended on the next few seconds.

The chairman was speaking, drawing attention to the various representations that had been made; the national federation, the small business organisation, the Country Land-owners, the electricity board's estimate of increased costs. He paused for a moment, looking over the gathered Councillors, before finishing "...and I think he might have a point."

That was a masterpiece of understatement, focusing the attention. There would be no rubber stamp here!

It was Councillor Lutey who proposed the decision be reversed and an overhead line permitted. A lady member seconded the motion and other councillors spoke in support. Councillor Berryman, the same person who tended Gordon on that first awakening after the appendix operation so many years ago had a few choice words to say, and Councillors Cocks and Cotton waded in, in support. Heads were nodding round the chamber as more speakers made their points.

Finally a vote was called. "Those in favour?" a voice rang out. Proceedings paused as a mass of arms were counted. "Those against?" A single hand rose, maybe someone supporting the Parish Council's contention that the line be underground. Perhaps all lines should be, but how many people could afford electric then? How many would like to pay to have their service buried even from 50 metres away, and this was 476 metres - a fortune. Anyway, at 11,000 volts it might be safer above, where no excavator digging a drainage trench would come unexpectedly across it.

Whatever the pros and cons it was passed! Relief was the feeling that hit; relief and jubilation! Scarcely aware of those around, some still awaiting their own fate, Gordon and Jan sat hands clasped, wanting to get up and run into the street, dash home and tell Steve - ring up Sharon and Chris with the news! Respect for the Councillors kept them seated, not liking to rise during the proceedings, listening without hearing as more numbers were called.

When they did arrive home, these happy tidings were received with polite attention rather than elation - subdued reactions marking how much family interests had diverged. Steve knew he was leaving in April, only the exact date still to be determined. His future lay in the Army, no longer in the valley; this decision would hardly affect him. A phone call located Chris, his surprise at being rung over such a matter, obvious - no one had broken a leg; what was so urgent? "Good. You'll be having real electricity then."

There was little curiosity in the statement, no realisation just how much had hinged on that decision. Sharon too, showed muted interest - pleased certainly for their success but turning quickly to her own progress, her friends and conditions at university in the winter weather.

For the parents this heady moment in life, this supreme triumph, was talked about on and off all evening. Books and television were cast aside, abandoned as the possibilities ahead, small points not previously thought of, now came under discussion. What would it mean for the house, for the site, for the future? These thoughts constantly diverted their attention, making it difficult to settle; the children's comparative disinterest hard to accept.

Lying together in bed later that evening, Jan spoke quietly. "How could things change so fast? Not many more weeks and he'll be gone." She nodded in the darkness towards the room across the landing, a movement unseen but unnecessary, for no one else was in the house, or even in the valley. "Think of the family celebration this success would have triggered ten years ago."

"They have their own lives now - a new generation. They still expect us always to be here for them though; somewhere to come, someone to come to in a crisis of their own."

"We're the old folk now, you mean? They'll never be in their forties?" Jan snuggled closer.

"Sure. Did you ever think about being so ancient when we first got married?"

A small fist punched him lightly. "Ancient nothing! I'm younger than you - most of the year anyway. Now we've got the permission, what will you do?"

"Well," he thought for a moment, working out a schedule. "Get Steve up about six in the morning and send him off to work early to finish welding those posts. We need them galvanised. At about one minute past nine, I'll ring the

Electricity board - get them to fix our supply before March... well, try to."

"Progress." Jan smiled in the darkness. "How long will the hook-ups take?"

"A week perhaps - I should manage ten a day; all the trenches are done, the cables sticking out ready. Need another day to wire the main control box when it comes."

Life it seemed, would not be too hectic; after all there were still four weeks until March. Slowly they drifted into sleep. Morning brought a fresh surprise. Steve had been taken off the posts onto another job, but he expected to be back on them shortly. How soon was shortly?

"I'll find out today."

As he left, driving away in the Maxi, the two parents moved to sit in the lounge; fifteen more minutes before they could make the phone call.

"You know one thing we could have now?" Jan waited, and seeing a small shake of the head, suggested, "A telephone answering machine. Then we won't lose bookings if both of us are called out. There won't be any children to help with the office this year."

"Sharon will still be home in the summer don't you think?"

"Not necessarily. She'll have her degree by then."

"Okay, an answerphone," he nodded reluctantly, "but some people don't like them and just ring off. We could get a deep freeze for the shop, start selling ice cream again."

More small talk filled the passing minutes until on the stroke of nine, Gordon moved across to the desk, lifting the receiver and punching in the number of that vital call to the Electricity Board. As he spoke into the phone giving news of the planning success, Jan listened from the adjoining room, hearing a plea for urgent action to get those overhead lines installed before the site opened in a few weeks time.

A long silence followed, then the words, "Really. We can?"

Shortly, the phone was put down, but as she rose to ask the details he lifted the receiver again, flipped open a small book and dialled a number. "Give me a price please, four inch concrete blocks... yes, a full load." There was a pause then, "River Valley Caravan Park... that's the one, down at Relubbus. When... oh, not until Monday. Okay. Go ahead." The phone dropped back into place.

Jan moved to stand by the desk and waited, expecting him to look up but he turned a few more pages of the little book and dialled another number. "A price for three and a half yards please... all right then, three cubic metres if you prefer. Yes, that's the mix, it's for a floor. How much?"

A silence followed, obviously explanations going on at the other end. "Do I get it today at that price?" Another pause. "Okay, go ahead. I don't want it too wet mind." The phone went down and he reached again for the little book.

Stepping closer, Jan put her hands around his throat and squeezed, taking them away as he pivoted round on the chair. "Don't you dare ignore me!" The hands still hovered, fingers outstretched. "Just what are you doing?!"

"Ordering concrete for the laundrette base and blocks for the walls. We'll be busy after all."

"Busy! You can't build a laundrette in thirty days!"

"The world was built if seven." Quickly he offered an explanation as a little fist drew back. "I can - or at least have a damn good try. The concrete is coming today to make the base slab, so we need some shuttering."

"What about the building inspector... what are you grinning at?" Jan paused, suddenly realising. "Hey! We're supposed to be short of money!"

"Money? No problem." Gordon's smile broadened as he quickly changed the subject. "The building inspector came on another matter last week, while you were in town. We've agreed what has to be done. It's easy using the existing foundations."

He rose, making for the door but she moved faster, blocking his way and laying one hand on a heavy glass ashtray on the windowsill. "The money?"

"Oh that? We can pay the Electricity Board by instalments, over ten years I think he said. That means we're rich again.

Simple?"

Taking the chance while she still absorbed this new information, he slipped through the door, turning again on the step to call back, "Bring a hammer and some four inch nails, time you did something useful."

His sudden sprint across the yard left her smiling.

Four days later the base had set, the first course of blocks already laid. Naturally these were cavity walls, but with only four sides and no internal partitions, three courses a day should be easy. A door frame stood waiting, the three windows expected tomorrow. Action! With luck the roof timbers, preservative treated of course, would arrive next week - at least that was the promise.

The building grew quickly, over two-feet higher each day, the three blockwork courses usually complete by early afternoon.

"I'm off to Camborne for those sinks," Gordon called, heading for the car.

"Don't get carried away - ordinary quality will be fine." Jan shouted back

Three stainless steel sinks were needed for inside the laundrette. A row of washing-up sinks fixed to the outside wall was also planned, but must wait until next year. Those rash words spoken earlier about being rich were not really true. Money was tight with the washing and drying machines still to buy, initial enquires showing commercial equipment to be expensive. Driving into the plumbing suppliers, the staff seemed in more chaos than normal.

"Hello John, what goes on?" Gordon approached a man with a clipboard.

"Stocktaking. What can I get you?" John moved aside as some men struggled by, their arms full of pipes.

"Stainless steel sinks - how much?"

"From about £35... depends on which one you want exactly."

"It's not one - four probably, should be a good discount?"

John wiped a hand over the seat of his trousers and smiled. Knowing about the caravan park he had half expected more than one. They had bargained often before, the discount always a compromise.

"How particular are you... about condition I mean? Will your lot expect perfection?"

"Why? Not perfection necessarily. If it's the shine I'm not worried, that wears off anyway, but they need to be decent."

The two men stepped to one side again as more pipes came by.

"As I said, we're stocktaking. Over the years a pile of sinks with blemishes has accumulated, a little dent or a small scratch, nothing very big, but since nearly all our stuff goes on domestic jobs, housewives won't accept them. Come on, have a look." He led off into one of the buildings, and after more bargaining, an agreement was reached.

As the car arrived home later, Jan saw the empty boot and asked, "Couldn't you get them?"

"Yes, they're being delivered. Wouldn't all go in."

"All? We only want three! You've not been buying spares again? Come on, how many?"

"Er... eighteen."

"Eighteen! You're mad! How long must we starve to pay for that little mental aberration?" She sighed, head shaking. "It's not safe to send you anywhere. All right, how much? I can tell from that stupid grin, they must have been cheap."

Gordon smiled back, being evasive. "I only asked for four, one for a spare, but... Ah," he saw the fist rising again and hurried on. "The price? Well it varied; you want the double drainers or the singles?"

"Double drainers?!" Jan took a step forward. "Why?"

"Touch of class." He tried to move back but felt the car behind.

"Do I get to hear the price, or would you like a high squeaky voice?"

Automatically his hand dropped defensively, the words coming quickly, "Five pounds for the single drainers, ten for the doubles. Three are for inside the laundrette, six for outside and six for another row of washing up sinks on the third toilet building. The three spares I'll put up the loft."

Ten days to opening. No overhead wires had appeared, but they were promised. "We'll be there directly," the engineer had said.

"Don't bet on it!" Jan thought, glancing through the window, seeing Gordon way up in the air. The timbers had arrived, work on the laundrette roof now in full swing. Taking a few hours off one afternoon another quick trip to Camborne saw two commercial washing machines and two tumble dryers placed on order at a cost of £3226 - equipment big enough to take a double duvet or perhaps a small tent! Paying by instalments for the incoming electric supply had indeed opened new horizons but even so, resources were shrinking fast!

Steve came home from work with the news that the posts were ready. A morning phone call to the galvanising works confirmed dipping could be done that day. By evening 56 posts had been taken to Plymouth, pickled in acid, dipped in hot zinc, loaded still warm into the car boot and driven back to Relubbus. A dozen leftover lengths of angle had been galvanised too, Gordon insisting they might be useful. Next morning saw the final roof tiles on, and by prior arrangement the plasterers arrived to work on the walls and lay the internal floors.

At tea a warning was issued. "They say they'll finish in three days, so don't let me find little fingerprints in the cement."

Steve looked blankly back at his mother, not understanding, the childhood memory lost with passing years, his mind on the future. Only a few weeks now until he left for the army.

Seeing no point in explaining, Jan asked, "How long until you go?"

"Four weeks and three days." A smile spread across the young man's face.

He wanted to leave, that was obvious. "Not," she thought "because he dislikes home, but for the adventure, for something new." That was natural - normal. Swallowing a lump in her throat she turned to Gordon. "If there are only 54 hook-ups, how come you had 56 posts made? No don't tell me; more spares?" Seeing the nod, she asked. "What were you doing with them down in the basement when it got too dark to work outside yesterday evening?"

"Drilling out the holes; hot zinc blocks them up. I fixed fifteen hook-ups today."

"What about the main control box?"

"That's undercover work. Saving it in case we get rain."

Quite suddenly men and equipment began to appear, the promised electricity supply becoming a reality - a pole erected, transformer mounted above, more poles bringing cables across adjoining fields. Things were happening elsewhere too. The laundrette glazed and the plasterers finished, all walls now smoothly coated inside and out, including the floor - good weather and constantly open windows drying the inner surfaces fast; decoration would soon be possible. A deep freeze cabinet stood in the shop, campers and caravanners could have their ice cream, other frozen food too probably.

Crawling up through a tiny access hole in the laundrette ceiling and wriggling into the roof space, electrical wires were routed down through conduits in the walls to various sockets for washing machines, tumble dryers, hair dryers, and even for customers to plug in their own curlers and stylers. A special socket with red warning light controlled the iron, so people would remember to turn it off - an improbable hope but the best that could be done. Another would serve a spin-dryer that might or might not be added later, and two long fluorescent tubes on the ceiling provided lighting.

"So you did finish in thirty days," Jan inspected the interior. "Now get on and paint the walls!"

Out came the white emulsion, a bit premature perhaps but the paint seemed to take okay. An arriving caravan hardly interrupted the work, the couple welcomed, made comfortable - then back to finishing the last hook-ups.

Progress!

The site was quieter now, the Electricity Board workmen gone, the incoming line finished, its overhead cables covered with an insulating plastic coating to guard against shocks from damp kite strings - after all, it was 11,000-volts!

In the house too, things were coming together, nearly ready for connection, wiring work having continued each evening. The scattering of electric sockets in various rooms was pleasing but of limited use, with very little equipment to plug in. Returning from ordering an electric cooker, Jan suggested, "I could get to like spending money!"

"Your Dad never told me you'd be this expensive when I bought you."

He hardly managed to get the words out before she dug him in the ribs with a finger; only a nudge as they smiled at each other, both pleased with the little spree - unwise perhaps, but just possible with the remaining resources. It couldn't actually be moved into position yet; the old gas cooker bought second-hand ten years ago must stay until the power was on. Still, just knowing a new stove was coming gave a buzz of pleasure.

All the rooms now had two types of lighting, but as yet only the little waterwheel lights actually worked. Both were operated by cords dangling from the ceiling, the mains ones with wooden macramé balls to pull on; the twelve volt cords still with little plastic cones. Why? Handsome way to tell them apart in the dark, naturally.

The great day came. Two men arrived to check the electrics and turn on the power! Poking a head round the meter room door, Gordon spoke to the senior man. "If there *is* anything wrong, be sure you find it."

He looked surprised. "People don't usually want me to; most don't even want me to look in case I do find something."

Every care had been taken with the hook-ups, every connection checked and rechecked - but there remained the possibility, the chance of human error creeping in. Fortunately, sensitive 30mA trips protected everything. Visitors were too valuable to electrocute!

When the men left, the power everywhere was on, the hook-ups working. That promise to caravanners had been kept! Every light in the house was tried - the gas cooker removed and replaced, the shop's new deep freeze switched on and tested, then as if in celebration, the year's second caravan drove across the bridge.

It was slightly disappointing to find this arriving couple not wanting electric. Jan asked them the following day if everything was satisfactory, hoping for some compliment, but they made no comments, not mentioning the new shaver points or the brighter toilet building lights at night.

Washing machines and dryers were still awaited, their arrival delayed but promised soon. The deal agreed was supply, installation and a one year guarantee. At £700 per washing machine and nearly £1000 for each dryer, nothing was being accepted unless it worked perfectly! Once they arrived, fitting should be easy - the plumbing already prepared, including three stainless steel sinks for hand washing.

A week later the equipment rolled up on a lorry, complete with a mechanic and his assistant. As the washing machines were eased into position and connected up, an armful of old working clothes shoved quickly in, provided an immediate test of efficiency.

Attention turned to the dryers. The first of these big machines was heaved from the lorry and lowered gingerly towards the ground, but slipped - descended the last few inches with a clang. The foreman hopped about a bit on one foot cursing with words mild enough not to upset a lady.

Watching the unloading, Jan had stepped angrily towards the dropped dryer, worried about damaged, but her attention now swung to the man, concern in her face. "Is it serious?"

Hoping on one leg, he reached the laundrette wall and leaned against it. "Give me a minute." The foot was lowered gingerly to the stony surface, lifted again with a wince and the man slid downwards to sit on the ground his back still against the wall.

Gordon smiled to himself, turning away from the performance and back towards the dryer. It didn't appear to be damaged but noticing the width, he glanced doubtfully towards the door, then back to the figure on the ground.

"You sure it will go through?"

The man rose surprisingly quickly, looked from dryer to door and back several times. Taking a quick step before remembering to limp, he produced a tape and measured the dryer, hobbled to the door and measured again. Head coming up in exasperation, he drew in a deep breath, lips moving to utter something explosive, but remembering perhaps there was a lady present, stopped short, saying with a shrug, "It's too big. The door will have to come off."

The word that formed on the man's lips had been clear. Hoping Jan had not seen and understood, Gordon stepped forward, holding out a hand for the tape and measuring again both the opening and the smallest dimension of the dryers. Straightening, he turned to the delivery crew.

"Waste of time taking the door off; it's still an inch too big. This is a standard size external door - it was up to you to let me know a bigger opening was needed. I did consult you before the place was built."

They scratched their heads, looking from machine to doorway. Checking the measurements again then asking to use the phone, the mechanic ambled off with a shrug to ring his office. He wasn't limping any more.

Returning, his message was brief. "The boss is coming over, said to wait."

Jan produced coffee for everyone, but was no longer smiling. Having done her share of manual work during the building, the chance of a further delay with the site already open annoyed her. Removing the door might be acceptable, even amusing, but not being able to get it in at all was ridiculous!

The boss arrived half an hour later. Collecting the cups, she gave him a dirty look. He turned away, produced a tape, moved to the door and measured every which way - no good. The workmen looking on, said nothing, just watched. It made him nervous. He went off round the side, his head reappearing a few seconds later.

"We can take that window out, it goes through there nicely."

"Who," Gordon asked, "is going to put it back again?"

"Well I thought perhaps if we get the dryers in, you could..."

"No. And it needs doing today! I'm not paying £2000 for dryers, then having rain drive in and destroy the electronics."

"OK. I know a chap who will do it this evening," the boss conceded with a shrug. He had tried but too much was at stake to argue.

Once the glass was out the four males worked together, lifting the heavy dryers through the shoulder high opening, having first put some timber and a thick cloth around the bottom frame so the drier could rest there when required. As the first machine was gingerly eased up and rested on the sill, two workmen dashed round to take the weight from inside.

Eventually, with both machines connected and working, the boss shook hands then departed. His mechanics in their truck followed behind, everyone pleased with the outcome.

Left alone, the two site owners looked proudly over the glossy new equipment.

"So this is what ran our funds down so much. And you say women like to spend!"

"We're still solvent - just about. Been an expensive year though; that cash we saved by paying the Electricity Board in instalments, it's almost gone."

True to his word the glazier turned up an hour later refixing the glass, leaving the putty to be re-painted after it properly hardened. Standing watching the man depart, Jan was thankful for an active afternoon, the bizarre method of installation holding her attention. Today was special for a less pleasing reason - Steve's last night sleeping in the house. From tomorrow he was no longer a young man drifting in search of a career; tomorrow he was a British soldier! A touch of pride brought a small smile as she gazed along the river, a smile that also held sadness. The last of her children, the babies she had once held so close... she swallowed, pushing the thought aside.

Later, as the three sat down to eat, she spoke with a flourish, a forced heartiness, wanting to make her son's last tea a happy one.

"The laundry equipment arrived today, the dryers were too big, they wouldn't go through the doorway."

Steve looked up, mildly interested but perhaps with half his mind elsewhere. "What did you do?"

"Sent for the boss. They took a window out and hoisted the machines through. Dad was helping, I just watched to see they did it right." Seeing Steve nod and look down, Jan tried again. "The foreman dropped one on his toe. Skipped about a bit and swore!"

Steve's head came up, real interest now in his face, turning to his father for confirmation.

"Yes, but they were very mild cuss words." Dad's comment was addressed to nobody in particular, but it was Jan who replied sharply.

"A man shouldn't swear at all in a lady's presence!"

Steve and Gordon looked at each other, smiles breaking out on both faces.

Quick to realise the significance, she drew herself up with a show of indignation, then seeing the smiles broaden, reached down for a slipper and threw it at Dad. "Don't be insulting!"

Dodging the missile, Gordon spoke to Steve. "I'll tell you why his language was so mild. When the dryer was being unloaded, Mum was watching closely. Both the workmen knew her concern was not for them but for the machine, in case it was scratched. She looked daggers when they fumbled letting it slip, but it didn't fall on his toe - missed by a mile. He danced around with Oohs and Ahs, then sank back against the laundrette wall. That was some distance from where the dryer now stood and it drew Mum's eyes in a new direction, making her forget about the damage. Women are so easily taken in."

Steve nodded agreement, both men laughing.

Jan, exasperated at the revelation but happy that this last tea was turning out so well, reached down for the other slipper and telegraphing the intent, threw it again at Gordon before joining in the laughter herself.

In the morning, Steve loaded his duffel bag into the car, gave his mother a farewell hug, and drove off with Dad to Penzance. The train stood waiting but its departure time wanted another ten minutes - a feature of end-of-line stations. Father a son stood talking briefly on the platform, then with no more than a clasp of the hand, Steve was gone, lost to sight in a crowded carriage.

Only at Easter with the return of several old faces, were the new facilities really noticed. Exactly a dozen units graced the valley, eight of them caravans but more to the point, four wanted electric hook-ups. The hair dryers in the laundrette were popular too, compliments flowing.

"You know what is best of all?" One woman asked. "You don't have to fiddle with coins and wonder when it will run out."

That was true enough, the iron, the hot water, the hairdryers; all were free - only the washing machines and tumble dryers had coinboxes and those found little use, hardly any coins entering the slots. Never mind, Easter was a short holiday, few clothes would need washing. That could easily change in summer.

With everything safely completed, the time had come to relax a little, to lay back in an armchair and argue over trivial tasks, like whose turn it was to sharpen the telephone box pencil and replace the scribbling paper. The pencil and paper idea had come in a previous year. A small piece of wood with a pencil sized hole in the top had been fixed to the wooden back-plate on which the telephone instructions were mounted. The pencil had remained there all season. The paper was just small pieces, about eight cut from a single foolscap sheet, each with a hole punched in the top and hung on a small nail near the pencil. Simple but effective, people liked it. Not that too many visitors were staying at the moment but as May approached, trade began to pick up.

Three ducks were sitting early, their shed getting messy - not due to these nesting ducks but to others who also spent the night inside and as ducks will, made continual droppings. The broody ducks themselves made no mess, bottling up their waste matter for a full twenty-four hours until they left the nest, dashing off to drop it at some distant point, a natural trait evolved over past ages to prevent predators being attracted by the smell. Usually these sitting ducks headed straight for the river and with a great burst released their load, the water around them turning dark and muddy. Some unfortunately, came round the house instead of going directly to the stream. Then, more often than not, a sizeable pool of evil smelling fluid would be deposited near the office door! This dropping had the consistency of runny tomato ketchup, but darker and very much more potent! It just *had* to be washed away, the smell truly obnoxious.

One problem of having several ducks incubating eggs was a tendency for each to leave the nest at a different time, so no period occurred in which the shed was empty and could be cleaned without upsetting the other sitters. What to do? The answer was simple; wait until one duck left for its morning wash and feed, then lift the others from their nests and carry them one at a time down to the river, leaving the shed empty for a quick clean up.

That morning Jan had been keeping an eye from the kitchen window, and gave a shout when the first duck appeared. Gordon, abandoning work near the laundrette, ran round to the shed. Leaving a shovel ready outside, he entered, gently picked a sitting duck off her nest and remembering how potent and explosive their droppings could be, took care to aim its bottom end to one side.

Striding round the corner of the house and on towards the river, he heard an urgent call from the kitchen window behind.

"Yes?" He looked over one shoulder, attention diverted, body turning, forgetting the bird in his hands as he twisted to see what was wanted. Maybe the duck had a sense of humour, just waiting for this opportunity, or perhaps the tail feathers brushing his chest triggered some hidden release mechanism - whatever the cause the duck chose that very moment to let go her entire load. Whoosh! Some flew up over the collar, dripping down inside, the jet's force spreading a thick viscous fluid around shoulders, under armpits, along the arms and thickly covering the chest region - from where it ran slowly downward over shirt and trousers. And it smelt! How it smelt!

Putting the duck carefully on the grass, he watched it waddle the few final steps to plunge in the river and wondered momentarily whether to join it. "Wretched creature," the thought came involuntarily with a smile, for he knew it to be his own fault. Turning to Jan at the window and revealing the full extent of the damage, he asked, "What did you want?"

"To warn you to be careful how you held that duck!" she was laughing.

He took a couple of paces forward.

"Don't you dare come indoors like that!" The window closed, leaving only a narrow opening, a voice shouting through the gap, "Wait by the patio!"

As he walked stiff legged across the grass, Jan dashed from the office door, grabbed the hose, turned the tap full on and making a big point of holding her nose with one hand, blasted the water straight at him. There was nothing to do but stand still and take the full force, and an unnecessarily thorough job she was making. In the valley, water pressure was high - normally an advantage!

"That's enou..." a jet aimed straight at the face cut the words short. Swallowing and lifting both hands defensively, he tried again, "That's enough!"

But she was enjoying herself, smiling broadly and taking full advantage of the rare situation. The jet continued to blast, switching to his right armpit under those defensively raised hands. Seeing him prepare to rush forward, she retreated rapidly towards the tap, whipping the hose away, "You're clean! Let it drip before you go inside."

May was pleasant, virtually all the visitors were retired couples, people themselves content with life and making few demands of any site owner; long warm days, trade slack enough to be easy - that would change drastically as the season matured! Of ten caravans widely spread in the valley, three had electric connections. Now these were available, an application had been made to join that special group of parks known as *'The Best of British'*.

People were happy in other respects too, meeting and chatting at new washing up sinks outside the laundrette, conversation showing they did indeed prefer them in the open air. The washing machines were now being used, as emptying the coin boxes showed, but one dryer had gone wrong.

"A thousand pounds and it doesn't work," Jan chatted as she walked across with a visitor who reported the fault. Careful inspection and reading the instructions yielded no clues. Never mind, better now at this peaceful time than in mid-season - the other machine was working well and both were under guarantee.

"It's the motor," a mechanic pronounced, having driven up in a service van and spent some time probing this and that. "Have to order a replacement."

A week and several phone calls later, no motor had materialised. Gordon lifted the receiver again, this time asking for the boss. "Look. It doesn't work. If you can't repair the thing, then replace it with a new one!"

"We can't. There isn't another in the country, at least not one that's any good to you becau..." The voice stopped, cut off by some terse, not very polite remarks as pent-up feelings surfaced. Peaceful time of year or not, things never stayed out of order at River Valley!

The voice on the line tried to explain. "Laundrettes normally work off three phase electric - all the spare motors are three phase. We're getting a single phase one shipped over from Sweden. I'd like to help but there's nothing we can do until it comes." The man paused, then added quietly, "Could be two months."

"Two months! That's very nearly the school holidays!"

As this exclamation exploded, a head poked round

the doorway, listening.

A few further angry words achieved nothing. Seeing the phone put down, Jan entered the room and hearing an account of the conversation, protested. "They claim to be a British firm. Why must the parts come from Sweden, and why so long? Ring the manufacturers."

"People on the phone pass the buck - a letter will be better."

Despite the time of year, any feeling of being at ease with the world had now departed. Consulting various booklets yielded an address. The letter set the case out briefly but clearly, stressing how they now bitterly regretted putting faith in the company. It was labelled 'Personal' and addressed to the managing director. Hurrying to catch the evening post, dropping that letter into the box did much to ease the pent-up anger.

Two days later a call from a very senior manager in this great company brought a profuse apology. One got the impression that someone had just stuck a rocket in a tender position and lit the blue touch paper.

"So sorry, a temporary problem," the voice claimed. "Not to worry, a motor was being flow in on a special flight - to be installed this very week."

Phew! That's service - the success toasted in cooking sherry, the only spirit in the house apart from Jim's whisky.

***

"Another one," Jan murmured to herself, watching the departing car. A surprising feature of late June was the number of people seeking an electric hook-up; the growth of demand sudden enough to catch many sites by surprise. Timing had been impeccable - people were touring the area, stopping at the office to ask one question, "Do you have a spare hook-up?" When the answer was yes, they insisted on paying for a pitch before driving off to reappear later towing a caravan. Trade had increased, fresh faces arriving just because of this facility. Life was becoming quite hectic considering school holidays were several weeks away.

Jim still helped occasionally - now with an improved

form of transportation, a disabled person's electric car, an export model capable of eight miles per hour. A numberplate fitted on the front read, *'Gramp one'*. Although not able to stay long with his worsening leg, he could now ride down from the bungalow more quickly in a crisis.

At this time of year Jan had no need of needlework. Halfway through her second big tablecloth she merely said, "It will keep." For Gordon too, hobbies were out. The Spectrum computer now ran on mains electric; a bigger machine must wait until autumn - time then to write a new program. For the moment, at the end of each day they wanted nothing better than to relax in an armchair with a book, or watch a short TV program, both of which were regularly interrupted by the telephone. Sometime before eleven a final walk round, the evening patrol, still checked that all was well - then to bed. They slept soundly.

Running the site without help was harder, no denying that. It brought home just how much the children had done. Nowadays of course, some liberal minded, politically correct idiot would try to stop it - say youngsters were not allowed to work because it's bad for them - nonsense, it sets them up for life!

The alarm still went off at six each morning, just time to rise, dress quickly and dash out, cleaning the toilets before many people woke, returning about seven. A host of small chores required attention before the shop opened at 8.15, but first breakfast - there would be no time to eat later. Probably even that early meal would be interrupted, some lady wanting a pint of milk or a chap asking for gas, and this year an extra chore became common - people tripping their electric. It was normal enough; equipment not used for some time became damp, causing a short. Ice packs too, were now changed in the shop, not by Audrey down at the bungalow.

With these rising demands there were hardly enough hands to cope, tempers tending to fray at times. For the most part however, they enjoyed the hustle and bustle, knowing the duration would be short. They enjoyed too, the money flowing in, lots of it, the new hook-ups boosting returns, finances no longer tight. They could afford now, to have help; it had been discussed once or twice, particularly one evening after a hectic Saturday. Earlier that morning someone had triggered their electrics for the third time, a line of caravans waited in the yard, a queue of people at the shop and half the morning newspapers had not arrived.

Next year might be even busier now the site's application to become a Best of British member had been accepted. Being invited to join this group of high class caravan parks was a landmark. River Valley was now in great company, including many top parks all over the country, and would be in the group's glossy brochure next year - an honour they intended to live up to.

CHAPTER 13

Grounded

Even as the peak season approached, rare unexpected lulls gave odd moments to throw oneself into an armchair, blow out a long sigh, and relax - collapse might be a better word. Such respites seldom lasted long! Evenings, after seven when the shop finally closed were quieter but people knocked at the door for advice or for something they had forgotten, or to book extra nights, a few late arrivals drawing up - and still the odd crisis occurring.

"Come on," Jan pressed the switch on the answerphone. "I've been cooped up in the office and shop all day. Let's walk round."

With a sigh, Gordon rose from the chair into which he had fallen only minutes before, but he was happy enough, strolling round looking at the site was one of life's pleasures, but that had been easier when the children were home.

As they left, a notice stuck on the door read, *'Back in ten minutes'*.

The walk was pleasant, an ambling pace, seeing with some pride the colourful array of caravans and tents, all with a good space between and surrounded by short grass, slightly browning in the sun. In a few places individual pitches with trees around were available, but caravanners seemed to prefer an open area for the company it gave - liked to see their neighbours, had chosen this form of holiday deliberately to meet new friends. One elderly couple put the feeling well, "We get enough isolation at home, could have stayed in our own back garden if we wanted that." Chatting briefly to other guests delayed the walk, causing a hurried return along the riverbank towards the house, uncertain what minor crisis might await them.

Near the bridge visitors were strolling around, plenty of people, but nobody waiting at the office - a relief and perhaps a touch disappointing? Pulling off the 'ten minute' notice that had been well exceeded, a gull on the grass in front of the house caught the attention. It sat hunched over, the posture uncharacteristic; disinclined to fly off in spite of nearby activity. People were passing quite close, some to inspect the waterwheel, others feeding ducks and trout off the bridge or looking at the notice board in front of the shop, or generally just sauntering past chatting together. Closer inspection revealed the gull's beak, one leg and part of a wing were tightly wrapped with fishing line. When approached it made off in a series of minor jumps with one wing outstretched. Fetching a long handled net used for rescuing ducklings that washed over the weir, Gordon caught the bird, discarded the net and walked over to sit by the office door. No way could it have eaten recently with the line wound round so tightly.

Passing over a pair of scissors, Jan sat beside him on the sun-warmed step, reaching over to hold the bird so his hands were free. The warmth of her thigh and the pleasant closeness of her body stopped him momentarily and he laid a palm across her hand. They touched a lot, sometimes from necessity but more often for no reason, just part of a way of life.

As he snipped the first pieces of line, her hands calmed and soothed the poor trussed up patient, a small crowd gathering to watch. Working carefully more line was gradually removed, yards of it, at one place complete with brass swivel. Sea line at a guess; thicker than anyone would use on the river, all tangled with feathers and difficult to dislodge. Bit by bit it unravelled. With the beak free, the gull pecked at his rescuers' hands, though no longer finding power enough to draw blood. A motorcaravan had drawn up, the couple seeming content to wait. As no one had fish, they climbed back into their vehicle, producing some ham. Pulled off pieces were quickly devoured, together with other small items that various children raced to nearby caravans to fetch. With appetite sated, a few slow steps to kneel at the river's edge and the gull was lowered in; it floated, drinking thirstily and in a few minutes flew away, obviously pleased to be free. The eyes of everyone followed its flight, smiles of satisfaction and pleasure all round. Most people are naturally sympathetic, even sentimental about animals of all types and particularly about birds; something that hopefully will never change.

"Lucky bird," Jan murmured as it disappeared. "Three weeks later and we'd have been too rushed to notice. Sharon's due home tomorrow."

Those three weeks still remaining before the school holidays might be the lull before the storm, but they were busy enough. Steve had been in the army, the Royal Electrical and Mechanical Engineers, for more than eight weeks undergoing initial training; square-bashing to those who have experienced it. His passing-out parade was due. It had looked impractical for both parents to attend, even with Sharon coming home for the weekend and Jim's limited assistance. What made it possible was that Audrey could help too, now that caravanners' ice packs were frozen in the shop rather than at her bungalow.

Rising in darkness at four o'clock the following morning, Gordon and Jan drove the 200-miles to attend. A smart body of young men marching across the parade ground recalled earlier times a generation ago, the military band, the straight arms swinging, every motion sharply in unison; proud moments, proud memories! Jan felt it too, though she had no such personal experience, her pride rising higher when Steve stepped smartly towards the rostrum to be presented with a silver cup for best shot, a feat entitling him to wear the crossed rifles emblem on his tunic sleeve. His main interest however was the training in mechanics he would receive over the next few years. All types of machine were included - tanks and their enormous transporters right down to the light vehicles of airborne divisions, the jeeps that would drop by parachute - and their mechanics must parachute with them! Working with engines was the career he planned to follow in civilian life too, if he should at some future date leave the army. The meeting after the parade proved great but early afternoon saw the homeward journey underway.

Ten days later, just before the school holiday rush started, another big day arrived. With Steve home on leave before his first posting, Sharon's turn came for distinction, the graduation ceremony at Exeter for her honours degree in Chemistry. Leaving Audrey and Jim to help Steve with the site, Gordon and Jan sneaked another day off to attend this once in a lifetime ceremony. Sharon looked impressive in a black gown and mortar board, with a blue silk V-shaped trimming at the neck.

"Our children aren't doing too bad," Jan glanced sideways then back, concentrating on the road ahead, moving out to overtake a slower car as they drove homewards. "Chris says he never wants promotion, in case it means more desk work."

Sitting in the passenger seat wondering what might go wrong at home in their absence, Gordon pulled his mind back to the present. It was true Chris enjoyed the street work, but those views on promotion could change. About to comment, he noticed the car they were overtaking had three children in the back seat; it triggered another line of thought. Children would arrive in droves next week.

As expected, Saturday hit like a minor hurricane! Sharon, managing on her own in the shop worked at full stretch most of the morning. Although now considering herself too mature for schoolboys, she smiled warmly at one or two lads in their late teens - turning a touch bossy when smaller children dithered over the choice of ice creams. The new fridges with frozen food and for ice packs added to the work but it was still newspapers that gave most trouble, people disappointed when their favourite title ran out - impossible to avoid, so difficult to anticipate how many of each title would be needed. Other things were selling well too; the postcards, a few pennants with the duck motif, and this year little plastic plaques, triangular in shape and just a few inches across with the site name and year printed on - people collected them to show where they had been. Sharon saw a whole display one evening inside a friend's caravan, all stuck to the cupboard doors.

Keeping people happy during the school holidays must naturally involve the younger generations. Of all the days of the week, Tuesday was probably the slackest - if any day could be called slack at this time of the year. For this reason Tuesday was chosen for a special purpose, an hour each week set aside as an identification morning for the children. They could bring to the office any flower, leaf or other item of nature, for Gordon to identify. No conditions were set other than a stated preference for specimens from the valley. He had been caught too often by plants from elsewhere, particularly Cornwall's coastal flora, salt in the air changing the form of species growing on cliff edges.

The percentage of children bringing in samples was not so great; less young people these days seeming interested in such things. Maybe a dozen would arrive, a few parents standing in the background. Most species from the valley could be recognised straight away, the name scrawled on a sticky label and placed round the plant's stem. Some specimens were shown under the microscope, the inside of a little purple wild violet was surprisingly pretty when magnified. Strangely enough the thing which most caught their imagination under high magnification was not a flower at all, but a piece of paper torn from a glossy magazine. Asked to name the colour, the answer was clear.

"Brown," young voices agreed in ragged unison.

"Are you sure?"

"Yes." They all looked again. "Yes," they were quite certain it was brown.

Each in turn peered through the microscope. Several, having looked through the eye piece, stared down onto the slide table under the lens thinking themselves cheated, believing that something else had been spirited there by sleight of hand - but no, it was still the original small piece of 'brown' paper. What they saw through the eye piece was not brown, but hundreds of small dots of many different colours, each dot too small to distinguish with the naked eye. Looked at without magnification the dots merged into a plain brown mass. It had nothing whatever to do with nature but certainly caught the youngsters interest, teaching them perhaps not to think that everything is just as it first appears.

A young girl moved forward, little fist rising, offering a small tightly clenched bunch. Taking the flowers, Gordon separated them, laying each in a line across the desk, the other children crowding round. It was best to say something about a plant, not only the name but what it was like in bud, how common it was, what sort of habitat it favoured or what insects might be attracted to it. At times only a leaf was offered, mostly by boys whose motive was more to score a point than to learn, but a description of the flower that would later appear roused their interest - they would check in the hope of proving him wrong, and in the process might always remember the plant.

Gordon picked up one of the samples, holding it out for the children to inspect, aware three adults in the background were obviously listening too; probably some were enthusiasts, much more expert than he was himself, the valley attracted such people.

"This is campion, our most widespread flower. I expect several of you have it?" Little faces looked down at cuttings in their hands, extracting and holding out a sprig of the flower. Only one young girl failed to produce a sample, hunting through her collection as the other children looked on.

Finding a host young eyes watching her, she shrugged nervously and chin rising, said with a touch of disdain, "I didn't collect any, they're too common."

Gordon leaned towards her, "Your name isn't Sharon, is it."

"No, it's Lily."

"Oh... well let's all look at this one a moment. There's something special about it." Attention swung back as he pointed. "See this small hole in the sepals... Um.. sepals are like petals but they come below and are usually green. In campion they all join up to form this little tube." He had seen the puzzled expressions at the word and tried to explain, then gave them time to look before leaning closer to whisper, "It's burglary really." Little eyes widened. Now he had their attention!

"Robber bees use these holes to steal the nectar. You see, many insects like sweet sugary liquids - you do too, I expect?" Smiles and nods confirmed this to be so. "Well the reason a plant offers nectar is to get its pollen to other flowers. When an insect takes nectar from the top, the yellow powder sticks to its body and is taken on to the next bloom. It's a fair exchange, the insect gets food and the flower gets its pollen spread. But..." he paused, leaning closer, showing again the base of the flower "when some bees reach the nectar through this hole instead of from the top, they don't carry any pollen, so it's cheating."

One of the other children picked up his piece of campion, holding it out proudly for everyone to see. Below the pink petals, another hole was clearly visible in the reddish green sepals. The three adults had come forward to stand close behind, peering with the children at this curiosity.

Another child offered a moth, something so numerous in the valley that only the common ones could be remembered. South's *Moths of the British Isles*, invariable provided an answer. One little lad lit up in a great grin when a spider he brought in a matchbox could not be identified; the other children looked at him in envy. With all the samples named, the session finished as it usually did, with a competition to identify the bird carvings on the tree behind the desk. These little meetings seldom passed without the phone ringing or someone coming to the office, but for the most part such interruptions were fended off, new arrivals shown to a pitch and asked book in later.

One woman came to the office door and seeing the group

inside, turned to leave. Jan hovering in the background, trying to deal with anything that came up, stepped outside and called after her. Coming back, the woman cast an eye at the still open door and the people inside, then moved closer to ask in a whisper, "Where have all the flies come from this year? We want the windows open but they keep coming in. There's even some in the toilets."

"Sorry, just a bad year for some reason. The hot weather perhaps - we've never had many before." Keeping her voice low and moving a few paces farther from the room full of people, Jan pointed at an adjoining door, "We've something in the shop that could help." Leading the way, she smiled, remembering.

The unusual insect numbers were only noticed recently but Gordon had taken immediate advantage, buying some fly-spray. Arriving home he with a case holding twelve cans, and protesting it was just to help customers, he had said defensively "Only fifty percent," when questioned about the mark-up, adding hurriedly, "We might get left with some."

The fly-spray did indeed sell slowly, nobody else even mentioned flies, no more tins purchased that week, but frosties, crisps, some sweets, chocolate, tinned salmon and other salad stuff were running down, sending Jan on a quick trip to Cash and Carry. This left Sharon managing the shop, though she had warned her services would only be available for part of the holiday. Gordon, dealing single handed with the office, rushed to and fro pitching a tent then sprinting back to sign-in the next caravan; the electric hook-ups nearly all in use. Keeping up was difficult, not unexpected but the pressure rising. At mid-morning two motorcaravans arrived together, a tent crossing the bridge shortly after. Another visiting couple wandered over to the office, a little queue forming, six people standing waiting while the first couple booked in, asking the cost and other details. Answering these questions, Gordon gave a silent sigh of relief as Jan appeared in the doorway, her arms fully loaded - and at that moment the phone rang.

With a murmur of apology to the queue, his hand reached out to lift the receiver. "River Vall..." he stopped, freezing in mid-sentence, feeling the hairs rise on the back of his neck as a female voice purred a lewd invitation, little giggles clearly audible in the background - the softly obscene entreaty so embarrassingly out of place in a room filled with people. For a moment he could say nothing, paralysed by a suggestion the like of which he had never expected to hear. "Pardon!" The word came in a gasp, aware that Jan had stopped in mid-stride, she and everyone else in the office watching him. The seductive young voice repeated her request, accompanied by more background giggles. He swallowed, feeling his own cheeks burning and sure it must show, struggled for a casual reply, managing only to gulp, "No thank you," dropping the receiver like it was hot, the hand withdrawing to rub automatically against his shirt, swallowing again then looking up to see every face in the room staring at him. "I... er," he turned to the nearest couple, "Two nights you said?"

The queue took time to clear, time in which to recover his composure, but with the last visitors safely pitched, Jan was waiting on his return to the empty office.

"Well, what got you into such a stew?"

"Stew?" Pretending not to understand he strode to the window, looking out at the ducks on the river.

"That phone call - you don't suddenly seize-up and go beetroot without reason. What happened?"

Turning he looked at her, his expression part smile part grimace, then signalled to two adjoining chairs and sank back before speaking. "It's not often a chap gets improper suggestions by phone from a young girl; a group of them I think."

The words were spoken quietly so Sharon in the shop should not hear. Jan shook her head, "Improper suggestion? Who were they?"

"She, not they. Others were there mind you; giggles in the background, but only the one voice spoke... teenage girl I think."

"Oh? You can tell, just like that, just by the voice. Expert on teenage girls are we? What did she say?!"

"I, er... she wanted me to put something hot into something quivering - had all the right medical terms too."

"Something hot..." Jan paused, realisation dawning. "What took you so long to say 'No'; thinking of having her call back later were you?" A pointing finger prodded, but the grin could not be concealed. "I bet they rang from our own phone box just round the corner. How far would you run if she issued that invitation in person!"

Though the site always had *some* empty pitches, the most favoured areas were often full and so it could be critical on any particular day, who moved first - those arriving or those due to leave. With this in mind, a departure time of eleven a.m. was requested during the school holidays, this ruling interpreted liberally, particularly with regular customers.

"Can we pay for another day," one couple called at the office as eleven o'clock approached. "We want to travel later."

"Our leaving time is just for guidance, I never even go round checking until after lunch. How much later?"

"We thought about midnight. Traffic is better."

"On the children's field aren't you?" Gordon pointed through the window.

"Yes, our two are playing with some other children by the river. They'll sleep on the journey home."

"Suppose we compromise. I'll charge you half rate, and in return you leave by ten o'clock - save waking other children? Half a day is our standard charge for leaving in the evening."

The time was agreed, money taken and they left the office.

"Were they happy?" Jan's head appeared round the doorway.

"Very. Happier than I am, anyway. That last tooth I had out back in the spring, there's a piece of bone working its way up through the gum. Can't stop touching it with my tongue - the end's getting sore."

"Ring Don, get it pulled out."

Don, a great dentist and their friend for many years, said to come in the morning. He worked unusual hours, starting very early and sometimes taking the afternoons off to go sailing - had a wonderful technique with a hammer and chisel - maybe those were not the right names for the tools but whatever they were called, it brought a tooth out clean and easy. On this occasion, no such drastic treatment was required; he prodded around with a metal probe, located the sharp slither and reached for the appropriate tool, asking, "Any other problems."

"No, bit sensitive one or two. I swill ice cold water round my mouth when I'm cleaning them. I figure those teeth are saying to themselves, *'damn that's painful, better grow some more enamel quick!'*"

"Masochist. It should work but normal people just use Sensodyne. Open wide."

The shard was gone in a second, Gordon asking, "How come you missed that bit?"

"We can't take all the bone out."

"Why not?"

"Patients would fall to pieces."

As the school holidays passed, so visitor numbers declined - a chance to recover! Trouble had started with the Parish Council over the fence along the riverbank footpath, but otherwise life settled to a slower more casual pace, with thoughts turning to improvements that might be undertaken this autumn. Following the jolt of nearly being caught out over electric hook-ups, they were determined not to be taken unawares again. Chatting to campers and caravanners during the season had revealed that some sites now provided a special cubicle with not only a WC, but a wash basin and a sanitary bin; comfort for those times when a lady was indisposed.

When numbers fell further and the third toilet building

closed, converting three toilet cubicles into two larger ones provided space for these extra facilities. Making an inspection when work was complete, Jan tried a hot tap at the small new wash basins, murmuring "Fine," then noticed a shelf fixed alongside. "That's a good idea."

"Thanks, anything for a lady's convenience. Ouch!"

Late autumn saw a similar arrangement added in the other Ladies toilets. Fortunately, the end compartment in these buildings was already bigger, making the job quick and quiet, done in early afternoon when visitors were out. Even so one lady entered, saw him and took a backward step, hurriedly pulling the outer door open again to check the sign. Apologising, Gordon left, saying it was time for coffee anyway - he was usually the more worried under these circumstances! As he told Jan afterwards, "Handsome young chaps can't be too careful."

"Where? Where?" She looked round, peering behind the door, then out of the window. "I can't see any!"

***

"Ah." A little convulsion jerked her body. A young wife lay tense in the darkness, wondering what had brought her so suddenly awake. She knew her eyes were open, but in the black silence there was nothing, not a wisp of an outline or a whisper of sound. So what had woken her - a noise from outside perhaps? Other tents were scattered over the valley floor, not too many now - September had brought an Indian summer of calm clear warm days but the nights were cool. Pulling the cover closer, she swallowed and easing herself to a better position, listened intently... something to her right moved, a small grunt then the faint sound of breathing.

Ah, that was Harry, her husband stirring in his sleep, but something still felt wrong. For a while she lay there, apprehensive; a tent in the middle of a field was not much protection, not like being at home with the strength of walls around. True there were others in the valley but not very close, the nearest tent perhaps a hundred feet away. Some paper rustled to her left! "A young rabbit?" The thought was comforting, they had watched some playing at dusk that

256

evening, surprised such furry little babies were born so late in the season.

She waited listening, but hearing no further sound wondered had it been imagination? Reaching to feel the ground gingerly took a little courage, a tentative sweep of the arm finding only the plastic groundsheet. Stretching farther, her hand touched a smooth but somehow knobbly half round stone. Something soft and fluffy had been expected; as exploring fingers tried to place the shape, it moved! The arm withdrew on impulse, freezing, still outstretched above the unknown object, intrigued but unsure, somehow unable to decide... Recovering she swung to the right, shaking the sleeping figure with an urgent whisper.

"Harry! There's something alive in the tent."

"Not me." With a sleepy grunt he slumped back on the pillow.

She shook again at the unresponsive form, "Wake up! It moved when I touched it. Good job I'm not squeamish."

Reluctantly Harry rose, felt around for the torch, stumbled, knelt on the other bed and aimed the beam downward. A tortoise blinked in the yellow light, its head disappearing. Moving closer an inscription on the shell read, 'Ennys cottage'. They offered some milk, not sure any was actually drunk but it went to sleep in a corner of the tent.

Next day it was still there, no head reappearing from the shell. Nor did it move as they left for a morning shower or during breakfast. Later the lady walked across to the shop and finding Jan and three people talking at the counter, she enquired if anyone had lost a tortoise. No one had, but the question and circumstances aroused interests that demanded explanation. As the story unfolded in great detail, Gordon left the office, walking quietly to stand listening in the shop doorway. Before mid-morning the small creature had been carefully returned to its proper home.

***

A shout rang anxiously out above the engine noise. "No, not up on end, the other way so I can roll it."

A lorry stood in the yard, its on-board crane unloading

a large wooden drum of electric cable. Four more drums already rested on the tarmac; this was the biggest, the cable nearly as thick as a wrist, over 100 metres of it, sufficient to reach a substation farther downstream - and costing a four figure sum! The large size should prevent voltage drop, so visitors' televisions worked properly. Cheaper to spend the money now and do the job right!

Only two caravans remained, Autumn well advanced, leaves falling, sycamore branches bare against a blue sky contrasting with the super golden brown of late October oaks. A small extra length of road had already been laid to give a turning point at the site's downstream end, and more stakes galvanised in preparation for the next batch of electric hook-ups. As the lorry manoeuvred round driving off across the bridge, two figures struggled to roll the massive drum to a suitable starting point. Reaching the desired spot, they rested a moment.

"A good husband would manage by himself," Jan suggested, breathing heavily and resting against a tree while Gordon unlashed a cord, letting the free end fall to the ground.

"Okay, I will. You stand on the cable end while I unwind the first length," He leant against the drum, heaving slowly forward. The cable started to unwind but almost immediately Jan slipped, overbalancing to stagger a few steps as it dragged along the road.

"Why are you laughing? I couldn't help it; the damn thing keeps movi..." pausing in annoyance, she demanded again, "What are you laughing at?"

"Of course it keeps moving. Er, I did warn you didn't I?"

"Did you hell!" A smile hovering, she stepped forward with one straight finger extending to prod. "Why?"

"I think you're wonderful." He jumped smartly back out of reach.

Jan's smile blossomed at the compliment though she well understood the implication - dumb blondes, it applied to brunettes as well - wonderful meant not only good-looking but dim, a standing joke between them. Pointing to the cable, she demanded again, "Why?"

"I thought you'd realise. Unless a drum is full, it naturally does that. The rim circumference is greater than each loop of cable - so it must drag."

She watched him roll the drum on, then draw to a stop and signal for help.

"We need to turn it round. Roll back the other way - it stops the same section dragging all along the road."

"Does it matter?"

"Might scrape the outer insulation off. I haven't paid this much for cable just to damage it. Once a good length is free we'll heave it a few feet sideways onto the grass. It will slide easier there, okay?"

Digging the trenches would start right away. There were rolls of thinner wire as well; it would take a good part of the winter to lay them all and reinstate the turf. This would bring the total pitches with electric to 130, not bad for late starters, and still with plenty of spare capacity in that thick cable if more were ever needed. However, getting the cable laid out on a flat surface was one thing, heaving it between trees and along the trench would be a different matter!

"I'll start after coffee," Gordon suggested as the now half empty drum came to rest. "Might finish by Christmas."

"Yes?" She looked sharply upwards as if something unexpected might fly by, something big and pink perhaps, her tone sceptical, knowing only to well his over optimism in estimating time.

Later that afternoon he found himself sweating in the weak October sunshine, swinging the pick with rhythmic vigour into hard ground, feeling drops of perspiration run down his face, dripping occasional off nose or chin, the discarded jacket hanging on a nearby bush. The cooler winter weather to come might not be such a bad thing after all. Basically he liked this kind of work, especially with no deadline - ample time for an hour or so now and then on a different task, the change easing muscles tired from continual digging. Many such diversions occurred naturally on a caravan park, arranging a variety of jobs not only easy, but inescapable.

"Phew!" He wiped his brow with a stained handkerchief, "Some folk pay at a gymnasium for a sweat not nearly as good as this."

Most of all, the enjoyment came from building or creating something good, something done in such a way that it would last. Even when they first arrived with their existence balanced on a knife edge, the best materials and building methods had always been used.

"Never build anything temporary," he addressed a chaffinch pecking among the excavated soil, but it flew off immediately. "Must have been a female," he thought defensively, knowing from the feathers that it was not. Laying the pick aside, he lifted the narrow spade to shovel out loosened soil, scraping a layer from the trench bottom in an attempt to keep it level - the action brought back another memory, a comment by a floorlayer about the toilet building. "Why bother so much? It's only toilets," the man had once said.

"Only toilets!" Gordon recalled his own explosive words. "How many people use your bathroom at home? Five maybe? Just you think of all the visitors using these toilets each day! Another thing, how many days of the week does your house get cleaned from top to bottom? My toilets will be cleaned twice *every* day - including Sundays! You say '*Only* toilets'. Nothing on a caravan park is more important!"

Tossing a final shovelful aside and reaching for the pick, he smiled, unsure now if the floorlayer had been pulling his leg, and looked round guiltily, checking if anyone were near enough to read his thoughts as he habitually read those of his bird companions. Blackbird and Robin had abandoned him temporarily. They searched the turf when removed and put to one side, but the ground now being dug was poor. Robin called once that day, flew up briefly while Gordon took a breather, leaning on the pick. The bird landed on a willow branch, cocked its head to one side and looked at the stony soil.

"Wasting your time there; worms only live in the top few inches." The message came clearly as he watched Robin fly off; imaging the bird's thoughts just a trick of idle brain cells needing something to occupy themselves. Eyes following the robin caught another movement; far away on a distant hill a red dot crawled across a tiny field - what did the tractor driver think about as he worked alone all day? Was he more sane or had he a dog in the cab to talk to? The scene along the valley was special, even now with the leaves falling.

"We are lucky to own this fantastic place." Fantastic, that was Chris's type of word. Fantastic but lonely. A new line of thought crept in as the pick swung again. Did they own it - or did it own them? Were they the valley's slaves? Men might come and go but the valley would always be there. How many slaves had it owned before? So far as was known, the first people arrived in Cornwall about the middle stone age, and like all early men they lived by hunting and gathering edible plants. Primitive people? How many today could find food from the wild vegetation around? The population density was lower of course in those early years, the people partly nomadic, moving on as an area became exhausted.

The pick hit another stone, a piece of quartz by the way it shattered. Was that a spark? Those earliest dwellers would have had one problem. Flint was uncommon in Cornwall. The fine grained crystal lattice of flint made a stone equally strong in all directions, making it possible to fashion spear heads and other tools. What must it have been like to live in those times; would this valley have been a favourable place? The swinging pick found a weak spot, sinking deep into softer ground. Was some ancient person buried here, by the stream? It could have been an ideal location; trout to supplement the diet and a climate warmer than the rest of the British Isles... No! It wasn't the British Isles then, nor England, not even the Celtic nation Cornwall later became. What language did they speak? Did they speak at all or just use signs?

"I could use signs. Leaning on a pick, wiping bare arm across damp brow... that would indicate I'm hot in any language." He paused, action matching thoughts.

With the warmer weather then, Cornwall should have provided easier living. Was that true? There was seldom any frost - that should make surviving winters easier, shouldn't it. Hm? Not necessarily. Hunters in frosty climates could kill extra animals in autumn, the frozen carcasses keeping until spring. You could never do that in Relubbus. Moreover, foliage dropped from trees here just as it did elsewhere; a little later to be sure, but it still dropped. No hawthorn or nettle leaves for winter vitamins, but fruit would keep. And fish were available all the year, and yes, salt for preserving - the coast only three miles away.

Salt had modern uses too; a visitor once claimed that in some parts of the country, stored caravans were kept dry in winter using salt to absorb condensation - who said that? Ah, Geoff and Sandra, the couple who rode a tandem.

By some 4000 years BC a less nomadic people, more skilled in the making of stone weapons, had settled at Carn Brea in the hills above Redruth. They were able to make primitive pottery. Did they visit River Valley?

Easing his shoulders, Gordon turned to estimate the distance dug that morning... fifty or sixty feet? Were those early people stronger and more muscular; would they have dug it quicker? At this thought the pick rose higher, thumping down with renewed vigour!

The bronze age, more than 2000 years BC, must have been good. Cornwall had the ingredients, the tin and the copper. Trade had started by that time, overland and by sea. Relics of the era were plentiful, stone burial chambers dotted the area, and stone circles like Stonehenge though not so large. Why did these early peoples place their settlements high up like Carn Brea? Think of the effort to carry supplies, fresh water, food, timber for burning; what advantage did it have? The natural one of course; defence! A hill top is favourite, especially with hand thrown spears. Did they too, dig trenches - as protection around their settlement?

"Need to be bigger than this one," Gordon stepped out and immediately back in, but with the left leg in front. As with all cable excavations this trench was narrow. Ten feet ahead the turf had not yet been removed; a job for the afternoon. The pick swung again as thoughts of the past returned.

The Romans, coming to England in the first and second centuries AD had not affect Celtic Cornwall as much as elsewhere, not spreading their domination in the same way in the far southwest. Finds of Romans coins however, told of trade with the conquerors. The pick swung again, striking stone; something sparkled, sunlight reflecting brightly from the loosened soil. The association of ideas and this sudden glitter made him lay the pick aside, stooping to lift... what? Oh, just another piece of Galena, hardly precious though it did contain small amounts of silver.

"Um, heavy for the size," he tossed the stone gently in one hand before putting it aside to take back to the office; visitors and especially the children were interested in such samples. Hearing a shout, he looked up to see Jan in the distance making eating motions. Lunch already? How time flew when enjoying yourself. Stepping once more from the trench, he collected the jacket still draped over a bush and made for the house.

Although trenching went easier with the mind fully occupied, muscles still felt the strain. Perhaps the shorter days were fortunate as November approached. Sharon, set on a career teaching and now working at Barnstaple as part of her training year, rang that evening speaking first to Dad, then chatting for some time to her mother. Eventually Jan put the phone down, turning back to the final stages of a large embroidered tablecloth.

"What," she wondered, "shall I start on next? Something different, a tapestry perhaps, a small one for a cushion or footstool."

Evenings were companionable; though the children had all left, they often rang or came back for a holiday at intervals.

One thing could be relied on in Cornwall, people would always want to visit. Happy in their own company, the two site owners often preferred to stay in, showing an interest in each others hobbies, watching a little television or just talking. They laughed a lot, private jokes, not necessarily very funny, just liking to laugh together. Watching Jan pick up a book, Gordon thought, "I suppose I deliberately try to make her laugh. She's beautiful then... her mouth, her eyes, I don't know?"

***

"Down to one now." Jan waved goodbye as a caravan headed towards the bridge. The remaining couple were bird-watchers with a motorcaravan; the man very knowledgeable on this subject. They too stood waving as their friends departed; a friendship formed during the holiday. Turning away as the car disappeared, the man saw Jan at the window and raised a hand in greeting, then pointed to the northeast.

Herons regularly flew overhead, landing by the river or on marshy pools opposite the house. With the valley now almost deserted it was no surprise see one, seventy or so yards from the lounge windows. Herons often stand like statues, waiting patiently before the head stabs suddenly downward, to rise again, a fish or a frog wriggling in that enormous beak. Waving an understanding, she watched the couple move off, then resumed her chores until Gordon returned for coffee.

While sitting drinking, the office bell rang. They looked at each other, waiting to see who would go. When another ring sounded Jan rose, muttering loudly about the idleness of men. Before reaching the door she saw the bird-watching couple, and wondered what caused their returned.

"It's still there." The man pointed again, standing back so she could step from the doorway and see for herself. For a while they watched together, looking for some flicker of movement, but none came.

"Not normal behaviour," The man's head shook doubt-fully, "It may be injured."

"Do you want to go closer?"

"No he doesn't!" the woman's remark was addressed at

264

her husband. "This wasn't a serious trip, just a few days to relax. We didn't bring Wellingtons and he's not going over in those shoes." She eyed the marsh with disapproval.

"Should I get Gordon to go?"

"Not yet. Later perhaps, if he wouldn't mind."

It was left at that - how much later not defined. Strange though, that it should still be there. No bird's patience was unlimited; if unsuccessful in finding food it would normally fly away. Before setting off again for work, they stood together looking across at the heron, concerned by its inactivity.

"We've been adopted," Jan suggested. "I think our bird-watcher would like you to investigate, but he said it's too soon yet."

Gordon glanced at the sky; clear and blue, though not particularly warm. "Okay. When I come back."

He left, hurrying downstream, anxious to get on. If the bird was still there later then he'd put on goggles and thick gloves and approach it. A beak that size and fast enough to catch a trout, well... it deserved more than casual respect - quite possibly the most dangerous of all local birds.

Returning for lunch, he dropped the tools in the service passage, saw the bird still standing in the marsh and reluctant to disturb it, decided to eat first. The meal made no difference; with the plates cleared away, peering again through a window it stood like a statue in the same spot. The bird-watcher was back too, standing on the riverbank.

Donning protective gear and joining the man took only a few minutes. "I hear you want me to take a look?"

"If you would. Got to be something badly wrong."

Heading across the bridge and over the fence, Gordon slowed, approaching carefully; the heron making no attempt to move away. At two paces, he stopped unsure, the bird's eyes were watching him but no movement from other parts of the hunched body. Another step would take him in range, best not give it time to think... he hesitated again; does a bird think or act from instinct? Lunging forward he grabbed the bill, holding it closed with one outstretched gloved hand before finally moving in to pick the bird up with the other arm over its wings, a hand under its chest. Carrying it back, a brief inspection in front of the house revealed a great gash down almost the entire length of the bird's front, like it had flown at speed into a thin wire and sliced itself open. Standing together the two men looked at the heron.

"As far as I know, no vets are open on Sunday afternoon," Gordon continued holding the beak while the bird-watcher inspected the wound more closely.

"It wouldn't help anyway. I work with the RSPCA. I'm not a vet but I've assisted one quite often. The best vet in the country could never save this bird even if the wound was fresh." The man shook his head.

Looking again at the cut, the flesh had turned yellowy black. "Should I put him back?

"Unless you've somewhere warm. Be dead by evening; it's an old bird anyway." The man didn't explain how he knew, but reaching out a hand, running it over the feathers, said "Do what you can," and walked away.

Very well, but little could be done apart from making its last hours comfortable. The bathroom was being retiled, the old ones stripped off, but this bird would never notice. Standing in the bath seemed the best place; it was warm and any droppings or matter weeping from the wound could be washed away later. Jan extracted a piece of fish from the small freezer cabinet of her fridge, brought quickly to room temperature by holding it under the tap. A small piece was offered, hoping a little food and warmth would ease the cold from its dying bones. The bird was not interested, one foot already in the next world, beyond thoughts of food.

Knowing it was dying, Gordon became careless. Due perhaps to the warmth, that long beak temporarily recovered some movement; opening it reached for his arm. The top section did no more than rest gently across the wrist, as if touching to draw attention or to say thanks. No pressure was exerted, the beak bottom hardly closing against the underside of the wrist, then it withdrew, resuming the previous forlorn statue-like stance. A glance downward to where it had touched revealed two streaks of blood across the entire width of the wrist - those beak edges like razors. The action held no malice, almost affection in the lightness of touch; while swabbing the cut with a Dettol soaked cotton wool pad, he wondered what a fit heron might be capable of. It died before nightfall as the bird-watcher had foreseen, sad though inevitable, the only bird they ever lost.

***

"Finish by Christmas, that's what you said!" Jan pointed an accusing finger.

"So I shall; the heavy cable anyway. I'll crimp the ends in the new substation this morning."

Each wire in this cable was the thickness of a finger; a special tool had been hired to make the connections. Some extra hook-up points were also ready but more lay waiting, the trenches far from finished. The third toilets too, were not yet switched on, armoured cable fixed to the rear wall led into the building but the internal connections saved for wet weather.

Jan's challenge had only been in fun, all should be ready long before opening day. She hunted out the plastic Christmas tree and decorations. It had lasted since the first year in the house; before that there had not been room - and yet, even without a Christmas tree, the caravan when the children were young had been special. Remembering those days Jan sat back on her heels, a silver ball forgotten in her hand. Though it could never be like the old days, a family reunion had been arranged this Christmas, all the children - well no longer children, she corrected her thoughts - all had managed to get time off and would be home.

They arrived separately over the following days, bringing uniforms for a photo session at their mother's special request. The best picture had Chris in his police gear complete with helmet, Sharon in her graduation cap and gown on one side and Steve in army tunic and peaked cap on the other. All were laughing together, caught in an impromptu moment by the erroneous impression Dad had managed to give, that the camera was not yet ready. It was lucky and unusual for all to get leave at the same time - really good to see them

267

together again. They still looked on Relubbus as their anchor, an unchanging spot in rapidly changing lives, a thing to rely on when needed. Such visits were always enjoyed.

This reunion would be brief, a few short days - days that saw all other work abandoned as they wandered round making a fuss of the ducks, visiting old haunts in the valley, running the lathe in the basement workroom - it still worked from waterwheel power. A few days of pure nostalgia, except one afternoon when the three split up, dashing off to meet old friends in the area. And then it was over; they were gone, leaving one by one in their own cars - all returning to steady jobs with careers ahead.

"We haven't done too badly," Jan clung to Gordon's arm as they watched Steve, last to drive off up the road. "In spite of all the work in their younger years and not being able to take them places, they're all doing well, all know how to stand on their own two feet."

CHAPTER 14

Little Angel

January saw the electrics complete, 130 hook-ups tested and ready, but visitor aspirations were now rising in other directions, the old black and white site brochures no longer effective. A new batch arrived with two pages of colour photos; Jan pushed another into an envelope and sealed it down, then thinking about lunch, headed for the shop. Not so much choice now, the shelves depleted after three months eating leftover stock, but many shelves of caravan accessories remained - and that case of fly-spray with only four missing - three of those Gordon had sold late in the season. Looking at them, Jan shook her head, remembering his outrageous sales technique. She had stood once, inside the house peeping through the slightly open communicating door to find who was being served, and saw him standing behind the counter talking to a young couple. Moving an arm in a sweeping motion in answer to something that was said, he knocked over a tin of fly-spray that just happened to be on the counter; it looked accidental at the time. Still watching, she had seen him pick it up, apologise to the couple, then look furtively round and lean closer as if to impart some secret. Holding out the tin he had whispered, "Some people buy these at this time of year, a squirt inside the caravan does wonders for winter storage."

When the couple believed every word and paid for one there and then, she had struggled to keep silent. Now, looking at the part empty case she shook her head again. Would they sell next year? Probably not - Cornwall remarkably free of flies and midges. On a shelf nearby rested another recent purchase, a device to handle rechargeable batteries now widely used in cameras and other apparatus - all part of keeping holidaymakers happy. In one respect however, there must be a decrease next year; they must not be left with so much food! Jan moved across to a shelf taking another tin of beans, a quick meal; more than an hour yet before she need start cooking. Taking the tin to the kitchen, she picked up a cleaning cloth and went outside, glancing up to where Gordon worked on the terraces, great steps carved out from the valley side when the old mine waste was removed. They looked a bit bare. A continuous mound of topsoil formed a ridge along the front edge of each shelf, a ridge placed many years before in response to something Chris said at the time.

"Dad, the shelves slope slightly towards the front to make sure no puddles get trapped if it rains, right?" The lad had waited for a nod of agreement before asking, "Well then, when people use those pitches, what happens if someone forgets to put the brake on a car?"

The family had been seated round the table at that time. Dad's agreement, "Yes, you're right. We're bound to get some women drivers," led instantly to scornful retorts and a mock battle between the sexes - something now remembered with pleasure. As the arguments died down, all had agreed a soil bank was needed. However, the future appearance had not been considered.

Now seemed a good to time remedy that by planting a few trees. A variety of foliage was needed along these edges, some short, some of medium height - on a caravan park all the visitors must be considered. The new planting should improve the appearance for people looking up from below without totally obscuring the view of those pitched on the shelves. With an eye to the future, if trees were to be planted, why not fruit trees, and if fruit trees then choose the greatest possible variety. Apples were favourite, cherry and plum too fussy about the soil they liked, and even more so for apricot and peach, but at least one of everything should be tried.

What about spacing? Say three fruit trees on each shelf... these would cost of course, but for the rest, seedlings and saplings of many wild species sprang up along the valley and would be free. Sycamore, ash, even oak could be used if the tops were cut every few years - and lower growing forms such as hazel, and some evergreens - laurel, escallonia, and euonymus. A few hawthorns might help but no blackthorn, too dangerous... and something perhaps to give a red tinge here and there, maybe berberis. That would do for starters. Drought might be a problem, particularly in the first year. Hm, a mulch of grass cuttings over the roots? The spring flush of growth would certainly provided that! This would be the last tree planting for the moment; over 700 had now been set and not one required by the planning authority. It was quite safe to put in plenty, they could be thinned out later if required, for no tree preservation order restricted the site. The old West Penwith Council was now disbanded, but in memory people may well think that they knew what they were doing. Their confidence in not applying such an order had led directly to extra planting. The odd tree might still need to be removed, but if anyone could find a better landscaped park than River Valley then it must be something special.

After lunch, the outside cleaning continued. Hearing a call Jan returned to the house and flicked a switch on the kettle, but it was dead. She had spent the last two hours washing electric hook-up points, removing bird droppings, green mould and various other stains from the white boxes, obviously a once a year job. For safety the main's switch had been thrown, cutting the current everywhere. Turning towards the table she pointed to the door, "You called me in, so don't just sit there; if you want coffee, go and switch on. By the way, your screws are going rusty."

Thinking this to be some slur on his mental ability, Gordon wondered what he'd done now, and looked back blankly.

"Literally, your screws are rusting; all the ones on last year's electric hook-up boxes. They're beginning to stain the plastic."

Hurrying away to switch on the power, he inspected a few before returning. Signs of rust showed on each one, zinc plating on the screws eroded away. Big dogs could cause it to happen but that seemed unlikely here; they would scarcely be expert enough to aim at every one. Anyway, the hook-ups were normally live and no great howls of anguish had echoed round the valley. So it wasn't dogs or foxes, just a case of poor quality screws - screw was the wrong word, they were small nuts and bolts. Returning for tools he extracted one of each type then phoned in an order for similar sizes in stainless steel, receiving a promise of immediate posting.

On the third day a heavy parcel arrived containing more than a dozen assorted boxes.

"Why so many?" Jan watched as he undid each pack, inspecting the contents, and saw one contained long stout woodscrews. "And what are those for? There's nothing like that in the electric boxes!"

"Er... thought I'd change the brass screws in the water-wheel to stainless... Stronger, make the wheel last longer. Constant dipping in and out of water softens the wood, allowing the screws to flex a little - brass is quite brittle under that sort of treatment - it's called work hardening." He turned away, reaching for another pack. Jan took the delivery note and picked up a pencil, jotting the numbers down.

"There are over six hundred!"

"Well... I thought..." he shrugged.

"Yes? Thought what? Most screws on site are already stainless - aren't they?"

"Not all. A few I used in the first year were only zinc plated. We should change them, this seemed like a good opportunity. We may need more in the future so..." he made a gesture, about to explain, but she stopped him in exasperation.

"Don't tell me! More spares, yes?"

He shrugged, put three of the boxes in his pocket, picked up the tools and headed off. Every hook-up, even the latest ones which had not yet had time to rust, had their

272

fiddly little nuts and bolts changed - not a hard job but murder on the knees, squatting at the low level boxes to carefully replace each bolt. In just a few days all were completed, costing less than twenty pounds compared to the original bill of over a thousand. Why on earth any manufacturer should use plated screws instead of stainless and risk their reputation for the sake of so little was a mystery that defied all logic.

The waterwheel should be easier, at least easier on the knees; rotating the wheel would raise every screw to the ideal height. Over the years an occasional paddle had come loose, either from constant movement or from stray branches washed down on the current jamming underneath. Replacing the existing brass screws should cure that - with luck no paddle should drop off for the next five years. Strangely enough, the last one to break free sank to the bottom rather than floating away downstream, so saturated had the wood become.

March saw the site in good shape, the transformer size already increased to cope with likely future demands and those extra hook-ups. Trade was good too, six caravans staying at the moment, mainly professional people who must use their holiday before April or lose it. With the winter's work finished and only this handful of visitors, life was easy, a chance to stroll along the riverbank indulging in a certain measure of self-congratulation - a nice, happy feeling!

The arrival of Easter with its short burst of activity, brought home their narrow escape. The speed with which caravans were converting to electric was amazing. Nearly half now wanted a connection. Even some tents needed one, a thing fortunately anticipated by putting eighteen hook-ups within the tent areas.

One early customer carried a magazine to the office. "You don't sell these in the shop, do you?" He pointed to a small picture showing a pillar with electric sockets. The small print also boasted of a light in the top.

"Sorry no." Reaching for a pen, Gordon took the magazine, scrawled something on a scrap of paper then passed it back. "We can charge your battery if it's any help?"

"I know, you did last year. My wife thought it might be nice to have power. Not to worry, it's only a woman's thing - her friend at home has a new caravan and keeps boasting about the electrics."

"Did you want anything else, there's not a lot of foodstuff yet." The shop was not kept open this early in the year, a note on the door telling customers to ring the office bell. As the man left, Jan asked what was scribbled on the paper.

"The firm's telephone number. We'll send for one; have a look at it."

When the parcel arrived with an invoice for £35, the robust plastic pillar stood some fifteen inches high with a light and two power sockets; ideal for inside a tent.

"How much do we sell them for?" Jan stretched the cord across office and lounge, testing how far it would reach.

"About £55 sounds good, what d'you think?"

"Pricey! Who'll buy it at a twenty pound mark-up... profiteering again?"

"Sure," Gordon rubbed his hands together, grinning. "But then I'm trying *not* to sell any." Seeing an expression of puzzlement, he explained. "We'll rent them to tents, an encouragement to stay longer. Older caravans might use one as well."

"Five pounds a night I suppose?"

"I thought we might hire them out free." He smiled, making a grab as she lifted the back of one hand to her forehead and pretended to faint.

Feeling his supporting arms, she let herself go and was lifted bodily to an armchair in the lounge. As her weight rested back on the cushions, she squinted cautiously through one eye, and seeing the grinning face above, closed it tightly again. With a moan, the left arm fell limply down, a shaky voice asking, "Where am I?"

Getting no response she opened her eyes and they looked at each other, both now smiling broadly. "You look like Gordon... would you pinch me please, I must be dreaming. Did I really hear you say free?"

"I did - and never mind the histrionics! The most important thing we're selling is space. We want campers to stay longer, talk about us to other people, enjoy something they can't get elsewhere. We definitely do not want to sell them a totem - that's what they call these things on the invoice, tent totems."

"Why not?"

"Once somebody has one, they can go anywhere to use it. If they're hired out, the campers may like them and come back next time."

"So that's why you're making them expensive," Jan poked at him.

He grabbed her wrist, fending off the jabbing finger. "Tents have enough in the car already, they may prefer to hire rather than carry something else. Anyway, the dearer the selling price, the more generous it will seem when we hire them out for free."

"Oh, generosity is it? I should have guessed!"

Easter passed, and while awaiting the arrival of spring bank holiday, Gordon walked all round the various roads and areas with the trolley and a pair of secateurs, clipping odd shoots of bramble, partly for the exercise, nothing else being scheduled at that time. Taking them downstream to the bonfire area, not used since the previous year, he sighted a nuthatch but lost it in the foliage and having emptied the trolley was about to leave when another appeared, flew up to a large old tree and disappeared into a hole. Withdrawing as quietly as possible, he hurried to the office. There would be no bonfires this spring! The book showed no record of any nuthatch nesting in Cornwall. For a week, no one ventured near the hole. An advert in the paper offered ex-Russian naval binoculars for £25 - it seemed worth a trip to Falmouth. Watching from a distance however, revealed no trace of the birds - perhaps they found the hole less than desirable. A pair did still feed from a container of nuts hung on a bush some distance from the kitchen window but they disappeared when the season for rearing young birds saw the nut supply changed to seed. The lengthening days brought not only nesting, it made the valley more active, extra caravans arriving and the phone ringing with enquires. Jan lifted the receiver one morning to hear Sharon's voice.

"I've got a job - teaching in a school near Banbury."

"When? You'll be coming down for the holidays?"

"No, well not the whole holiday. My training year doesn't end until July. I'll be home then, but not to work this year. I'm taking a house with three other teachers; renting it but we have to fix up the rooms. I'll need a decent car."

The conversation continued until a ring on the shop doorbell cut it short. Hurrying through and finding the customer wanted a length of clear waste pipe, Jan stretched up, standing on toe tips in an attempt to reach the coil from a high shelf - it wasn't often asked for. About to fetch a stool, she saw a man walking towards the shop, waited for him to enter then stretched up again, knowing the coil lay beyond reach, but flicking an eye towards this new customer with a look of, "Oh dear, if only I were taller."

Quickly he stepped forward, lifting it down and carrying it to the counter. The woman still waiting to be served, smiled quietly, "Two feet should be enough."

With a left over newspaper laid to protect the counter, a big carving knife cut into the plastic, the pipe rotated a little before cutting again - an attempt not to mark the paper though it was unlikely to be sold now.

By the time Gordon returned from pitching two tents that had arrived together, the shop was empty. Repeating the conversation with Sharon, Jan said, "She'll be down as usual, but not to work. Steve tells her cars are cheaper down here, do you think that's true?"

"Second-hand ones, yes. We guessed she wouldn't be helping this season."

"Just as well we advertised in the club magazines for wardens. When are they coming?"

"Next week. I wanted them here before the Dutch Rally but it doesn't really matter."

Standing together, they glanced across the almost empty

front field; a single caravan parked near the entry point was erecting the Dutch ANWB flag. By evening the grass would be covered in caravans, twenty-four of them and three motor-caravans, all retired couples on a rally from Holland, a direct result of joining the Best of British group of caravan parks. The leader had arrived nearly an hour ago, other caravans would dribble in singly or in groups during the morning. An hour after everyone else, the mechanic should arrive, deliberately last to help anyone with problems on the road. River Valley was popular with the Dutch, nice people to work with, the rally booked to stay for three days, their longest stay on the whole tour so the leader claimed. By early afternoon it was good to see the front field looking colourful again, bringing a hint of busier times soon to come.

A week later the wardens arrived in their caravan, a couple from Yorkshire, Granville and Dot - Dorothy really but she preferred the shorter name. In their early sixties, both were ex-club wardens so had the best of training. Arriving in May gave them time to settle before the peak period, taking over the midday cleaning, work at which Dot proved particularly efficient.

***

"What are those for?"

A lorry loaded with paving slabs had drawn up near the office.

Gordon pushed past, not replying, clearing the steps with a leap and shouted to the driver. "Follow me."

Watching them disappear round the corner, Jan clenched a fist. "Right. I'll teach him to ignore me!" For a moment she considered going on strike, but with trade getting busier and so many old friends among the customers, that was impractical. Looking round the room for inspiration, her eye fell on the steaming cup - coffee she had made just before the lorry arrived. Picking it up, she hurried to the kitchen, then lifting cup from saucer, poured it slowly and deliberately down the sink with a little huff of satisfaction. Taking a teaspoon and adding more coffee powder to the cup, a smile crossed her face as she turned on the cold tap, topping it up, stirring the contents and carrying it back to the office, sitting down to sip at her own hot brew.

The lorry left, most of its load still aboard - that was a relief, but what were they for? She wouldn't ask again, that was for sure; her fist clenched in annoyance but the shop bell rang, calling her away. When Gordon returned she was already back in the lounge. Sitting at the desk he lifted the cup, screwed up his face in distaste and called across, "Hey, this coffee is stone cold."

"Is it really?" She sat down, ignoring the implied request, waiting for an explanation of the paving slabs, watching his face; seeing something false in that apparently vacant expression. When he rose, carrying the cup out, she followed, seeing him tip it away, grab a teaspoon and look round for the coffee jar. As if she were not there, he started looking, opening each cupboard and examining the contents.

Her turn to smile; she had thought of that, and watched as his hand reached for a bowl on the top shelf. "There's sugar in that one."

He took it down anyway to check, then bent to a low cupboard.

"That's saucepans, you'll be needing those later." Jan spoke again.

A hand reaching for the door stopped, frozen in mid-air. He drew back and stood nonchalantly up; fingers drumming for an instant on the worktop were pulled away, thrust in a pocket to silence them.

"By the way, did I tell you this wonderful idea I have for paving slabs?" He swung towards her with a big smile as she grinned back, knowing she had won!

"No you never did - slipped your memory I expect? Like a coffee would you?" She reached in the bread bin, pulling out a loaf and rescuing a jar from behind. "Go ahead, I'm listening."

"Each slab will be cut into four pieces, Granville can help. We'll take them right down the site in the trailer so nobody hears." He stopped, a gesture suggesting that all must now be clear.

"Oh good, I've always wanted fifty broken paving slabs." Sarcasm strong in her voice, Jan poured boiling water into the cup.

"Not fifty, that doesn't divide by four." Seeing her move to the sink and tilt the cup, he hurried on. "Forty-eight, from a dozen slabs. When they're finished, we'll pile them by the dustbin area. People who insist on using those infernal throw-away barbecues can collect one to save our grass."

The grass was taking a hammering anyway, losing its green; June had been hotter than usual. Now in early July, the turf lay brown and lifeless - time to water perhaps? After sunset, with most people safely in their caravans the hose was rolled out, something never attempted before. Waiting for darkness had advantages; fewer cars to run over the hose and water would evaporate more slowly! Three hours later, around 2am, those few areas tackled had been thoroughly watered. A farmer had once advised that wetting the top few inches did nothing but harm. "Saturate it thoroughly," he had said. That at any rate had been achieved! Jan coped the next morning while he slept in; the whole procedure repeated the following night and again for the rest of the week. At the end of that time, the watered grass grew no greener than anywhere else and had cost a fortune at the meter! The project was abandoned; rain must come eventually.

"You could er, go out tonight and do a rain dance," Gordon suggested. "They wear very small costumes."

"You'll be lucky!"

There the conversation ended and as days passed the dry weather continued. With school holidays about to start, the only grass still green grew northeast of trees or under hedges. No mowing was needed and the river had shrunk; down a good two inches lower than seen before. Fortunately the tarmaced roads banished dust clouds that once rose from every passing car; the state of some incoming vehicles making it obvious not all sites had gone to such expense.

***

"I want to see my pitch first!" A man stood truculently

279

before the desk, the queue of other new arrivals waiting behind him stretched across the office and through the open door, one couple still standing on the office steps. Beyond that, the yard was full with caravans and cars. Gordon had just left with a caravan and motorcaravan travelling together, but should be back shortly.

Jan looked up at the unsmiling face. Often people were grumpy and ill-tempered after a long drive. She too felt impatient; this last Saturday in July was great, but incessantly busy. With the peak season in full swing, life had been hectic, hours of sleep short - in spite of having assistance now, they still did the morning cleaning themselves and that had not long been finished. An urge to send the man away was tempting, but people usually cheered up when offered a choice of nice pitches. "See Gordon when he comes back... he may need to clear the queue first," Jan knew the words had come with a touch of hardness and regretted it, but the pressure to get on was unrelenting. Adopting a sweeter tone she asked, "Would you mind waiting outside please. I must book in the next caravan."

Planting his feet more firmly, the man drew himself up. "I'm staying right here for the boss, not taking orders from an office girl!"

A jolt of anger gripped Jan, a ripple of unease running through the people behind. Momentarily she froze, then an idea struck. Office girl? Did she look so young? A smile slowly spread, bringing a response in the waiting faces; the tension eased, good feeling returning, magnified as knowing smiles passed back and forth, better humour engulfing the room. Many were tired having travelled through the night, tiredness not helped by more waiting to be booked in and shown to a pitch - but this sudden rudeness and the answering smile broke the spell. The man at the desk reddened, his discomfort obvious, it brought more joy to the faces, more happy good spirits.

Jan felt better, in control now, mistress of the situation again, her voice light hearted as she spoke. "Let me tell *you* something. This *office girl* owns the joint!"

The deliberately down-market expression and following pause were effective. She might have left it there but couldn't resist. "That boss you're waiting for is my husband, and you know what husbands do?"

The man swallowed, not sure what to say.

Jan looked up at the women beyond, "They do as they're told!" Seeing heads nod in agreement she turned back smiling, "Now you want to book in, or you want to wait?"

Bicycles became more numerous and with the roads now smoothly tarmaced, dangerous speeds were being reached by some children. For the most part, young people responded better to a little discussion than a blank command of "Don't do that." An occasional quiet word kept this hazard within reasonable limits, but only just. Another problem in the making perhaps?

By midday arriving families had filled the area nearest the office, many of the children, as was normal, shouting at the top of their voices. This was nothing unusual; they came very often from more crowded environments with higher background noise, where the loudest voice got most attention. During the afternoon many left for the beach, other equally noisy ones arriving. Jan walked over to the office door and looked out as shouts rang back and forth; they were obviously happy - past experience forecasting the voices would quieten as days passed. With a shrug she closed the door and turned back.

"Well?" Gordon was watching her from the desk.

"Nothing. Those last two boys that arrived..." She shrugged again.

"Make good town criers. Want me to speak to them?"

"No... perhaps... No, they're happy enough - everyone else might not be though. Pity to spoil their fun on the first day. They may be better when more children come back from the beach?" The suggestion carried little conviction.

"Okay. I'll wander over." He rose, went to the kitchen, then left by the office door, walking round to where the children played. Some ducks lay in the shadows under the hedge watching his approach but not moving as the boys continued to shout and race after a miniature version of a soft beach ball. The simple act of pulling some bread from a pocket changed the ducks stance, their heads rising and alert. When he threw the first piece they were up and running. Gordon squatted on the ground as the small flock gathered round; he heard a shout, saw the ducks prepared to take flight and turned to see the lads pelting forward. With a finger to lips and a motion, he signalled to come on slowly, passing a piece of bread to each boy. Shortly the three were seated on the ground whispering to each other and surrounded by beaks, all taking pieces from the hand. With the bread finished, the ducks waddled off to the stream for water as they often did after food. The man and two boys followed, sitting on the bank watching, Gordon pointing out the differences between mallard and muscovy, and indicating the ripples where a trout rose to the surface for a fly. He spoke in a quiet voice, hardly above a whisper as discussions turned to the area in general, the nearest beaches, the recreation field and other matters of interest to young minds.

No one had mentioned noise, but having discovered for themselves that voices could be heard without shouting, and perhaps from concern for the ducks, the youngsters were exuberant but quiet. He left shortly after. The effect might be short lived but on previous occasion volumes had not usually returned to former levels; as an added advantage the boys might now come to him with any problems. It would be easier too, to get their help if needed - they had already agreed to watch for anything upsetting the ducks.

Of course not all children were likeable, a few were a pain in the... what is the word? Anyway, next to the laundrette lay the chemical emptying point. This special drain for disposal of fluids from portable toilets was shaped like a big cardboard box sunk in the ground - except it wasn't cardboard but smooth cement with rounded corners. A four inch pipe in the bottom led away to the sewer and as is normal with drains, this pipe had a trap at the bottom - that is, it descended then bent upwards again before leading the effluent away. This upward bend trapped water in the pipe, preventing sewer smells from escaping.

Such systems usually have a tap above to wash out the toilet container, and sometimes a water flush to keep the pit clean. Always looking for ways to improve, a special novel system had been arranged with this particular drain - the washing machines in the laundrette also discharged into the concrete dish; all that soapy water helping to keep it fresh and sweet smelling. It would be a fair bet that this was normally the most hygienic and cleanest chemical emptying point in the county. This year however it had a drawback. Some mother's little angel thought it fun to drop rocks and boulders into that four inch pipe! They stuck in the bend causing a blockage. When the next chemical toilet was emptied, all the nasty effluent could no longer run away, it welled up, lumps of debris floating around the concrete dish. A discharging washing machine added to the volume causing it to overflow. Another man coming to empty his toilet bucket, saw the result and hurried across to ring the office doorbell just before lunch.

"What's happened at the emptying point, it's flooded, not running away. We're off today; plan to travel right after we've eaten. Is there anywhere else...?"

"I'll fix it, hold on." Gordon reached for a pair of rubber gloves, collected a drain rod and they were off. At the drain a murky soup still rose almost to the rim, several squelchy looking brown objects floating lazily on the top - a stain across the nearby concrete showed where it overflowed. From the liquid surface to the start of the exit pipe was about nine inches, and from there to the bottom of the bend almost as far again. Probing with the drain rod encountered something hard and knobbly in the bottom of the pipe. It needed no genius to guess some little terror had filled it with stones.

"Damn! Guess who's going to put an arm down eighteen inches through that mess, then grasp each stone and pull it clear." Gordon spoke with a grimace, then seeing the man's reaction, pointed a finger quickly at himself, "Me!"

The visitor who had taken a quick backward step, now

smiled doubtfully, gazed at the disgusting fluid and pulled a face. Glancing down at the container still in his hands, the man's expression asked, "When?"

"It'll take a while; if you still fancy your meal, go and eat. By the time you finish I'll have it clear. My lunch is due too... hope we don't have stew!"

When the man left, Gordon fetched a pail and another smaller container, lifted a nearby manhole lid and bailed out what was possible to lower the level a bit, deliberately trying to catch the major pieces of floating debris. Stripping to the waist and pulling on a right-hand glove, he suddenly stopped and listened; then leapt to the nearby laundrette door, bursting in. One washing machine was working!

"Has it been going long?" concern imparted a demanding edge to the question.

The woman, confronted by these urgent words, the bare torso and that single thick rubber gauntlet, stepped back in alarm, "Oh! I just started. Is something wrong?"

"No. Not to worry..." about to explain, he caught a hint of fear in the face and decided better of it, glancing up at the electric control box and wondering if the power should be cut? Surely the job would be finished before it discharged. Leaving quickly he stretched a thick elastic band around the glove top in a vain effort to stop the evil stuff flowing in, then emptied almost an entire bottle of Dettol into the repulsive brew, saving just a little to smear over the arm, elbow, and up the biceps. This was it then; no further precautions that came to mind... taking a deep breath the arm plunged downward.

The number of stones was considerable, they came out with varying difficulty, some awkward to grip. Fortunately, once a few were removed, most remaining effluent flowed away, only hand and wrist now submerged. One stone had washed well round the bend and was hard to reach. He could feel this final obstruction with the end of a finger and worked it gradually outwards - at least he hoped it was the final one. Just as two fingers achieved a grip, the washing machine started its discharge, soapy water shooting everywhere. Somehow news had spread and a group of campers were gathered, watching from a little distance.

One regular visitor wrinkled her nose and whispered, "Not to worry. Just what he needed to clean that other stuff away!" Turning, she asked, "Anyone feel like telling him he should have switched the washing machine off first?" A few grins showed but nobody offered.

Only partly hearing these comments from the watching group, Gordon continued to kneel, hanging on by fingertips. There were two choices; to let go the precarious grip and risk not being able to reach the stone afterwards, or endure the full flow of suds and water which had now mounted to the top of the dish and was overflowing, its normal drainage impeded by his own arm blocking the pipe. Removing a knee from the rim of the dish to avoid wet trousers, he bridged in an awkward fashion, gradually working the stone out against the flow of the suds. To a great cheer the offending object came away and was held up with a flourish, then quickly lowered again as water ran down the arm.

Round at the tap to which the garden hose was fixed, he carefully squirted the soiled arm, then with a tablet of soap and a towel put there beforehand, got clean and dry as a voice called "Lunch!" Somehow, news of the murky task had preceded him; arriving at the house the door was locked, Jan inside making 'No' signals with her hands and pointing to the patio. A plate of salad rested on the white enamelled table that stood with four garden chairs outside the lounge window. Turning back to her laughing face he bunched a fist and made as if to drive it through the glass. She held up a hand, palm outwards signalling stop and turned the key, opening the door. Gathering up the salad, he took it to the dining room table and sat down.

"Would you prefer something hot?" Jan asked.

"What did you have in mind?"

"Brown Windsor soup?"

CHAPTER 15

Ticks

Rising early as usual and peering between the curtains, the site slept; not a movement among that mass of caravans spread across the adjacent field. Downstairs Gordon filled two jugs with corn - breakfast for the ducks before cleaning started. Emerging from the basement, a movement through the lounge window caught his eye, a Kingfisher settling on the bridge parapet. Must have flown upstream from the estuary where they nested, its colour arresting - powerful even before the sun had risen. Stopping in mid-stride, he called softly, "Look out at the bridge." For perhaps twenty seconds the bird crouched eyeing the water below as if ready to dive but it never got the chance. A Jay flying from willows beyond the far bank, swooped down as if in attack.

Why? Few birds had more dissimilar feeding habits, neither in any way a threat to the others well-being. Apart from hawks, different species seldom bothered to attack each other. Did jealousy at the smaller bird's vibrant blue cause the sortie? The Jay had a blue streak on its leading wing edge; maybe it didn't like being outshone - conditioned to fight for territory against birds with blue markings? Whatever the cause the Kingfisher skimmed off, inches above the river surface, disappearing from sight round a downstream bend, knowing perhaps that the clumsier Jay lacked control enough to follow. Such visits were rare, a nice start to the day, something mentioned to several early customers. As morning wore on the site came awake, the phone, the shop, more arrivals; an unending but happy quest to satisfy visitors. Thank goodness the new wardens, Dot and Granville, were doing the mid-day clean and helping to mow the grass.

Towards evening someone was in trouble with electrics, a common enough problem on touring parks. When a caravan and its equipment had lain unattended since the last holiday, dampness and condensation often triggered a fault. Normal industry standards dictated that six hook-ups be protected by one safety switch, so when such a fault occurred, then Bang! Off went the electric to six tourers - not always six of course, sometimes only four or five were connected.

Invariably someone would arrive at the office complaining! Turning the power back on had become a fine art, done immediately by whoever was free at the time. Usually nobody knew what caused the short, and consequently the faulty piece of equipment, whatever it might be, was still turned on. Naturally the system failed immediately, the six caravans again losing their supply. A little logic generally revealed the guilty party. Each electric box also contained six overload switches, one for each caravan. Switching these off and on, invariably located the culprit; testing that caravan's equipment, one piece at a time, found the faulty item.

Problem solved? No! Too much to hope! By a kink of human nature some owners disliked being wrong and chose to argue, insisting it was nothing to do with their caravan; some even went so far as to plug the faulty item back in. Had the argument lain solely between caravanner and site owner then the stand-off might have continued, but with up to five neighbours clearly showing disapproval the guilty party seldom persisted.

"There's an electrician list in the laundrette," Gordon suggested to one such visitor, pausing with another idea as he turned to leave. "If you've a heater in your caravan, try drying the faulty gadget thoroughly overnight. Don't re-test until your neighbours leave for the day. If it fails again, scrap it and come for me, okay?"

Some were more difficult! That evening the supply to six caravans failed for the third time. Try as he might, no fault could be found in any of the units. Eventually, stretching various leads to more distant hook-ups isolated the culprit!

It was Lionel and Doris's caravan, an elderly couple, old regulars and particular friends of Jan's Dad; the two often supping a tot in Jim's bungalow of an evening. Another couple, Frank and Ruby, also old friends, had been helping trace the fault, or rather trying to, for the search had been fruitless. Frank used his electrical test meter on everything possible in Lionel's caravan. Not a single fault, not so much as a flicker of the needle, everything apparently perfect - yet within half an hour, the electric was off again. As evening wore on the problem persisted but by juggling gadgets and a process of elimination it came down to a brass light fitting. When switched on, this light worked perfectly, but twenty minutes later the electric failed once more. Inspecting the lamp again, Frank noticed the fitting was warm and it dawned on him that as the lamp gradually heated, the brass stem must expand and cause a wire somewhere inside to short.

"You could use it ten minutes at a time."

"If it can short, it can probably give a shock." Lionel unplugged it permanently.

Problem over - but he was subject to a fair amount of ribbing by a group regulars who knew each other well.

Jan was pressing some shirts and a blouse. She had an ironing board of her own in the basement, but for small things it was quicker to dash across and use one permanently set up in the laundrette. A woman came in, her hair wrapped in a towel.

"Wish they had hair dryers near the ladies showers!" She spoke loudly, passing quickly on through an opening in a polished wood partition that surrounded the hair drying and information room towards the rear of the building.

Aware she had not been recognised, Jan made no comment, just gave a nod keeping her head down, finishing the blouse then set the iron on its stand, flicked the switch and left. Crossing back to the office, she glanced upward; no sun today and a touch wind. "Would I feel the same if I were on holiday?" A day without sun did make people prone to complain.

Later at tea, she broached the question with Gordon - he was gazing vacantly out through a window at something as she explained the chance meeting. "That woman may have a point. When long curly hair is wet, it's not so easy to put a sweater over your head to cross to the laundrette. A woman wouldn't want to walk across the yard in just her bra and..." She stopped as he swung suddenly round.

"Where?"

"Down boy! You weren't listening to me... just caught the last few words. Come on, admit it." Jan watched him gather his thoughts, knowing from the stance, the expression, that a denial was coming. "Little boy caught pinching sweets," at the secret thought she couldn't resist a smile, aware he would bluster some excuse.

"No, I was listening," Gordon insisted. "Er... she couldn't get her sweater on and her hair wouldn't curl, but I don't know why she ran across the yard in only a wet bra... Where is she now?"

"Why? What did you intend to do about it?"

"Not a thing. Honest. I'd turn and look the other way normally, only I can't have women running around naked. Well I can't, can I? Why are you laughing?"

"What about the girl on the top terrace, the one that had half the males on site strolling up there apparently just to look out across the valley? Oh yes, I heard about it. You went for a look too; no good you denying it - I was told. Did you make her cover up? What was her name... Ah, Domi..."

"Never mind what her name was. And no! I didn't tell her to cover up. How do you approach a girl who is lying there, long slender limbs, nice little waist, every bit of her suntanned to perfection, body stretched out, head resting on some sort of pillow, golden tresses moving softly in the breeze, odd strands blowing across smoothly rounded..." he paused for breath, making a motion, both hands held out horizontally, knuckles upwards, moving them apart as if over two mounds. "Of course I couldn't see her properly, didn't really look. I, er..." He tailed off with another small gesture "...can hardly remember."

"Why is your colour rising?"

Unconsciously he lifted a hand to his face, then seeing Jan laugh, protested defensively, "Must be warm in here. What did you expect me to do? Walk right over to her, stand looking down and say, *Hello hello hello, we can't have that sort of thing here.*"

"Stop imitating policemen. What would you do if she made a grab for you?"

"Cry '*Help!*' Mind you, I do tend to lose my voice in moments of panic."

Jan stepped forward, punching his chest gently. "Now listen, I'll tell you again. I met a woman in the laundrette. She didn't know who I was and grumbled about having to come right across from the showers to the hair drying room, okay? Well can't we fix up a hairdryer in the Ladies toilets? We've got electric now."

"No." Gordon shook his head.

"Why not, or do you like the thought of..."

"There isn't room, that's why. I looked into it last year. Apparently, to comply with regulations, a hairdryer on a flexible cord must be ten feet from any source of water. I expect that's metric by now, say three metres. Our buildings have toilets along one side, basins and showers on the other. You can't get ten feet from water. We could have the type that's fixed to a wall, like hand dryers but higher. Can you see women wanting to use those, trying to get their head at all angles to get their hair dry? We'd get grumbles all the while."

"Pity. Could we make a hair washing arrangement over those sinks in the laundrette?"

It was certainly a thought. The little room at the back already had two hair dryers, each with its own mirror over a little bench, and stools and a red carpet.

"Yes, I can probably fix it. Temperatures might fluctuate a bit when the washing machines cut in... should be minimal though. I'll fit the adjustable type, some people like it really hot, others not so much."

"Water might get on the floor," Jan warned. "Wouldn't

damage anything will it?"

"Not really. Might make it look messy; depends how much."

"Could you fix a system to prop that door open - gets hot in there this time of year. Oh yes, and don't forget the spin dryer."

"Right, nothing like keeping a chap busy. You'll be wanting it all done before coffee break?"

"If you want a coffee ask for it, don't hint!" Despite the severe tone, a smile hovered, one finger rising to shake in his direction as she prepared to say more, but he interrupted again.

"It says in the book I'm reading that a good woman should anticipate her man's every need, even before he knows it himself. He should never have to ask! I'm just helping you to be a good woman."

Jan opened her mouth, closed it again and looked round for a missile, didn't see anything she was prepared to throw, hesitated, then with a gleam in her eye started to remove her blouse.

"What are you doing!"

"You said, *'A good woman should anticipate her man's need?'*"

Eyes opening, he made to grab her but in a single fluid movement she swung sideways, one arm thrusting forward, knee slightly bent as a swordsman might lunge for the kill; the outstretched palm pressed flat against his chest forcing him back. Easing the now bare shoulder suggestively and bending to rub a cheek gently against it, she looked up under lowered eyebrows and whispered sweetly, "When my little jobs are done."

A ring of the shop bell called them back to reality but these brief interludes of fun kept them sane. Buttoning the blouse she hurried off. A man wanted cornflakes, the last packet; several lines now running low. Around eleven the following morning when the early rush had passed, a trip to cash and carry with a detour to the builders merchants secured both cornflakes for the shop and a shower fitting for hair washing. Returning, Gordon stood in the laundrette considering the row of stainless steel sinks. Which one? Second from the end maybe? Yes... another idea was vaguely forming... it would have to be that one. Now, how to start? The plumbing first; best get that over while most people were out for the day. Inserting a Tee junction and tap saw the water back on in under fifteen minutes. The remaining pipework and crawling about in the roof space to extend the electric supply, took longer. By comparison, a system for holding the door open was done in a flash - a length of cord with a hook to catch the handle; the hook home-made, bent up from extra stout wire. There had been interruptions, quite a few; lunch of course, then a tent arriving, someone fishing in front of the office and a car that wouldn't start. Granville dealt with the car, he was good at that. Not having to worry about the midday cleaning also helped.

Satisfied, Gordon returned to the house. Only one thing left now. Hurrying inside he sank into a chair, pleased with himself. "All finished except the spin dryer. There's a power socket ready; just a matter of buying it."

"Get a good one, not something cheap," Jan warned as they drank.

"You think I should go right away?" He looked at his watch, nearly three o'clock. "Which is better then, Currys or E.T.S. Is there a sale on anywhere?"

Penzance was not a large shopping centre but adequate, easy enough to find what you want provided it wasn't too unusual. The search was short, the machine fitting easily, sideways in the car boot. Back home, it took twenty minutes to fix the drain, then plug in - and the spin dryer was working.

Pushing a load in the drum, Jan pressed the automatic timer button and it hummed into action. Thinking to save a few minutes, she hurried back to the office for a key to empty the washing machine coinboxes. No one had ever broken into one but Gordon, careful and suspicious as usual, insisted they be emptied regularly on the basis that if anyone ever did break in, they would find nothing worth stealing and not come back. She looked down at the keys, a little hand printed tag said 'Tumble dryers'. "Another of my dear husband's precautions," she shook her head, knowing these were for the washing machines. Arriving at the laundrette door, a glance inside was enough to send her trotting back to the office. "I think you better come and look!"

He came quickly but she was already halfway across the yard, a short sprint and they arrived together; she stood back holding out a hand inviting him to enter. The spin dryer now rested near the far wall, the electric lead stretched to its furthest extent, its drain hose trailing on a water-splashed floor.

Mopping up and lifting the machine to its proper place, a press of the button and they stood back to watch. Like some hovercraft, the dryer floated off, transporting itself across the room. A foot reached out blocking the path and it stayed - very little required to stop the forward march, only vibration making it move. A plywood base with a little wooden upstands on three sides cured the problem. The job complete, he walked back carrying the tools, wondering if it was too early to claim that promised prize.

As the season passed its peak, trouble about that fence along the footpath rumbled on, but that was nothing new, pushed from the mind by a more immediate concern. Certain shelves in the shop had taken on a depleted look - the annual balancing act between customers' needs and not having too much left when the site closed. Last winter a case of shredded wheat had lasted into the new year by which time they both hated the stuff. Fortunately, many shelves now held non-food stock that had no sell-by date, the postcards for instance and all the caravan spares, but even these goods were not immune to the passing of time.

Gas mantles that once sold like hot cakes were suddenly out of fashion; two boxes with twenty-four in each sat on the shelves. At the present rate of sales they might take five years to clear - and positively nobody would want mantles by then! High up on the top shelf was a gas hairdryer; it fitted over a normal caravan gas stove and had a blower that worked from a car battery. Five years ago that was the latest thing, a status symbol among caravanners; now when showing it to a customer one day, a group of people in the shop gathered round as if it were some archaeological treasure. Oh well, they hadn't made too many mistakes and people were generally pleased. Installing hook-ups had certainly saved the site's fortunes, the new hair drying arrangement delighting quite a few and all the laundrette machines were working well. What more could tourists want?

By early October, Dorothy and Granville had gone, promising to return as wardens next year. With only three caravans remaining and the shop closed, Jan and Gordon slipped off for the day to a business meeting, leaving Jim in charge. With his worsening leg now severely restricting movement, a note on the office door directed any arriving customers to his bungalow, but none were expected.

This would be their first ever attendance at a 'Best of British' conference, where the group of top parks discussed tourist problems, latest trends, and how to keep visitors happy. Happiness meant return trade, something to be treasured! After the meeting, a banquet rounded off the evening; not dinner jacket and bow-tie but fairly smart, well-dressed ladies elegantly eating smoked salmon while discussing how best to extract accumulated hair from basin plug-holes. The company was stimulating; knowledgeable people with a common purpose. An owner with a few hiring caravans on his touring park described how one was all but destroyed by a newly married couple.

"The girl... this young wife, she left a note apologising. Not used to cooking she had boiled a large tin of spaghetti - just placed a saucepan of water on one of the gas rings then popped in the unopened tin, not even piercing the lid. Being unsure how long it would take, she let it boil merrily away until the tin exploded." The man paused looking round the attentive faces. "When my cleaning staff went in, spaghetti hung from the ceiling, walls, cupboard doors, some tangled in the bedclothes - and all hard, two days old at least; no attempt made to clear it up. The couple had left early -

divorce I should think!"

The account finished, other voices offered advice. Mostly these discussions were good-natured, a little criticism levelled by one site owner at another park because its toilets had old fashioned doors rather than modern flush ones. It didn't really matter, there was no bitterness, the good-natured chat all aimed at improving standards. One point raised was an industry requirement for hook-ups and other electrics to be tested every third year by an independent firm and a certificate obtained. River Valley didn't have one - it would have to be arranged. After the meal, the party broke into small groups, chatting together. Paul, one of the founder members, was talking.

"There *are* other ways of impressing visitors; making them feel welcome is the secret. A woman telephoned one February some years ago to make a booking; she was buying a caravan, taking it to France for a month, sailing back to Plymouth then wanted to stay at Kennford. I wrote it all down like we always do - the details and the dates she wanted, then passed a few pleasantries before ringing off. Two months later I looked at the bookings coming that day, read up my notes and in due course she arrived, introducing herself. Welcoming her to Kennford, I asked how she liked the new caravan, and had she enjoyed France. *'How can you possibly know that?'* She was delighted - been coming ever since because no one was quite as clever as that Paul at Kennford!"

A howl of banter greeted this punch line, the talk continuing as other tales were told. Departing eventually, Gordon and Jan headed for home, expecting to arrive shortly after midnight. Next morning they slept in, rising late to find no problems had arisen; a quick phone call arranged that electric inspection.

Three weeks later, on 30th October 1985, another early morning call had them rushing to Jim's bungalow. Audrey was in a coma - breathing but totally unresponsive. Something had happened in the night. The doctor arrived promptly, she had suffered a severe stroke. Phoning immediately for an ambulance, Penzance Hospital had no beds, neither did Truro; he persevered, finding one eventually at Tehidy. Jan followed the ambulance and sat for a while at the bedside but could do nothing - little prospect the Doctor said, of Audrey regaining consciousness. Returning home she found Jim cooking his midday meal.

"Can you manage?"

"Audrey would want me to carry on." That was all he said; didn't want to go to the hospital, not until there was news. He had seen people die in the army, handled it in his own way. Jim had always been tough, he may have been old now, his body weakening but his mind was still strong.

The call came next day; she had died. Jan stayed with her father, sending Gordon off to the hospital. He came back later with Audrey's case. That night in bed they clung to each other, the emptiness hard to accept; it was Jim's loss really but they felt the sadness keenly.

"Did you see her?" Jan asked.

"No. They just gave me her stuff. I think I signed something. It didn't seem possible; twenty-four hours ago she was talking about the garden. Walking along those empty corridors with her case in my hand... that was the most desolate thing I've ever done."

Winter was lazy, well lazy compared to the previous ones - some work to do but no great projects, no grand improvements demanding attention. Smooth bare cement floors in the toilet buildings were painted with red resin to seal any dust and to look more posh; a road dug into Area 6 was filled with stone ready for tarmac and as normal, bushes and trees were being trimmed both on site and along the entrance road.

Thanks to a good summer season, finances had risen; a little spending seemed reasonable enough - Audrey's death still achingly fresh, bringing home the shortness of life, a 'spend it while you can' feeling. A new ride-on mower had been discussed, something bigger and faster, but driving to Truro and seeing the actual price Gordon drew back, taking

Jan's hand and walking away.

"No, it's not meanness, merely business prudence."

"Yes, of course." Deliberately sounding sympathetic, she steered a route apparently by chance to a dress shop, rightly guessing that something far more modestly priced would meet with little resistance. When the pleated skirts she fancied happened to be substantially reduced in a sale, she liked them all - looked good in them too!

"It's so difficult to choose. There're all nice," she swayed lightly from the hip displaying yet another.

Sitting in a chair watching, he enjoyed the display but sighed in apparent resignation, shaking his head and turning to the assistant, "Okay, one of each please."

Carrying the six skirts, each a different tartan pattern, they strolled from the shop both happy, Gordon still muttering. Smiling at this pretended disapproval, Jan leaned closer to whisper, "You realise they'll all need christening," and saw his expression change!

Browsing in various windows, a real computer caught the eye, something with more scope than the present spectrum. With the mower price still in mind, this computer seemed relatively cheap and was also carried home. Over the following weeks a new program developed. Writing in a different language, persuading the computer to calculate and print more elaborate bills was complex, ideal for passing a pleasant hour after the continuing winter task of tree and hedge trimming - so good to sit with an interesting mental challenge instead.

Jan however, was not always pleased with these efforts. Working on a large embroidered tablecloth and rising to collect some silks, she cast a glance to where he sat at the computer. The program was becoming quite refined, she had practised printing bills and had come to like it but resented the continual alterations. He spent hours on the task, the improvements invariably requiring a different sequence of keys to be pressed.

"I hope you're not changing it again, there can't be anything else to do. Leave it alone!"

"Don't you want it improved?"

"No, keep it simple. Works fine the way it is."

"I thought it could help with the shop... save us money, make life better for the customers."

"How?"

"What is the most perishable thing we sell?"

"Ah... milk, I think... well anything fresh. Maybe bread but we can sell stale loaves for the ducks, so milk - or bananas or peaches in hot weather?"

"Wrong, they'll last at least two days, we've something that only lasts one." He waited, watching, seeing her lay the silks absently aside and walk over to the desk, guessing she was mentally working her way through the shop shelves.

"One day? Nothing spoils in one day; if it did you wouldn't stock it! Go on, tell me what..." She broke off, pointing a finger. "Newspapers!"

"Yes. How many mornings pass without us either getting left with some or being grumbled at for having sold out? With this sequence I'm writing; we take everyone's order when they first arrive and enter it in the computer. That way I can add them up each morning and order the exact amount." Gordon motioned towards the machine with both hands, fingers outstretched like a magician on stage about to pull a rabbit out of a hat.

"A real genius wouldn't need to add them up, he'd make the computer do it, but..." Jan paused, a dismissive wave of the hand saying no such genius existed here. She also thought that when printing receipts, it should display a fancy heading. "Hardly any sites give computer bills to their visitors; that's bound to make ours a topic of conversation. Caravanners will show it to people they meet on their travels. Make it print the site name in really big letters."

The final heading, set in bold type, included the full address and telephone number, all done automatically - no need for expensive pre-printed paper. Provision was made for a caption at the bottom; it could for instance include the latest special offer in the shop.

"Like those cans of fly-spray you still haven't sold?" Jan suggested.

As the winter progressed and days shortened further, Gordon slipped often into the basement with some lame excuse about reoganising shelves and oiling the lathe. He guessed Jan suspected something; that was unavoidable but keeping the parts separate and hiding them away, the secret was preserved.

The object of this clandestine work was a bird table, a masterpiece to go outside the kitchen window - she had wanted one for some time. Designed after the fashion of a Swiss Chalet with no walls, it had a floor, and above this a pitched roof overhanging at all edges. The construction must be ultra lightweight - that was essential! This was no common bird table on a post - rather it would swing to and fro' suspended in front of the window. No trees grew nearby from which it could hang, but he wasn't an engineer for nothing!

Slender timber sections and thin plywood were crafted into an intrinsically strong shape that included convenient perching points and places for hanging nuts, every part coated in preservative then stained, given three coats of varnish and glued and screwed together. It would be suspended by nylon cords - the structure's lightness allowing these to be slender. The cord might need renewing after five or so years, a pity but anything thicker would look ugly. Never mind, cord was cheap enough - sold in the shop for tent guy ropes and bought at wholesale price!

As Christmas eve approached, Jan mentioned often the lack of presents under the tree, hinting that some people just didn't care for their wives - didn't love them any more. Seeking a diversionary tactic Gordon strutted up, stood as tall as he could, gazing down into her eyes with an intended James Bond twinkle.

"You can unwrap me for Christmas."

It doesn't do a lot for a chap's ego when he makes an improper suggestion and his wife falls about laughing. He could get a complex.

At 6am on Christmas morning, while everyone else still slept, he crept from a warm bed and down the stairs.

Sharon, who arrived home the day before was also still in bed, no surprise there, no one expecting to see her before nine. Unlocking the office door quietly while his hands were free, he hurried to the basement, gathered everything required, climbed the stairs again and out through the office, depositing the lot at the far end of the house. Pushing the lead of the electric drill through a window opened earlier, he popped back inside to plug it in. Twelve fixings were required, the positions already marked out; it was only necessary to drill the holes, slip in plastic plugs then screw the various fittings to the wall. Simple. He stole off to fetch the extendible ladder, leaning it against the end of the house close to Sharon's bedroom. So far, no one had woken - that was about to change. Once the drill started, no one slept any more!

"What's going on, it's only 6.15?" An annoyed voice shouted through the window.

He looked up to see two faces pressed against the pane above, trying to see but prevented by the angle and not wanting to open the window in their night clothes. Good, that suited very well, preserving the element of surprise. No need to worry about neighbours, no other house could be seen in any direction. A small cottage hidden by trees lay some distance to the west, but even that was not within shouting distance.

"Go back to bed, I'm not ready yet!"

A long length of slender timber no more than two fingers wide, shone in the morning light, preserved and varnished like the bird house itself. Fixed to the wall several feet above the kitchen window, this timber pointed horizontally outward, its far end supported by a rope from high on the gable. Thin wires at 45 degrees in each direction provided sideways stability in a wind.

A few minutes later the bird table suspended by thin white cords hung six feet from the kitchen window, swaying fractionally in a gentle breeze. From its bottom swung four wire containers filled with nuts. On the table itself lay a variety of seed, bread, bacon rind and other tasty morsels, together with nesting material in a small net for the birds to pull at when springtime came. A small waxy Nitelight candle on a saucer completed the image; it should have been burning but wind snuffed out the flame - a cardboard sign scratched out in black ink, read "Dicky's All Night Cafe."

When the two girls descended fifteen minutes later, both ladder and tools had disappeared but the curtains were still closed.

"All right then, what have you been up to?" Jan demanded.

"Yes, I would have slept another two hours! My friends will never believe I was up before seven, and I'm supposed to be on holiday!" Sharon spoke with apparent disgust but had been too curious to stay in bed.

"Draw back the curtains." Gordon's hand swung out in a gesture of invitation.

Jan swept them aside with a simultaneous thrust of both arms. "Ooh! I like it." Gazing through the window, taking in the scene then peering upward at the method of support, she turned with a happy smile, "Clever!"

As good a reception as could possibly have been hoped for. With a nonchalant shrug he waved a hand, "Oh it was nothing."

"You big spoof... I know when you're pleased with yourself!" She stepped close with a kiss and a hug.

Leaning back, he drew a breath in mock alarm. "Hey, not in front of the children!"

As she hugged him again, Sharon lashed out with a clenched fist, but lightly, "What do you mean - Children!"

January saw the tarmac gang back again, a short visit finishing the road into Area 6, one of the dog areas along the riverbank. Last summer this area had been full, the grass deteriorating where so many cars drove over the same tract of ground to reach their pitch. This new tarmac would solve that problem but dog pitches had run short - doggy people liking the situation with the river walk so conveniently near. Last year one witty customer had suggested, "Area nine should be for dogs too."

"The hardstanding?" Gordon had shown surprise. "We keep it for bad weather or for heavy motorcaravans. Most people want grass."

"I do too, and we're happy by the river, but sometimes I'd like hardstanding just to be alone. You could change the area name then; instead of just Area nine, why not add a letter, call it the K9 area?"

That had been back in August, and though the suggestion had appeal, it lay too far from the footpath to be practical for dogs.

As more weeks passed and the new season started, news arrived of a new Tourist Board scheme for grading caravan parks, offering the public a definitive guide to standards for choosing their holiday destination.

"Should we join?" Jan passed the paper over. "Seems a good idea but will they expect clubs and games rooms? Will we get marked down for not having entertainments?"

A customer came in and the letter was laid aside, but reading more thoroughly later made it clear that only quality mattered; toilets, tidy pitches and electric hook-ups were the essentials. Being in on the first year must be good, an application rapidly posted and the inspector's visit awaited.

As Easter arrived and trade increased, the new paper ordering system was well received, particularly by those customer who chose to sleep late, happy that their favourite paper would still be waiting; newspaper sales rose considerably. A fresh ripple of disagreement over the footpath had faded away at least temporarily, complaints about dog mess sending Gordon off with a shovel, removing all traces but knowing more droppings would soon appear. Still it was worth the effort, the path enjoyed by visitors and locals alike. Promising himself to clean it more often, he wondered how practical that promise would be when the site was really busy.

After lunch, the wind began to rise - pleasant enough in the hot weather but Jan, taking a phone message round to a caravanner, noticed Dot and Granville, the wardens who had arrived only the previous week. They were taking down a partially collapsed awning from a caravan whose owner was away, struggling to get it clear before damage was done - all part of the service. Later the wind continued to rise, reaching a strength seldom seen in the valley. Not too many tents had come for Easter, but those present might find sleeping difficult tonight. None had ever been lost or even damaged in the valley, but that could change! How fierce would this wind become? At nine o'clock the laundrette was locked, preventing overnight noise from the machines, and with luck, that should be about it for the evening!

Around 9.30 a tile on the roof clicked; Jan looked anxiously out. "Pity there's no shelter for people from the tents if anything does happen."

Taking the keys, Gordon re-opened the laundrette, then visited each tent telling them the building would be open all night. It might at least give peace of mind.

Morning found nobody asleep on the floor; the wind had moderated, causing no damage. Rumours filtered back later that some coastal sites had been less fortunate. The storm had done something else too. An early warning system set up by the police brought news that someone in the area had used the night's bad weather to break into coinboxes on campsites. "Empty them every evening, or better still change the slots to work on tokens rather than cash," a voice on the phone advised. About to ask where the break-ins occurred, Jan was stopped by a long ring on the doorbell. Seeing a man waiting on the step she said goodbye, replaced the receiver and hurried to the door.

"My electric has gone again. Directly I switched the kettle on, same as before." The voice held accusation rather than apology. Jan took the details, promising it would be fixed soon and making a suggestion. "If you're using a full sized kettle, turn everything else off until it boils. We use five-amp trips on all our sockets, like most sites."

A week later in that quiet period immediately following Easter, these overload switches were converted to ten-amp, removing for good the kettle problem, and slotmeters in the laundrette were changed from coins to tokens as the police had advised - tokens available in the shop. That cleared all the minor changes, or so they thought!

"You really need street lighting." A tourist board inspector had arrived to assess the site's new grading, a likeable chap, his comments interesting and to some extent flattering - one point of conflict, this request for lights. Arguments that people did not visit a remote Cornish valley to be lit up like Oxford Street, were sympathetically listened to, but lighting formed part of the marking system. A compromise was agreed; lamps to be placed by the washing up sinks and one outside each toilet building. Other suggestions included more signs, a roof over the emptying point for chemical toilets and some means of flushing it.

The extra signs were easy; small ones made by a local firm. Over the washing-up sinks a series of neat labels reserved one place for clothes and the rest for crockery. The inspector had suggested, "It will avoid grease from plates or dishes getting on clothes and at the same time stop crockery being contaminated by residues from babies nappies." There had been no need to say more. Ug! One could easily see the wisdom of that! Good idea.

Now, as the little signs were being fixed, Jan walked down to watch, asking, "Why that particular place for clothes washing?"

"The inspector's choice, it's for dirty nappies too."

"Did he say it had to be that one?"

"No. Just reached out his hand and made a motion over the sink." Gordon took an apparently casual step backwards.

"I suppose the end one is..." Jan broke off, rounding on him. "I'll thump you! Dirty nappies - made a motion over the sink! Stop taking the Micky."

Later inside the Ladies, a small plaque declaring 'Sanitary facilities,' appeared over the door of those toilet cubicles that also had a hand basin and waste bin. Fair enough. It was not so much that a woman needing these facilities could not find them for herself the inspector had explained, but the sign would give the impression such cubicles were reserved for that purpose, and might deter others from using it, thereby ensuring its availability for a greater period of time. That too, was very true. Another sign inside the laundrette declared, *'Last wash 8pm, lockup and one hour later'*. The 8pm could be changed to 7pm or 9pm, giving more flexibility for early and peak season respectively. All the signs were plastic and should last indefinitely without repainting; they were or course, fixed with stainless steel screws. The dustbin yard too had a smarter sign; the old one, painted in a hurry at a Council Inspector's request some years before, had become a little tatty and was due for replacement anyway. All in all, as far as signs were concerned and considering the low cost, the inspector's visit had been well worthwhile.

A roof over the drain for emptying chemical toilets was no big job, a few short courses of concrete blocks, some roof timbers and a couple of clear plastic sheets. Nice quiet work for the slack mid-afternoon period, and near enough to the office if a caravan arrived. The walls were rendered and decorated, a small three cornered hand washing basin installed, and a flush system to clean the drain.

With tourists still relatively scarce, a couple of afternoons saw lights installed as agreed outside the various buildings, all the work done quietly and cleared up before most people returned in late afternoon. Few even noticed, except for the lights at night, and there the generally expressed view was a doubtful, "Yes, all right but let's not have any more." A survey over the following weeks, showed 80% of customers against street lighting in any form, many having come to get away from such things. The park had however, achieved its five ticks, the top grading in the scheme's very first season!

Lengthening days brought increasing activity, and not only by holidaymakers. Jan's bird table pulsed with life - blue tits, great tits, green finches, the occasional robin, a pair of Cole tits, and even a male Chaffinch had found his way onto the swaying platform, though more often this species preferred ground feeding with the Blackbirds. From time to time the smaller birds would disappear, put to flight as a Magpie or a Jay glided in. They collected both food and building materials; in a month's time when young fledglings started to hatch, the nuts would be withdrawn and more bird seed made available. Rarer visitors mingled with these common varieties, the greater spotted woodpecker, a tiny willow tit and a pair of nuthatch. A song thrush with a splendidly marked chest appeared several times but lacked either the courage or perhaps the inclination to fly to the table. It seemed to prefer mid-height branches, taking ivy berries, reputedly poisonous - to people at any rate. Jan noticed its funny way of eating.

"Why does that thrush only take berries that are below him when the ones above are much closer?"

Gordon watched with her for a while before offering a reply.

"I think thrushes, often being ground feeders, naturally look downward for their food. One feels a certain affinity with the bird - I've always had a preference for things beneath me."

He was a shade slow stepping back.

CHAPTER 16

Susan

The ducks were being prolific this year, four muscovys sitting in the shed, and three Mallard with nests under conifers around the entrance yard - there may have been more but these ones the family were aware of and were being careful that no one else should find out. They watched each day for the sitting birds to come off and eat, and as the season developed, several hatched. The flock had increased to nearly seventy ducks with one mallard still sitting. Susan, Gordon called her, and though he never mentioned the name, Jan heard him once call softly and saw the duck come running. Rough calculations suggested the eggs had about a week to go. Often, ducks are creatures of habit; this one came for food just after nine most mornings, though occasionally it was later. Today she had not yet appeared. Called away to a leaking standpipe, Gordon rushed off with a new tap and two wrenches, returning shortly with the faulty one.

Jan, having been asked to keep watch, met him at the door. "No sign yet. Go and check; see she's all right."

He had already left food in the usual place but none the less, put the tools down and strode off, slowing to approach the nest with care, trying to look casual so no one would suspect. But something was wrong. Susan was easily recognisable, a shade lighter than normal, a pretty little duck for whom he felt considerable affection. If you knew exactly where to look, the feathers were just visible through branches that hid the nest, but one wing appeared spread out, not at all the demeanour of a sitting duck. Looking casually round again to check no one was near, he stooped, reaching under the conifer, knowing it would not disturb the bird for they were close friends, but concerned all the same least he leave a scent the fox could follow.

Fingers touched a feather; there was no welcoming movement. Dropping a knee to the ground, he stretched farther. The wing was stiff! With great concern now, knowing but not wanting it to be true, he pushed forward, hand gently touching, probing. The body was cold! A great sadness gripped him; he swallowed, vision blurring, feeling the water in his eyes and blinking it back. Dead. This was her first time, she would never experience the fluffy heads of a new brood under her wings now. A child, a young girl, approached. "What are you doing?"

For a moment he could not speak, fighting to mask the emotion that threatened to spill over. He wanted the girl to go; no one could share this moment, it was between them, between him and the duck who had given her trust. Keeping his body hunched over so the child would not see, he forced himself to reply, speaking quietly, "Nothing, just checking for rub..." He stopped, appalled at the word that had almost come, "...for things." It came out with unintended gruffness and the child ran away - he hardly noticed, fingers gently running over the smooth feathers as if they might breathe life... Kneeling there, his head bent in a simple prayer; he knew it was silly but... one finger touched an egg. It was cold! With a trace of panic he felt the rest. They were all cold. It was down to him now; the only thing he could still do for her. Already he blamed himself for the death, for not moving her inside the shed. Would he fail in this too?

Quickly he rose, sprinting to the office, down to the basement, grabbing a small cardboard box, urgency in every movement, jumping up the stairs three at a time, snatching a towel from the bathroom rail, stopping a moment of fold it neatly and with care to form a nest in the bottom, then out through the door, clearing the office steps with a mighty leap and on towards the bush. Moving the duck tenderly to one side, he reached for the eggs, transferring them quickly but carefully before racing off holding the box out in front, not stopping to answer someone's question; he didn't know who, nor heard the words they had uttered. In the office he cleared away papers with a sweep of the arm, placed the box down and quickly turned on the desk light, pulling it close over the eggs to warm them in the only way he knew how. What to do now? He looked down at the brightly lit eggs, partly obscured by the lamp, and bent to peer beneath... there were twelve. Hatching eggs without an incubator was said to be difficult. Were they dead already? No they mustn't be! There had to be a chance.

Think! He gazed down; they were too flat, should be more moulded to a nest shape, and more insulation underneath. Yes, but these eggs must remain under the light, letting the warmth creep back into them. How... another cardboard box! Right. He hurried off, finding one, adding a wad of newspapers to offer insulation, each folded so the outer end rested against alternate sides of the box, starting to form the proper nest shape. Good, but what about moisture? The nest humidity must remain high; Susan would have seen to that herself, carrying water back in her underfeathers. Ah, trickling water down onto those upturned newspaper ends and letting it run down between the sheets should do the job - better be warm water - to evaporate slowly and stop the nest getting too dry. Half a pint a day might suit but play it by feel. What next - the nest shape? Corn! Yes, plenty of that, sacks of it down in the basement; the ducks' main food. Several jugfuls quickly emptied into the box made a thick bed for the eggs, a bed which would hold them in the right shape and help to even out the heat.

Okay, it was ready but must be preheated before the eggs were transferred. They had best remain in their present box under the existing desk light for the moment. Borrowing another flexible lamp from Sharon's room, one used only when she was home, solved the preheating problem. For a quicker start the light was lowered to within a few inches of the corn - later it would be lifted and a thermometer used the ensure the exact temperature.

The immediate crisis over, Gordon's thoughts returned

to Susan. She would be pleased with what had been done - but would she still be happy in a weeks time? By then they should both know. "Don't be so stupid," he lectured himself. "She'll never know. What you need now is to dispose of the body." Black thoughts of revenge and anger suggested the carcass be bated with poison and left, bringing retribution when the culprit returned, but those thoughts were thrust aside. Susan should be buried.

Jan, now sitting in the lounge reinforcing buttons with a needle and thread, saw him descend the basement stairs and return with a shovel. She had offered help preparing the nest but received no reply, and seeing an intensity in his expression had made no further attempt to intrude. Now she watched him with mixed feelings, guessing the intent and sensing his wish to be alone. Her own emotions were conflicting - sadness mixed with a feeling of exclusion - a long time had passed since they had not shared each other's thoughts. They had lost ducks before; why had this one affected him so deeply? Well aware that he still loved her, she wondered for an instant if he had found Susan more attractive.

On returning he failed to say where the body was laid to rest and Jan never asked. Before lunch she watched as the eggs were transferred to the new container, each held in front of the light and three found to be infertile - nine left, but no way to tell if any remained alive. A thermometer now lay alongside the nest, the lamp height adjusted to maintain an appropriate temperature.

"What will you do with them? Leave the box here or move it into Sharon's room." The comment was casual but she hoped he would move them to the little bedroom at the rear. Customers would ask questions and there seemed no chance of success.

"Um... not sure." He opened a drawer, pushing the contents to one side then the other, searching. "Ah." Taking a black felt tip pen, he moved the lamp from the box, reaching to mark the top of each egg with a large cross, turning to explain. "Susan..." he stopped, not meaning to have said the duck's name aloud.

"Susan?" Jan pretended not to know.

He looked at the carpet, shuffling and turning aside. "It's her name, she knows... used to know when we spoke, when I called her..." He stopped, giving a little shrug of the shoulders, turning the palms of both hands momentarily upwards and back as the arms sank unhappily down. "Don't mind, do you?"

There was something poignant about the movement and the way the question was asked. Jan took his hand, squeezing it without comment, then prompted, "You were explaining the crosses?"

"Er... the duck..."

"Susan?"

"Yes, Susan. She would have turned those eggs every day, lovingly turned them over with her beak to stop the ducklings resting too long on one side. I saw her do it only yesterday, she let me watch... don't laugh; most ducks will stop if anyone is near."

Jan checked her expression. Just for an instant the improbability of a duck consciously making so deep a friendship had seemed ludicrous, but she saw no laughter in his face; he really believed it. Perhaps it was true? She waited.

"Well," he looked down at the eggs again, "How she knew which ones had been turned I can't tell, but I should never remember. I don't know how important it is but this way at least I'll do it right. I'll turn them now, then again each night and morning; crosses down in the daytime, crosses up overnight - if anyone looks they won't see the marks. Okay?" He reached in, carefully turning each egg, then from a jug trickled warm water onto the newspaper edges; it was sucked in and carried away like a wick; none falling directly on the eggs. That should maintain the humidity - checking the thermometer he pulled the lamp an inch lower.

"How do you know what heat to use?"

"All birds have a high blood temperature, about five degrees higher than our own, Fahrenheit that is," Gordon paused, looking suddenly anxious, "I wonder if the strong

311

light will affect them; it's dark under the mother. Wait..."
He took a stride towards the door, stopped again, then
hurried back to the kitchen, opening a drawer and easing out
a plastic carrier bag, separating it from a whole host of
others tucked tightly inside - bags brought back with the
shopping. Leaving the office he made for the original nest,
not really wanting to destroy it but needing the feathers.
Back in the office he spread them thickly over the eggs and
thermometer, then took away the lamp and lifted the box.

"Where are you taking it?"

"Down the basement. I can't help light from the lamp
but I *can* avoid sunlight." Another lamp stood on the bench
below; he pulled it over the box and spent the next hour
dashing downstairs at intervals to check the temperature and
adjust the lamp height. Jan shook her head but said nothing,
seeing little prospect of a happy outcome. The eggs had
been cold, a live duck would never have allowed that...
but she could see he must try - or live forever wondering if
the ducklings might have been saved. So far as they knew, no
visitors were aware of the little tragedy, the morning rush
over before the discovery was made.

A single caravan arrived early in the afternoon, followed
shortly by a tent. It was not yet the really busy season and
life was easy, time enough to pop downstairs every ten
minutes if needed, but nothing further could be done now
the lamp's correct height was established. He slipped down
again as they were about to turn in for the night.

"Are they still there?" Jan asked with mild sarcasm.

"Yes, and the crosses are now at the top. Set the alarm
for two o'clock."

"Two o'clock! I will not!"

"We must. Supposing the bulb goes during the night.
The eggs could be cold by morning. I'll have the clock my
side, you needn't wake."

"Oh sure!"

Someone was shaking him. "Wha...What's that noise?"
"The blasted alarm. I can't reach. Turn it off!"

"Okay, give me time, where... Ah. Good. There! Loud isn't it, but I don't suppose anyone heard?"

"If they did, and somebody asks - I'll tell them it was accidentally set for the wrong time. I'm not having people know the truth; it would be all round the site before lunchtime. Who said, *Leave it my side, you needn't wake up*?" Reverting to her normal voice she spoke with feeling, "Some chance!"

"Okay, so you're a light sleeper. Is that my fault?" He opened the wardrobe door rummaging inside, "Where's my dressing gown?"

"You're not going to the North Pole, get on with it and come back to sleep."

"I'm not going down like this!"

"You should wear pyjama bottoms like normal men."

"What do you know about normal men?"

"Nothing. Absolutely nothing! I can promise you that. What are you afraid of?"

"I've told you before, a young chap like me must protect his body from delinquent girls. Remember that phone call and..."

"Delinquent girls? In your dreams! Anyway the house is locked, bolted and chained like Fort Knox! Even the Dagenham girl pipers couldn't see you, far less break in."

"Oh yes they could. They..."

"How? Go on, tell me! Every curtain is drawn so the overhang faces towards a blank wall, I doubt superwoman could see in here." Jan snorted in exasperation, folding her arms and waiting for a reply.

"Those ventilation bricks in the basement. If someone crouches down outside and puts an eye to the slits, they can see in, not easily but by moving their head..."

"I'll move *your* head in a minute! If you don't get that stupid inspection done and get back to sleep, I'll move it right off your shoulders!"

It did seem time to retreat. Not having located the gown, he grabbed the trousers laying nearby, saw her reaching for a vase and hastily left closing the door, pulling them on outside on the landing.

Downstairs in the basement all was well, the light steady, the temperature correct. Thinking they would expect to hear some external sounds he chatted for a few moments, telling them what fine ducklings they would be, then thought of explaining what had happened to their mother but decided against; it might be too traumatic for ones so young. Before departing he looked shiftily towards the vents, then leaned close and made a dozen soft quacks to settle them for the small hours.

The following night was simpler, Jan had taken the clock back to her own side of the bed. He never even heard the alarm, she switched it off immediately, then struggled to shake him into wakefulness. A Dressing gown hung ready over the open door. There was no chatter as he left, but on returning and suggesting, "There, that wasn't so bad," he received the mumbled reply, "Go to sleep. I'm thinking of having you certified."

In the morning she looked drawn.

"Of course I'm tired," she snapped an answer, "I can't sleep. I lie there waiting for that damned alarm to ring. It's your fault; how much longer?"

Later in the day, they walked together to the bridge to feed the trout. Another couple joined them, old customers, friends for many years.

"Your wife is looking a bit tired," the man commented sympathetically.

"Yes, we've had a little problem that kept us..."

"More than a problem I should say." Jan interrupted. "Well after midnight a man came round ringing the doorbell to change a gas bottle. I couldn't get back to sleep for ages. Come on." She grasped Gordon's hand, pulling him towards the office. "There's work to catch up on."

Mounting the steps she pointed, "Inside!" shoving him forward as he made to step through the doorway; following him in, closing the door and leaning her back against it preventing any chance of his leaving again. "You were going to tell them!"

"Why not? They're old friends."

"I don't mind *you* looking a fool, but you're not making me look one too. No one else would get up every night to look at eggs that will never..." she paused, aware of his deep concern in the matter. "It's not very likely you'll succeed you know. I wish you could but I think..." she stopped again, not able to say more.

Gordon offered no immediate reply, well aware the chances were slim and getting less by the day, but he owed it to Susan to keep trying. Was he being unreasonable? "I could sleep down in Sharon's room and take the alarm with me?"

Jan sighed. "No. You're a stupid old fool but I do love you." She smiled, took his hand and moved away from the door. "What other woman could have such excitement in her life?" A touch of sarcasm coloured the whispered comment as they hugged, then leaned back to smile at each other.

"What's with this telling the customers lies? Woken by a man wanting gas? Where did that come from?"

"We did have one once. That chap who had a young child and wanted it for the two o'clock feed. You got up and fetched him one, remember?" She saw him nod and they hugged again. "I had to stop you. Grabbed the first thing that came to mind, didn't have time to consider."

"Do you care so much what people think?"

"Not normally. But they'll laugh and..." she hesitated, "you don't find this amusing do you. It's more serious than you let on, isn't it?"

They had let go of each other but still stood close. Now he turned away, but she had seen the look in his eye and knew the smile was forced when he turned back.

On the fifth evening a faint chirp sounded as the eggs were turned. For a moment he stayed absolutely still, without moving so much as a fingertip, a great leap of hope inside but hardly daring to believe. It could only have come from inside an egg. He lifted it gingerly to an ear, knowing that ducklings could talk even before hatching but still not sure it was so. The chirp came again. It *was* true! He tried another, and another. Four certainly, were alive. An impulse to shout the news almost had him running along the corridor and up the stairs... another glance at the nest stopped him; seeing only four crosses and realising the other five eggs had not been turned, stayed his hand. He had picked them all up to listen but in the excitement had not paid attention putting some down again without turning. Quickly that omission was rectified. The slight delay allowed time for thought; these chicks were alive but how many - and were they strong enough to hatch? He would say nothing, just carry on as before with no change of routine.

Two days later the first eggs were pipped, and by evening three ducklings had broken free of their shells. Careful inspection showed each had all the right features but seemed less sturdy than those hatched in the normal way. All the other eggs except one were pipped, a pimple of raised shell cracked by an egg tooth on each tiny beak. Good, but as the following day arrived it became obvious that in spite of wetting the shells regularly with a finger as the mother would do with wet feathers, the rest of the ducklings were too weak to break out by themselves. They would need help; certain other changes too, must be made. Some of the feathers must be removed and shallow containers for water and chick starter crumbs added to the box. Two things were now necessary; first to help the weak chicks out of their shells, not all at once but a bit more each hour, and secondly to dip the beaks of the stronger ducklings in the water. They would probably not eat yet; for the first day of their young life ducklings tend not to feed, rather they absorb the yoke from their feathers. That single remaining unpipped egg was a problem. Gently Gordon chipped a hole - it was alive, the beak moving weakly.

A day later, only this last one remained in its shell, the rest beginning to fluff up but several without the strength to stand properly. Nevertheless, the time had come! Hurrying upstairs and trying to maintain a deadpan expression, he moved close to Jan, taking her hand and guiding her towards the basement door. At first she failed to understand and resisted, but then somehow sensing his mood, she followed - not saying she had guessed, still fearing to be mistaken. The light was off as they felt their way along the corridor to the workroom - surely that was wrong. With her hand on the bench she waited; the light snapped on.

"Oh! So many. Cute! Are they all right?" A typical mother's first question.

"Not really, but they may be. Several are weak, and one very doubtful." He showed the duckling still in its shell, then lifted two lively ones, putting them in her hands. "These are fine, and this one. The others, well... we won't know for a few days. When we're sure, I'll carry them back up to the office for visitors to see. They like hands. Put those back then hold your hand palm down, just here." He indicated an empty corner. Jan lowered the two back with their brothers and sisters, then placed a hand in the corner. Immediately three ducklings moved underneath.

As the day went on, small tweezers provided a means of giving food, a single special chick crumb placed in the beak of those not yet able to stand steadily enough to feed themselves. The one in real danger could only lay on its back, kicking feebly and was just not going to make it, but even so a single crumb was placed in its beak every hour throughout the day, continuing even after the others were all feeding themselves. Next morning, nine fluffy yellow ducklings emerged from the basement to live on the office desk, warmed now by the desk lamp. At day-five from hatching, the hopeless duckling took a first bite of food on its own, and as time went on the light was moved gradually higher, reducing the heat.

Each evening they came into the lounge, sitting on a towel-covered lap watching television, or playing on the carpet. The lamp stayed on during this time keeping the nest cosy for their later return. A box of tissues lay handily close to wipe up little droppings, and with the tissues eventually exhausted, a toilet roll served the same purpose. Later still they swam in the bath, and as spring matured towards summer, were put in a large cage outside. These ducklings were mottled, darker patches in a mainly bright yellow fluff, lightened gradually to cream as they grew; tubby little birds playing in and out of a large tray of water. Finally, June saw their release to the river with the other ducks, the cage left available with the door almost closed to stop bigger ducks stealing their food. Occasionally a toddler would try to chase them - they seemed to know when to run, diving in the river to escape but coming out again as soon as an adult appeared. More often it was other children that defended them, particularly young girls who would sit on the grassy bank offering bread or just holding out a hand for the little beaks to investigate.

As the summer went on, the site never had a tamer, friendlier brood, in fact they were now almost fully grown ducks. Gordon was mother, his hands the only things they saw in their first days of life apart from each other. This seeing each other was important, preventing them imprinting as a single duck can - at least they knew they were ducks - but to them humans, and two humans in particular, were friendly giants, not things to be wary of. Their easy assurance with people even made the other ducks less timid - not that River Valley ducks had ever been that, but this year they were exceptionally amenable to being handled. Not many wild Mallard will let themselves be stroked and enjoy it, but these did. All the females were named though with the differences in plumage so small, it was difficult for most people to remember which was which and address them with their proper title.

Watching this brood taking bread from some children one day, Gordon said quietly, "Susan would have been proud of them."

"She would," Jan nodded. "If your affections ever stray, it will be a female duck, not another woman, yes? Tell me the names again."

"That one is Sable," he pointed and a duck immediately started towards them. "See the dark patch of her beak?" He reached into a pocket, and keeping the hand turned backwards, knelt on the ground. Sable came to the hand, nuzzling round it until she found the bread. "Look, that's Olive, the one with the greeny tinge to her beak. Audrey, has a greenish beak too, it's a common colour but watch for a white tipped feather on one wing." He looked around for more but the others were moving off at a run towards someone throwing bread farther upstream. "I'll tell you the others another time, but that one," he pointed along the bank, "the mallard with the very dark feathers, that's Eileen, the backward duck; she still has impaired vision on one side but no other weakness. She's very bossy with the other females."

"What about the drakes?"

"You can name them. I'm not really interested in males."

***

Dot and Granville, the two wardens were still helping but only for an hour or so each day. Just now their caravan was empty, they were off shopping in Truro. Jan glanced through the office to see Gordon appear from the service passage in the nearest toilet building carrying a saw in one hand, a large plywood sheet grasped in the other. Intrigued, she watched, seeing him disappear round the building then cross towards the laundrette. Resisting an urge to dash out, she waited, moving back into the room but still having a clear view. Moments later he emerged again, running back to fetch a carpenter's stool and a handful of tools. What exactly they were, was difficult to see.

It was mid-afternoon, most people out. Slowly she moved forward, grasping the knob, leaving the door wide open and starting stealthily across the yard. Half-a-dozen paces and the phone rang, a bell high on the gable wall clanging out across the valley. "Damn!" Swinging round she raced back, running up the steps, swinging the door closed and reaching to grab the receiver, not wanting him coming to investigate as he surely would if it rang for too long. The call was a booking, something most welcome - but couldn't it have waited another ten minutes? Taking the details she held her voice steady, grabbing a deep breath now and then between the words. "Yes. Oh certainly... Of course. Yes do." Putting the phone down while still scribbling the last note, an irrelevant thought demanded, "Why is the customer always right?" Rising, she hurried out and ran soft footed across the yard hoping it wouldn't ring again for just a few minutes.

Peering round the door, she watched silently. He had his back turned away, the wood balanced on the stool as he sawed down one side. Would he jump if she spoke now? Better not in case he slipped. Carrying out any piece of work without discussing it first was unusual. She stayed silent but he stopped, somehow feeling her presence, turning slowly, some unknown sense betraying her position. Only her head was showing, there would have been ample time to sway back out of sight but she stepped forward.

"Oh yes. And what are we making so secretly? Don't I get consulted any more?"

"Ah, it's..." he waved an arm, giving himself time to think. "Women shouldn't be so nosy." She was right, they habitually discussed any new project, but an argument that morning had strained relations; nothing great, just a small disagreement about a customer; it was bound to happen occasionally as the site began to get busy.

"Okay, so don't tell me - I'm not *that* interested anyway."

"It's a pair of stocks, like in the old days, for locking up women who argue with their husbands." He looked at her feet, then up to her head and down again, turning to looked from one end of the board to the other as if measuring it.

"Better make it six inches longer." She was smiling now, looking *him* up and down, the little dual bringing good humour back.

" Okay, it's a notice board, double sided so you can turn it over to show a fresh lot of leaflets quickly. I still have to varnish it."

It seemed unlikely. Jan glanced at the polished wooden partition walls only partly covered with pamphlets and posters; there was miles of space already. A notice board would be superfluous. About to challenge the proposition, she pointed to some chunky timber pieces lying on the floor but the phone rang out again. Eyeing him with a warning glance, she turned and ran.

At lunch an air of intrigue settled across the table, many a quiet smile but no words. Only once did the phone ring but Jan carried on eating, knowing he would never risk loosing the booking. With the meal finished she moved to the fridge, opening the door slightly and standing so as to conceal the contents.

"Oh, we're out of milk. I'll get some from the shop, I need to check the fridge anyway." Hurrying out, she tore a piece of selotape from the roll, stuck it quickly over the shop bell contact, opened the door and raced to the laundrette. No sign of the so-called notice board could be seen. She ran to the service passage in the second toilet building, not finding it there either but the smell of varnish was strong. Grabbing one of the many tins of Vim stored under the workbench, she sprinkled white bleach powder lightly on the concrete floor, walking backwards to the doorway and stepping out, stretching over to place the tin on the corner of the bench.

Towards mid-morning the following day, when Gordon had gone off with a caravan to find a suitable pitch, Jan slipped from the office. Dot and Granville had not yet started cleaning as she raced across to the service passage. The smell of varnish was strong again! Looking closely at the floor showed someone had trodden in the powder, but the marks went no farther than a ladder leading to the loft space. "So that's where it is?"

She looked upwards, putting a foot experimentally on the first rung - the ladder was loose, not tied to anything, its steep angle causing her to step back. Never mind, she knew where it was.

A few days passed, interesting days with that edge of fun, before Gordon returned to the house one afternoon ostensibly for coffee, but with a smug look on his face.

"Well? Is it finished or still hidden in that loft?" Jan saw his mouth drop momentarily open... and then they were smiling at each other. She thought about pretending not to want to know, but decided to put it another way. "No chance I can escape seeing it I suppose?"

He stepped to the doorway, raising a hand and making a finger clicking motion, indicating that she should follow, like someone signalling a dog to heel, only the fingers refused to click. She smiled; he never could do that. She lifted her own hand and a sharp click rang out - they grinned again at each other, both hurrying to the door.

On entering the laundrette she saw it straight away, a new table-like work surface fixed to the wall where the last sink ended, making an L-shaped corner. Underneath, leaning against the wall was a baby bath - the intention clear.

"Brilliant!" She reached for the bath, putting it on the table but he shook his head, taking it off and placing it on the sink's draining board.

"Use the hair drying shower to fill it." He demonstrated, taking the flexible chromium lead, turning on and letting water spray in, then turned off and lifted one end of the small oval bath so the water ran into the sink and away. "The new work surface is for changing nappies. You approve?"

"Yes!" She punched him lightly. "You didn't think I believed that tale about the twin-sided notice board did you? Come on I'll show you." She made to move off but he grabbed her hand, pulling back.

"There's more." Leaning against the new table he put both hands backwards and with a great heave, plonked his butt on the surface, then bounced up and down a bit. Repeating this on the drainer where the little bath would stand, he lifted a finger, "You know why, don't you? They've got to be..." The hand rose, and as it descended they said in unison, "Strong!"

Leaving the laundrette, a small diversion and she showed the white powder on the service passage floor, explaining its purpose. Honour satisfied on both sides, they walked back to the house hand in hand.

Visitor numbers were increasing, camping spaces getting short. Tents covered Area 2, many were new to the site but that was normal; young couples who first found the valley using a small tent would come again for a few years then suddenly turn up in a caravan. Not everyone chose this route, a few families stuck to their tent year after year and not only for cost; Isa and Brian for instance from Peterborough, had certainly not economised on their latest tent - some just found camping more to their liking.

Earlier in the year, one of the campers started feeding a hedgehog. The first night they heard a noise but saw nothing; guessing the animal, whatever it might be, was after the bag of scraps left outside. Morning found the bag tipped over, its contents nearby on the grass. The following night a saucer of bread and milk replaced the scraps, and peeking through a gap deliberately left in the entrance flap, the family watched a hedgehog in the moonlight. After that it came shortly after dark every evening, expecting to find a meal, not even concerned when they left the front of the tent wide open to watch. Because of this nocturnal friend, the family booked an extra week, but eventually they had to go - leaving behind a problem.

Having decided tents were a good source of food and not having its appetite sated at the usual spot, the hedgehog visited other tents in its quest, snuffling and burrowing to see what might be found. When word got round among other campers, many families began leaving something out. As the weeks went by the spiky animal would even go inside to eat; probably the best fed hedgehog in Cornwall, soon to be in need of Weightwatchers!

It was inevitable one must suppose, that just as had happened previously with the tortoise, a recently arrived family unfamiliar with its habits should receive a visit. A lady in just such a tent put her hand out of bed one night - and screamed! Tales reached the shop in the morning. Several nearby tents had been involved, people running about half dressed, shouting, lights coming on; no one knew where the hedgehog had gone. Most were more annoyed that the creature might have been frightened, than they were at being woken in the night, but generally it seemed a subject of amusement.

When the poor lady came into the shop, a group of women were still discussing the nocturnal wanderings of their men. Seeing them, stopped her suddenly in the doorway, unsure whether to enter or run back to the tent. Nervously, she stepped inside.

"I'm so sorry to have caused all the fuss. I'm not normally that nervous but I woke up in the dark to hear rustling in the tent, put my hand out kind of automatically and touched this spiky thing!" She gave a little shudder. "I quite like hedgehogs, it just didn't occur to me that one could get inside our tent. Lying in the dark, just woken up and still sleepy, I was barely awake when it moved under my hand. I just shrieked. My husband says it's a good job he hasn't a dicky heart. Good job I haven't either, I should have passed right away on the spot! Hope I've not frightened your hedgehog away completely, everyone seems so attached to it."

The lady turned to another shopper, explaining yet again - she may still have been a little in shock or perhaps it was her normal manner, for it seemed she couldn't stop talking, still chatting as the other campers left. Gordon continued to listen sympathetically, wondering how to escape. He would have to be more careful and warn everyone who pitched on that area!

Late July as usual, bristled with activity; one lived for the moment, made snap decisions - not always the right ones - and hurried on. A happy month but with little time to rest. Jan at last managed to make coffee, intending to carry it to the lounge when the bell rang again. Leaving the cups she hurried from the kitchen, opening the office door to a youngish woman with light brown hair and an unhappy face.

"I'm sorry, your spin dryer... it's stopped working. I may have, um, done something wrong?" Her voice was uncertain, questioning.

"I'll come." Jan slipped the catch as she left.

The spin dryer had indeed stopped; the laundrette filled

with an acrid smell. Opening the lid, the clothes had been rammed in filling every inch of space, totally overloaded.

"Did I... um, was it my fault?" The woman asked nervously.

"Yes, overloaded. You certainly forced them in - and how! They take less than half this amount." Jan sighed, forgetting to be diplomatic, the seasonal pressure placing tact at a premium. Regretting the bluntness she turned, "Never mind, we'll fix it." Reaching up, opening a window to disperse the smell and placing the stay-open hook on the door handle, she hurried back towards the office. Fifteen minutes later Gordon was driving off to Penzance for a new spin dryer. With the wardens not yet returned from a shopping trip, Jan was left on her own, dodging between office and shop, life a bit frantic! Gradually as mid-morning approached, things became easier, most people leaving for the beach. There was even time to tip away the cold coffee and make a new cup, but another caravan drawing up again prevented her drinking it.

A couple who she failed to recognise came to the office, but apparently they had been the previous year. This time they had two grandchildren in the car. Taking the money and leading them off to a pitch, Jan headed towards the front field; three places were vacant, caravans that had left this morning. Swinging left at the corner, a horn sounded loudly behind caused her to turn. The car had stopped, the man stepping out. "Not that way; round behind the house where we were last year."

"Sorry, that area is only for adults."

"Yes but we don't want a pitch out here," the man pointed to where other youngsters were playing. "It's full of children!"

This was what she hated; why did these things happen when Gordon was away? Did he slip off deliberately? A fist clenched at the irrational thought. She looked again at the children in the back of the car, then at the man. "There are other areas, smaller ones but mostly with older children, not ones where your grandchildren would find new friends so easily."

"I still don't see why we can't..." A voice inside the car caught his attention and he bent, listening, then straightened again. "Can we move later if we don't like it?"

"Oh sure," Jan nodded, it would be Gordon's problem then. "Follow me, there are three pitches available. You can choose."

Fifteen minutes later she was looking at the new spin dryer in the back of the car, and by lunchtime it was fitted and working - another morning survived.

"What have you got to smile at?" Jan asked as they ate, tucking the food away at speed and hoping the office bell would stay silent. She didn't know why but she was smiling herself.

"Don't you feel it?" he lifted a fist, punching an imaginary target. "Don't you feel a tingle when everything goes wrong and you fix it. All these people's holiday relying on us and we don't let them down? Doesn't it give you a zing."

"Yes, I suppose it does." Her smile broadened, "But I'll give you a zing if you keep disappearing just when I get a difficult customer."

That afternoon two things happened to make life even sweeter. Firstly the woman who burnt out the spin dryer came in with her husband; they had seen the new one in the laundrette and insisted on paying for it. Gordon took the cheque, thanking them, explaining after they left that he had really intended to refuse the money, but thought that doing so might make the woman feel uncomfortable.

"Oh yes, I'm sure!" Jan punched him lightly.

Towards evening, the lady from the caravan that had wanted the adult area, came to the office to say they were very happy on children's field after all, and that their grandchildren had made friends with a young family from the next pitch. Great when things come together!

August was easier this year with Dot and Granville managing the midday cleaning, much of the mowing and helping any customers with car trouble. Now in the school holidays, families were more common than couples, the site's balance of population changing. With vastly increased numbers of children, bicycles were causing concern. One lad, sweeping at uncontrollable speed down the steep, smoothly-tarmaced road from the terraces, had panicked when the mower appeared crossing the road ahead. Unsure which way to turn, he hit the machine a glancing blow, denting it severely, then careered off onto a grassy area, narrowly missing two parked caravans before crashing into a belt of gorse. The boy escaped with minor scratches but considerable shock.

Back at the office, this incident posed a problem. "What do we do? It's only a matter of time before someone gets badly hurt. Suppose he hit a young toddler instead of the mower."

"You've seen his parents."

"Yes. Told them it might be safer if the bicycle wasn't used any more, but other children will be using theirs?"

No easy solution came to mind, perhaps the smooth tarmac was not such a brilliant idea, though it came in for much of praise - as did the laundrette which was now open later. The little figure *9* had been screwed into position to make the sign read '*Last wash 9pm, lockup one hour later*', Granville had the key and generally locked the door, since his caravan was nearby. Often enough people ignored the sign putting a coin in and starting the wash cycle much too late. Insisting on locking up on time to stop other machines being used, Granville gave these latecomers a choice; take the washing out or collect it in the morning. "The guv'nors start cleaning early, they'll open it for you then."

Mostly it went smoothly enough, the explanation that machine noise might otherwise keep babies in nearby tents awake, was usually accepted. One evening two families travelling together set the machines into action at five minutes to ten and refused to leave. A man from the nearest tent came up to complain and loud words were shouted. Gordon hurried across, trying to cool the situation but positions had become set, no one prepared to lose face. Turning with a shrug as the argument continued he strode off, heading towards the office but doubled back, slipping round through the dustbin yard to cross the road quickly and unlock a small building housing the main electrical gear. Opening a large white cabinet and swinging back the big door, he studied a bank of switches in the dim light, found the one marked 'laundrette' and flicked it. Locking up and taking the same circuitous route back, he found the laundrette in darkness, all the machines stopped. Jan was there too, attracted by the shouting. The aggrieved families, knowing who she was had drawn around her complaining loudly. Granville and Dot standing to one side were also involved.

Gordon's reappearance triggered another round of hard words but he merely shrugged. "Nothing I can do. The automatic timer switch has cut in - it won't restart until seven tomorrow morning. Don't worry though, I'll be up at six to clean the toilets; when the power comes back on I'll pop another token in and restart the washes - unless you'd prefer an early call?"

That offer shut them up, the tone of the conversation changing, even an apology for not reading the notice on the wall.

Gradually numbers declined, the strain easing, sad in one way for they enjoyed the struggle of mid-season, you knew you were alive then! So many people depended on their judgement, their ability, certainly never a dull moment - and never a day off! With instant decisions demanded, mistakes were made of course, the pace exhausting at times; but they loved this constant challenge!

Such efforts however, were not sustainable. September and quieter times came as a relief. Just twenty caravans remained, only two with children, the rest mainly retired people. Great! So easy to please, so much time to relax - luxury! The coming winter held promise too, no great projects planned for the immediate future, the site now exactly as most visitors liked it. A few might want clubs and entertainment, takeaways, games rooms and the like, but the vast majority would hate such things. People who came inland away from the beach mostly wanted nothing more than a quiet peaceful place to relax. Perhaps the decision to avoid such things was just laziness but neither Jan or Gordon thought so. The valley had ideal surroundings; trees, birds, ducks, the river; why spoil it? Plenty of places offered frantic activity - activity mostly designed to part people from their money; at least a few sites should be kept for those who holiday to relax and unwind. It is written somewhere that ants have had the good sense to stay unchanged for the last 30 million years. How do they know what ants were like that long ago? Specimens preserved in amber are identical to today's ants, even to small parasites that live on them. River Valley had become very like the ant, disinclined to change - not in respect of quality or facilities, but in the basic concept - that it should provide a tranquil place for those seeking peace.

Developing the site's computer program might appear to contradict that aim for nothing could be more modern, but it was more a hobby, not affecting the valley's atmosphere. Besides, it pleased the visitors, the little printed receipts still a novelty seen on very few sites.

The program was in fact becoming quite sophisticated. For the benefit of foreign visitors, it now printed bills in several languages, the information fed in from translations done by visitors themselves, or in one case by a more devious route. While discussing a Dutch language bill with a visitor from Holland, the man mentioned a brother-in-law of Hungarian extraction living in Vermont in the USA. Addresses had been exchanged, a letter sent and in a few weeks the computer could speak Hungarian - well perhaps not speak, but it had every word required for the bill. The touch of a single key at the right time, would produce a printout in Hungarian, then automatically reprint in English.

"Hi Desi, how are the family?" a passing thought acknowledged the help. Noticing Jan standing by the window, Gordon stood up, stretched and wandered across watching Francis, the biggest and oldest Muscovy drake, seeing off a young contender. "That's ten languages now in the computer,

329

pressing H will give you Hungarian."

"Single letter codes are better. Why must we press NL for Dutch?"

"What single letter would you choose? D is already used for German, and N is for Norwegian. Remember the chap who translated Norwegian for us and in return I gave him that book, er... *Sleigh Ride*. Put my foot in it, didn't I; told him it was about Finland really but that was almost the same as Norway - like telling a Scotsman he's almost English! We need someone from Spain now?"

"Better hide Francis then."

"Why?"

"Spanish people may not like sharing a site with Francis Drake."

Jan had also acquired a pen-friend in the USA; Anne, from down south near Jackson. Life in general was easier too. There were still physical jobs ahead, hedge trimming, painting, trimming back turf that encroached on the road edges, but they could wait for winter. At the moment, a little cleaning, changing gas bottles, seeing in the occasional caravan that still turned up; just enough activity with ample free time - an ideal life! Odd things, of course, cropped up now and then. The drain leading from the centre toilet building blocked for the third time in a week. There had to be some basic cause for that - by now every jot of roughness should have worn off the pipework; most years not a single drain blocked in the whole season. Closer investigation showed the fault to lie with a particular tree. Near one corner of the centre toilets, a supposedly dwarf conifer, Green Pillar, had grown to many times the expected size, its roots penetrating the sewer pipe. The cause of this spectacular expansion was not clear, a wrongly labelled species perhaps - but now that it was feeding on really nutritious stuff, the growth could only be expected to accelerate! Cutting it down might be drastic but a definite cure, the stump left in place rather than disturb neighbouring plants. That drain never blocked again. Pity to lose a tree but a host of others were doing well, the entrance looking increasingly attractive with conifers of various sizes, textures and colours in the Cornish walls ahead. Those visitors still arriving should be impressed, many slowed when approaching the bridge, stopping to gaze at them, and in both directions along the river.

Everyone loved the stream. How many years had it flowed through the valley? Before man, no doubt. Did dinosaurs once drink from its waters? Who knows, it was all part of the great continent then. Lizards, tiny ones about the size of a finger, still lived around the site if anyone looked carefully on a sunny day. The photo album showed a picture of Sharon aged ten with a little lizard on her jumper, just like a brooch. They were seen by campers sometimes, basking in the hot sun then shooting off to hide when approached - it was quite normal to find people coming to the office and asking what they were. Quick eyes too saw trout when they jumped, but most people just heard the plop as a fish dropped back into the stream, turning heads to find only a circle of ripples spreading across the water. One morning a salmon more than two-feet long, a monster for this small river, swam upstream to rest in a shadow cast by the bridge. Word spread and people came to look but none could tempt it - smaller fish were rising, racing the ducks to snatch bread thrown on the water, but the big fella just lay on the bottom, nose into the current, causing some merriment, particularly among the women present when their men failed to induce it to rise.

"There," A woman pointed "An intelligent fish, must be female."

"Why?" her husband stood one knee raised with a foot on the parapet, tossing in another piece of bread.

"Knows when to keep its mouth shut!"

CHAPTER 17

Fluffy

The approach of October saw less caravans, only eleven staying, not so much money but friendly, even more time to stop and chat. After talking with one couple about the ducks, about Cornwall in general, other sites and just anything that came to mind, Jan returned to the house, her determination renewed. For a week or more she had quietly striven to achieve an aim, not nagging, not even arguing, just working a word in when the opportunity occurred. Now she must try again.

"A visitor told me today about the toilet buildings at Wood Farm up in Dorset, said they were all tiled. Wonder what ours would look like? Are we right to keep putting it off?"

Gordon made no immediate reply but shuffled uncomfortably from one foot to the other, looking out across the river. Six weeks ago, as the peak season faded away, tiling had hardly been considered, certainly not for the immediate future. Chatting more leisurely to the autumn customers however, had made him uneasy. Nowhere had a nicer setting than this valley; were they really falling behind again? He turned back to reply. "I know we'll need to soon, but it's expensive. Shouldn't we wait a year or so?"

Why were people never satisfied - expectations always rising, a constant battle to stay in the race as standards rose. Later that week another couple spoke of the toilets at Wild Rose park in Cumbria. Standing chatting to these caravanners, listening to the description, knowing River Valley's facilities were being compared unfavourably, was a new experience.

The couple concerned were not even aware such comparisons had been made but it was there, hidden in what was not said.

Just how expensive would it be anyway? Tentative enquiries were made; local tiling firms contacted and chatted to, each refusing any indication of price without inspecting the job. Reluctantly, firm quotations were requested. Over a period the letters arrived, even the cheapest asking more than the toilets originally cost to build, years of high inflation taking a toll. Nevertheless, a firm was chosen, a timetable agreed. Once the site closed at the end of October, Gordon would remove all doors, basins, cisterns, mirrors and hooks from each building. The toilet pans however, would stay. Cemented solidly to the floor they could not be moved; the tilers must work round them. An English tile was chosen; dearer than Spanish but the biscuit (the body of the tile) was stronger and should last indefinitely. The pattern, Glade Pearl, by Johnson Tiles, had a subtle mottled creamy surface with a faint border, its pale colour selected to preserve the toilets' light, airy quality - a patterned tile in pink on the same background to be randomly scattered at a rate of one pattern for every twenty plain tiles.

The floor would be covered too, in reddish flecked, cushion edged tiles; that is to say the edges slightly rolled over to prevent visitors feet catching against any sharp ridges. Anti-slip floor tiles were chosen for inside the showers, in front of the urinals and at the outer door threshold, to prevent slipping in these vulnerable places. Four inch high curb tiles laid as a skirting, would join floors smoothly to walls making cleaning easier - a really professional job!

So much for the planning. It seemed straight forward enough - should be finished by Christmas. However, niggling doubts persisted on the wisdom of dismantling all three toilet buildings at one time. What if the work was delayed? Building firms had been known to take on more than they could manage. Get everything in writing; that was the secret!

"You can type out an agreement," Jan warned as she saw him busy at the desk, "but what makes you think the tiling boss will sign it?"

"Firms worry most about getting paid. I've included a clause showing payments are due when each building is complete."

Sure enough, this strategy succeeded, the contract duly signed and Gordon set to work.

"How much more?" Jan asked as over a hundred doors, basins and cisterns were carted through the house and down into the basement. A mass of mirrors, taps, toilet roll holders, coat hooks and the like soon followed.

With everything clear the tilers arrived and straight away a problem arose. Existing paint must be stripped from the walls before a tile was laid, otherwise they would soon come loose - or so the mastic firm advised. Fine, but this paint stubbornly resisted. It was scraped, softened with hot air blowers, doused with paint stripper and scrubbed with wire brushes, all to very little effect. Completion by March when the site reopened, began to seem doubtful, the outlook bleak!

"Whose silly idea was it to tile the toilets anyway." Jan demanded one evening.

Already uptight at the delay, and well remembering her little hints and nudges three weeks ago, Gordon gripped the arms of the chair, stiffening and moving forward. "Never hit a lady," the warning thought conjured a tempting picture of that nice scene from 'The Taming of the Shrew' where Petruchio puts Katharina over his knee and wallops her bottom. "Nice idea!" Mumbling the comment under his breath, he sunk back again in the chair. It had been a long hard day. Removing paint was the contractor's problem but he had worked with them since early morning trying to move the job on, changing from one tool to another and back again, endlessly. Progress was being made, but so slowly!

For the tiling firm, this extra cost in hours and wages proved unacceptable! A pair of sand-blasters were hired, two young chaps and a compressed air machine. On that first morning, one man entered the building carrying the blasting hose. He looked like a spaceman, another hose supplying fresh air directly to his helmet like a diver. Seeing clouds of dust that shortly spumed from the doorway made the need for such precautions clear; impossible to breathe inside the building otherwise. The man at work was not even visible when looking through a window in that room of flying dust.

This drastic remedy certainly proved effective, a single day saw the Gents side stripped of every inch of paint. As sand-blasting moved to the Ladies, Gordon helped clean up paint and sand particles left behind, then assisted the three men, all expert tilers, fetching and carrying for them but never actually laying any tiles.

"Leave it to the experts," he answered in reply to Jan's query one lunchtime. "We're paying them after all, and there *is* another reason. If any tiles come loose, they can't say I laid them!"

"They'd never do that - would they?" Doubt sounded clearly in her voice.

"I'm not giving them the chance! One job I *am* doing each morning before they arrive is to sound all the previous day's tiles, tapping them with a pencil. Any hollow ones I mark with a felt tip pen. The mastic firm says adhesive should cover ninety percent of the surface. The chaps objected at first, but taking out a couple of marked ones showed less than half the tile in contact with adhesive."

As days passed the bedding improved, the tiles more solidly stuck; less and less hollow ones appearing. Those few found still had to come out, but to save precious minutes Gordon handled much of this removing, which was time consuming and fiddly, easy to chip an adjoining tile, a need to be patient and careful. Then one of the lads would slip in a new tile, properly bedded - the work of a moment. As an aid to push tiles more firmly into the mastic, one tiler produced a rubber hammer, pressing each firmly into position. A day later another hammer appeared, again of rubber but larger. These tools were shared from time to time and acquired names.

"Pass me Relubbus Number One," a voice called and a hand tossed him the smaller hammer. A short distance to one side someone was already pressing softly away with

Relubbus Number Two. Very few tiles were now marked with a cross in the morning, though every single one was tested. So far as one could tell, all work was of the highest quality; it had to be with Gordon constantly watching, and because he was always there, helping and saving them time, he could see everything was done properly and ask for remedial action when needed.

As Christmas approached Jan was increasingly worried, and she was not alone! Not even the first Gents was complete, some floor tiles still to be laid. No chance yet to refix the basins and other fittings or connect the new pipe-work for hot and cold water, and for drainage. Ten weeks only to opening day! Would it be ready?

Steve's arrival home pushed these worries aside, a bright spot, news of his army friends, of manoeuvres, of baiting the sergeant and the consequent five mile run in full pack - fit young men in the prime of life. But this was no regular leave. He was going abroad, joining British forces in Belize, jungle country not too far from the equator; the Gulf of Mexico on one side, Caribbean on the other. Expecting heat, insects, discomfort and a certain amount of danger, Steve was nevertheless pleased at the prospect.

"It includes a sea diving course," he said by way of explanation. No further details were offered but under close questioning it emerged that instruction on underwater equipment and diving techniques would be received over many weeks in clear warm waters teeming with tropical fish; a prospect looked forward to, its details gleaned from a returning soldier. Early in January, departure day arrived but Steve was not at home, he had left the previous morning announcing his intention to spend the night with 'a friend'. From his preparations and appearance Jan made the assumption that this friend was female and guessed at his desire to get for one last time, something that might be in short supple in a jungle army base! She thought about it again after the lad left, torn between wishing him success and concern about what sort of girl it might be.

Now, just a few hours before he must catch the train,

she wished he would return, wanting to cook him a meal before leaving. Looking at the clock she moved to the window eyeing the sky - it was cold outside, a few flakes of snow whipping across, driven by strong wind, the first snow in the valley for more years than she cared to remember.

With an hour to go, Steve arrived, ate a hurried meal then with Dad driving and Mum in the front passenger seat, they set off for the station. Snow was still falling lightly; little flakes here and there swept along by the wind. It presented no problems, the six miles covered quickly as they chatted but towards Penzance the flakes began to thicken. The train was in but not yet due to leave; with Steve's kit installed in a carriage, they stood on the platform talking. A roof overhead kept the weather at bay but along towards the engine, driving snow swept across the tracks, visibility dropping. In spite of a reluctance to part, it seemed unwise to hanging on; best get back while the roads were reasonable. With a final hug and clasp of hands, they left, waving and hurrying away to find the car already white, the windows partially obscured. Heading homeward the intensity increased, blizzard like, driving into the windscreen in such volume that seeing became tricky - but stopping seemed equally unwise, something could easily run into them and anyway, it might get worse. The road surface was now completely white, a depth of two or three inches already laying. Arriving eventually at Relubbus, they stopped at Jim's bungalow, hurrying in to check he was okay and report Steve's safe departure. Restarting again afterwards proved difficult, wheels spinning, gradually finding traction and sliding uncomfortably on the road surface. As the speed increased, drifted snow hit by the front bumper flew up over the bonnet, obscuring the screen, the wipers at maximum speed struggling to clear it.

"The tilers won't get here tomorrow." Jan stood by the window after they rushed indoors, looking up at the driven flakes. "you realise that in twenty-four hours Steve will be sitting in 95 degrees or more with the sweat running off him."

In fact he was not so lucky. A phone call that evening found him still in London, the train had sat for three hours at Penzance station. Cornwall really had no idea how to deal with this sort of weather! A few days later all traces of snow were gone, the tilers working again and better still, Friday saw the first Gent's completed. Great! Progress at last!

While surplus materials were carried off to the Ladies, Jan started cleaning, washing away at those toilets left in place during tiling. Rubbing off bits of mastic and trying to bring back the lustre, the pans did not respond. In the end, she called Gordon over.

"Something's wrong, they won't shine!"

He tried, but with no better effect. No matter how vigorously they were rubbed, these pans still looked dull and dirty. Adhesive perhaps, stuck to the surface? A closer inspection revealed the truth. Sand-blasting! The glaze was breached by thousand upon thousand of little pits; the black plastic seats too were destroyed, their surface no longer shiny but roughened like course sandpaper. In alarm they looked hurriedly around; the ceilings had been similarly blasted - everything, even glass in the windows was pitted!

Serious! Catastrophic perhaps? Just for a start every toilet in the building, both Ladies and Gents, must be removed and replaced with new ones. A surveyor was brought in to provide independent evidence if needed, then the tiling firm boss phoned. Subcontractors were his responsibility, though no reflection on his own men, for he had hired the sandblasters in good faith as specialists. Notes were taken and records made, together with innumerable photos; an investigation showing the other buildings just as bad. The entire site's loos must be replaced, and weeks were passing, action needed! No time for insurance approval - it wouldn't be the first occasion necks had been stuck out and risks taken!

It's an ill wind they say, that blows nobody any good. A quick trip to the plumbing suppliers found their staff delighted with this sudden order for thirty WCs, a standard pattern in white.

"Just had a new delivery... over there," the man pointed

at a mass of white pans in one corner of the yard. "Not had time to stack them in the storerooms yet."

"I could save you the trouble, collect them myself today if the cost is right?"

They haggled for a while before agreeing a price that did not include delivery. That suited Gordon well; he wanted to examine each one, rejecting any with chips - after all, these would be River Valley toilets! Six fitted in the car, each covered in its own blanket for the journey to ensure they arrived in prime condition. The first batch driven home was carefully unloaded and stored in the sitting room.

"I'll nip off for another load. Re-check them while I'm gone, will you? And watch your hands." With that he left.

Carefully inspecting each loo, Jan discovered two with a bad glaze inside the pan; sharp protrusions certain to catch disposable nappies and sanitary towels, for in spite of being asked not to, many visitors still flushed them down the loo. It paid to take care when searching for these blemishes - they could easily tear a probing finger.

An hour or so later, six more toilets rested in the lounge and two from the original load were on their way back. With a sigh Jan looked at the little array, dropped on her knees and started the inspection, finding only one faulty. By teatime, thirty pans graced lounge and office, most destined to remain for some time, much to the surprise of various friends who visited as the days passed - in Wales she might have acquired the name, 'Jan the loo!'

Tiling was continuing but not fast enough! One of the men had a problem. "Your floors are a damn nuisance near the shower doors. All angles and changes of slope - these kerb tiles are difficult to cut!"

A solution was found but again it took time. As the tilers marked the required cuts, Gordon went quickly to the basement, emerging later with the tiles ground to shape on a carborundum wheel normally used for sharpening tools. Stuck into place with mastic, they finished those difficult corners perfectly but it was taking too long! The next batch marked, were put aside to be shaped that evening when darkness prevented outside work.

As days passed, Jan watched the constant activity; glaziers arriving to replace those sandblasted windows, the three tilers constantly at work and a group of contract painters arriving to blitz the damaged decorations. These painters only came at weekends, moonlighting perhaps from more permanent work. Meanwhile there were old loos to remove, new loos to install, basins and cisterns to re-erect and a maze of pipework to replace. Time had run short, pressure mounting!

"What were you doing last night, the bedclothes were everywhere!" Jan put breakfast on the table; it was still dark outside. "You should sleep like a log, not be restless."

"Restless? Had a bit of a dream, that's all."

"Oh yes? Defending me from a hoard of young men?"

"No quite. We were building a palace in the desert. This King had lots of wives and... "

"Don't tell me. You had to keep them all happy?"

"No, I was building them a new bathroom. They wanted rose pink loos, dozens of them, all to be carried across the desert on my back, this chap with a whip driving me on - and when I reached the palace, the loo wasn't allowed inside until the chief wife herself had inspected it. I waited there, but the King wouldn't allow her out until all the loos were ready for inspection. Twenty-nine times I trudged across that desert, the line of loos outside the palace gates growing longer every day. On the thirtieth trip with the very last loo, I was so exhausted that I crawled the last mile, fighting against a wind that howled across the sand. Almost within reach of those palace gates, a fearful sandstorm drained my last strength, and I collapsed, but in falling I managed to take of my tunic and drape it over that final beautiful pink china loo. Lying there helpless, the sand stinging my almost naked body - my fingers locked onto that tunic, holding it in place as I passed into unconsciousness." Gordon paused, taking a long slow sip of coffee.

"I don't know how much time passed, but someone was holding a cup to my lips. I drank and they helped me up, steadied me as I staggered across to the palace gates. There stood my long line of loos all pitted and ruined by the storm! That other one was useless too, my tunic blown away by the wind. The King looked out from his window and saw them; nothing imperfect could stay near a palace. He bellowed to the guards. I must pick each one up and take it back! Another thirty times across that terrible desert.

"But unbeknown to anyone, the chief wife had watched from the harem window, and felt sorry for me. That night she crept out and collected all those damaged loos, they were just like the ones we have here. She smuggled them one by one down to a hidden basement in the castle, carried them down with their own fair hands. I offered to help but she said, "No you must rest, I command it." Wives can be so wonderful sometimes."

Gordon rested back with a tired flourish, shoulders sagging, looking sad eyed at Jan across the table, waiting for her to speak.

A pretty head shook. "No Chance!"

More days passed and work continued. As they were removed those pitted loos did go down the basement and Jan actually did do the carrying - well, most of it! The old toilet seats, however, found a different home - another hole in the ground in the little wood adjoining the house, an ideal place for a decent burial, all thirty of them. A sense of humour helped preserve sanity. What would some future discoverer make of this secret cache hidden in the ground?

By then, the pitted surface might well be thought to be just the effects of time, the assumption made that someone had buried loo seats in prime condition. Would they come under the hammer at Christies as rare archaeological treasures and be whisked off to great houses around the country? Could some Earl or Duke have one as his Country Seat? What about a suitable headline? "Buried Toilet Seat Mystery, the police have nothing to go on?' Who would decide if it was treasure-trove? Ah! How about the Privy Council? "Control yourself Gordon, the stress is getting to you."

For six weeks the work forged on, plumbing and replacing toilets early every morning and at weekends, helping the tilers during the day, cutting any special tiles in the evening; an unvarying routine - until mid-February saw a sudden break, a romantic interlude that called for a trip to London.

Chris was getting married! His choice of bride surprising, a social worker, a profession of which he formerly disapproved - but a very good looking one! Her name was Lesley. Choosing Valentine's day for the marriage was certainly romantic, but he better never forget their anniversary! The bride looked super, a happy day, several off-duty policemen in attendance. The best man's speech, referred to Chris's previous 'John Wayne' outlook, recalling a promise, "I'm never getting caught by a woman!"

When the floor was cleared, Chris and Sharon watched in surprise as their parents danced together, something they had never seen or suspected. Steve unfortunately was still away in the jungle.

Returning to Cornwall, the tiling continued; a minute inspection of the previous days' work finding few faults. In the end, it proved impossible to complete everything by opening day but enough was ready to satisfy any visitors during those first few weeks. One regular caravanning couple arrived at the weekend and having looked in the first two toilet buildings, the man wandering down to find Gordon working in the third.

"Can I carve my name on one of the tiles?"

"Hello Harry. Not unless you want four foot high letters in red spray paint on your caravan!" The men grinned at each other. "Good to have you back, do you like them?"

"Great, except..." Harry's grin broadened, waiting. "One of your pattern tiles is upside-down."

"What! Where?" Gordon's voice rose in alarm but he got no reply, just a shaken head and happy departing smile.

At the door, Harry stopped, "Tell you next year - unless you find it first."

Unexpectedly a letter arrived from Steve! This relatively

short message told of jungle heat, of great diving in the warm clear waters, and of Fluffy. Jan scanned the letter quickly then read in more detail, giving a little shiver even at this second reading. Fluffy was the company pet, a ten foot long python that slept coiled round the rafters in the barracks, dropping from time to time onto a bed or a passing shoulder - they kept it well fed! There were tarantulas too and other little beasties, but diving on the reefs made up for everything. Putting the letter aside, she wished it were longer, wondering about the food, the native girls, the other soldiers... but Steve was never one to elaborate; he must have felt homesick to write this much. Gordon was out working with the tilers again, she would show him later - they must reply this evening.

Easter saw the final tile laid and plumbing complete - even the putty on those replaced window panes had matured and received its quota of paint. After all the problems, the effect was terrific; they looked really splendid! Maintaining quality had caused arguments but mostly good-natured; the tiling firm could be proud of their achievement. Payments had been made at intervals as work progressed but now with the final bill, the question of compensation arose; the cost of all those damaged loos, of the painting and re-glazing - money already paid out that must now be recovered.

"Just deduct the cost and send a cheque for the rest," Jan suggested; a sound enough idea. However, the tiling firm would require invoices, evidence of the damage to support their own insurance claim - a need anticipated and photocopies made.

"Sure, we could do that," Gordon agreed. "But I don't want them asking later for more. I'll go over personally; they should give a written quality guarantee too." He picked up a closely typewritten sheet together with the copy invoices, collected a coat and made for the car. The journey took roughly thirty minutes; the reception as anticipated, was less than cordial.

"You should claim it from the sandblasters. They did the damage, not our tilers."

"They were *your* subcontractors, I've no contract with them; it's down to you to recover the money. You said they were insured."

"Their insurance may not pay," the tiling Boss hesitated. "How much are you figuring to deduct? Those loos and seats were old; wouldn't you have repainted those ceilings anyway. Expect everything new at our expense, do you?"

Gordon looked at him across the desk; for a while they sat there, sizing each other up... they had met often during the work and seldom agreed but regularly reached a compromise. "Our loos were in perfect condition when you started, and yes the ceilings would have been repainted; they always are." He paused, but seeing a smile appear on the face opposite and a stout finger raised as if to point, he rushed on. "Don't get excited. If I hadn't been putting all the damage right, I'd have painted them myself, all it would cost would be a tin of paint to..."

"And your time. That must be worth money!" The interruption cut in decisively as a fist thumped the desk, awaiting a reply.

Drawing a deep breath Gordon smiled to himself. "I'm glad you mentioned that. For six months I've worked non-stop, repairing damage, helping your men. Check the invoices. How many hours of my time have I charged you for?"

A look of concern crossed the face opposite and the office went quiet, no sound but the shuffling of papers. In a moment the man looked up in surprise and perhaps relief. "None?"

"Hadn't we better agree before I change my mind?"

They were both smiling now, the head across the table nodding. "Go on then, I accept. Sign the cheque."

"Sure. After I get two things. A written agreement that this amount," Gordon pointed across the desk to a figure in pencil in a corner of one of the invoices, "is the final bill and settles everything. I also want a five year guarantee that they won't fall off the wall!"

"You'll be lucky. Five years? No way!"

"The adhesive makers specification says tiles must be

in contact with the grout within thirty minutes of mixing. You didn't stick to that. I was there all the time remember. A section of wall was spread with adhesive, then the tiles pressed in. Some sections were quite large. If tea break came before it was finished, the last tiles were well over thirty minutes before they hit the glue."

"It's standard practice. Everyone does it, those tiles will stick - you know that! Hell, you should, you went over every damn one and made my chaps take off all those that sounded hollow. Nobody in my life ever inspected our work as you inspected it. Those tiles will last forever!"

"Then you shouldn't mind giving a guarantee?"

"Phhh... I'll promise that no complete section of wall will come loose. No one can say if a single tile somewhere might not..." He raised his hands, a request for understanding.

"True." Gordon rested an elbow on the desk, looking down, thinking. It would be unreasonable to expect a firm to come for single tiles. Anyway, singles were no problem, he just wanted some insurance against a major catastrophe. "Okay, how about any group of four tiles that come..."

"Twenty-four?"

"Six?"

They settled for a dozen, the agreement was written out, signed, stamped and the cheque paid. Compromise was generally best; both were happy.

Later that afternoon back at River Valley, two proud owners walked again round the buildings, delighted at the splendid effect. Visitors were scarce so early in the season, but several who had stayed in previous years commented on the improvement. The work had certainly been worthwhile. As they stood looking, a woman entered, stopped short ready to retreat, then recognising them, relaxed.

"Startled me, finding a man in here. Tour of inspection? I never would have believed it; when we left last year they were fine but, well, ordinary. Now..." she gestured, gazing round, "terrific. Will you do the laundrette walls too?"

"No! I never want to see another tile!" Gordon's reply came automatically, but immediately he doubted its truth, wondering if in a few years tiling the laundrette would prove irresistible. In spite of all the difficulties he would have no hesitation in using the same chaps and the same firm again. The only question was, would they be prepared to come?

Noticing a far away look, Jan nudged him and he came back to the present, seeing the other woman now waiting uncomfortably, obviously not sure whether to continue with her business or wait until he departed. With a few clumsy words he excused himself, turning to the door feeling slightly awkward.

"What's the matter?" Jan sensed his mood as they stepped outside.

"Nothing, just felt I didn't belong. Told you we should have gone in the gents." He squeezed her hand and they started towards the office but after a few steps she pulled back, turning again to look at the building.

"The insides may be super but I never remember a spring when the outside looked worse."

Normally at least one toilet building was painted each winter, but there had been no time - and it was more than that. This year the outside walls looked grubby, mainly from those sand-blasting dust clouds that burst forth at every window and doorway to settle where it would, unavoidably coating outer walls to a greater or lesser extent, depending on wind direction. Rain had washed some away but it remained patchy; poor compared to normal standards for starting the season. Scrubbing a small test piece with a brush and soapy water did wonders; it came up fresh and sparkling, emphasising the shabbiness elsewhere. Treating three whole buildings that way would be impossible, but that too was solved the following day.

"He'll fall off!" A woman from a large elaborate tent had wandered over. Jan, dragging a cable to give more slack, smiled in acknowledgement, glancing up at the roof where Gordon, pressure washer in hand, stood balancing on the ridge cleaning dirt and moss from the tiles.

"Why does lichen grow so much here?" the woman called to the roof above.

"It likes clear air. Grows a lot in the arctic too, some animals live on it," the reply floated down.

"Ask him if you get many reindeer in Cornwall," Jan whispered.

The woman grinned and shouted the question. No answer came back but suddenly the air around them was full of spray, putting the ladies to flight.

By evening, all roofs, gutters and walls were clean, the hired machine returned. Everything was ready, and just as well. Although visitors to admire this new smartness were still scarce, a letter arrived from the Automobile Association. A message to savour! River Valley was shortlisted for that premier award, AA Campsite of the year - one finalist among eighteen sites from England, Scotland and Wales. What such a win could do for next year's advertising was incalculable!

Some days later a taxi drove slowly across the bridge, parking opposite the house. The driver stepped out, wandered back to the river, then strode casually towards the office.

Meeting him at the door, Jan asked, "Waiting for someone?"

The man smiled, obviously pleased with himself. "Expecting visitors are you? This is River Valley?"

"Yes," she nodded and waited, not understanding.

"I had a phone call. Got to meet someone at the airfield next Tuesday and drive them here - someone important, coming by private plane. I came over today to check the route." He smiled more broadly, then turned, walking away.

"Who?"

The man swung round, head shaking, "Secret, not allowed to tell. Could be handy if your car breaks down though."

On Tuesday, the taxi returned with his special passenger; an AA man for that 'Campsite of the Year' inspection. They departed an hour later with no clues how the site had fared.

Magpies are spiteful, destructive, stupid birds. Spiteful and destructive because they raid other birds nests, and stupid for an entirely different reason.

Walking round with a message, Jan saw a visitor cleaning his caravan but something else caught her eye. As the man called a greeting and they fell into conversation, she looked pointedly towards the car.

"Oh those." The man followed her gaze. "I woke a few mornings ago to a tapping noise outside the caravan. Leaning over and easing back the curtain I could see nothing; then a movement near the ground caught my eye as the tapping restarted. Our car was parked quite close alongside, like it is now, this magpie madly attacking a hubcap! I was about to rise, open the door and chase the silly bird away when the noise stopped. Looking out again, it still crouched there, wings held out threateningly, feathers fluffed up to launch another attack. My wife Carole lay asleep; I shook a shoulder waking her - she was annoyed, not at all inclined to believe me. Another flurry of tapping made her lean to the window. It was light outside but early, dim enough so the stupid bird couldn't see us inside the caravan with only the one curtain drawn aside. We knelt there on the bed together, laughing at its silly antics, assuming it would soon give up. When it came again early the following morning and the next day too, it ceased to be amusing. Today I cured it." He pointed to towels that now hung over all four wheels. "Easier than taking off the hub caps."

Magpies' spitefulness extended beyond fighting their own reflection in shiny hubcaps; they would attack and carry off young ducklings too, a vice that made them River Valley's least favourite bird. More than that, a destructive streak had appeared, strong black beaks pecking putty still soft where the toilet windows had been re-glazed due to sand-blasting damage. They were clever too! Several times Gordon hid nearby with a handful of stones but somehow they knew. Once a magpie did head for the window, then suddenly changed its mind, veering off in another direction. A makeshift scarecrow erected nearby met with no success - they ignored it. Adding a pitchfork and a scarf that billowed in the wind were similar failures. Even a picture of an eagle cut from a glossy magazine and stuck inside the window did no good. Jan suggested a photo of Des O'Conner.

It was mainly a single window being worked, one on the gable end over the Ladies loos. However, putty was disappearing so rapidly that another pane must come under attack soon. At a busier time of year, more people might have forced the birds to hunt elsewhere but this early in the season, visitors were few. Somehow the magpies must be deterred for a few weeks... but how? By autumn the putty should have hardened.

For several nights, as a result of his determination to stay awake and solve the problem, Gordon fell asleep quickly. "A matter for the little grey cells," he thought, and those cells promptly shut down - hating magpies apparently as good as counting sheep when it came to dropping off. One night however, probably from something eaten, sleep did not come and in the morning he hurried down the basement stairs. The solution lay somewhere here, amid copious quantities of what Jan called junk. There were spare loos, wash basins, a stainless steel sink, a stack of doors, some manhole lids in case a heavy vehicle damaged those sprinkled around the site, six boxes of plumbing fittings - but not what he wanted. Freshly painted signs for the site entrance lay against one wall and behind them two similar signs from many years ago, their paintwork worn and cracked. Jan had tried several times to get these old ones thrown out.

"Look at them! Don't tell me they'll ever be used again!"

"Suppose some vindictive person backs a large lorry into the existing signs one night, and into the new signs the night after. These will make a second reserve." He had dodged back out of reach, nipping through the doorway, racing along the basement corridor with Jan in hot pursuit.

Remembering, he smiled and moved on. In another room, three long fluorescent fittings for the toilet buildings together with five spare tubes lay in front of other electric fittings. He delved behind them without success and moved on to shelves stacked with boxes of wall and floor tiles matching those in the toilet buildings, stockpiled in case the pattern be discontinued. Where could they be? Against the wall lay spare shop shelves, some with wire baskets for vegetables and two boxes of shelf fittings. An old square biscuit tin still retained the goat equipment from when Judy supplied all their milk, including swivel stakes and even the great green worming pills that had only once been used. Smiling again at the contents and the memories, he looked round the room, seeing the vast stack of dustbins in one corner; they kept better down here in the winter, protected from possible frost; twenty were already outside for the visitors but over seventy remained. With a sigh, he moved on to the next underground room, finding wheels and belts, spares for the waterwheel gearing, a host of paint tins, boxes containing all manner of other spares, and a pile of gleaming chromium taps. "How come I left them here?" These were purchased when the plumber's merchants had a sale; they should be stored with the other plumbing fittings. Shaking his head he moved on; some spares were kept in the toilet building loft but surely he hadn't... Ah! There they were! He remembered now, each wrapped in a black plastic bag for protection; spare mirrors like those in the toilet buildings over every basin - must be about thirty. Taking two from the top, quick steps hurried upstairs then away in a downstream direction.

Reaching the third toilets he knocked loudly and hearing no reply, entered the Ladies with some care, ready to retreat, but no lurking female waited to pounce. In a few moments he wedged the mirrors tightly inside the window that was loosing putty, wired it closed and made good his escape.

Not another piece of putty was lost. Where all else failed, the mirrors succeeded - the stupid bird never took another mouthful. That damn magpie had beaten itself, so busy with the reflection, a fight it could never win!

CHAPTER 18

Stools

The site was busier now, everyone pleased with the tiling. They particularly liked the soap dishes, set snugly back into the blockwork and finishing flush with the tiles. The suggestion box too, was full of compliments, except one comment scrawled in a childish hand demanding a BMX track. No chance! Bikes were problem enough already. A more serious letter however, asked for stools in the showers, the writer finding it no longer possible to lean against the walls when pulling on trousers. That seemed odd, but whereas the old rough surface had remained largely dry, steam now condensed more quickly on the tiled walls, invariably making them damp.

"Someone mentioned that a few days ago but I had a queue and forgot." Jan picked another note, scanning it through. "They like the non-slip tiles. These stools, where do we get them?"

"I'll try Trago Mills, might as well go now?"

"Well don't be too long, and don't get carried away. We only need twelve."

"And a spare perhaps - the odd one could get pinched." Gordon reached for the car keys, hurrying off.

Arriving at Falmouth, a look round the store found no ordinary stools with legs. Disappointing. Some fancy circular ones were on show, made entirely of coloured plastic. "Too expensive," the thought came automatically as he looked at two in a bathroom display, guessing they would exceed £15. "Not really what I had in mind, not enough of them anyway." He turned to leave but having come so far, changed his mind and intercepted a nearby assistant.

"Have any proper stools, do you?"

"Only those, Sir." The assistant pointed.

Gordon shook his head but too late, the man strode off, picking one up and bringing it back. "They come in three separate parts; assemble them yourself." He pulled up the seat top, showing two cones joined together with a single nut and bolt. "Very simple, you just drill the plastic, only we don't supply the bolts. Here, try it."

Taking the offered stool and sitting on it, swaying to one side then the other, it seemed strong enough... but hardly what was needed - poor design, nasty upper class thing, not at all what campers would want. He rose, picking it up to hand back.

"One pound fifty pence each," the assistant volunteered.

Gordon froze in mid-movement, then trying to seem casual, turned the stool over, seeing it in a fresh light. Actually, the design was not so bad. Yes, he looked closer - it couldn't rust and stain the tiles, a great advantage. Light too, easy for cleaning, first class all round really - visitors would like them! "Okay. Do you have any more like these?"

"No. sorry." The man seemed reluctant to go looking.

"Not in your stockroom?"

"Shouldn't think so. Need another one do you?"

"Another twenty!"

"Twen... hold on, I'll get someone to look."

Fifteen minutes later he was on his way home; the boot, the back seat and passenger seat, all covered in tightly stacked stool parts. Even the missing nuts and bolts had been found in another department.

Looking out through the office window, Jan saw the car arriving home; someone walking towards the shop prevented her meeting it. When she returned he was sitting at the office desk, apparently concentrating on the ledger. A small upward curl at the corner of his lips told her he was pleased.

"You got them then." She made for the office door but he was up in a moment, swinging her round.

"You make the coffee, I'll fetch one in and assemble it."

The holes were drilled by the time coffee appeared. Jan set it down and watched as the nut and bolt were tightened and the seat cover slipped on. Picking the stool up and looking it over, she nodded. "Good. Twelve we said, or did you get that spare one?"

"No." He rose, turning to look through the window.

Having seen the little smile, she asked again, "Two spares?"

Not receiving a reply, she walked across to the desk, upended the packet of bolts, and started counting, putting the last one down with a bang. "Twenty-five!"

He turned towards her. "Twenty-two actually. I got three extra bolts just in case."

"Oh of course. How much?" The demand came fiercely loud as she stood waiting.

"Sh!" With a warning finger rising to his lips, he stepped hurriedly towards her, looking quickly outside then leaning close to whisper, "One pound fifty, well a bit less actually - got a ten percent discount."

"Why the secrecy?"

"We might sell some in the shop. Five pounds each seems reasonable?"

Giving way to Jan's look of disapproval, Gordon shrugged, "Oh, all right then," and with a felt pen marked the stool at £4.99. One stood in the shop for a week but remained unsold. It was not however, entirely useless. An elderly caravanner who came each morning, took to sitting on it while his wife did her shopping. As trade built up and shower usage increased, the stools were well received but those tiles that looked so good and attracted so many compliments, gave rise to a further complaint

Every shower cubicle had hooks for hanging clothes, rounded ones with no sharp corners, in anodised aluminium - a manufacturer had even been found whose anodising was thirty microns thick rather than fifteen, to last unblemished over the years. However, one thing had not been foreseen. Clothes that hung on these hooks now picked up moisture as steam from the shower condensed and trickled down the tiles, something that had not happened when the walls were rough. That problem too was fixed, and in a manner that would draw people's comments way into the future. It proved the most effective and perhaps the cheapest improvement ever carried out.

Although the site was busy, a week remained before the school holidays. With Dot and Granville now helping, getting away for an hour would be easy enough. When Jan, serving at the counter, saw Gordon walking around with a notebook checking shelves, she naturally thought he was off to Cash and Carry. Two hours later the car reappeared but instead of parking by the shop, it came to rest on the far side of the yard.

"He needn't think I'm carrying stock from right across there!" At the silent thought, she stepped to the desk, grabbed the ledger and pen, pretending to be busy, not even looking up when the door opened - expecting some sarcastic comment about women sitting around as usual. However, Gordon strode straight past, opening the basement door and disappearing down the stairs.

Rising quickly to follow, she stood listening by the top step looking down into the darkness, then hearing returning footsteps, was just fast enough to regain her seat at the desk before he hurried past with a large cardboard box. Hearing the clink of metal she knew something was inside.

Reaching the car, opening the door and positioning his body to obstruct the view, he extracted from the box a coil of rope, a knife, a screwdriver, a hand drill and a few other items, tossing each onto the car seat. Leaning forward he waited while a holidaymaker walked by, then carefully lifted a bunch of red roses from the passenger foot-well, put them in the now empty box, closed the flaps and hurried back to the office.

Unable to fathom what was going on, Jan waited, not sitting again at the desk but standing by the door. "Just what is it you're doing!"

This was no idle question, her finger jabbed towards him. With swift evasive steps he shoved the box on the desk, dodged back into the lounge and turned away to stand looking out at the river and waterwheel.

Slowly and deliberately she approached, standing silently behind. After a while her hand reached up, touching lightly the hair on the back of his neck, pleased to see him flinch and jump aside. They were facing each other now, her finger reaching out to prod his ribs.

"Ouch! That's not very nice after all the trouble I've been to." He looked deliberately towards the box on the desk, his smile not very well disguised.

Jan turned to follow the gaze; she had assumed the box was empty. Hearing the unmelodic rendering of a once popular tune, she looked back to find him staring innocently at the ceiling, whistling without volume, a silly grin on his face. Clenched fists and a threatening step forward caused the smile to slip. Seeing arms thrown defensively across his chest, she smiled but could wait no longer, hurrying off to lift the box flaps, reaching inside for the roses, holding them for a moment before swinging round. "Okay, so what did you do - crash the car? Is that why you've parked it over there?"

"No, honest. I just saw them in a shop and thought it's a little while since..."

"Little while! How many years? Anyway I love them." She moved towards him, really pleased but just a little needled at being strung along. Moving close with the intention of planting a little kiss, she noticed some caravanners feeding the ducks not far away and waved to them, holding up the flowers, then reaching up with her lips, knowing he would duck away looking for somewhere less public. When they hung together in the privacy of the hallway, her happiness was complete - two could play tease.

As she left to place the flowers in water, Gordon made off in the other direction, collecting tools from the car and a stepladder from the service passage.

Fifteen minutes later, he called her to the Gents side of the first toilet building where Dot and Granville also waited. In the first shower compartment, a plastic carrier bag hung on a rope - this rope rose, passing over two small pulleys screwed to the ceiling, its end hanging in one corner of the cubicle.

As Jan watched, Dot reached forward pulling the loose end down until a loop in the rope slid over one of the existing clothes hooks. The plastic bag had now risen, hanging well above any shower splashes and not touching the wet tiles. Clothes stored in this bag should stay dry!

Working at odd times over the next few days saw the showers in all three toilet buildings equipped with this arrangement. The plastic bags were temporary, Dot already crocheting better ones, open textured in orange nylon fishing line - easy to pop in the washing machines. Visitors loved them! Over the years several families were to turn up solely because some friend had told them of the shower basket system. It went down well in the site's grading inspection too.

"How did we do?" Standing at the office doorway, Granville nodded towards the inspector's car disappearing along the track towards the village.

Jan, sitting reading at the desk, looked up. "He left a report, went over it before that last caravan arrived. We've still got the top grading, five ticks again, but he wants a roof over the washing up sinks down at the third toilets. Is Dot any better?"

"That's what I came over for. I'm taking her off to the doctor."

As the June days passed, Dot's condition deteriorated and eventually the couple were unable to continue - a sad farewell after all their help but Granville felt the greater comfort and convenience of their home might aid Dot's recovery.

Days were harder with no one helping; Jim's leg now preventing him leaving his bungalow. The site had originally been arranged for two people to run but the shop made that more difficult. Cleaning the toilets before breakfast was no different, they had always handled that, but the midday clean must now also be done - and they could no longer do it together; someone must watch the office and shop! Jan found herself stretched, running between counter and office, darting back and forth, inevitably keeping customers waiting - and that phone kept ringing! Meals too became more difficult with visitors constantly demanding attention.

One morning she struggled vainly with a queue while Gordon strode away to pitch a caravan. Coming back, he noticed the dustbins overflowing and had grabbed a pair of rubber gloves when someone stopped him to complain their electrics were off. Simultaneously another caravan drew up in the yard and some young lad was chasing the ducks! Which to do first?

Calling across to stop the child, he turned to the man, promising to fix the electric soon then led the newly arrived couple to the office. Asking how many days and tapping the details hurriedly into the computer, he pressed a trifle too firmly on the zero key, producing 100 days instead of 10. The bill spewed out by the printer was enormous!

"Three hundred and... No!" He stopped, looking at the offending piece of paper, cursing silently and forcing a smile, passing it off as a joke. Showing the offending bill while cancelling the entry and re-typing with more care raised a laugh from the couple, but took time, delaying those other waiting chores.

"Can we keep it as a souvenir?" the lady asked.

About to nod in agreement, Gordon stopped himself. Suppose these were revenue people in disguise? Quickly he sought an excuse.

"I better keep it to put my accounts right later. By the way, you may notice some areas are almost empty now, but don't be tempted; they're for families with children when school holidays start next week. I try to get young people of more or less the same ages together, so they find friends easier." Taking the money he locked the office and led the caravan off, hurrying now, jogging rather than walking to save time as they headed for a pitch. Life was intense - and the real peak still to arrive! Those empty sections glimpsed at a distance looked incongruous but it was natural - one could say inescapable that more areas must be used for children when the schools broke up. Seeing such areas empty, couples often asked for these apparently more spacious pitches. Giving the reason usually changed their minds but with no wardens now to help, time was often pressing, long explanations best avoided.

The morning had already been fairly frantic, with newspapers late and someone backing into a standpipe, the water gushing everywhere and requiring immediate repair. Gordon slowed a little as he led the caravan on; areas 3, 4 and 5 were all reserved for couples, offering freedom from ball games and at least some quietness for the busy time ahead. Area 5 had three caravans - room for just one more, still with twenty feet clear on both sides. This latest visitor reversed smoothly into position. 'Thank goodness for experienced drivers', the thought had hardly come when a tall man emerged from a nearby awning, shouting abuse and pointing across at the empty area behind.

The newly arrived couple who had just stepped from their car, now looked doubtful, their unhappiness increasing when the tall man shouted across at them, "Go on, move off, pitch somewhere else!" then turned muttering loudly, "They take your money then don't give a damn!"

If so many other jobs had not been waiting Gordon might have tried to explain, to placate; even a bit more sleep over the past week might have stayed his tongue but this abuse was uncalled for. Already wound like a steel spring with tension, he swung on the shouting man.

"Take your money you say! Come to the office - I'll be delighted to give it back!" Speaking tightly, eyes blazing, something within spoiling for trouble, he stood for a moment watching doubts enter the other angry face, then swung away, heading off to fix the electrics.

"What's the matter?" Jan asked late that evening, lying together in bed.

"Something I made a mess of." Explaining the incident, Gordon paused, "I ought to have moved *him* back onto the empty area, then put children all round... no, that's wrong. I should have explained, but he was rude and I was stretched. Things like that can make you short with other people as well. Not one of my better days."

A comforting hand reached out. "Will the new wardens turn up tomorrow?"

"Not Cynthia and her husband, that's at the weekend, but Janet and Des should come - they promised to, anyway."

By Sunday, the new wardens located from rapidly placed small adds, had arrived; capable, eager and anxious to help. Working just a few hours on alternate days, they handled the mowing, the midday toilet cleaning, checked dustbins and topped up toilet rolls.

Jan and Gordon still rose early for the morning cleaning and were busy later in the office, in the shop and pitching a mass of arriving families during those first weeks of the school holidays, but life was certainly easier - well mostly it was.

"You'd better come and look at this," A caravanner stood at the office door.

Expecting it to be something nearby, Gordon rose from the desk. Following but not realising they were going so far, he glanced back once at the open office door, thinking it should have been locked. The man led across the bridge, walking on up the road to stop near a bend, the verge on one side overgrown with ferns. Kneeling, he pointed, "Look."

Something brownish apparently grew on the surface. Closer inspection revealed several fronds of fern had forced their way right through the tarmac.

"Pteridium aquilinum... bracken to most people. Go through practically anything. It's near the edge now but you wait 'til next year! They'll ruin your road."

"How can I... we never use poison sprays - the visiting children you know, so how do I stop them?"

"Drain the roots, keep cutting them down or better still pull them out; too late this year - wants doing in Spring. You'll probably get bitten, they harbour midges."

Two caravans sweeping down the road, ended the discussion, causing a dash back to the office.

As time passed and Autumn came and the wardens left,

a few caravans still dotting the site. Several were empty, stored more or less permanently, the owners using them at intervals, saving time and petrol by not having to tow. Only one toilet building was now open, the daily routine easing, with no grand projects in prospect other than a roof over the washing-up sinks that the Tourist Board inspector had requested.

"Okay, so how long will it take?" Jan asked.

"A week maybe. Just a timber frame with clear plastic sheets above."

"I'll believe that when I see it. Treated timber straight from the ground?"

"Sort of." Gordon sketched the outline on a sheet of paper. "We'll set lengths of galvanised angle iron upright in a concrete foundation so the timber legs start six inches above ground. Stop it rotting. Good?"

"Oh great. This foundation; who will mix the concrete?"

The construction took only a week, in spite of several refinements, some for visitors' convenience, others to make it stronger. With that task and a little painting completed, the winter of '87 was easy, an ideal, balanced, unhurried life; small jobs could always be found but with time for leisure, time to do whatever one wanted - the life perhaps that people imagine when they dream of running a caravan park.

"It's a great feeling," Jan threw a handful of bread to the ducks as they wandered together downstream along the riverbank. "This is how it should be. Wish we'd had so much time when the children were young."

A strong wind rattled the roof tiles one night making sleep difficult, but morning revealed no damage other than a single tall tree leaning badly over where some gust had caught, tearing one side of its roots from the ground. Never mind; if it had to fall this was the ideal time of year, and it might be saved - probably a lost cause but with the foliage cut and branches lopped, those roots might take a fresh grip.

From the top rung of a short ladder Gordon reached the lower limbs, swinging himself upwards. Below Jan shifted the ladder away, clear of falling branches. Removing some boughs and shortening others, he climbed higher, finding a new perch from which to work. This time of year was lonely but good to feel free, no one breathing down your neck with impatience, no queue; freedom to choose your own pace. Finally the top branches were cut away before working downwards, reducing the trunk height in sections. Finishing when the shape seemed satisfactory, he looked for a way down. Jan had returned to the house, the ladder now resting some distance away. Directly below, strewn around the tree, fallen boughs lay everywhere. Tossing the saw well clear and swinging down through the shortened branches until his feet hung some eight foot above the ground, he aimed for a small patch between the debris below and let go hoping for the best. All was well, a slightly turned ankle providing an excuse to leave the clearing up for another day.

In the morning's post amid the usual array of junk mail, nestled one official looking envelope. Such letters often spelled trouble.

"What is it?" Jan demanded.

Rising from the desk still reading and flipping over the pages of a legal looking document, Gordon came to a halt near the lounge window staring out, apparently at the water-wheel, his eyes scanning along the riverbank before replying.

"It's the footpath?"

"Not again. We've given our land free already - half a mile of it! What more can they want?"

"Nothing," he smiled. "This is an extinguishment order."

"Extinguishment?"

"The old footpath fifty-two and footpath seven no longer exist; at least they won't provided it all goes through. People have until 14th December to object."

"You mean it won't be public any more... after all the trouble it's caused?"

"Tempting I agree, but it's not like that. The new wider footpath will be created automatically when the old one is extinguished. Since the river was straightened many years ago, the exact position of the path has never been properly established, but people naturally want to follow the stream. Closing one and opening it on the new line should make everyone happy."

"Some hope!"

Like most compromises, no one had achieved everything they wanted but the conclusion proved amicable enough, most people having some cause for satisfaction. To achieve this result however, River Valley had conceded a three foot widening of the path without any compensation other than the Council agreeing to erect and upkeep a kissing gate at the downstream end to stop straying cattle, and to erect a fence along the path line. It had however been a long drawn out and sometimes bitter struggle. Although news of this settlement was good, Gordon set off downstream feeling slightly sore. True it was a splendid path, deserving the attention and most people had acted well enough - but one or two had been at least a little vindictive.

Still thinking about it, he started cutting the previous days branches to a size suitable for loading on the trailer. This little area had trees on three sides, just the type of place Blackbird liked; plenty of cover and fallen leaves thickly carpeting the ground. Naturally his feathered friend soon appeared but Gordon sunk in his own sombre thoughts forgot at first to acknowledge its arrival. Reaching to drag clear a branch under which the bird was scratching among dead leaves, he checked himself just in time, apologising automatically and seeing Blackbird look up in response to the spoken words. Stepping back to rest against the trailer he took the opportunity of a breather, looking back at the yellow beak and bright eyes, the sideways tilt of the black head suggesting it might speak.

"Brooding a bit are we? Nearly pulled that one on top of me didn't you?"

He had never lost the habit started in those first lonely years, of imagining his companion's thoughts, and now sought a reply to the bird's question. "Sorry. I was thinking about some people who..." he hesitated; it wasn't easy to explain in a way a bird would understand. "Well, these

362

people, not many mind you, just a few... have been unnecessarily unpleasant."

"*Holding a grudge will do you no good! Listen, suppose I find a worm but before I can eat it another bird comes along and we fight. I'll see him off of course, the one in possession usually does, but having won I must put the matter aside, not chase after him... else you know what happens... the worm escapes! Waste of time, holding a grudge, think of the effect. If you'd like to strangle someone but don't actually intend doing anything about it, what will your hate achieve? Nothing! In fact if he or she comes to know how you feel, it may even cheer them up. And what will it do to you? Hate always acts to depress the person who feels it, spoiling their enjoyment of life. You only get that sense of supreme well-being when everything is right with the world - that never happens if you're busy hating someone. Forget it. You can't change the past, give a wave and a smile next time you meet; perhaps you'll be friends again - even if you don't succeed, the effort won't be wasted - that little wave may really get them worried!*"

"I know you're right, and in any case I'm pleased with the outcome. The better the path, the more people will walk past and see the site."

"*Now you have it! Another thing; suppose you've two pals. One you argue with, then afterwards put those differences aside and are friends again. The other pal has never given you a cross word. Which friend is the most reliable?*"

"The one I haven't argued with of course."

"*Are you sure? One day something may happen to cause such an argument. Can you be certain he will behave afterwards as well as the other friend did?*"

"Um. You may have a point."

Shaking himself back into action, Gordon carefully lifted another branch from the far side of the tree before dragging the trailer off. He didn't want to frighten Blackbird away... this coming winter would be lonely enough without that.

"How will this petrol trouble affect touring?" Jan reached to switch off the television. They had been watching the news, an item about the shortage in America, a shooting at a petrol station, customers fighting when stocks ran low. The new season had started, but would so many people come to Cornwall if petrol became short and the price increased?

"I don't know. That big twin axle job..." Gordon pointed through the window. "The man told me he does fifteen miles to the gallon when towing. He couldn't really have a smaller car for a caravan that size."

"You think people will stay nearer where they live?"

"Might have to if they can't get the petrol. Might stop in Devon, save themselves eighty miles each way; nearly eleven gallons for that one." he glanced again out onto the field. "Tents would be less affected, and smaller caravans."

"Like our little Eccles and the mini-van when we first came down over twenty years ago? How thirsty was it... mind you not many families would even think about anything that small now."

"About thirty to the gallon but remember the load it carried. People who store their caravans here should still come."

"We've talked about statics before. Maybe it's time to start, have some for hire so people can travel light in smaller cars and..." Jan paused abruptly, "But not if I have to clean them all!"

Of the 250 units permitted on site, 170 could be statics - big caravans that didn't move; just stayed permanently jacked up on concrete blocks, wheels hanging clear of the ground - in fact they need not actually have wheels. Legally, such caravans could be sixty feet long and twenty feet wide. Enormous! Far bigger than the house.

"I suppose it's inevitable eventually. Petrol stocks may be vast but not unlimited. This crisis may pass but another will come." Gordon rubbed his chin.

"You think it's the future then?"

"Well probably, at least to some extent, if you look far

enough ahead. I prefer our existing type of trade, there will always be tourers, motorcaravans, and certainly tents, but perhaps not so many. We should save them the best pitches - not best, most convenient is what I mean; all the pitches in them main part of the site, with the toilets suitably near."

"The statics will each have their own facilities? "

"Sure. A toilet, shower, television, microwave... the lot. People always want more and that's worrying. You remember the chalets we saw at the caravan show, those with pitched roofs that come in two halves and are fixed together on site," Gordon paused, and seeing a nod hurried on. "They look so much better. I know they're dearer but will people expect that type of thing in a few years?"

"Could we have them? Does it really matter?"

"We'd have to get planning approval... and yes, it probably does matter. Suppose at some time in the future most people do ask for better quality - for chalets that is. Anywhere offering rows of square statics could quickly go downhill. That would frighten off our tourers, be bad for the village too."

"We'll be retirement age in ten years; will it really affect us?"

"Possibly not, but I'd like to leave a successful site, not something rough and substandard. Once a place starts to run down, it's hard to stop - you've seen parks we couldn't get away from quickly enough."

And there the matter was left. Des and Janet the previous season's wardens had arrived back, but no luck as yet in finding another couple. Other hopes were also unsuccessful; despite reaching the final group in that coveted 'Campsite of the Year' competition, the title went to another park. Bookings too were down, increased advertising preventing a bigger fall but numbers were discouraging; maybe the petrol situation? Ah well, it was early in the season yet.

Seeking any improvement to make the site more attractive, six better quality hand dryers were fixed, one in the Ladies and one in the Gents of all three toilet buildings. Eight had been bought from a special offer in a caravanning magazine, the spares smuggled quickly downstairs before Jan saw them.

The use of these dryers, like most other facilities, was free; only the washing machines and tumble dryers had slot-meters.

Cleaning the toilets shortly after six a few mornings later, Jan called, "Get me the broom will you; this floor is covered in sand."

It happened again the following day, not all over, just in the vicinity of the new dryers. Discussing it with the wardens later in the day, Des had the answer. "We get it too, at the midday clean. You know why... someone dries their swimming trunks here because it's free."

Another week slid by, a continued lack of people triggering more discussion on the future. The big twin unit models that looked like chalets were undoubtedly far better in appearance but like all caravans, each must be separated from adjoining chalets by at least a six-metre gap, leaving less open ground for trees and bushes.

An alternative did exist but spelled harder work. Chalets built of blockwork with a tiled roof, required no fire gap. They could be built in pairs, halving the number of separate units and leaving extra open space; the shapes were more attractive too - more expensive though, something to be done gradually, over many years. In a way, that expense was good - too valuable ever to become run down! Properly built bungalows did not deteriorate with the years. Plans were drawn up, discussions held with the Council, a letter sent asking the Chief Planning officer's opinion - but with no intention of starting until the season ended.

In June, with splendid weather, numbers were not great, caravans still scarce. When one drew up in the yard, Gordon hurried to meet it.

"Hello." A blonde lady alighted from the near side. "You've a space for us?"

"Sure. How long?" There was no real need to ask - the site would certainly not be full.

"Several years if you like. I'm Eileen." Seeing no sign of understanding in the blank expression, she wagged a finger. "You're supposed to be expecting us. We're the new wardens, this is Peter."

"Oh, yes well... er, follow me to a pitch." he hurried off, disconcerted and a little uneasy. Who were they, and from where? One of those phone calls replying to an advert perhaps, but none were expected today?

As the season developed this couple joined Des and Janet, taking turns with the cleaning, Eileen serving at times in the shop. The extra help allowed Jan more freedom, more chance to chat with customers. Having an extra person serving in the mornings, shortened the queue as milk, breakfast cereals and bottles of gas were collected. The newspapers however, still took most time. The special system where everyone reserved their favourite paper was popular - so popular that over seventy percent of visitors now ordered a copy of at least one title. To make sure they reached the right person, customer's names appeared on the top of every one. Obviously they did not get they by magic but were hand copied from a list on the computer screen. However, the pile was now so thick it took considerable time to find the one required. A trivial adjustment to the program improved this situation, automatically sorting the list into alphabetical order; no great thing but it made finding the right paper so much easier, increasing the speed at which customers were served.

In early July, a letter arrived from the Chief planning officer. Opening it and scanning through, the conclusion was read aloud; '*it is my view that permission is likely to be granted.*'" On the strength of that advice, the chalet scheme was submitted for planning approval.

Caravanners' and campers' opinions had also been sought; many approved of the idea, perhaps they too had their eye on petrol costs, some expressing the hope that relatives would hire a chalet for holiday reunions. Most however, wanted the touring and camping areas kept separate and unchanged.

One bright spot in the year's figures was the number of small tents from overseas, many coming through the new Best of British brochure, River Valley's entry sporting a picture of St. Michael's Mount. Jan had booked in several from Holland and as another arrived in the office, unsure about the price, she made an offer that had often been successful in the past.

"You can camp on the hill, looking out over the windmill; make you feel at home." Two heads nodded, and they paid for three days. Dutch couples loved to camp on a hill.

Steve too was home; now fully trained he had left the army to work locally on heavy vehicles, visiting often but living nearer his job - and his girl! Seeing him regularly provided a welcome diversion while awaiting a decision on the chalets. The first news came in mid-September, a report to the Planning Committee recommended chalets be accepted instead of caravans. Encouraging tidings, but would that Committee agree? Disappointment soon followed, the application agreed in principle but a decision held back pending preparation of a legal document restricting the valley's use. The inference was simple - agree to these conditions or lose the permission. Naturally the document took time to prepare and as months passed, local opposition gathered strength. Understandable of course; most were not voting for caravans rather than chalets - they didn't want either in the valley. The caravan permission however, already existed, obtained by the previous owner over twenty years before.

Jan walked across the room then back again. "We only want to do something better. Why do people object?"

"Human nature. Only see what you want to see. When we do retire, what will happen to the valley?" Gordon moved to the window, looking out. "I'd like to see tourers forever but sooner or later someone will install those 170 caravans."

"What happens when visitors want something better?"

"If the caravans are cheap enough, people will use them. When the paintwork gets tatty with age, that's when the trouble comes. If your prices are really cheap, you can't afford new ones; have to keep the old ones going or buy second-hand. Be a rougher site then of course, but that may eventually be unavoidable without the best accommodation. Quality is the only real answer."

Chapter 19

France

Two weeks before the season ended, a minibus arrived - apparently filled with older teenagers, eighteen to twentyish, not the sort of party ever accepted. Greeted with an explanation that groups of young people were not catered for because of an absence of suitable activities in the valley, a somewhat older man, thirty perhaps, stepped forward. He appeared to be in charge.

"We're a party of bird-watchers from university on a field trip, just for one night; twelve of us and two tents. The last thing we need is entertainments."

That seemed fair enough, worth taking a chance; not many other people about who could be annoyed even if these students were a bit boisterous as teenagers were naturally apt to be. They booked in, paid and were shown to a pitch on the empty camping area with nobody else nearby - the three remaining caravans a hundred metres away.

Once both tents were up, the party marched off following the river, not unduly noisy but not so quiet as most bird-watchers. Around midday they marched back in groups, lots of activity around the tents no doubt indicating the preparation of a meal before all left in the minibus, perhaps seeking coastal birds. For some reason that departure was a relief; something about the group feeling wrong. Several times that afternoon and evening Gordon looked across towards the tents but darkness fell several hours before the party returned, voices shouting intermittently from tents to toilets, the time almost midnight before silence fell.

In the morning all was quiet as Jan rose at six, shaking

the sleeping figure beside her into wakefulness, then hurrying ahead to start on the toilets. Collecting cleaning gear from the service passage she was surprised to find a gas heater burning and hear water running. Someone having an early shower? Outside again, her eye caught something else - she pulled up sharply, reaching down a dubious finger to check. A ring of white frost like substance coated the bottom of one of the big red gas bottles. Strange. The finger touched... "Oh, it *is* ice!"

Quickly rounding the corner another surprise awaited; the Ladies door was wide open. That never happened before; normally the mechanism automatically closed it. Running forward, she found the room full of steam, the far side hardly visible, particularly towards the top. Crouching to find clearer air and moving forward, one shower was running but the building empty. Stretching a hand towards the tap she pulled back sharply, surprised by the temperature; no wonder there was steam! About to reach in and turn it off, a thought came - her hair had only been set yesterday! If a wetting was unavoidable, perhaps someone else should do it. Still crouching, she made for the outer door, noticing now why it stayed open; a piece of wood rammed underneath. "Might as well remain that way until the steam disperses." The murmured comment came while hurrying back to the office.

"Gordon! Come on, we've got trouble."

A face appeared round the hall doorway, "Trouble?" He stepped into the room still doing up shirt buttons and reached for the ducks corn jug.

"Leave that! Someone left a shower running - the place is full of steam, come and turn it off."

"Couldn't you... Ah, the hair-do? I suppose it doesn't matter if I get soaked?" He was already making for the door, Jan following as he raced across the yard. She caught him when they paused together peering into the steam filled room. Turning, he saw a grin on her face.

"You just want to see me get soaked."

A small nod and a broadening smile as she leaned back against the wall, confirmed his suspicion. For a moment they stood watching each other. Placing a foot on the step, ready to rush in... another idea occurred. "Ah!" He turned, striding deliberately away round the corner to the service passage, reaching to turn off the main water supply. The hiss of the gas burner died, hot water no longer running. Returning, he found her waiting by the step, a smile on both faces now.

"Cheat!" She punched him playfully on the arm as they entered the building, reaching to open windows and check the showers. Though water no longer ran, one hot tap was on - full on, it took a dozen turns to close.

"Must have been running all night; did you see the frost round the gas bottle?" Jan reached up opening the last fanlight, the room already clearing. "Look at those Daddy Longlegs." A finger swept round, pointing to craneflys thickly dotting the tiled walls, all of which dripped with moisture from condensing steam.

"Drawn to the lights last night when someone wedged the door open. I'll collect them for the ducks, they haven't been fed yet." Gordon moved across, picking bodies from the walls. "Will you clean the Gents if I carry on here?"

Finding the Gents in good order, Jan cleaned and returned ten minutes later to see him still collecting. "How many?"

"Two hundred and ninety-four so far, but I keep finding more." He held up a coffee jar, displaying the numbers.

"Get the hose out. The walls are already saturated, we'll spray them down."

Returning indoors later, they chatted as eggs were slipped into boiling water, a quick easy breakfast. The Ladies had been washed down and left to dry, both gas bottles checked and one changed. The other was almost empty - two bottles wasted in that single night.

"The only caravans on site now are regulars, been coming for years." Jan buttered some toast. "Must have been those students; will you say anything?"

"No, don't give them the satisfaction; we could never prove it. Everything is working again, act as if nothing's happened... but we'll check again when they leave! My fault, I should never have taken them; I thought bird-watchers would be okay, particularly the girls."

"No more parties of young people then?" Jan raised an eyebrow.

"Not even from theological college!"

More time passed, 1989 rolling in, January, February, but chalet permission was never granted. The only remaining avenue, an appeal to the Environment Department, the hearing not expected until June, another delay - frustrating! Jan wanted a break.

"We could get away, off somewhere on holiday. Eileen and Peter will feed the ducks and keep an eye on the place."

Under normal circumstances she might have expected yet more resistance, but continuing worry about the future was affecting them both.

"Okay, France should be warmer if we drive far enough south - anything to make you happy." Watching a beaming smile blossom, he really did want to please her, but there was something more. It offered a chance to size up the opposition, to find what continental sites offered; how French visitors might be attracted to Relubbus. More importantly, did they use chalets on their caravan parks? And why should English families want to cross the channel when they could enjoy themselves better in Cornwall! Tactfully he made no mention of these thoughts.

Jan however, was well aware of the intention! A casual observer might think that looking at someone else's toilets rated very low in the holiday enjoyment stakes! That would normally be true, but when first plotting the holiday she had enquired casually, "I wonder what French sites are like?"

The trip was quickly planned, the prospect lifting spirits; the first proper holiday in twenty years.

The crossing from Plymouth to Roscoff took five hours, the sea pleasantly smooth. Arriving just before dusk, the first hotel was almost empty but comfortable. A good night and an early start next morning gave the chance to dash southward while the weather lasted, the hotel patron warning northern France could be very cold in the early months. He was right; they had left Relubbus with temperatures exceeding fifteen degrees centigrade and thought that by travelling south the climate would naturally get warmer. Wrong! It was far, far colder! Everywhere the Breton road signs warned of ice and slippery roads; even several hundred miles farther south it was still colder than at home but the feeling of freedom, the release at being away, not having to think about planning and Councils - it was great. Picking campsites from a directory and following the roadmap to locate them, all were closed. No wonder in these temperatures! Gordon, having rehearsed the words carefully, explained in halting French that they owned a park of their own. This led in several cases to a tour of the facilities and such discussions as language permitted. One camping ground on the west coast was gradually being eaten up as an enormous sand dune encroaching from the sea at a rate of three metres a year. Others in the Loire Valley at Tours, and in the Dordogne seemed mildly expensive compared to England, and along the coast at Biarritz the prices were frightening. Jumping back in the car they motored inland to pass the night near Foix.

The morning route rose steeply into mountains, pausing in Andorra to look at another caravan park. Even this early in the year it was open - the caravans so close together you could pass cups of tea through the window to a neighbour.

"British fire officers would throw a fit." Jan suggested. "I'm glad we didn't bring *our* caravan." She had learned a little Spanish before the trip but it proved of limited use as Catalan was the language commonly spoken. The hotel was reasonable but cold and deserted. Once during the evening a phone sounded along the empty corridors. Gordon rose automatically then pretended cramp in the leg had caused him to stand, but saw Jan smile and knew she understood.

With snow beginning to fall outside, they moved on next morning, briefly entering Spain, then back into France by the Mediterranean coast near Perpignan. Even allowing for the closed season, very few of the many sites visited came up to Cornish standards but most offered letting accommodation, some just caravans but the better ones sporting chalets. Which group would River Valley belong to? Some things in evidence would never be allowed at home; urinals on outside walls, electricity lines tied to trees with what looked like string, pitches with hardly a blade of grass even though they could not have been used for many months - but the people were nice, especially with anyone attempting to speak French. Near Perpignan they stayed at a small hotel, more a guest house really, and walked down to the beach to lean against a rail on the promenade overlooking the Mediterranean. An icy wind cut through jumpers and overcoats, producing many a shiver.

"No wonder they all close until later in the year," Jan pulled her coat tighter while looking round the small town for somewhere to eat.

Stopping at a sort of antique shop with lots of copper work and old ornaments in the window, Gordon muttered, "I don't see any brass monkeys."

"Are you surprised?" Jan asked with another shiver.

He didn't realise she knew.

At breakfast a couple from an adjoining table waved a greeting, speaking in French but the accent was from Germany, recognised from many such visitors to Cornwall.

Hearing a hesitant reply and guessing the reason, the German asked, "Shall we continue this in English?"

Speaking slowly, hunting for the words, Gordon insisted he must stick to French in order to become more fluent. It was not his intention to be rude but the other couple now turned away, concentrating on their food.

The French landlady however, busily preparing another table in the corner, looked across with a beaming smile of approval, and later was obliging enough to read a long list of words onto a tape brought along for the purpose, so the proper pronunciation could be listened to and practised on future occasions. It should help when speaking to French visitors next season; at least, that was the intention. Thanking her warmly, they left next day in search of somewhere less windy. Parking along the way to walk round a town in search of lunch, Gordon stopped at a shop selling clothes, leading the way inside.

"I need a hat. Insulation against this weather!" Seeing a puzzled expression, he tried again, patting the flat of one hand against the head. "Er... un chapeau?"

"Non. Je suis désolé mais..." the assistant speaking fast, regretted they did not sell hats but gave directions to a shop some distance away. Though Gordon's French was still very limited, Jan was surprised when without hesitation he led the way outside, walked up the street, turned right at the traffic lights, took the third turning on the left then the second on the right and fifty metres along was a shop, its window full of gents headwear. She was impressed. Hiding his own surprise at this success, he chose a soft French cap; easy to fold and pop in a pocket.

Driving gently along the coast aiming eventually to reach Nice, they were in no hurry, visiting towns and churches, eating in one place and staying the night in another, enjoying the country but never able to get warm. Another two days of shiver-making wind turned them inland, perhaps for more shelter but they came after some time to a grassy verge, stopping for a coffee from the flasks and to study the map. After a while Jan, in the driving seat having taken a spell at the wheel, put away the empty cups and wound down a window, simultaneously turning up her coat collar.

"This is the road to Lyon." Gordon pointed ahead, glancing down to where his finger marked a point on the map then bent to look more closely, nodding confirmation. "It is."

"I know."

"How?" he looked up.

"It said so on that big sign about a mile back. In French of course, L-Y-O-N," she spelt out the letters one at a time, counting them on her fingers as to a child, leaning back sharply as he made to slap her hand. In that moment as they laughed together, he pulled her close and their lips met - amazing how much better life had become - and how much nicer the prospect of life in their own warm Cornish valley now seemed. This trip had at least made them appreciate home, pushing worries about planning into perspective. Pity about the wind; they had laughed about that too for a time, but it kept them mainly in the car.

"You know what lays beyond Lyon?" he whispered.

"Paris?"

"Or Roscoff. Which would you prefer?"

"The ferry you mean, and home? It *must* be warmer there!" Jan nodded, reaching to close the window.

Having decided on Relubbus they determined to return smartly, still amazed at travelling a thousand miles nearer the equator only to find it colder than home. A visit in summer might be nice but leaving the site in someone else's charge after mid-April was out of the question.

Seeking the quickest way back they chose the motorway, finding it empty of traffic. No doubt people used minor roads rather than pay the toll. Driving non-stop through the night, taking turns at the wheel, they pulled off the road at Jan's request next morning, and into a rest area with toilets. Directly the car stopped, she dashed off, leaving Gordon to investigate food being served from a big caravan to one side of the parking area. This was no Joe's Snacks as seen in English lay-bys - far more grand, in keeping with French reverence for food it stretched at least twenty feet, the full length counter spotlessly clean. Six chefs in tall white hats and white coats cooked each order directly on the hot plates of a row of gleaming stoves that lined the rear wall. Egg and chips seemed a safe enough order, but on receiving it he was disappointed to see the egg still yellow and runny, not basted at all. Too late to complain; knowing the French liking for lightly cooked food he should have spoken first. Arriving back in the car to find Jan already there, he slid into the seat.

"Ah, looks nice; thanks." She whipped the tray away and started eating.

"That was for me! You were supposed to get your own."

"Pretend you're a gentleman; go fetch another. Um, good chips but this egg is nearly raw."

Off he went, leaning on the counter and trying to explain to one of the chefs in limited French that the British prefer their eggs well cooked. "Can I have mine turned over?" He spoke in a mixture of language and hand signals, correcting as he went and making flipping motions.

"Mais Oui, certainement," the chef nodded. Someone else took the money and found change while this second plate of egg and chips was prepared. The finished meal looked fine, egg, nicely browned and crispy on top.

Back at the car Jan asked enviously, "How did you manage that?"

"Just skill and a fantastic knowledge of the language."

The first forkful however, revealed the awful truth! The egg had been cooked on one side, just as before, then scooped from the pan and put upside-down on the plate.

"You did say, *'skill and knowledge of the language'*, didn't you?" She looked at him with a touch of a roguish grin on her face, leaning over to pinched another chip.

Taking the empty plates back, he spent some time trying to explain in French, how the English like their eggs. The chef who had cooked the meal listened, the other chefs gathering round. Several French customers joined in, a little crowd gathering, intent on the attempted explanation, helping here and there with a word until the meaning was clear, but with every sign of disbelief that anyone should want an egg cooked on both sides. Everyone was arguing, hands waving in the air, people interrupting each other, several talking at the same time and turning back to Gordon for confirmation. Finally, as understanding dawned, one chef shook his head with incredulity and looked at the others, raising both hands, palms upwards, "Les Anglais...?"

Hard luck on the next Englishman who likes his eggs sunny side up!

Arriving back in Relubbus one mid-afternoon was like a breath of spring, much warmer than during the entire trip through France. A good night's sleep in their own bed made things even better, and in the morning they fed the ducks, stroking the feathers as pieces of bread were taken from the hand - a real welcome home. With Peter and Eileen still asleep in their caravan, that first walk round revealed little change - buds on the trees were fatter, bushes highlighted with those first white blobs of pussy willow - a promise of spring yet to come.

The break had been cold but good, those planning worries now less deep - for a while at any rate - but not forgotten. Try as they might the odd questions slipped out; the options, the chances of success, what to do next? A decision to purchase four static caravans of various sizes was partly to test the letting market and partly window dressing to demonstrate the appearance.

The arrival of this new accommodation did one thing; it emphasised how easy the siting of caravans was compared to building chalets. Jan mentioned the fact wistfully one evening as they sat together.

"You don't really want the easy option, do you?" Gordon asked.

"In a way it's tempting. I know chalets will look better but the work building them..." she broke off, looking vacantly out across the valley, then asked quietly, as if to herself, "If we do get chalets and make the place really super, would the children take over in the years to come?"

No answer came as they sat together watching the sky gradually darken, silent minutes ticking away before he spoke. "We needn't build them all, just make a start, set the standard. The petrol problems may go away for a while anyway."

And so it was left, thoughts pushed aside - the decision anyway not in their hands - but periodically those hidden concerns were triggered again. One morning, 21st April, an early visitor paid for a copy of The Times in the shop, reappearing shortly after to toss it on the counter and point to an article. There, in black and white, was the evidence! Due to a shortage, gasoline prices had raced from $170 a tonne to $270 - an enormous percentage rise. What would that do to touring trade?

There were other worries too; an unexpected visit from the District Council. Mr Lodge, Assistant Director of Environmental Health appeared on the doorstep to make an inspection. They could only expect the worst; the Council were out to get them!

A few days later a letter arrived. Realising from the envelope that it referred to this recent visit, Jan opened it with some trepidation. Scanning through, a smile spread slowly across her face and she turned reading aloud.

"*I am writing to compliment you on the excellent conditions on the site and the exemplary manner in which the site is run and maintained.* There! I knew I liked him." Quickly she read on. "*I would have no hesitation in putting forward your site as an example as to how others should be run.*" A fist punched the air in triumph. "It's dated the seventeenth, how about that?"

The phone rang. Laying the letter aside, she reached for the receiver. "River Valley Ca... Oh, hello Chris." Her voice held a touch of concern; calls at this time of day were unusual. She listened, replying at intervals. "Really... When do you move... How much..." The conversation continued, finishing with a short account of the latest happenings at Relubbus. Replacing the receiver, Jan looked across the room with an even bigger smile.

"He's a sergeant now. Promotion!"

***

Summer arrived, trade picking up; not too many children yet, just the odd teenager, no doubt having finished their final exams. New wardens, Don and Christine arrived, such changes normal in the industry; people often preferring a different part of the county every few years; some even became wardens on the continent. Peter and Eileen were still helping - having the extra hands made life better - more help for visitors too, and more eyes to keep watch. Even so, a problem had arisen. Reports were being received of two teenage lads walking around among tents at the lower end of the site and making a nuisance of themselves - climbing over hedges from nearby fields, tossing stones in the river, playing with the standpipe taps, spraying water at each other and at tents or anything else within range. No complaints mentioned anything destructive but these lads made campers uncomfortable, uneasy about going out and leaving their possessions. Patrols in that area had been increased, without success. One afternoon a camper called in at the office. "They're back again, those lads - just walking about."

"Thanks." Gordon made for his bike, slipped on cycle clips and headed off as he did so often when leading visitors to more distant pitches. Wanting to hurry he was careful not to go fast; children were told not to speed so he mustn't either. Approaching the downstream end, the two teenagers came into view, walking away across the bottom section of grass. Seeking to use surprise, Gordon speeded up, approaching quickly, intent on speaking to them before they could run off. Leaving braking until the last moment he aimed to slide the cycle to an abrupt halt beside the pair - this sudden appearance intended to impress - but it had to be timed right! They still hadn't heard the approach, hadn't looked round - the distance was closing rapidly - his hands grasped for the brakes... wait, not yet, another ten feet, wait... now! He squeezed hard, feeling the bike slide then suddenly tilt - felt himself lift and sail headlong over the handlebars, striking the shoulder of one teenager as he shot between, rolling automatically into a ball.

The lads froze, unable to immediately comprehend - the cycle veering off to crash into a bush as this human projectile shot neck-high between the pair like a cannon, hitting the turf with a thump, rolling right over and springing up to face them. A mouth dropped open, then closed, swallowing... tense seconds passing.

Suddenly the taller lad took off towards the river, Gordon leaping in pursuit, almost within grasp, the dog after the rabbit, belting along for a hundred metres before the almost forty year age difference took its toll, the younger lad haring away.

Catching had never been the intent; the cause of this mad chase unclear - adrenaline probably from that flight through the air! Strolling slowly back, he grinned to himself. "Idiot. Me not him." Arriving at the fallen cycle, he looked idly round and seeing a slight quiver in a clump of gorse, walked quietly over to stand looking down at the other lad. "You can come out now. I'm not dangerous, not crazy... only wanted a word."

It transpired the lads were after a girl, someone they met at the beach who said she was staying on site, but a girl without a name. Not finding her, they had wandered around waiting but bored and as teenagers will, had found their own amusements. The other lad now reappeared on the far side of the hedge, standing in the neighbouring field. They moved closer, talking across the foliage.

"There are only four girls of your age group staying at the moment. Next time call in at the office and I'll walk round with you, see if we can find her. Evenings are best, most people are back then."

The group parted, Gordon recovering his bike and heading for the house, the boys walking off across the fields. They never came back. Whether it really was a girl that drew them to the valley would probably never be known.

As the year progressed, reached a peak and began to wane, nothing had happened on the chalets front - the Public Inquiry still months away. During the busiest weeks it was easy to forget but as trade declined, those old anxieties tended to re-emerge. Still, brighter spots did occasionally occur.

"What are you looking so smug about?" Jan asked as she left the shop, leaving Eileen to continue serving now the early morning queue had gone.

Gordon sitting at the desk checking figures on the computer looked back at her, pretending not to understand. "Smug?"

For a while the stand-off continued, but shortly he asked, "Who do you think booked in today - staying in a tent?" It was hardly a question, there was no way she could guess. "John Simmons... you know, the Tourist Board inspector, the one who gives us our grading. I offered him free but he insisted on paying. His wife is quite attractive."

***

"Not yet." Jan whispered the words softly, nestling closer, her hand sliding up under his pyjama top, pulling him forwards, fingers opening to drag nails gently over the warm flesh, wanting him to wait but it was no good! She could feel his impatience, his need - but it was not for her. He had been restless all night, waking many times, his sleep shallow. She too had slept badly, waking when he did and now it was morning; still early, still dark but he wanted to rise, to get up and on with this vital day. She had tried to delay him, tempt him, using her body... but his mind was too full, to concerned with what lay ahead. Understandable of course, after all those years of work and dedication to make River Valley the best. What did destiny hold? At some future date maybe many years ahead, the valley's fate could turn on this day - would it be showpiece or slum? Decision time had arrived. The Pubic Inquiry would open in just a few hours!

At breakfast, eaten as the sun rose, Jan saw him toy with his food, without appetite, saying little; rising to walk round the room, look out at the waterwheel then sit again. An hour before necessary he climbed in the car and drove off - more nervous than she had seen him for many years.

Parking the car, there seemed no point in arriving this early. Walking uneasily along the high street, The Buttery on the corner of Morrab Road at least offered somewhere to sit. He was still sipping coffee when a man he later recognised as the Council's Barrister entered, took a nearby table and started deep discussions about River Valley with someone Gordon had seen before in the Council offices - one of the District Council's staff possible, though he could not be sure. Imagination perhaps - association of ideas... but who else would be discussing the site? Not wanting to eavesdrop, he left without finishing the coffee. Had he stayed and listened, then the coming events might have seemed less dramatic.

For the hearing, both a legal and a planning expert were retained. As they outlined the case, it seemed sound and sensible, including strict rules on the length of season to prevent permanent residential use. That was understandable and proper. Since permission for caravans already existed and this application actually proposed a lesser number of better looking units, what was the problem? Looking round those faces in the hall however, one could see hostility to the project, occasional murmurs of disagreement - the belief that stopping chalets would somehow stop caravans too. With the case for granting permission finished, the advocate sat down and a hush descended over the hall.

The Council's barrister rose to his feet. This was the moment some in that room were waiting for; to see this proposal torn to pieces! Attention focused on the solitary figure as he glanced down, perhaps at some papers on the desk, then towards the inspector. His next words drew gasps of disbelief. The District Council, the planning authority who had caused this appeal... they were offering no evidence!

Unsure of what it meant, Gordon reached towards some papers on the wooden surface in front, and found his hand shaking. He could only guess that having inspected the evidence, the letters and minutes of the committee meetings, the planning law and all the circumstances, this learned barrister found the position indefensible. What else was there to think? Voices were raised in the hall, angry voices, but the Inspector called for quiet. Everyone would be heard - and so they were.

After the Inquiry was over, the Inspector, the man in charge, the man on whom everything appeared to rest, announced he would view the site, inviting along anyone who wished to come too. Having completed that inspection and listened to all the comments, he promised an early decision. That meant the results could be expected in a few days, a week at the most. This usually indicated a cut and dried case, and since the District Council had offered no evidence it seemed unquestionable that permission would be granted.

The days of waiting passed slowly, until one morning the phone rang. Late autumn was the only time of year when calls were rare. Eagerly the receiver was lifted, a greeting and a few words exchanged, then an explosive reaction.

"That's ridiculous! You can't mean it!"

Jan looked up, surprised at the force and incredulity in Gordon's voice. A long pause followed, obviously listening to someone before speaking again.

"Can they do that? Is it legal?" Another pause, and he laid the receiver down.

The second bombshell had fallen. Slowly, he turned, his face drained of colour. "They've cancelled the Inquiry!"

"Cancelled it?" She couldn't understand.

"The District Council has got together with the Government department..." he hunted for words to explain, "I don't know exactly who - must be the Environment people or the Inspector. Somehow they've decided among themselves that there's going to be a re-trial!"

And that was that. Cut and dried with no possibility of argument. The Inquiry just held was to be set aside. How strange that the Council who had offered no evidence should be consulted but not the applicant? Gordon and Jan heard only after everything was decided. What went on here? Natural justice seemed to demand equal treatment for both parties. This new hearing would be expensive. Could they afford it?

"Who do we know," Gordon asked "with power enough to wipe out an Inquiry where all who wanted to speak were given every opportunity? Has it ever happened before or is this unique?"

A week passed, a bad week! Jan's father, Jim was taken off to hospital and from there to a nursing home that offered twenty-four-hour care; a place four miles away in Hayle. They visited him straight away, not waiting for the usual visiting times. He was drugged and in some pain but tough to the end, trying not to let it show. Returning home, passing Jim's now empty bungalow, this new sadness added to the gloom, giving a bad night.

In the morning a strange thing happened. A copy of a letter mysteriously appeared, a letter on District Council paper and addressed to the Planning Inspectorate. Someone obviously thought the applicant should see it - but who? Who had sent it? Sitting at the desk reading again the contents, Gordon gazed blankly towards the window, one hand drumming an unconscious tattoo on the desk. Clenching a fist to stop the nervous fingers, he rose from the chair and headed for the kitchen.

"We've had a copy of a letter, one I'm not sure we were meant to see."

"What sort of letter?" Jan wiped her hands on a tea towel, reaching out for the copy, but he held on to it, reading sections aloud.

"...the Public Inquiry held on 5th October 1989 was curtailed when the Council's Barrister resolved to offer no evidence on behalf of the Council. Such an action was directly contrary to the clear instructions which he had been given." Gordon stopped, holding out a hand, palm upward in an expression which said 'Can you believe that?' They looked at each other, unsure, before he spoke again.

"Would a Barrister come all this way and then do the exact opposite of his client's instructions? Why should he?" It was hard to understand.

"What about that morning before the Inquiry when you were having coffee in the Buttery and saw him talking with the Council man. He must have said something then; surely they must have known?"

"I can't be sure it was a Council man. I'd seen him in the Council building... a lot of people go there, not just Council officers. But why on that particular morning should he want to meet anyone else? I can't even be sure it was the Barrister either, though if not it was his double - and they *were* talking about the enquiry. Perhaps we're being paranoid, imagining things - this whole business has got so I'm not sure of anything any more. You'd have thought the Department of the Environment would at least have given us chance to express an opinion. It seems very one sided, just consulting with the Council - especially since it was their man who offered no evidence!"

This idea, this resentment, kept returning but it did no good. Unjust it might be, but nothing could be done; the new inquiry would take place. For those opposed to this application, it was a victory, a cause for smiles but the emphasis was all on *'stop the development'* as if defeating the chalets would somehow wave a magic wand and the existing permission for caravans would also disappear.

On the site, very little work needed doing this winter, just as well for events had robbed them of the incentive. Some messages of support had been received, and considering the population of the area, not that many had attended the hearing, but it was depressing to be counted as the villains.

"We didn't even get the original permission," Jan sighed one evening. "If someone else owned the valley it would probably be covered with big static caravans by now. People would be pleased enough then to have chalets instead!"

They talked of giving up the appeal - just using the existing permission and bringing on the big square caravans to make up for diminishing tourers. Such accommodation must eventually become substandard but that was in the future; for a while they would be fine. There was another possibility; let someone else take the hassle - the idea of selling up was discussed. Depressing thought.

"Why think only of a few dozen protesters?" Gordon asked. "Think of the hundreds of holidaymakers who would prefer the better appearance and nicer accommodation chalets will provide."

It was all very well to say that, but the protesters were local people, folks they liked and wanted to be friends with. He moved across to look out over the stream. "If only the petrol situation would improve, the site could stick to tourers and tents - I like them best anyway."

"Could an electric car pull a caravan?" Jan turned back from the window.

"No, I don't think so. The range would be too short and

the batteries too heavy. Besides, the chalet permission if we do get it, will ensure this valley is always a quality site, not a place of falling standards. Rough places attract rough people."

And so it was left, set aside, some trenching work for new services being used as a diversion to ease thoughts about the future.

On 19th November something happened to drive these thoughts away. Jim died, his 85th birthday less than a week away, the cake Jan had made now standing forlornly in one corner of the kitchen. Jimmy James, (Arthur George on his birth certificate but always called Jim) would be missed. Some caravanners came down for his funeral, travelling 200 miles each way, a tribute to a grand chap; grocer's boy, guardsman, boxer, policeman, a great tough-guy who would help anyone.

Later, Steve moved into the bungalow, a temporary measure while working in the area. He really fancied to travel and hoped later to get a job in Germany - higher wages over there, increasing the attraction. Whether he would achieve that aim remained to be seen. He had acquired an old motorcaravan and was working on its renovation, an early Volkswagen, the split screen model so sought after by collectors. Gordon called in to see it one day and was talking to Steve when they fell into conversation with someone inspecting Relubbus bridge, a man called Peter from the Cornwall Archaeological Unit, who on being asked about its age, admitted they had no precise figure.

"What we can say is that these pyramid cappings are circa 1850, and the plug and feather marks make it after 1800. That means this bridge was rebuilt less than 200 years ago. If it had wedge-marks, that would have been earlier, between 1500 and 1800." He pointed, "Those rough stones at the bridge ends were to deflect cartwheels, avoiding damage to the main stonework."

Spring, 22nd March 1990 saw the re-trial, the new inquiry underway. Two years had passed and even now it was not straightforward. Only a day was allotted, the inspector booked elsewhere for the morrow. It overran, causing a six week adjournment until the 4th May and after all that, the appeal was lost!

"How could something that a barrister felt unable to defend, and where the inspector was prepared to offer an early determination, be lost? Who could have...?" Gordon shook his head, still not able to understand; a mystery perhaps never to be fully unravelled.

Ah well, disappointing but never mind; disappointing too that only a fraction of the cost of this hearing was paid by the Council even though it would have been unnecessary but for their side's actions. But that's life!

Chapter 20

Escape

"Ah, a postcard from the States. She's in Philadelphia for the weekend."

Sharon was on the Fulbright Exchange, teaching in a school at the southern end of New Jersey, not far from New York - a one year job swap with an American.

Waiting until a head poked round the doorway, Jan passed the postcard over, offering a tentative suggestion. "We could visit, look at America and see the tourist trade over there? Sharon would love to show us around; Peter and Eileen can manage here." With autumn progressing, that was true enough; getting away presented no problem.

"Probably be pleased to get the place to themselves," Gordon nodded in agreement. Staying in the valley seemed somehow less attractive after the big failure.

A coach tour was booked, a 3000 mile trip from Los Angeles right across the States, finishing in New York, a trip scheduled to take two weeks, leaving another week with Sharon before returning home. This was their first flight in twenty years; years in which holidays had been a few short breaks to see the family and one ferry trip to Europe.

"Are you nervous?" Jan knew his dislike of heights.

"No, not really." The answer was relaxed, dismissive; 'As if I would be,' the manner said, but looking from a window shortly after take-off and seeing the ground far below, his fingers gripped the seat. Silently controlling an unaccountable urge to get out and walk, his face set in a mask to show nothing, growing accustomed to the height after a while, like those tower cranes at work he forced himself to climb years ago. Eleven hours passed, some in fitful sleep before touchdown in Los Angeles where a minibus carrier, something between a bus and a taxi, whisked them away to Pasadena to join others at the tour hotel. A day at Disneyland saw Jan spinning around in a monster cup and saucer, riding a roller coaster, a mini submarine, the monorail, the river boat, returning exhausted but happy, sleeping soundly to wake at six for a leisurely breakfast before the coach rolled off towards Las Vegas, city of bright lights and gambling.

"You're lucky," the tour guide addressed them over the coach's microphone, "You'll be almost the last visitors to use this building - it's being knocked down shortly."

Great! What was it, unsafe or totally dilapidated?

"No, no," the guide shook his head in answer to someone's question. "It's just too small. A bigger building will rise on the same plot. Be ready in less than six months - in time for next season's start..." he broke off at another question from the rear, "How many rooms? Oh small, just over six hundred I think." His expression showed contempt for the size.

It proved comfortable enough; perhaps the conversation had not been so casual Gordon thought, looking at the guide with a new respect and wondering how the technique could be applied to caravanners. That dampening of everyone's expectations had definitely resulted in delight at what might otherwise have been considered mediocre. After the journey and still feel some affects from the flight, they retired early but rose at 4am. Peeking through the curtains, the streets outside still blazoned with neon signs and lights of every description, cars were passing and people walking just as they would in mid-afternoon. Did this city never sleep? Hurriedly they dressed, making for the nearby Excaliber, a relatively new hotel or casino or whatever these vast gambling houses are properly called. The floodlit outside was more than matched by its interior, not crowded but still with dozens of people. Las Vegas may be the greatest place in the world for non-gamblers! Breakfast was offered for a song, as much as one could eat for the equivalent of a pound sterling, a sop to draw in custom for the main purpose - the machines! Food was one of the trip's highlights, Americans eat well! Not necessarily wisely but well! This was some city; almost everything cheap, not in quality but in price like the food, and all designed to attract the gambler. A few dollars *were* fed to the hungry machines just to say Las Vegas had been played, but no success expected or achieved, nor was it particularly desired. The big gamble had been years before, giving up everything to buy their Cornish valley - after that small bets were easy to resist!

The coach stopped at a host of famous places across the continent; the advantage of such a tour - experienced guides knowing just where to visit, the Hoover dam for instance, that years ago had been known to a generation of students as Boulder Dam.

"I think," Gordon said as they stood looking at the tall structure, "if I've got the right one, they have a special system of using surplus electricity to pump water to a lake on higher ground during the night when not so much power is needed, then at breakfast time it runs back down through turbines to reclaim the current for peak demand. Do you think we could find a way to do that with our waterwheel when the batteries are full?"

"If I hear about work back home once more, I'll push *you* over the edge and through those turbines!"

"You can't. Bound to be a steel mesh to stop floating debris entering - just like we have bars in front of our waterwhee..."

A little fist punched him. "You won't float, I'll wrap one of those bars round your neck first! We're on holiday! Stop thinking of problems back home."

"I must."

"Why?"

"Makes the trip tax deductible... well partly."

She hit him again but gently, with a small grin and shaking head. They flew the grand canyon in a small aircraft, went for a boat trip on Lake Powell, then into Indian territory, and stood at Four Corners, with part of a foot in four states, Utah, Colorado, Arizona and New Mexico.

It was here they discovered the most primitive toilets in the world! Entering a door in a row of small shack-like constructions, one was confronted by a toilet seat but no sign of a chain or any means of flushing it. Fighting the smell and looking down through a hole in the pan, a vast chasm stretched off to left and right, and way below a sea of what appeared to be mud. A trickle of water falling from an adjoining toilet made it clear this was not really mud at all! Ugh! Treading warily, Jan quickly left, heading for the coach's onboard facilities.

After purchasing a few handmade pieces of polished blue stone mounted in silver, they swept onward through Monument Valley, scene of so many westerns - heading for the John Wayne museum. Big John worked this area a lot and it was here the tour stopped for food.

"Order something local. Be adventurous," Jan urged, not believing for one moment that he would.

"Beans on toast... beans are traditional cowboy food," the explanation was added hurriedly at her grimace - he ordered a Mexican Taco.

The Mesa Verdi was terrific, perhaps the biggest possible contrast to Las Vegas, now so far behind; a special place for Indians, for wild game and as it turned out, also for mornings. They rose real early but sunrise over the Mesa Verdi was worth it, watching the first rays appear and shoot across the prairie, a herd of buffalo like shapes silhouetted by its brilliance. As this ball of orange fire cleared the horizon they strolled off to locate breakfast. So far each morning Jan had ordered thick pancakes with maple syrup, they usually came in batches of five for each person - all of which regularly disappeared!

"I must start to diet." She commented as they ate. Later there would be a good opportunity to see how she did that.

Snow coated the top of the Rockies as the tour moved on, then swooped down to lower levels at speeds well above the legal limit, coming eventually to Dodge City. No hope of a slug in the Last Chance Saloon, no drinking on a Sunday - this was Kansas, 'the bible belt' someone said, but a meal in the Golden Nugget proved memorable. Rib eye steak was chosen, cooked to order and in due course would be carried to the table by a waitress who meantime poured the coffee. Laid out across one end of the eating house was an immense display of every type of salad and fruit one could imagine, together with soups, and well - just about everything. Soup seemed the proper place to start; Gordon chose clam chowder - it was good. He followed as Jan rose again, collecting a great plate of salad, including fresh strawberries and pineapple that Americans like to mix with normal salad items, hesitating at several dishes holding unknown contents but she threw some on anyway, again whispering the instruction, "Be adventurous!" Returning to the table a girl arrived with two huge steaks, and an invitation to "Top yourselves up with salad whenever you like." She reappeared moments later with a steaming pot having noticed the coffee cups were empty. Jan finished her steak and salad, commenting that more of those strawberries and some cream would finish the meal off nicely. So it should, considering the size of the bowlful she returned with. Gordon having finished his steak, wandered off to find a separate and extensive dessert table, returning with apple pie and something reddish, probably cranberry sauce.

"That looks good." She took a final strawberry from her bowl, wiping the spoon round the dish to gather the last of the cream, then asked, "Where from?"

Following the pointed finger she departed to collect an identical helping. That apple pie was really super, hardly surprising - this was after all, America. Both went for '*a tiny bit more*' and this time just for a change, added cream. Seated back at the table the helpings were not really any smaller than the first ones - must be the dim lights?

Jan glanced upward, then back at the dish and shrugged. Gordon watched her savour each mouthful with sensual pleasure, and eventually with the dishes scraped clean, they leaned back in the chairs as a girl refilled the coffee cups again. Life was good.

While sipping the hot liquid, the tour guide passed by,

his name was 'Will'. Leaning over he advised quietly, "Don't miss that chocolate fudge, it's really the best on our whole trip!"

"We shouldn't..." Jan hesitated, watching Will walk away.

"No, of course not. He'll be disappointed though, if we don't try it. Not fair after the trouble he took to let us know, do you think?"

"We could taste just a nibble perhaps?"

They sneaked off back to the dessert display - and again those tiny bits didn't actually turn out to be all that small.

"Difficult stuff," Jan excused herself softly to someone sitting on the next table. "Sticks to the spoon, very rich, hard to serve a small quantity; barely leaves room for enough cream to cover it."

"Top up with cream half way," the stranger advised.

She nodded her gratitude, a beaming smile spreading at the thought. Sitting back enjoying another coffee, they surveyed the bill - converted to sterling, it cost less than three pounds a person. Leaving a hefty tip for the girl, they reluctantly departed, Gordon whispering, "We should tell everyone visiting Dodge City to eat in the Golden Nugget, *especially if they're on a diet!*" he emphasised the last words.

"Spoilsport." But she hugged him in the evening light, too happy to be affected by a little hinted criticism.

The arch at St Louis was impressive, some piece of imagination by its creator - and so the coach trundled on to Kentucky, Virginia and the Shenandoah National Park. Trundled is perhaps not a proper description, for it regularly broke the speed limit, thundering along but at one point slowed suddenly to a relative crawl, bringing surprised looks and questions from the passengers. The tour guide, Will, picked up his microphone, "Nothing wrong folks. If you watch to the left you'll see a gas station ahead. That's where the sheriff sits checking traffic speeds."

Sure enough, a uniformed figure sat at a bench over-looking the road, a police car parked nearby, ready perhaps to give chase. His hand rose to wave as the coach passed, some shouted words lost in the engine noise might have been "Catch you next time!"

Washington was a grand place but apparently to be treated with suspicion. The guide warned to be careful and go everywhere by taxi, but Georgetown he said, was safe. By daylight they saw the Jefferson Memorial, the White House, Capital Hill, Arlington National Cemetery, The Monument, George Washington's house and a great complex of museums. That night, six of the party joined together to visit Georgetown and met the Guardian Angels. These pink jacketed chunky looking chaps, walked the streets swinging baseball bats casually by their sides, their presence generating confidence.

An early call next morning and the coach swept onwards, to Philadelphia and the Liberty Bell complete with its famous crack, then finally on again to New York.

"Now listen," the tour guide warned. "Hotel rooms in New York are small - no I mean it - rabbit hutch size! So you know what to expect."

The announcement was greeted with some disbelief, for all across America the motel type rooms had been in the large to enormous range. He was right though; the hotel on Times Square was grotty by comparison. Never mind, it would be little used. They were off at seven next morning, and before that, a six hour tour had been booked taking in New York at night. Up the Empire state building, a ferry past the Statue of Liberty to Staten Island and back again; here, there and everywhere. As always in the States, food was not forgotten - the tour stopping for a seven course Chinese banquet. Jan was suspicious, the contents of each course somewhat obscure; filled however with holiday spirit and a certain recklessness, they ate everything regardless of what it might be. On the same circular table sat a dozen people, a party from South America, a couple from Germany and another couple from Canada, a rich variety of accents all talking together in English - and there, in Chinatown in the middle of New York at well past midnight, was a Greek lady who had a friend living in Helston! That was nine miles from home. Small world. Back at the hotel there was time for maybe four hours sleep before leaving to collect a car.

"Driving in New York is an experience at the best of times," the tour guide had cautioned.

They were about to find out! Neither had used a right hand drive vehicle before, and certainly not an automatic. Learning to handle such a car in the morning rush hour in the centre of Times Square may seem foolhardy, but there was little choice. With some apprehension, Gordon climbed behind the wheel of a sparkling white, brand new model, a type never seen before, much less driven. An attendant handed over the keys and turned to walked away.

"Hey! How d'you drive this thing please?"

The man turned, stepped to the car, a black arm reaching in to point. "Stick the key in there and press." He moved off again without another word.

Apart from the main routes, virtually every street was one-way; so much they knew from the previous night's tour but that was the coach driver's problem then and the streets had been relatively empty. Now it was different, more traffic and the Lincoln tunnel must be found, driving on the right hand side of the road in a very strange car with every other street showing no-entry. New York drivers, not known for making allowances, were heavy on the horn and short on patience. How would they fare?

"Piece of cake!" Gordon insisted, rolling his eyes and holding up two pairs of crossed fingers as the car eased slowly from the subway garage, into traffic. Tensely they followed the stream of vehicles, hoping not to bump or be bumped, searching the road ahead for the sign. "There!" Jan pointed to the right. It was almost upon them! They swept round the corner, found the Lincoln Tunnel, got everything perfect and in short order were on the New Jersey Turnpike. Talk about beginner's luck! Fifteen minutes down the road, they spotted their old tour coach. It rested stationary, pulled in and being booked by a traffic cop. For three thousand miles across the States the driver had broken every speed limit in the book and got away with it; here travelling empty, they nailed him!

Sharon's school was found without a hitch, a short tour of inspection offered and accepted. Her flat was medium sized but adequate, the air-conditioning essential even in October, but noisy. Days while she was teaching were partly spent looking at Caravan Parks or rather Trailer Parks to give the local title. Some were quite good, the emphasis mostly on hard ground to support large motorcaravans, called RVs or Recreational Vehicles. At the weekend Sharon acted as guide to the Amish country, with evenings for sightseeing or shopping.

On the first visit to a supermarket, they manoeuvred with care, still suspicious of that 'Collision Damage Waiver' signed when collecting the car. Many vehicles in this parking lot were old and dented, the area far from affluent. A big American, probably waiting for his wife, leaned lazily against a pickup truck in the next line. Idly he watched as Gordon stepped round to open the doors for Jan and Sharon. When they stepped from the car, the man slapped an arm against his side.

"Now I've seen everything!"

The hand rose, pushing back a wide brimmed hat, then stretched out to gesture with raised palm, "What the hell..." Slowly the head shook, that hand rising again to take the hat, striking it against his knee, "Gee!"

Gordon, somewhat at a loss, just said, "Hello."

Detecting the accent the man nodded in understanding, "Ah, you're English," as if that explained all.

Eventually the time came to leave; the trip had been great - the country and particularly the Americans so easy to like. They were friendly, easygoing and not nearly so much in a hurry as those visiting England in a caravan. Thinking of Americans who had stayed at Relubbus carried thoughts back to Cornwall and the site; the wardens had been left in charge, a promise to ring up regularly largely forgotten, calls being placed only twice in the whole three weeks.

Landing back in England and driving off to Cornwall, leaves in the valley were already falling - it was good to be home. Prompted by Jan's rampage in Dodge City, partly as a jest and partly to fill the lengthening evenings, Gordon started writing a diet program on the computer; it might well be needed if the States were visited often! Rapidly this project became more than a joke as interest grew and nutritional facts came to light. Certainly it offered a quicker way to count calories, but there was more. Research revealed that official recommendations existed for daily targets of some thirty different nutrients. Interest deepened. If the computer could count calories, let it calculate everything else at the same time - it would be no extra work. All a person need do was enter the type of food and how much, for example:-Banana, 95g.

Once that was done the computer would display all the vitamins, minerals, protein, fats, fibre as well as the calories. Not only that, it would add them all up throughout the day, giving running totals at any time, and comparisons with the recommended daily targets - and all without any extra work from the user. Favourite recipes too, could be fed in and given a name the computer would recognise, and figures for different types of food could be compared before deciding what to eat.

Another handy feature helped to keep the diet healthy. Pressing a key would display all the vitamins, and show any shortages over the past day, or week or month. Another key would display a list of foods rich in that vitamin so the deficiency could be rectified. The same could be done for minerals and other nutrients.

Dieticians are apt to say "Eat a balanced diet," as if that were the easiest thing in the world. This program quickly revealed a 'balanced diet' was in fact, quite difficult to achieve, particularly for instance in Calcium, or Vitamin A, or Iron and some other minerals. However, the system could never be marketed; that would need scientific testing and medical approval. Never mind; persuading the computer to work out the various figures had occupied many a long evening and taken minds off that still unresolved problem - River Valley's future.

**

"How did it go?" Jan asked as Gordon appeared in the doorway just before dusk.

"Another thirty metres. Nearly finished now."

A trench was being dug, a long one, half a mile from house to downstream boundary. Work had started the previous winter, continuing intermittently; the trench contained a sewer and a series of empty pipes, five of them, each perfectly straight and level. Laying nearly three miles of empty pipe may sound bizarre but it was not so mad. These were merely ducts inside which smaller pipes would be slid; for the water main, a TV aerial cable, an electric cable, and a telephone line.

"And what about the fifth pipe?" Jan had once asked.

"Well, er, we might... you never know what other service caravans may want one day. After all, who knows what the future holds?"

"Oh, a spare - half a mile of pipe that's no earthly good to anyone!" Seeing him about to protest, she demanded, "Go on then, what could you use it for - trained mice running along with messages round their necks?"

Gordon had not been able to find an answer but had carried on anyway. At ten metre intervals along the whole line, little chambers were built giving access to these pipes, a row of galvanised manhole lids stretching away into the distance.

"Okay, so when you've finished the pipes, what about caravans?" Jan asked.

"I still think ordinary ones will spoil the valley. The chalets would have been better, just 80 nicely shaped pairs. Now we're back to 170 long metal caravans - well not us necessarily, but someone eventually will."

"Is there any alternative?"

"Possibly." He walked to the window, gazing out over the empty valley. Now in November most trees were bare, the bushy willows still retaining a sparse coating of leaves; this foliage though turning yellow, looked almost black in the gathering gloom. The river ran by as always, a few drakes sleeping along the very edge, close enough to tumble in if a fox came - most ducks already locked safely in the shed for the coming night. Turning back, he sat on the low sideboard, the room still in semi-darkness. "The site's quality depends on the people we attract - you agree?"

She nodded. Nothing was truer than that!

"Well, to keep them coming we need to offer something as good or better than our competitors. We don't have the beach, so appearance is everything. They need to love the valley and at the moment they do; it's quiet, sheltered, pretty - and we get our priorities right."

"Like you getting in the river and clearing the reeds just upstream of the bridge where people first stop their cars to look?" Jan smiled, "And how each spring you make up and re-turf where the current washes the bank away in front of the house?"

"That sort of thing, yes - wild flowers for the butterflies and not being afraid to tell people if they do things that upset other visitors - a loud wireless or leaving a groundsheet down too long and ruining the grass for the next person. Sure, but that's not going to be enough. If dearer petrol stops some people towing caravans and more visitors seek to hire accommodation, then we must provide it in a way that our type of people like - considerate people who care about the countryside, care about how things look and about their neighbours, people who drive quietly if they come back late - you know."

"Yes," Jan looked at him suspiciously, nodding her head. "I know something else too. Out with it! You're working up to some new scheme?"

"One thing in particular will help keep the site attractive. Where we need big caravans, let's use the twin-unit type - the ones with pitched roofs; they look so much better, the designs and finishes are really improving recently. Some of this year's models look just like a proper bungalow. They're expensive - need a longer season to justify the cost. I'll have to make a fresh application; another Public Inquiry too, probably. Would you mind?"

"Mind?" She sank back in the chair. "Do I get a choice?"

So they tried again - third time lucky, perhaps? This application sought to lengthen the season and confirm that twin units were permitted; the ones that came in two parts and bolted together on site. Such units complied with the legal definition of a caravan; they would be less work too, arriving by lorry and quickly ready for occupation. The extended season, if permitted would allow opening through Christmas and into early January.

The year flew by with letters passing backwards and forwards but the matter had still not been agreed, and with little prospect of a resolution, it went again to appeal - to a Public Inquiry. That was arranged for the 13th August 1991, more than three years since the Council were first approached about chalets. Leaving the site for a whole day in the school holidays was not easy, but there were now three pairs of wardens working alternate days; Ron and Jean having joined the others. With this help, Jan would have to manage.

At the Inquiry everyone gathered yet again, the various arguments laid out for consideration.

"Why," asked the inspector, "do you choose the fifth rather than the first of January as the closing date?"

Standing in the witness box Gordon shuffled nervously, "We get quite a few Scottish visitors. I thought it unwise to send them home on new year's day."

When it was over, not one clue indicated the possible outcome. Busy August days went by, Autumn came, then winter and the new year and still they waited - but it was worth it. Third time lucky! Early in February 92 the decision arrived. The Inspector's findings confirmed that the original planning permission did include those nice looking twin unit mobile homes! Tents were mentioned in the decision, so camping was now legally confirmed, although the right to tents had long since been established. He granted the extended season too. So at last the position was clear; or was it?

A few days later another letter arrived. Gordon opened it, scanned the text, drew in a deep breath and sat heavily in one of the armchairs.

"You'll never believe this!"

"Believe what?" Jan looked up sharply, drawn by the tone.

"The Public Inquiry, that final decision in our favour - it's not final at all!" Wiping a hand across his chin he rose again, kicking the wall in annoyance, forgetting the slippers were thin. "Ouch! It says here, *'the views of the Inspector are not binding in law'* can you believe it? At any time the District Council can still challenge our right to twin units."

"Will they do that?"

"They had to pay some of our enquiry costs, not as much as seemed fair to me, but I doubt they'd try again? Still, anything is possible - it's too risky."

Further negotiations with the Council yielded first an opinion from their solicitor that the planning was sound, but even that was not sufficient. It had to be agreed by the Councillors.

A letter dated 4th June 92 gave the final approval. After four years it was at last agreed that the original planning permission did allow any type of caravan, including those in the shape of chalets!

Jan waved the letter with a wry smile. "Is it too late now?"

The question hardly needed asking. They had talked over the possibilities a lot recently. Circumstances had changed, a recession underway - no time to start major expansions! And another thing, they were four years older, retirement not to far in the future; five years possibly - eight at most.

"Too late? Yes, I think it is." Gordon smiled back. "At least the recession has lowered petrol prices; visitor numbers are rising this season. Pity about the first permission, we could have made that look super, something the county would be proud of - might even have persuaded one of the children to take it on after we step down."

"Or the grandchildren. Chris phoned this morning; Lesley is pregnant; early next year we'll be grandparents!"

Several people were seen walking towards the office, not in any hurry but in a laughing group, the man holding some sort of container at which the others were looking, sometimes pointing, all with varying expressions of merriment. The leading trio were recognised as John and Gerry, and their daughter; a family with a big tent pitched well downstream. Automatically the letters MPG came to mind. Why was it so much easier to remember car numbers than names? The office door stood wide open, combating the hot weather - beyond lay a field packed with caravans, every pitch round the perimeter in use; so it should be at the end of July - no one ever parked in the middle, that was playing space for the children. The approaching group came on, still laughing, John handling the plastic container nervously in one hand, like it might explode - arm extended away from the body ready to drop at the first sign of danger.

Meeting them at the door, Gordon looked at the ring of expectant faces, then at the plastic tub that had once held ice cream. Guessing at some sort of live specimen he asked, "Where did you find it?"

"Kellie, our daughter came running, pointing towards the river and asking what was the big green thing on the tent opposite. We all went to look; not too near mind you - even from that distance you could see it was an insect." John paused.

Grabbing the opportunity, Kellie took up the tale. "We sent Dad forward for a closer look - he's not so valuable as the rest of us, if it was going to eat anyone it might as well be..." she paused, pointing a finger and grinning at her father. "He wouldn't go too near and came back quickly saying '*I don't know what it is but it's pretty big!*'"

"I went quite near enough. And what about afterwards?" John protested "They pushed that container into my hand, telling me to catch it!"

"Mum remembered seeing a sign you put up on the

notice board, inviting us to bring in anything unusual for identification," Kellie explained. "So Dad took his life in his hands and went over and put it inside... well he didn't exactly put it in, I mean he didn't pick it up - just leant over at full stretch, held the tub below and knocked it in with the lid. We made him do the carrying; that thing might eat its way through the plastic!"

John eased the lid, passing it over. "Some sort of huge mysterious insect. Can you tell us what it is?"

Dropping the lid on the nearby windowsill, Gordon looked down at a bright green creature, two inches long with enormous back legs. "It's a Great Green." He eased it out onto the edge of one hand and put the tub down.

"Great Green what?"

"Grasshopper."

Disappointment showed clearly in the watchers. John shook his head despondently. "I'm deflated, feel about two inches high! Thought we'd found something really rare. Is it safe?"

"Perfectly. Doesn't bite or sting - just sings by rubbing a back leg against its body. It's often called a Great Green Bush Cricket these days, that's different from a true Cricket. They *are* rare in most places, not in the valley though - listen for them at dusk. Here..." The creature was offered.

John held out a dubious hand, letting the insect be eased onto his palm. At first he was unsure, then turned, showing it to the others. Two hands reached forward but without any real intention of making contact. Suddenly the creature started to move, not jumping but crawling along. John tried to shake it onto the grass outside but it clung on.

"They do that," Gordon warned, "like glue. Here, scrape it gently on the edge of the tub, then let it go in some tall grass. That's one reason we don't cut round the edges."

They took it away, no doubt showing the creature to others in passing. Much later, news came back of its careful release. "We put it in the hedgerow and named it Gordon."

***

"Stop that!" Jan waved a warning finger. "What are you

doing this time?"

"Putting in Welsh. That young couple staying on Area 3, she gave me the words - teaches Welsh at her school."

"Leave the computer alone. Don't keep making it more complicated!"

"Complicated? Oh, I see. When you're sitting comfortably, I'll explain." Gordon spoke as if to a child. "Now listen careful. If someone from Wales, books in and you want to give them a Welsh bill, do everything as normal until the computer asks *'What language?'* This is where it gets difficult. You press W."

He ducked as a cushion sailed across the room. There had been several arguments recently, the program becoming increasingly sophisticated and Jan resenting changes as he continually made it do some extra little thing - occasionally a matter of importance but often like a crossword addict, unable to resist playing with it.

Mostly the program was good - if someone pressed a wrong key it did nothing, merely asked the operator to repeat the entry - making the program Jan-proof, he called it, but some wrong keys the machine could not detect. Pressing 'E' for Electric instead of 'A' for Awning would definitely give the wrong answer. This had happened on the previous day and Jan, still annoyed, blamed the program for what had been her own wrong entry. That was unusual. She used the computer more than anyone and seldom made a mistake, but on this occasion, several other people waiting in the office had witnessed the error, causing some embarrassment.

Gordon, standing nearby ready to take the visitors to a pitch, had been foolish enough to laugh! Jan re-did the entry, putting the matter right but afterwards refused to use the computer again, keeping any arrivals chatting until he returned to the office, then insisting he booked them in - standing behind him and watching, making it clear she was checking his every move. An edge of annoyance had crept in, a mild irritation leaving neither prepared to give way. It was inevitable of course, that with the pressure of preparing each visitor's bill, rushing off to take them to a pitch then dashing back again for the next, he eventually pressed a wrong key and the machine spewed out something ridiculous.

"Men!" Jan waved a hand to the visitors, a gesture that proclaimed all males useless, masking a smile of triumph and turning back with a sweep of the hand, "Come out of that chair; better let me do it or we'll be here forever."

As the day went on, she continued preparing the bills, working in the odd comment to various customers about that earlier mistake, laughing with them over the error. Hearing these remarks made at his expense, Gordon bided his time and was out working on the dustbins when the chance came. Seeing Jan slip to the laundrette with an armful of clothes, he hurried back to the office, taking advantage of her absence to make another program alteration, typing in a small new sequence and a secret codeword to govern its operation.

Later that day, more old customers drew up in the yard, a couple who first came some ten years ago and were good friends. Surreptitiously typing in the secret codeword, Gordon left the office on the pretext of topping up toilet rolls in the Gents.

Left on her own, Jan welcomed the visitors and for a while stood exchanging gossip. Thinking another caravan might sweep down the entrance road at any time, she moved to the desk, asked how many days they would like and prepared to type in the necessary information. At the first touch of a key, a message in large print flashed across the screen.

"Go Away! I want a man!"

For a moment she was dumbstruck, mouth opening to curse, cutting the word abruptly short - the visitors' presence remembered. A quiet snort of anger escaped as her finger reached to press hard on a key; nothing happened! More keys were pressed - no gentle touch but stabbed down in frustration as the screen remained unchanged. Realising the couple were watching, she drew back in the chair clenching her fists.

I'll murder him! Look!" The screen swivelled sideways, allowing them to read the caption. "We had an argument about the computer," Jan explained, rising and hurrying to the door. "Gordon!!!"

He had been waiting for the call, knowing it must come. Leaning out of sight against the far wall, he forced away the grin and walked to the office. "Yes, dear?"

"I'll give you *yes dear*! Fix that machine." An arm stretched out, pointing.

Saying "Hello," to the visitors and exchanging a few words, he walked across to the computer and paused, pretending to read, then spoke as if to the screen. "Want a man do you? Very sensible; well done Nogdor." He reached to pat the monitor with approval, then sliding into the seat, entered the special codeword to turn off this new sequence, typed in the details and out came a perfect bill.

Taking a cheque he glanced sideways with just a touch of triumph, turning quickly back to the still laughing caravanners.

Seeing his grin, Jan's face hardened, she wanted to... suddenly an idea came, a smile of her own slowly spreading as she spoke. "You don't think this problem could be contagious, do you? Will all my kitchen equipment suddenly *want a man*?" The last words were said with emphasis.

Gordon looked up sharply. "No! The infection is over - forever, honest!"

Chapter 21

The Tapestry Frame

"There - it's finished." Jan held up a square of cloth, a ring of flowers decorating the dark background. It should have looked good but she was disappointed, the effect spoiled by wrinkles and distortions. This one was for a footstool and would be better when pulled tight.

She fancied bigger tapestries but working with loose material the finished picture could never be smooth; it twisted and warped as work progressed - and when the size increased, so did these wrinkles. Evening hobbies were in fashion again with daylight hours drawing in, the shortest day next month.

"I need to keep the material stretched," she picked up a needlework magazine, several had been bought just for this purpose. Together they scanned the pages looking at tapestry frames, seeing good features but all with some drawback.

With the site closed, it was easy the following day to slip off to Truro and gaze in the windows. A variety of shops offered frames but all with drawbacks, many obviously made for economy, though even these were moderately expensive!

"Look," Jan pointed to a large wooden square, mounted on two tall legs.

Gordon bent closer to read the price tag, drew in his breath, straightening to nod reluctantly, "Yes. If you like it."

"Thanks, but no. I'm pointing out the faults, not buying. Look again; how would you work at that one?"

"How should I kn... Um; need to stand in front. I suppose you want one to sit down at?"

"Wouldn't anyone? Those long crossover bits at the back; if we buy it could you cut them out so I could get a chair up close and my legs underneath? "

"Only if you don't mind it falling over; it's where the strength is. Anyway, in the evenings you sit in an armchair - you need something wider."

"That's fine some of the time but it won't always be an armchair... too long in the same position is uncomfortable. Sometimes a high stool near the window would be nice, so I can see outside. We should look for adjustable height."

Gordon shook his head. From what they had seen so far, it looked unlikely. "If we do buy one, I might be able to adapt it a little..." A new thought occurred, "If it's too short I can fix that."

"How?"

They were still standing outside the shop window. He glanced behind, checking no one was in the way, then stepped quickly backwards. "I can cut six inches off the legs of your stool."

Rounding on him with raised fist, Jan stopped suddenly as two people walking along the pavement stared at her. Embarrassed, she turned away, lowering the arm, catching a movement inside the shop and found a woman watching from behind a stand of wools. Feeling her colour rise, she glanced quickly to the left. Gordon had moved, pretending not to be with her, standing in front of the next shop with a small smile on his face as he apparently concentrated on a window full of baby clothes.

"Right." Her neck snapped back to glare fiercely through the glass into the other woman's eyes, resisting a strong urge to stick her tongue out. They faced each other briefly before the woman inside looked away, adjusting something on the wool rack, then disappearing with a tiny backward glance.

"Hm!" Jan blew a snort.

Gordon watching surreptitiously, half expected her to paw the ground like an angry bull and charge in his direction but she turned the other way and strode off along the street. In the end, he had no option but to follow, catching up as she was turned into a coffee shop having salvaged her pride.

He knew instinctively that she would sting him for the most expensive cake on the menu to complement the coffee, but the little charade had been worth it! Neither spoke as they sipped the hot liquid, looking at each other across the table, both trying to hide smiles. Jan lifted her fork, delicately filled it from the oozing wedge of cream and fruit that the waiter had called Wicked Delight Gateau, raised it, ran a tongue suggestively round her lips, opened her mouth slightly and still holding his gaze, slid the confection inside as if performing an exotic act. There were better ways to bring a man to heel than shouting at him!

Sipping another hot coffee, the discussion of frames resumed.

"I must be able to turn the work over to keep the back tidy, and while I'm doing that the tapestry must remain tightly stretched. For a really big tapestry, I'd like to move the material up as work proceeds so it's always at a convenient height. It would be nice too, if the frame would tilt at a different angle; whatever position I happen to find most comfortable at the time."

"Glad you don't want much... getting complicated isn't it?" Gordon shook his head, frowning, but in the back of his mind an idea was developing, an idea he definitely did not want her knowing about yet. "Okay, why not sort out what we need but wait for the January sales to buy?" He watched her expression but she was not suspicious, the suggestion of buying in the sales very much in character and easily believable. In truth, January was not too far off and would be soon enough; she was working on an embroidered table-cloth at the moment. Cross stitch work did not distort like tapestry; good results could be achieved without stretching the material.

Over the next few days, whenever Jan went shopping he secretly worked on plans for a frame but one like no other on the market! He would make it for Christmas, including all those features discussed and a few ideas of his own. Smuggling in the wood was the first hurdle; that needed the car, which meant Jan could not be out shopping at the time.

The answer was simple; buy the wood and leave it in the bungalow at the site entrance, do most of the work there. Some tale about extra shelves should provide an excuse - easy enough to walk down sometime and bring back a few pieces to work on in the basement.

The timber was bought, hidden away, and construction started. Basically, the task fell in two parts - first the square frame, then some sort of stand to mount it on.

Okay, the frame that actually held the tapestry was just four pieces of wood fixed together in a big square. Simple? Not really. When fixed to the stand it must pivot right over so odd ends of wool on the back surface could be kept tidy, and it was special in other ways too. Jan had mentioned her wish to move the tapestry up as work proceeded, keeping it at the most comfortable working position - fine, so the top and bottom members must be rollers. She had also said the material must remain stretched.

"Well..." Gordon pondered how best to reconcile these objectives, keep it tight yet let it move. "A single removable pin will fix the top roller but the bottom one needs something to get the tension just right." A ratchet was the answer, allowing the material to either run free or be tensioned up just a few millimetres at a time. That would both permit movement and allow the exact tightness to be achieved. He nodded to himself and realising he had been muttering, looked round quickly, though it was virtually impossible for anyone to approach undetected. With such a system the tapestry could be any length - floor to ceiling if needed. "Good. This ratchet; I better have one at each end of the bottom roller so the material stretches evenly."

Sorting out a length of mahogany some 10cm square, he sneaked it down into the basement and set up the big waterwheel lathe. With the timber in position, one hand reached for the Frankenstein switch. The enormous machine was American, said to have been shipped over on lend-lease arrangements during the war. Starting-up this lathe originally produced a surge of current that the waterwheel alone could not supply, putting stress on the storage batteries. This special switch, a long handled lever fixed to the wall, started the machine slowly by stages - the name 'Frankenstein switch' came from the children, after one that operated a monster in some film they once watched. As the motor moved smoothly into action, he set to work, chips flying as wood spun against cutter, dub, dub, dub, the sound lengthening at each pass as corners disappeared until a smooth round form remained. More machining to shape, then hand cutting the ratchets and finishing with fine grade sandpaper, produced two mahogany knobs that should contrast well with the varnished pine of the frame itself. Lifting one, a palm ran over the surface feeling the smoothness; a comfortable size to fit the hand.

As time went on it became necessary to admit that something was being made for Christmas, the workroom declared out of bounds. Jan promised not to enter, not even to look when alone in the house - but would that promise be kept?

With the square frame now ready, attention focused on a stand to support it. First the armchair problem; the stand's legs must be wide enough apart to slide easily past the arms of any chair. They were not really legs but tall wooden triangles coming to a point at the top, some 80cm in the air - say about hip height. Simple so far, but these legs would not stand upright on their own; they must somehow be fixed together.

Two things were important. Firstly there must be no timber along the floor at the front, otherwise the stand could not be drawn up close to a chair! Secondly, if the cross bracing so often seen at the back of stands were omitted, then the frame could be drawn up over a chair or even over a bed - useful if later in life if someone became ill. Fine, but without diagonal braces, where would the stability and strength come from? That needed thinking about.

Gordon spent the afternoon trimming bushes; one thing you could say about the valley, there was never a time - never would be a time - when work ran out. Something could always benefit from a little attention. Snipping away required no concentration, giving time for thought. On the pretext of sharpening tools, he had spent last evening doodling on the basement bench, sketching possible solutions without much success. Having a naturally cautious nature these scraps of paper had been scored up into tiny pieces with a razor knife, then shuffled up together and separated in three piles, each hidden in a different place. The frame, so far as it had progressed, had been dismantled and hidden in case Jan's curiosity overcame her promise. Now as he worked on, trimming a branch, leaping with outstretched arms to snip a slender bramble high above, the chance to think was welcome. By evening inspiration had come - steel corner brackets would give the necessary stability.

It was Steve, sworn to secrecy, who welded the metal. With these brackets screwed solidly into position, the triangle-shaped legs stood rigidly upright, supporting the square frame above. A few tests proved this sturdy combination slid easily over any armchair. Fine, it was already better than anything seen in the shops, but this was a present for someone very special - nothing less than perfection would do!

"Now didn't she say the height should be adjustable? How?" Converting the rear part of each triangular leg into a double member, solved that. It slid upwards to five different positions, sufficient to cope with the very highest of high stools. The same technique made the stand's width adjustable too - just in case a frame for wider tapestries was ever needed. What else could be added? A small adjustable foot at each side would combat uneven floors.

Concealing the amount of time going into this project meant working down at the bungalow or in the basement when Jan went out shopping. If loving care measured a gift's value, then this frame was better than any present Napoleon gave to Josephine! Apart from the steel brackets that Steve had welded, every member consisted of wood without a single knot - not easy to find these days; the man at the builder's merchants had mumbled to himself as knotty samples were rejected. Each piece was sawn, planed, rubbed down with several grades of sandpaper, the final one so fine it felt soft on the hand - every corner slightly rounded so no hand or wool could catch, then treated with preservative and three coats of varnish. But the present was still incomplete.

A pair of small matching boxes about the width and depth of a hand were made to hang on the stand, for waste wool ends and for tapestry tools. The box for tools had three small holes drilled near the bottom - a needle pushed into these holes would pierce a polystyrene foam block and stay safely held until needed. Magnets fitted one on each side provided an alternate place for needles; various hooks for scissors and the like were also added. What about patterns or sketches? Several sizes of board were prepared, with hooks to fit over the top roller, one big enough to turn the whole frame into a drawing-board or painter's easel.

Two friction discs allowed work to be set at any stiffness or in any position, or to swing over for trimming the reverse side - a strip of webbing attached to each roller made it easy to sew the tapestry on.

When all was done and assembled late one afternoon, it shone like a piece of furniture, magnificent! And yet something was missing... it needed a tapestry! What plausible excuse would allow a trip to Truro? Some mower part? Yes, a fuel filter; that would do. An hour later, an assistant in one of the needlework shops held out a tapestry, put it to one side and reached for another. The choice was extensive, the selected scene had a stream and bridge not unlike the one at River Valley. A roll of plain tapestry cloth was also purchased, both hidden in a bag and the bill paid. Not really liking the plastic carrier, its name and logo with obviously feminine connections, he hurried off, making for the car when something in another window caused a hesitation. One of Jan's magazines had shown a set of tapestry tools - needles, clips, stitch-rippers and little brushes for keeping the surface clean. Most tools had already been found but not the right kind of brush - and here was the exact thing in a window - except this was some sort of cosmetic establishment. The name above the window said Body Shop. A swift leftward glance took in the street, a handful of people wandering around; turning casually in the other direction found several others. He wore no watch, but looked down at his wrist, trying to give the impression of waiting for someone, then gazed again at the window and that little round headed brush; the card alongside said 'Blusher'. A hand reached up nervously touching a cheek, to be hurriedly withdrawn - an association of ideas probably. Moving to the doorway, he stepped quickly inside and across to a free assistant, a young girl; they were all young girls - his first instinct on entering had been to look for an elderly salesperson.

"You have a little brush in the window; got a round head..." he stopped, unconsciously lifting one hand, the finger making a little circle, worried she might think he was being insulting, "...the brush." He dried up, wishing now not to have come in.

The girl, a ripple of amusement in her face, turned away. Moving to one side she lifted a small stand with perhaps a dozen different sizes and shapes, offering it forward. Briefly he reached out, touching the one required then looking up towards the ceiling, wanting to whistle or hum but knowing it would only attract attention. "Be cool, blend in," the thought came as the brushes were whisked away, the assistant pulling open a drawer to extract something wrapped in green.

"This one?" she unfolded the tissue, holding the brush towards her cheek and rolling it suggestively between fingers. "Shall I wrap..." She stopped as the brush was whipped from her hand , disappearing into an inside pocket.

Passing a five-pound note he mumbled gruffly, "They're good for engines."

Back at home these latest items were laid on a bench. That was it. No further possible improvements came to mind, the frame in every way the very best he could make it. Others might not realise, but Jan would know the love that went into it. Next time she left to drive into town, the various parts were wrapped with Christmas paper in nine separate bundles of various shapes, including that tapestry kit of a little river going under a bridge and the roll of plain tapestry cloth on which could be worked any design she wished.

Preparing this particular part of the present posed perhaps the most difficult challenge of the whole process - last time he used a needle was as a youth in the forces.

Jan was intrigued by the extra parcels appearing in the pile of presents under the tree. Though she might guess something of the gift's nature, there was no way to realise its comprehensiveness.

A few days later, up in Buckinghamshire, the family gathered at Ivy's house, or rather part of it did. Only Sharon and Steve were able to come as Chris was on duty in the police but Gordon's sister Jane, her husband Bill and their daughters Emily and Andrea were there; a merry occasion. Jan's present added to the fun; each parcel she opened yielding another piece of wood and a gale of laughter since no one knew what the pieces were for. The roll of blank tapestry material emerged from its wrapping to give a clue, she turned it over in her hands, stopping suddenly at the sight of a small heart, worked ham-fistedly into the material, an arrow passing through had GC by the feathers and JC at the point. For a minute she sat looking at it, turning with a happy face to stretch out and squeeze a hand.

Assembling the parts took only a few minutes, mostly with wing-nuts that needed no tools, the whole frame soon erected and looking grand.

Back home in the valley a week later, further improvements evolved as the first tapestry was worked on. Where to put the wool? A series of 84 hooks mounted on a new wool rack, hung the little multi-coloured skeins in neat rows that automatically moved up or down if the frame height was raised or lowered - just as easy to reach from a high stool or low armchair.

An adjustable lamp bracket too, was added, and another for a magnifier. To stop any wrinkles across the material, a lateral stretcher fitted in any position, moving when the work moved. Short lengths of strong plain material were attached, one to the top roller, another to the bottom; fixing a tapestry to these allowed the pattern to be wound higher or lower when working near the bottom or top edges.

Many people coming to the office admired the frame, one elderly gentleman offering a word of advice.

"Apply for a patent. It will take time, so put drawings, details and a photograph in an envelope, go to the post office and send it by registered post to yourself. When it arrives, don't open it. Keep it for ever as evidence if someone tries to steal your design."

A patent was applied for, the letter sent from Goldsithney Post Office. It came back the following day, three clear date-stamps 14th Feb 94 across seams in the envelope.

Struck by the fact that it could bring pleasure to anyone bedridden or in a wheel chair, attempts were made to contact firms in the industry, the design offered free on the basis that instead of a royalty, every tenth frame would go to charitable organisations. Having seen the photographs, John Lewis enquired about stocking it, but this frame was so much more complex than the simple frames currently on offer - no manufacturer would produce it at a saleable price. The idea fell through, the design made available free to a charitable organisation dealing with immobility; they were keen but again cost prevented any mass production.

"Not having much luck, are you?" Jan reached for more wool, selecting another colour from three dozen small skeins hanging near at hand. "Shame. For someone on their own or people who can't get about much like those in wheelchairs, this would be terrific."

"I know," Gordon moved across to where she sat at the frame. "The materials are cheap, about £30 but there's a lot of work in making one - they all say it's too expensive - even charitable organisations must consider the price. It would be good to give something back to the world, sort of say thank you for our own lives together, but what more can we do?"

"Write about it one day perhaps - publish plans and drawings of how to make it, and invite everyone to use the design."

"Need someone good at woodwork, but many men are... we could suggest that in return for the free design, they make an extra one for somebody less mobile or for an

417

organisation helping elderly people? It could help anyone bed-ridden too; just lift the legs and slip it under, then leave it at the bottom of the bed when not in use."

"Be nice if they called it the Jan and Gordon frame?"

There the conversation lapsed. Pity there was no way to get a mass of these frames to those who would really have appreciated them. A working example was sitting waiting at River Valley for any charity who wanted to copy it - or even for a profit-making organisation come to that, provided they would give one in ten to good causes. How many lives could be cheered up for a fraction of the Greenwich Dome's cost?

CHAPTER 22

Contentment

"There's no water!" Jan ran towards the door, calling with quiet urgency. It was almost ten minutes past six in the morning; waking late she had rushed ahead to clean the toilets.

Gordon, left behind and hurrying to catch up, was locking the office. He looked up in surprise to find her running towards him. "What do you mean, no water?"

"Come and see!" Not waiting, she was off, reaching the Gents door just ahead, bursting in to push down a hot tap in demonstration. It was dry, no water gushed from the nozzle.

Stepping into a shower, Gordon turned both taps - nothing. Pulling the door open, he tried a tap on the outside wall without result, then left at a sprint for the other toilets, forcing the Gents door open on the run, checking taps and shower again, then burst into the Ladies to find Jan already there, her hand on a tap.

"Damn!" She shook her head. "More than four hundred people asleep in their caravans and tents... and no water!"

For a moment they looked at each other, unsure what to do, then Gordon grabbed for the door handle. "The meter!"

He leapt through the doorway and was gone. Following, she glanced at the field of sleeping caravans, then ahead at the fleeing figure, and chased after, crossing the bridge and catching him near the water meter. Neither carried tools to lift the lid, but none were needed. The meter that clicked every few seconds under normal operation, was going off like a machine gun!

419

"Hell... it's running full bore! The three inch main must have split. Got to find it. You check the standpipes." And he was off again, to the service passage for the manhole lifting tools, grabbing them and running down the site, seeing Jan race off towards the nearest standpipe.

Within five minutes, the leak was found - in a manhole just past the third toilet building where the three-inch main reduced to two inches, the Tee-shaped fitting blown apart by the pressure. Standing, manhole lid still in hand, Gordon looked down appalled, watching the flow as if it were pound notes, which in fact it very nearly was! Snapping into action he dropped the metal lid back, not expecting it to clang so loudly in the morning silence. Regretting the sound, praying everyone would sleep late on this particular morning, he held both hands out as if to somehow silence the noise - then raced off again, catching sight of Jan and signalling her towards the house, not wanting to shout with caravans and tents covering every pitch; visitors who were due for a rude awakening soon - no water to wash with! Hoping they would all have full water carriers and spurred on by the thoughts of money flowing from that broken pipe, he streaked up the road, found the metal turnkey, yanked off the lid to the water valve, fumbled key onto spindle and twisted madly until it would go no more. Resting for a moment, panting for breath, he leapt again towards the bridge, crossing to stop by the meter... it was silent. "Phew!"

But no time to rest! Jan was back by his side now; he turned to her, "Okay, it's off. The two-inch 'Tee' piece on the end of the main has exploded. I need a new one. Need to bail out the manhole first - find me a bucket and jug."

She stood watching as he raced off. Nobody, absolutely nobody, kept spare two-inch fittings. It was hopeless; they would have to wait at least until the builder's merchants opened, and even they might not have one in stock! Shaking her head she hurried to the service passage, searching quickly and emerging again, bucket and jug in hand - just in time to see Gordon leave the house with two adjustable wrenches and a black plastic fitting.

"You had one?!"

"Of course." For the first time that morning he smiled. "Didn't doubt it did you? Give me the bucket; you stay here and warn the visitors. If any of the wardens wake up, have them fetch water from the river for flushing loos."

Arriving back at the burst pipe at speed, he lifted the lid and started bailing. Bucket after bucket was hauled from the hole and thrown across the road but the water level never altered. Muttering to himself he tried to go faster, "Of course. This is the low point; quarter of a mile of three inch water main is draining into this manhole - filling up as fast as I can empty it." Ten minutes later the level began to drop but now the pipework below was in the way. The bucket must be filled using the jug - it was slower! Of necessity as the level dropped he lay flat on the ground to reach. Trying to save time by flinging the water from this prone position, the whole bucketful fell short of the crown of the road and ran back to soak him - worse, the first customer had appeared, heading for the Gents. A quick call stopped him.

"Sorry, no water; burst main. I must bail out before replacing the fittings."

"Can I help?"

The man stayed, standing above, flinging the buckets that bit farther so the water ran cleanly away. With the pit nearly empty the wrenches came into action, forcing the shattered fitting loose enough to unscrew by hand. Taking a roll from his pocket, Gordon wound sealing tape onto the threads before tightening nuts on the new fitting. That did it, the pipework was reconnected. Making sure blocks of wood that took the end thrust were wedged in position, he dropped the cover back so no one would break a leg, then raced away to turn the water on. At twenty minutes to seven, all taps and showers were working again - thirty minutes of frantic effort, and hardly a soul from the parks mass of holidaymakers ever knew the sweat that was shed on their behalf.

"I woke two of the wardens." Jan, stood looking out over the site where a few people were now stirring. "Asked them to do the morning clean for us; told them why."

Gordon lay back in an armchair, wet through, partly from water that had run the wrong way and partly from perspiration.

"When things run smoothly, that's fine, but at times like this I'm shattered."

"Never mind, poor old chap." She stepped away from the window, a hand reaching to pat the unresponsive shoulder before dropping into her own armchair. "How many sites could have done it - how many finding a shattered water main could repair it before anyone knew?" Another thought occurred. "How many would have been stupid enough to stock a spare two-inch fitting!" They smiled across the room at each other. Guessing he had not the energy to argue, Jan spoke again.

"I suppose you'll want to slip off and buy another one?" Seeing a small shake of the head, her smile broadened. "Good, 'bout time you learned some... why the big grin? You haven't got...!"

Receiving a small nod, she reached for a cushion.

He caught it, tossing it gently back. "I just happened to have two. Special discount when we bought some other pipes. It's not fittings I'm short of, it's energy. I can't keep up this sort of thing for many more years. Time we thought about retirement. Any chance of breakfast?"

***

Jan and Gordon stood together in the lounge looking out across the valley; near at hand some ducks played in the river, sunshine glinting off the water. With the summer season waning again, more intervening years had flown. Today was their ruby anniversary; forty years of married life. As the old song said, it didn't seem a day too long.

Chris, always strong on common sense and still in the metropolitan police, had risen to the rank of Inspector. He and Lesley, now in a bigger house, recently had a second child Jack, who weighed into this world at ten pounds six ounces.

Sharon still worked in Northamptonshire, now a senior teacher with a widely spread network of friends across this country and America, so many in fact, it was surprising she still came home to Cornwall.

Steve had left the army and was studying again; taking a degree course at Loughborough University, a course on Engineering Design, and was specialising in computers.

And Grandma Jan and Grampa Gordon, what about them? They were happy as ever; no chalets yet, the petrol crisis now completely passed and everything fine - super surroundings, a business with no stress and just as much or as little work as either wanted to do. The ideal situation, except for the odd panic and the school holidays! Cornwall really was the place to live; not much changing. Ivor and Pam, with Diana and Tom were wardens now. Yesterday clearing up in the basement Gordon came across six large jars of Bramble Jelly, still solid and with no signs of mould, from that time he over-cooked it fifteen years ago. Jan was right, it would last forever. The coffee jar with Sharon's hair inside lay hidden in a box, and alongside it something only a few years old - that unopened letter they sent to themselves about the tapestry frame.

Something else happened in the basement recently. Chris had visited with his four-year-old daughter. Like many young girls, Katie was afraid of the dark but holding granddad Gordon's hand she descended the basement stairs without any lights, the pair stealing quietly across an underground room, feeling their way round the heaps of stored items and hiding behind a cardboard box in the far corner. So quietly did they crouch together, that Chris failed to find them in the game of hide and seek. The visit had been short but it brought back memories.

"How time has passed. Do you remember that morning in the shop when a picture of Samantha Fox appeared in one of the newspapers; a chap collecting his copy opened it and said 'That's my daughter!'." Jan moved to sit in her favourite armchair as they chatted nostalgically over times long past and those piles of accumulated junk. "Where did we bury that horse drawn mower? Seems so long since our first little caravan and those baths under the bridge. That line of pipes Chris laid when he was only eight, while we rushed Steve off to the doctor - it's never leaked has it?"

That was true, all the underground services still in fine condition, the site retaining its unbroken top Tourist Board grading of five ticks, and still holding that *'Best Site in the Southwest'* title, for the competition had never been run again. No tiles had fallen from the toilet walls, even the single upside-down pattern tile remained; the tiling boys had done well. That curtain Jan asked for over the front door just after the house was built some twenty-five years ago - she was still waiting. This season would be the 27th at River Valley - how many people had they made happy in that period? The most frequent comments had been delight at the shower baskets - in some way they caught people's imagination. A few folk had been upset of course, over the years for various reasons, it could hardly have been otherwise; Gordon regretted that.

Time to think about retirement soon, and a move to Jim's bungalow just down in the village. Who would own the site then? Could a buyer be found who would care for the valley as they had themselves?

"What will we do with our time?" Jan asked, stretching comfortably.

"Write about the valley, perhaps?"

Would caravanners and campers visit them at the bungalow - they did hope so.

END

Epilogue

I write now, from retirement. Jan and I have sold River Valley but we still live in Relubbus in the bungalow right at the site entrance - watching the caravans arrive and leave as Audrey and Jim once did. Many old touring friends still call to see us, some new faces too - we enjoy the company, miss not seeing so many people now we've left the site. Call in if you can or write to us - be nice to hear what you think. If any of your friends ask, we do a mail order service for the books, signed copies post free, helps to keep us in touch. There's a contact address on the last page.

Chris has reached Chief Inspector now but for a short while he's acting Superintendent on a special job. Lesley, his wife is now a district nurse, the grandchildren doing well; Katie is eight and Jack five, the generations moving on - in a dozen more years we could be great grandparents? That would make Ivy, my mother a great, great grandma. Sharon is still teaching, thinking of a new house, dashing off occasionally to America. Steve has found his niche in computer work, designing machine tools; high-tech stuff.

Jan and I are pensioners with a couple of acres of wild land to potter in and a house full of mementoes - you'd never believe the junk we've accumulated, things we look at sometimes and remember. For instance, there's the packet of carved wooden sausages once used for display before the site shop had electric, and an old plastic propagation dome with a long abandoned wasps nest inside. The two halves of that old St Hilary billiard table now form a bench across the back of the garage, and the tree of bird carvings is here too, in one corner of the dining room. Happy memories! Oh yes, our bathroom towel-rail is like the ones in the third toilet building, a stainless steel grab rail from the seat of an ancient bus - and no one has ever found out the history of that old brick path underwater across the river.

Brian and Eileen manage River Valley now and live in our old house, a nice couple, you'll like them. John and Michael, the new owners, call in from time to time, offering their experience. Perhaps they'll tell their story some day?

And having read the series, you wonder how much is true? Virtually everything; once or twice the exact timing may be a touch out, April perhaps instead of March, and only Christian names have been used but the people concerned will recognise themselves. The conversation too, is recreated as faithfully as possible though probably not word perfect. Often it comes from talking to people after the event as with the lorry driver who moved Jim's furniture. Many of those little titbits of knowledge that crop up from time to time came originally from caravanners and campers. I have to admit too, that I really did talk to Robin and Blackbird. And those little romantic moments with Jan; they were also true.

Oh yes, that reminds me, we have a retirement friend; Tiger Lily. She lives in the Sunroom, in the corner above my rocking chair. Have you guessed? Tiger Lily is a spider (a Common Cross I think) about 8mm across the body. I feed her regularly on dead flies, not too squashed or she doesn't like them. I offered the first ones with a pair of tweezers that tended to catch in the web and made her angry. A needle proved better, she takes a fly easily from the end but still sometimes gets tangled. On one occasion my finger caught in the web; Tiger Lily tried to bite it - I could feel the two distinct points of her fangs trying to push through my skin - they failed to penetrate, or perhaps she was playing with me. Since then, the needle is greased before impaling a fly lightly on the end - that seems to have solved the problem. When she's hungry Tiger Lily comes to the bottom of the web, waiting for a fly to be offered. Thinking that flies will get scarce when winter arrives, we've taken precautions. You know those little black canisters that films come in - they are ideal. Ours may be the only house in Cornwall with a store of dead flies in the deep freeze. We have a cock pheasant, a wild bird that Jan has tamed enough to come to the back door for peanuts -

actually within reach of her hand but she never tries to touch it - never betrays the trust. There are squirrels and rabbits too; the rabbits were a pest at first, destroying flowers in the wall but they've stopped that, so we like them now. Be kind to animals, it makes you feel good.

We never did find out anything more about that cancelled public enquiry. Chatting to various legal people since, it seems it really may be unique - unless someone out there knows different? Ah, sweet mysteries of life!

We still walk regularly round the site, and it's still nice - good to see a hedge that needs attention and to say, "I haven't got to do that." But there might be just a tinge of regret, a yearning to go back thirty years. Could I have done better? Almost certainly, but I did do something right - I persuaded Jan to marry me!

Happy camping and caravanning.
Gordon Channer.

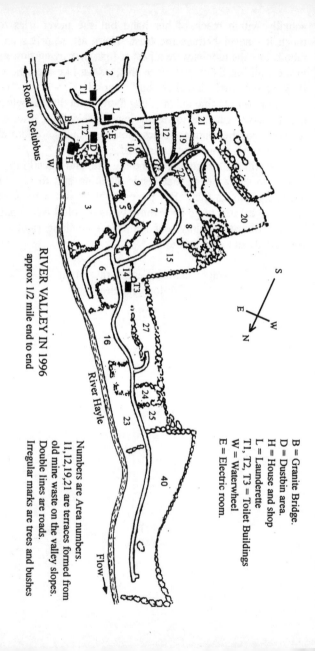

RIVER VALLEY IN 1996
approx 1/2 mile end to end

River Hayle

→ Road to Relubbus

Flow →

B = Granite Bridge.
D = Dustbin area.
H = House and shop
L = Launderette
T1, T2, T3 = Toilet Buildings
W = Waterwheel
E = Electric room.

Numbers are Area numbers.
11,12,19,21 are terraces formed from
old mine waste on the valley slopes.
Double lines are roads.
Irregular marks are trees and bushes

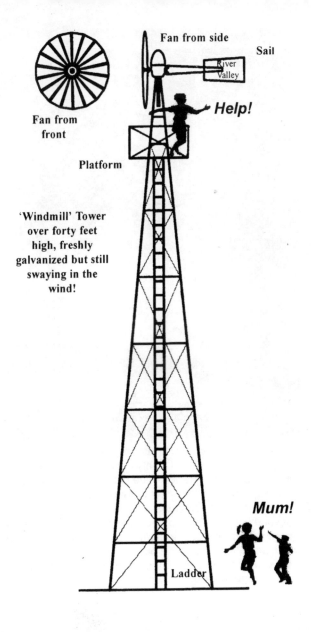

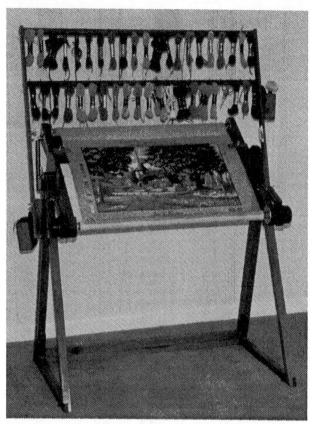

The Tapestry Frame. Never mind if you're a top class joiner or just an enthusiast with plenty of time, please feel free to copy or adapt this design - see next 6 pages. No one is saying the frame is perfect or that nothing will ever go wrong - its up to you to test your work thoroughly before anyone uses it! I am no design expert, but this one has given Jan much pleasure for many years with no obvious faults and I hope it will give equal enjoyment to others. For those who take up this offer, consider making a second copy for someone elderly or less mobile than yourself.

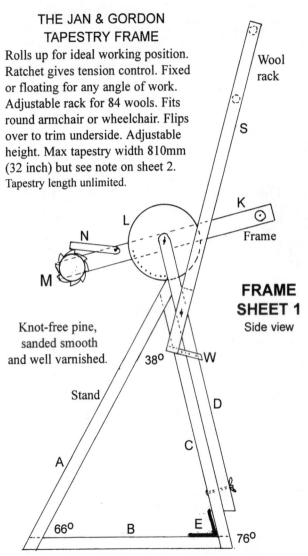

THE JAN & GORDON TAPESTRY FRAME

Rolls up for ideal working position. Ratchet gives tension control. Fixed or floating for any angle of work. Adjustable rack for 84 wools. Fits round armchair or wheelchair. Flips over to trim underside. Adjustable height. Max tapestry width 810mm (32 inch) but see note on sheet 2. Tapestry length unlimited.

Wool rack

S

K

Frame

L

N

M

FRAME SHEET 1

Side view

Knot-free pine, sanded smooth and well varnished.

38°

W

Stand

D

A

C

66°

B

E

76°

Member D can move up and down and is fixed at the desired height by two bolts into member C.

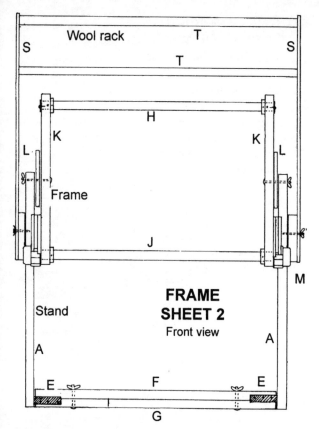

E = metal brackets holding stand legs to members F & G
M = hand tensioning knobs on ends of member J (see sheet 5)
Nuts & Bolts. All are metric 6. Generally wingnuts are used.
If required to fit over bed, or for wider tapestries, just lengthen
members H J & T by 100, or 200mm. The Stand is already
width adjustable by this amount. Members T, each have 21
brass cup-hooks facing forward and another 21 facing backward, making 84 wool hooks. There are 8 special washers cut
from aluminium and extended to make tool hooks under
wingnuts K1 D1 and at T1. Two matching timber boxes 100 x
110 x 50, hang from these hooks for tools and waste wool ends.

FRAME SHEET 3

How it all fits

H1 is 35mm metal washer
screwed to each end of roller H.
Z is position of lamp bracket
not show here (see sheet 6)

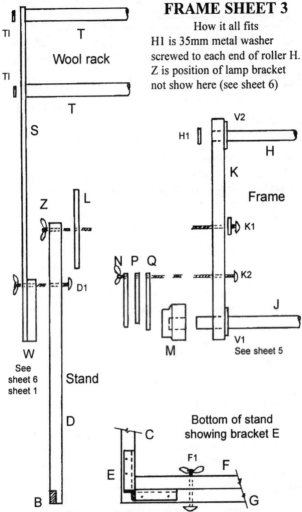

K1, K2, D1, F1 are M6 bolts. One washer under each wingnut.
K1 fixes frame K to stand D.   K2 fixes three ratchet pawls to K.
T1 = washers under woodscrews that fix S to timber rods T
V1 is metal washer slotted to roller J stopping K moving inward.
V2 is as V1 but with 4 holes to line up with 7mm hole in K
Pushing 6mm bolt through one of these holes fixes top roller.

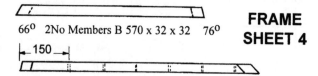

66°   2No. Members A 900 x 32 x 32   38°

Members A, B, C, are half jointed and screwed at the angles shown.

66° 2No Members B 570 x 32 x 32 76°

FRAME SHEET 4

|← 150 →|

76°   2No Members C 847 x 32 x 32   38°

Dotted lines show 7mm holes which must be at exactly 100 c/c.
Increase hole size if greater tolerance needed.

65 |← →| |← 220 →|

76°   Member D 870 x 30 x 30   Semi circular end.

Dotted lines show holes as in member C. 20mm from the RHE
is a 7mm hole to take bolt K1 (see sheet 3) connecting Stand to
Frame. This bolt passes through K, L, D, and lamp bracket Z,
finishing with a wing nut. At 220 from the RHE is a 7mm hole
for mounting the wool frame.   2No.

|← 170 →| |← 305 →|

2No Members K   610 x 45 x 32   V

The 29mm holes at 35 from each end are for frame rollers H, J.
The 7mm hole at 305 from RHE is for support bolt K1, (see
sheet 3). The 7mm hole 170 from LHE is to support the ratchet
pawls N,O,P. The undimensioned 7mm hole is to mate with
those on the perimeter of disk L. (for fixing angle of frame).
V is 7mm hole for bolt that fixes top roller J via washer V2.

|← 150 →| |← 150 →|

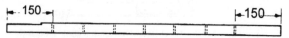

Members F, G, 900 x 32 x 32 Both are identical but turn 180°
horizontally and vertically. Dotted lines show 7mm holes at
exactly 100 c/c. (see note on member C)

The cutaway portion is 115 long, for steel bracket E, 2.5 thick.

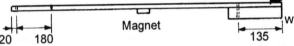

28 wooden rollers. J=960 H=870 2No T=1020
H and J have a narrow slot 75 long 5wide and 5deep
cut from each end towards the centre to take special
washer V to prevent inward movement of member K
2No each. Washers V1, V2 from 3mm Aluminium.
V2 has four 7mm holes, for a loose bolt into K

V1

V2

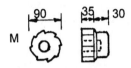

M

2No. Mahogany Ratchets
Hole 28 dia. 40 deep.
Fixed to J by grubscrew.

Q

N

P

Ratchet pawls. 2No of each.
20 x 9 Q=145 N=136 P=127
7mm hole, 10mm from end

Magnet

W

20   180

135

Member S, the wool frame supports, 2No. 835 x 32 x 12
At 20 and 200 from LHE are two 4mm holes for wood
screws that fix members T, and T. The RHE is stiffened by
a 150 x 32 x 32. The 7mm hole at 135 from the end if for
a 6mm bolt that fixes wool rack to stand member D.

L

L1

**FRAME
SHEET 5**

Member L, 200mm diameter x 12mm
plywood. Friction disk allowing frame to
be set at any stiffness.Centre 7mm hole
for bolt K1.(sheet 3) This disk is also
fixed to member D by a single counter-
sunk woodscrew at L1. The series of
7mm holes,15mm c/c 12mm in from rim,
line up with a hole in member K to fix
the frame solidly in any position. 2No.

90   90

Horizontal stretcher - 685 x 32
x 12, is loose,not fixed. It lies
across members K, K, clamps
to the material and moves up
and down with the tapestry.

76°   135   100   E1

135   76°   E2   100

FRAME SHEET 6
The metalwork.

Two steel brackets made from 29 x 29 x 2.5 angle, allow the omission of any cross-members, thus letting the stand be drawn up to an armchair, wheelchair, or over a bed.
E1 fits to left hand side members C & B leaving a 110mm section jutting out at right angles, which faces downward to fit over member G (see sheet 2)
E2 fits over C & B on the right hand side, the 110mm jutting out section facing upward to fit over member F.
Each bracket is drilled for at least 12 woodscrew, 4 into C, B, G on one side & 12 more for C, B, F on the other.

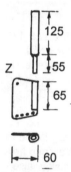

Z   125   55   65   60

The lamp bracket Z, has a 7mm hole at the top and is fixed by bolt K1 (see sheet 3) to stand member D. The 4mm holes below are for a woodscrew also into member D. Choosing which hole to use changes the lamp angle. The tube welded to the bracket, and the extension tube both have an internal diameter of 12mm, to take a lamp with a 10 or 11mm end. Bracket for LHS has tube on the opposite side.   2No.

Members W 140 x 16 x 3. Steel or aluminium, drilled for fixing with a woodscrew to the bottom of the wool rack. (See sheet 1) The end, bent over at an angle, catches on D, preventing the frame falling too far backwards.   2No

W

Y   B

Adjustable foot at front of members B. A 50mm length of 8mm threaded bar with a welded on 45mm circular plate. Screw tightly in a predrilled hole, to compensate for uneven floors.   2No.

Birds common in the valley   roughly in body size order.

Goldcrest	Wren	Longtailed tit
Blue tit	Cole tit	Great tit
Pied wagtail	Grey wagtail	Goldfinch
Chaffinch	Robin	Bullfinch
Yellow hammer	Hedge sparrow	House sparrow
Linnet	Nuthatch	Blackbird
Song thrush	Mistle thrush	Starling
Greater spotted woodpecker		Green woodpecker
Magpie	Jay	Jackdaw
Rook	Crow	Ring Dove
Wood Pigeon	Barn Owl	Kestrel
Teal	Buzzard	Common Mallard
Pheasant	Heron	Mute swan

Migratory Birds

Blackcap (Apr-Oct)	House martin (Apr-Nov)
Sand martin (Apr-Nov)	Swallow (Apr-Oct)
Swift (Apr-Sept)	Cuckoo (Apr-Sept)
Spotted flycatcher (May-Sep)	Fieldfare (Oct-May)

Infrequent visitors

Willow tit	Tree creeper	Wheatear
Reed bunting	Skylark	Kingfisher
Common Sandpiper	Woodcock	Bittern
Merganser	Cormorant	Stonechat

Steve - Chris - Sharon

Jim   Jan's Parents   Audrey

Frank   Gordon's Parents   Ivy

Little friends

Those wasps that lived in the kitchen, on the worktop in one corner between sink and stove. See them rise from their nest in the plastic dome, up into the clear container then along the plastic pipe and out through the hole in the wall, coming back with aphids to feed grubs that will be the next generation of wasps. Years later, another nest rescued from under a caravan, lived here too.

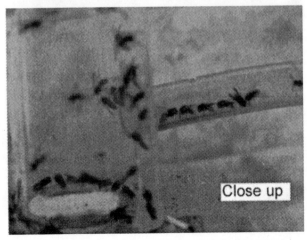

Close up

LADY DI, BOD, & MIN

IN TRAINING

MIND THE CLAWS

A DANGEROUS BIRD?

JAN'S WATERWHEEL
CAKE

JAN & GORDON with BOD & MIN
In the house, with the painted wall behind.

STEVE with MIN, an abandoned young tawny owl
This is a novel, not a bird book. The owls were
present for just short time then released to the
wild, but taking these photos proved irresistable!

The Valley of Dreams Series.
by Gordon Channer

Village by the Ford	£6.95	0-9537009-1-7
House by the Stream	£7.95	1-86033-583-7
Wheel on the Hayle	£7.95	0-9537009-0-9
A Buzzard to Lunch	£6.95	0-9537009-3-3
Follow that Caravan	£7.95	0-9537009-4-1

Best enjoyed if read in the order given above.
There is an experimental web page with more photos
entitled:- www.Cornishbooks.co.uk

The series is available through your local bookshop or can
be ordered direct (post free in UK) from, Cornish Books,
5 Tregembo Hill, Penzance, Cornwall, TR20 9EP
Email   Dreams@Cornishbooks.co.uk